MOLL FLANDERS

RIVERSIDE EDITIONS

RIVERSIDE EDITIONS

UNDER THE GENERAL EDITORSHIP OF

Gordon N. Ray

MOLL FLANDERS

Daniel Defoe

EDITED WITH AN INTRODUCTION AND NOTES BY

JAMES SUTHERLAND

UNIVERSITY COLLEGE, LONDON

HOUGHTON MIFFLIN COMPANY

BOSTON · The Riverside Press Cambridge

Daniel Defoe: 1660–1731

MOLL FLANDERS was first published in 1722

INTRODUCTION

by James Sutherland

I

In the market bookstall of the old Scottish town in which I was born, copies of *Moll Flanders* were regularly exposed for sale tied up with a piece of string: a distinction which they shared with Boccaccio's *Decameron* and a work dubiously attributed to Aristotle on the generation of animals. Whether the string was honestly intended to preserve the immature reader from corruption, or whether it was meant to suggest that this was a work of such flaming indecency that it must be bought at all costs, it would be hard to say; but it is certainly true that *Moll Flanders* was long looked upon as a highly improper book which only the lower orders of society would wish to read. As one of Defoe's contemporaries put it:

> Down in the kitchen, honest Dick and Doll
> Are studying Colonel Jack and Flanders Moll.

Although Defoe's novel, like Moll herself in her old age, has now become respectable,[1] it still raises certain problems of interpretation which are not easy to solve. What had Defoe in mind when he wrote this story? What was he trying to do? What sort of reader was he writing for, and what purpose was the book intended to serve? Did the journalist in him get the better of the moralist?

The paradox at the heart of *Moll Flanders* is how Defoe — an essentially respectable and law-abiding citizen, and a member of a godly religious sect — came to write a story in which the heroine is a woman who had been for twelve years a whore and a thief (not to mention a transported felon), and who is yet so sympathetically treated by the author that he may almost be said to have ended by becoming one of her many lovers. To a middle-class nonconformist like Defoe, Moll was outside the pale; if she had ever knocked at his front door he would have sent her about her business. And yet, having written her story, he has managed to leave his readers with the feeling that she was a woman whom it would have been rather fun to meet. Defoe has therefore been accused of hypocrisy, of writing with his tongue in his cheek, of trying to have the best of both worlds; he has compiled, it is suggested, a catchpenny tale for lovers of pornography, and has then added some perfunctory moral

---

[1] Except in Eire.

reflections which he knows we shall skip. It must be admitted that this is a plausible inference if we consider only the title-page, which seems to be designed to persuade the startled apprentice to part with his sixpence, and the preface, which has an air of protesting too much. Again, when Moll is in Newgate awaiting execution, and has arrived — so she says — at a state of true repentance, she tells us about this at some length, and then breaks off to add:

> This may be thought inconsistent in itself, and wide from the business of this book; particularly, I reflect that many of those who may be pleas'd and diverted with the relation of the wicked part of my story, may not relish this, which is really the best part of my life, the most advantageous to my self, and the most instructive to others; such however will I hope allow me liberty to make my story compleat . . .

Defoe appears to apologise here, through the mouth of his erring heroine, for inserting a passage that must bore those of his readers (surely the majority) who will read the book only for what Moll calls "the wicked part"; at all events, he is obviously aware of the fact that some at least of his readers will be of that sort. As a journalist of thirty years' experience, Defoe knew what the public wanted, and he must have known very well that the fortunes and misfortunes of the famous Moll Flanders would appeal to those readers who wanted only sensation.

Yet to assert that *Moll Flanders* was written with only such readers in mind would be wide of the truth: Defoe was not a simple person whose motives can be accounted for in a few cynical words. He was an odd mixture of the puritan and the artist. The two are not, of course, incompatible, as anyone can see who has read *Pilgrim's Progress*. The complicating factor with Defoe is that he was rarely either the pure artist or the pure puritan, and that the two elements were sometimes in conflict, and often imperfectly integrated. Less than a month after the appearance of *Moll Flanders*, Defoe published a work with another of those long descriptive titles, but with a very different content: *Religious Courtship: Being Historical Discourses, on the Necessity of Marrying Religious Husbands and Wives only. With an Appendix of the Necessity of taking none but Religious Servants.* By "historical discourses" Defoe meant discourses telling a story; the book is a series of fictitious dialogues, interspersed with narrative. It is, in fact, a literary hybrid, falling between a religious play and a religious novel; and though it is now almost forgotten, it ran through about as many editions in the eighteenth century as *Moll Flanders*. In *Religious Courtship* the puritan side of Defoe found uninhibited expression: the book is both godly and practical, the work of a man who had once intended to enter the nonconformist ministry, and who always retained something of the preacher in his strange make-up. *Moll Flanders,* on the other hand, is the work of Defoe the artist; and the artist accepts life as it comes to him, and is as much concerned as the critic to maintain, in the words of Matthew Arnold, "a free play of the mind on all subjects which [he] touches." But the life of Moll being what it is, and Defoe being what he is, his puritan conscience keeps breaking in, and when that happens, Moll is made to comment — not always very convincingly — upon her own moral shortcomings and the wickedness of the life she is living.

If, then, the reader of *Moll Flanders* is left in some uncertainty about the author's attitude to his heroine, it is owing to a sort of double vision in Defoe, rather than to a deliberate attempt to write a sensational best-seller and then give it a spurious air of respectability by adding what a recent critic has called a "comminatory coda" of moralising. It is clear that Defoe was fascinated by criminals, and not merely as a social problem (though that certainly interested him), but as individuals. He wanted to know what led them to a life of crime, how they thought and felt when they were at work on a job, what effect this antisocial life had upon their character, and how they differed from other members of the community. Moll, too, is no ordinary criminal: everything — even thieving — can be well or badly done, and the Moll Flanders whom Defoe has imagined develops into a highly proficient thief. As such, though she never obtains Defoe's moral approval, she clearly wins from him the admiration that we always give to intelligence and skill. Defoe is at some pains to distinguish his heroine from the blundering crooks with whom she is from time to time associated; she evades capture for so long because she has courage, presence of mind, quickness of apprehension, and, as time goes on, all the know-how acquired from the successful practice of her profession. Defoe would have admired all these qualities in a London tradesman; it is a pity that Moll should apply them to the purposes of theft and whoring, but the qualities themselves remain admirable and fascinating. Above all, Moll has the toughness, the resilience, the ability for mere survival that usually go with indomitable energy and great physical stamina. She would always be the one to crawl out unhurt from the debris of a bombed building, the stewardess to survive the crash; and if she were marooned on a desert island, she would, like Robinson Crusoe, retain her sanity, take stock of her resources, and proceed to make some kind of life of it. Simply as a human animal Moll is an impressive specimen, and the deepest impression made by Defoe's story is the abundant vitality of this woman living by her wits in the jungle of eighteenth-century London. "Though a quarrel in the streets," Keats once wrote, "is a thing to be hated, the energies displayed in it are fine." It is because Moll keeps on trying that we cannot refuse her our sympathy; she is the will to live, the head bobbing above the waves, the human life battling with circumstances. In contemplating her struggle to survive, the artist and the puritan in Defoe came near to being reconciled; for what delighted the artist simply as experience also won the approval of the puritan as human effort. For over sixty years Defoe himself had been involved in a similar, if less immoral, struggle to keep his head above water; and pondering the chequered life of the woman he had created he might well have reflected: "There but for the grace of God go I."

II

Imperfect — or more precisely, perhaps, intermittent — though he may have been as an artist, Defoe had to an unusual extent the power of putting himself in the place of other people, and of realising in sharp detail an event or a scene. His greatest triumphs may be said to be in the field of imaginative reporting. When, for example, he comes to Moll's first theft he sets the scene with such careful attention to detail that he fixes it in our minds, and gives to it that air of authenticity which, for Defoe, is almost the justification of fiction:

> Wandring thus about I knew not whither, I pass'd by an apothecary's shop in Leadenhall-street, where I saw lye on a stool just before the compter a little bundle wrapt in a white cloth; beyond it stood a maid servant with her back to it, looking up towards the top of the shop, where the apothecary's apprentice, as I suppose, was standing upon the compter, with his back also to the door, and a candle in his hand, looking and reaching up to the upper shelf for something he wanted, so that both were engag'd, and no body else in the shop.

There are many such dramatic moments in Defoe's fiction: moments in which the clock seems to have been temporarily stopped, and eternity hangs on the event. Here the effect is due not only to Defoe's strong sense of fact, his delight in recording the actual, but to his equally powerful awareness of the awful hour of temptation. Moll is at a turning point in her life; she is faced with a sudden choice between right and wrong, and she is about to give way. If she yields, the next step will be easier, and the next easier still; soon the moral implications of thieving will hardly trouble her at all, and she will concentrate only on her technique.

The phrase "imaginative reporting" may seem to beg the question. Why should we distinguish between what Defoe is doing in the passage just quoted and what Jane Austen and George Eliot and Henry James are doing in their novels? An answer to this question has been given by Mr. Ian Watt, who suggests that all Defoe's novels "make formal realism an end rather than a means, subordinating any coherent ulterior significance to the illusion that the text represents the authentic lucubrations of an historical person." [1] This is a shrewd comment, and it certainly helps to account for our feeling that when Defoe has given us so much it is a pity he hasn't given us the little more that would have transformed his prose narratives into genuine novels. His method of telling a story is always the same: the hero or heroine — a sailor marooned on a desert island, a pirate, a soldier of fortune, a courtesan — narrates the events of a lifetime from childhood to old age, dwelling on certain episodes or situations and hurrying over others, moving from one kind of environment to another, now prosperous and now in extremity.

> Toiling, — rejoicing, — sorrowing,
> Onward through life he goes —

and the story goes with him. Defoe's task, as he saw it, was to *be* a sailor on a desert island, to *be* a London citizen in a plague-stricken city, to *be* a female adventuress and thief; to see and feel things as each of those characters would have experienced them, and to throw their story into a plausible autobiographical form.[2] In this, to a large extent, he succeeded; and if plausibility or verisimilitude does not comprise his whole aim as a writer of prose fiction it certainly absorbs much of his attention. The autobiographical form, too, was a singularly convenient one; for it would legitimise careless writing, repetition, and garrulity, and would absolve him from forming any regular plan.

It is, indeed, the want of planning, the sort of planning (to go to the opposite extreme) that Henry James brought to bear on his novels, that makes it necessary to classify Defoe's stories among the primitives of prose fiction. There is every reason to believe that he wrote

---

[1] *The Rise of the Novel*, 1957, p. 117.
[2] A typical example of Defoe at work is his handling of the situation that develops in Virginia when Moll discovers that the man she has married, and to whom she has borne children, is her own brother. What will a woman in such circumstances feel, and what will she do? What will be the reactions of the mother? If Moll tells her husband the truth, how is she to do it? How will he take it? etc. etc.

his stories as Sir Philip Sidney seems to have written his *Arcadia* — making them up as he went along, and having little more idea than the reader of what was going to happen next until it happened in his mind. In the writing of fiction he is one of the great improvisers rather than one of the planners. Sufficient unto the day were the pages he had just written: there would be more to be said about Moll tomorrow — if he had leisure to go on with the book. On no other basis can we account satisfactorily for the numerous repetitions, loose ends, and abrupt transitions in Defoe's stories, and for their general formlessness and apparently artless spontaneity. In his later years — such was his remarkable output — Defoe must have regularly had several books in hand at once; and only a writer of unusual inventiveness and fluency could have kept up the flow of imaginary anecdote which forms the staple material of his fiction.

In so far as he was an artist, then, Defoe worked by fits and starts. He was capable of realising intensely whatever he happened to be writing about at the time. Nothing could be better in its way than a scene in the early pages of *Moll Flanders,* where Moll, lying ill in bed, hears the family talking about her in the dining-room downstairs:

Alas, says the old lady, that poor girl; I am afraid she will never be well. Well! says the elder brother, how should Mrs. Betty be well? they say she is in love. I believe nothing of it, says the old gentlewoman. I don't know, says the eldest sister, what to say to it, they have made such a rout about her being so handsome, and so charming, and I know not what, and that in her hearing too, that has turn'd the creature's head, I believe, and who knows what possessions may follow such doings? For my part I don't know what to make of it.

Why, sister, you must acknowledge she is very handsome, says the elder brother. Ay, and a great deal handsomer than you, sister, says Robin, and that's your mortification. Well, well, that is not the question, says his sister, the girl is well enough, and she knows it, she need not be told of it to make her vain.

We don't talk of her being vain, says the elder brother, but of her being in love; may be she is in love with herself, it seems my sisters thinks so.

I would she was in love with me, says Robin, I'd quickly put her out of her pain. What d'ye mean by that, son? says the old lady, how can you talk so? Why, madam, says Robin again, very honestly, do you think I'd let the poor girl die for love, and of me too, that is so near at hand to be had? Fye, brother, says the second sister, how can you talk so? Would you take a creature, that has not a groat in the world? Prithee, child, says Robin, beauty's a portion, and good humour with it is a double portion; I wish thou hadst half her stock of both for thy portion. So there was her mouth stop'd. . . .

The man who could throw off such a passage as this was well on his way to writing the first naturalistic novel in English; the dialogue is entirely effortless, it helps to differentiate and define the various characters, and it carries the story forward easily and imperceptibly. Over this little scene, too, in the dining-room of a middle-class family in Colchester, there hangs a cloud of suspense: the eaves-dropper upstairs has a guilty secret which, if once revealed, would lead to her being driven from the house. As she listens, her lover (whose sincerity she has now too good reason to suspect) talks about her in a bantering way, while his younger brother discloses to the whole family the fact that he is honourably in love with her and wishes to make her his wife. Defoe was writing this sort of realistic dialogue almost twenty years before the publication of Richardson's *Pamela* (1740). The pert, hoity-toity conversation of the two sisters has something of the complacent gentility of Pamela, but comes even nearer to the middle-class genteel vulgarity of the Branghton girls in Fanny Burney's *Evelina* (1778). Yet this promising situation in the Colchester household, which would have furnished Samuel Richardson with material for a long novel on the theme of Virtue Betrayed, is abandoned by Defoe just as it has begun to interest us; the scene shifts abruptly to a completely new environment and a new set of characters, and the Colchester family fade into Moll's for-gotten past, never to reappear in her story.

Defoe's novels are full of abrupt transitions, and when he has decided that it is time for a change of scene he can be quite ruthless. Moll's married life with the younger brother is dismissed in a few words:

> It concerns the story in hand very little to enter into the farther particulars of the family, or of my self, for the five years that I liv'd with this husband, only to observe that I had two children by him, and that at the end of the five years he died. . . .

There follows the usual stocktaking (Moll finds herself a widow worth £1,200), and a new sequence of adventures begins. This is De-foe's normal method as a storyteller: he proceeds rather like someone giving a lantern lecture, flashing his slide on the screen, talking about it for a short time, and then passing on to the next slide, and the next. (He writes, of course, in the tradition of the picaresque novel; but the literary ancestry of *Moll Flanders* is to be found rather in the pamphlet lives and confessions of actual criminals.)

III

In the picaresque novel the hero is sometimes the least interesting character in the book. His main function is to be *there*, to be on the spot, to have things happening to him, and, above all, to meet with other people and so introduce them to the reader. In the novels of Smollett, for instance, we are much less interested in Roderick Random than in many of the minor characters; less concerned about Peregrine Pickle than about Commodore Trunnion, Lieutenant Hatchway, and Tom Pipes. But this is hardly so with Defoe's stories; and of all his heroes and heroines Moll Flanders is perhaps the most attractive. Defoe makes a genuine attempt to enter into her circumstances, and to see things from her point of view; it is his minor characters who are apt to receive a rather summary treatment.

Moll is an odd — and, to some readers, a baffling — mixture: she has a hard shell, but she is not hard-boiled. In view of the life she has led, we might expect her to have become brutalised, insensitive, a woman with an eye for nothing but the main chance. She is certainly calculating and mercenary; but, as Defoe has presented her, she has also retained the capacity for feeling; and her conscience, if not always immediately operative and sometimes conveniently moribund, is by no means dead. Here, it is sometimes argued, Defoe has departed from strict probability, and has created a character who could not at one and the same time do what she does and feel what she feels. If the reader of *Moll Flanders* gets that impression about Defoe's heroine, he has the choice of three possible explanations. He can say, in the first place, that Moll's flashes of generosity and affection and her occasional twinges of conscience are not true to character, and offend against what the older critics called "decorum" — that Defoe, in fact, has made the mistake of substituting what would be his own feelings in the same circumstances for those which are proper to the character he has created. It would be difficult to deny that this may sometimes have happened, for all Defoe's heroes and heroines have something (and sometimes a good deal) of himself in their composition.

But there is a second explanation, which is more to the credit of Defoe as an author. Moll presents the same sort of paradox as Shakespeare's Macbeth. The hero of Shakespeare's play is a noble and sensitive soul who shrinks from evil, and who then, having told us in unforgettable words how heinous such a crime would be, proceeds to murder his sleeping king — an old man to whom he is indebted for many favours, and his own guest. Before and after the deed he feels, and *expresses* himself, as any honourable man might feel who had been compelled to be a horrified onlooker of the crime, but as the criminal himself would surely not. Macbeth has now "stepped in blood," and as the consequences envelop him he proceeds to wade in it; but to the last he has the feelings of a sensitive moralist and the utterance of a poet. Psychologically, all this may be thought to be incredible; but Shakespeare willingly sacrifices psychological realism for the over-riding purpose of making us realise a situation. Defoe, of course, was no Shakespeare; he wrote at a lower pressure, and his motives were more mixed. But one of his aims in *Moll Flanders* is to make us realise what Moll had been doing, and that what she had been doing was wrong; and if he had presented his heroine as a mere hardened offender who never thought twice about the consequence of the crimes that she was so constantly committing he would have defeated his purpose. Moll would have been a less inconsistent character, but she would have been living in a moral vacuum; and, as a hardened criminal, she would have been no more interesting than a baseball player seen only in his professional capacity, with no private life and no personal problems other than those connected with his batting record.

There remains, however, a third explanation of Moll's inconsistent behaviour, which, if accepted, would absolve Defoe completely from all charges of blundering and incompetence. Moll, it may be argued, is inconsistent because that is what she was, and what most people are. The drama of the ancient world, and the literary criticism that was based upon it, accustomed readers to expect fictitious characters to be consistent; but in modern literature characters are often so much more complex that we have become used to a large measure of inconsistency, and may even be rather bored by the sort of character who always acts in accordance with our expectations. What is there, after all, in Moll's contradictory behaviour that we might not find in a robust and good-natured woman who has taken to a life of what is for the most part petty crime? Defoe devotes a good deal of his attention to Moll's reactions immediately after her first theft, and her various reflections seem natural enough. She slept little that night, and was still very much worried next day:

> Then I was impatient to hear some news of the loss; and would fain know how it was, whether they were a poor body's goods, or a rich; perhaps, said I, it may be some poor widow like me that had pack'd up these goods to go and sell them for a little bread for herself and a poor child, and are now starving and breaking their hearts, for want of that little they would have fetched, and this thought tormented me worse than all the rest, for three or four days.

"I was impatient to hear some news of the loss" is surely right: the wretched bundle she had taken was presumably only one of many objects stolen that day in London; but this is Moll's first theft, and because it is of such vast importance to *her* she naturally assumes that it must be in the news. Again, the thought that the bundle may have belonged to "some poor widow like me" is perfectly natural, and so too is the further extravagant vision of the owner and her child starving and breaking their hearts because they have lost their all. Such morbid thoughts spring from Moll's heated imagination, for she is still a newcomer in the world of crime, and she sees the whole episode in human terms, and not just (this will come later) as a successful "job." Her second theft, when she leads the child up a dark alley and steals its necklace of gold beads, provokes in her what at first sight may seem to be a strange reflection:

> The last affair left no great concern upon me, for as I did the poor child no harm, I only thought I had given the parents a just reproof for their negligence, in leaving the poor lamb to come home by itself, and it would teach them to take more care another time.

As Moll herself explains, poverty is beginning to harden her heart, and she has already reached that stage in which she is prepared to put the blame for her crimes on someone else. The loss of the child's necklace would teach its parents not to put temptation in a poor woman's way; they did wrong "in leaving the poor lamb to come home by itself." Why this sudden tenderness on Moll's part for the child she had just robbed? She had previously shown little enough tenderness for her own poor lambs, the lawful and unlawful issue of her body, who had mostly been "taken off her hands"; and as for this particular child, she has already told us that immediately after removing its necklace "the devil put me upon killing the child in the dark alley, that it might not cry," but the very thought had almost frightened her out of her wits. Why, then, has it now become "the poor lamb"? Moll, it might be said, is looking back on the incident with the normal feeling of a good-humoured woman to a little child, a child that had certainly done her no harm, and might even be said to have done her a good turn. But it is really her desire for self-justification that is responsible for this apparent tenderness: Moll has conveniently shifted all the blame on to the parents, and it is her indignation with *them* that finds expression in this concern for "the poor lamb."

We make a mistake if we think that Defoe can never be subtle, just as we make another sort of mistake if we do not admit that he is often careless and forgetful of what he has written. As Moll grows old in crime, Defoe is concerned to show us how her moral arteries harden, and it may now be objected, more plausibly than ever, that such a woman would no longer be capable of the tenderness and the moral scruples that Moll continues from time to time to show. But to say that is to have too rigid a conception of human character. If character "sets" with advancing years, and certain attitudes become fixed, the stiffening process is rarely absolute. Most people remain, like the English climate, unpredictable; they have their cold days in summer, and their warm days in winter, and a period of apparently unrelenting rain may suddenly give way to the kindest of blue skies. "A foolish consistency," said Emerson, "is the hobgoblin of little minds"; it has certainly proved to be a bugbear to many literary critics when they discuss characters in fiction. Moll has the inconsistency that comes from being alive; she lives for the moment, and she changes with circumstances. Does she contradict herself? Very well, she contradicts herself. She is large, she contains multitudes.

All three explanations of the apparent contradictions in Moll's character and behaviour may be valid at one point or another in Defoe's rambling narrative: he sometimes spoke his own mind through the mouth of his heroine; he occasionally credited her with thoughts and feelings which, if not really appropriate for her, help the reader to realise the full significance of the life she is leading; and he saw in her, as often as not, a mixture of good and bad, generosity and meanness, strength and weakness. As a creative writer Defoe was an author of mixed motives, and of varied interests.

IV

In the course of an abnormally active life, he had been among other things, a merchant, a political journalist, and a secret-service agent; he had stood in the pillory and had been more than once in prison; he had travelled widely. When such a man takes to writing fiction, he has certain advantages over the author who has led a sheltered and purely literary life. As a London merchant he was naturally well-informed on shops and shopkeeping, on goods of many sorts, on shipping and cargoes, on banking, and so on. His familiarity with such matters enabled him to give his stories a wonderfully solid and authentic background; he did not have to "get it up" for the occasion. The world of trade and commerce was, of course, a natural environment for such an adventuress as Moll Flanders. Defoe's knowledge of the underworld of London seems to have been considerable; some of it he probably acquired when he was himself a prisoner in Newgate, and some of it from his later experiences as a journalist attending the trials of criminals, and possibly interviewing them in prison. In the course of his career as a secret-service agent for Robert Harley and others, he had ridden over most of England and much of Scotland; and though his travels outside Great Britain were probably not extensive, his knowledge of other countries — very useful for a man who had once traded in wine, tobacco, and other commodities in a big way — was remarkable. In *Moll Flanders,* then, Defoe was writing about a world with which he had long been familiar, giving a new kind of expression to subjects which had always interested him and which he had often written about before.

But however much the contemporary background comes into the foreground in Defoe's stories, what interests him most of all is still the individual human life, and especially the drama of the human soul struggling with circumstances. The moments of greatest tension in *Moll Flanders* are nearly all connected with temptation, with the choice between good and evil; and if Defoe himself had not been so sharply aware of the difference between right and wrong, if he had not (with all his tolerant knowledge of the world) retained his capacity for being shocked by immorality, he would never have succeeded in holding our attention as he does. It would be wrong to suggest that this awareness of good and evil is no longer to be found in the modern novel; but the twentieth-century novelist is so much alive to the social and economic and ideological forces that mould human character, and to the psychological problems which these create, that he tends to content himself with *accounting for* human actions rather than presenting them in a moral setting. In narrating the progress of Moll from childhood to old age Defoe by no means neglects the influence of environment, education, and heredity; indeed, it is part of his purpose to show how these help to account for the sort of woman that she became. But, for Defoe, she is still a moral agent. *Moll Flanders* is not — what it might be in the hands of a twentieth-century novelist — a mere case history; it is a story of sin and crime, beginning with fornication, and going on to adultery, bigamy, incest, and chronic theft. However much Moll may be the unhappy victim of circumstances, the fact remains that at each turning-point in her story she is free to choose between good and evil. Defoe never lets us forget (because he never lets Moll forget) that she is ultimately responsible for whatever she does. If the modern reader is ready to forgive her, that may be a tribute to his charity, or perhaps only an indication of his indifference to moral issues. But he cannot say that Defoe was indifferent; for Defoe faces the issues squarely, and draws from them, time after time, what seem to him to be the inescapable conclusions. To tie up copies of *Moll Flanders* with a piece of string is worse than unnecessary; it is misleading.

TEXTUAL AND BIBLIOGRAPHICAL NOTE

Moll Flanders carries the date 1721 on the title-page of the first edition, but was not in fact published until January, 1722. A second edition followed in July, and a third ("corrected") in December, and reprints continued to appear at frequent intervals all through the eighteenth century. Defoe's story was perhaps less popular in the nineteenth century, but in the twentieth it has probably replaced *Robinson Crusoe*, among adult readers, as his most widely read book.

The present text follows that of the third edition, whose numerous corrections are almost certainly the work of the author himself. For the purpose of this reprint a partial modernization has been carried out. Capital letters and italics have been made to conform with modern usage; but the spelling of Defoe's printer has been left undisturbed except in a few instances (e.g. "whether" for "whither") where it might prove confusing. The absence of all points of quotation from the dialogue follows the practice of Defoe's printer, and should not disturb the modern reader. On the other hand, Defoe's (or his printer's) use of commas, semicolons, etc., is sometimes so misleading that it has been necessary to make a considerable number of changes, although, in general, the punctuation remains closer to eighteenth-century than to twentieth-century usage.

Acknowledgment is made to Basil Blackwell, Publisher (Oxford), for allowing the editor to make use of the Shakespeare Head Press text of *Moll Flanders*.

Modern biographies of Defoe include Paul Dottin's *Daniel Defoe et Ses Romans* (3 vols., Paris, 1924), James Sutherland's *Defoe* (London, 1937; 2nd ed. 1950), and John Robert Moore's *Daniel Defoe, Citizen of the Modern World* (Chicago, 1958). A briefer study is Francis Watson's *Daniel Defoe* (London, 1952). Discussions of *Moll Flanders* will be found in Virginia Woolf's *The Common Reader* (first series: London, 1925); in Mark Schorer's "A Study in Defoe: moral vision and structural form" (*Thought*, vol. xxv, 1950, pp. 275–87), and in Ian Watt's *The Rise of the Novel* (London, 1957).

CHRONOLOGY

1660	Daniel, son of James Foe, tallowchandler, born in London.
1680–92	A London merchant, trading in stockings, wine, tobacco, and other commodities.
1692	Bankrupt.
c. 1695	Starts a factory for manufacturing bricks and tiles.
1697–1701	Becomes known as a political pamphleteer. Calls himself Defoe.
1701	*The True-Born Englishman. A Satire.*
1702	*The Shortest Way with the Dissenters.* For writing this pamphlet Defoe was found guilty of seditious libel, sentenced to the pillory, fined, and imprisoned for several months. Second bankruptcy (1703).
1704–13	Writes and publishes *The Review.* Acts as a government secret-service agent in Edinburgh and elsewhere.
1715–18	*The Family Instructor* (2 vols.).
1719	(1) *Robinson Crusoe.* (2) *The King of Pirates.*
1720	(1) *Memoirs of a Cavalier.* (2) *Captain Singleton.*
1722	(1) *Moll Flanders.* (2) *Religious Courtship.* (3) *A Journal of the Plague Year.*
1723	*Colonel Jack.*
1724	*Roxana.*
1724–7	*A Tour thro' the whole Island of Great Britain* (3 vols.).
1725	*A New Voyage round the World.*
1726–7	*The Compleat English Tradesman* (2 vols.).
1731	Dies, April, in a London lodging-house.

NOTE: Defoe is now chiefly remembered for the works of fiction that he wrote in the years from 1719 (when he was in his sixtieth year) to 1724. A complete list of his separate publications — on politics, religion, history, travel, economics, education, etc. — runs to about 400 titles.

THE FORTUNES
AND MISFORTUNES
OF THE FAMOUS
MOLL FLANDERS, &c

Who was Born in Newgate, and during a Life of
continu'd Variety for Three-score Years, besides her Childhood, was Twelve Year a Whore, five times a Wife
(whereof once to her own Brother) Twelve Year
a Thief, Eight Year a Transported Felon
in Virginia, at last grew Rich,
liv'd Honest, and died
a Penitent

Written from her own Memorandums

THE PREFACE

THE world is so taken up of late with novels and romances, that it will be hard for a private history to be taken for genuine where the names and other circumstances of the person are concealed; and on this account we must be content to leave the reader to pass his own opinion upon the ensuing sheets, and take it just as he pleases.

The author is here supposed to be writing her own history, and in the very beginning of her account she gives the reasons why she thinks fit to conceal her true name, after which there is no occasion to say any more about that.

It is true that the original of this story is put into new words, and the stile of the famous lady we here speak of is a little alter'd, particularly she is made to tell her own tale in modester words than she told it at first; the copy which came first to hand having been written in language more like one still in Newgate than one grown penitent and humble, as she afterwards pretends to be.

The pen employ'd in finishing her story, and making it what you now see it to be, has had no little difficulty to put it into a dress fit to be seen, and to make it speak language fit to be read. When a woman debauched from her youth, nay, even being the offspring of debauchery and vice, comes to give an account of all her vicious practices, and even to descend to the particular occasions and circumstances by which she first became wicked, and of all the progressions of crime which she run through in threescore years, an author must be hard put to it to wrap it up so clean as not to give room, especially for vicious readers, to turn it to his disadvantage.

All possible care, however, has been taken to give no lewd ideas, no immodest turns in the new dressing up this story, no, not to the worst part of her expressions; to this purpose some of the vicious part of her life, which could not be modestly told, is quite left out, and several other parts are very much shortened; what is left 'tis hoped will not offend the chastest reader, or the modestest hearer; and as the best use is to be made even of the worst story, the moral 'tis hoped will keep the reader serious, even where the story might incline him to be otherwise. To give the history of a wicked life repented

3

*of necessarily requires that the wicked part should be made
as wicked as the real history of it will bear, to illustrate and
give a beauty to the penitent part, which is certainly the best
and brightest, if related with equal spirit and life.*

*It is suggested there cannot be the same life, the same
brightness and beauty, in relating the penitent part as is in
the criminal part. If there is any truth in that suggestion, I
must be allow'd to say, 'tis because there is not the same taste
and relish in the reading; and indeed it is too true that the difference lies not in the real worth of the subject so much as in
the gust and palate of the reader.*

*But as this work is chiefly recommended to those who know
how to read it, and how to make good the uses of it which the
story all along recommends to them; so it is to be hop'd that such
readers will be much more pleas'd with the moral than the
fable, with the application than with the relation, and with the
end of the writer than with the life of the person written of.*

*There is in this story abundance of delightful incidents, and
all of them usefully apply'd. There is an agreeable turn artfully
given them in the relating, that naturally instructs the reader,
either one way, or another. The first part of her lewd life
with the young gentleman at Colchester has so many happy
turns given it to expose the crime, and warn all whose circumstances are adapted to it of the ruinous end of such things, and
the foolish, thoughtless, and abhor'd conduct of both the par-
ties, that it abundantly attones for all the lively description
she gives of her folly and wickedness.*

*The repentance of her lover at the Bath, and how brought by
the just alarm of his fit of sickness to abandon her; the just caution given there against even the lawful intimacies of the dearest
friends, and how unable they are to preserve the most solemn
resolutions of virtue without divine assistance; these are parts
which to a just discernment will appear to have more real
beauty in them than all the amorous chain of story which
introduces it.*

In a word, as the whole relation is carefully garbled [1] *of all
the levity and looseness that was in it, so it is applied, and with
the utmost care, to vertuous and religious uses. None can, with-*

[1] sifted.

out being guilty of manifest injustice, cast any reproach upon it, or upon our design in publishing it.

The advocates for the stage have in all ages made this the great argument to perswade people that their plays are useful, and that they ought to be allow'd in the most civiliz'd, and in the most religious, government; namely, that they are apply'd to vertuous purposes, and that by the most lively representations they fail not to recommend virtue and generous principles, and to discourage and expose all sorts of vice and corruption of manners; and were it true that they did so, and that they constantly adhered to that rule, as the test of their acting on the theatre, much might be said in their favour.

Throughout the infinite variety of this book, this fundamental is most strictly adhered to; there is not a wicked action in any part of it but is first or last rendered unhappy and unfortunate; there is not a superlative villain brought upon the stage but either he is brought to an unhappy end, or brought to be a penitent; there is not an ill thing mention'd but it is condemn'd, even in the relation, nor a vertuous, just thing but it carries its praise along with it. What can more exactly answer the rule laid down, to recommend even those representations of things which have so many other just objections lying against them, namely, of example of bad company, obscene language, and the like?

Upon this foundation this book is recommended to the reader, as a work from every part of which something may be learned, and some just and religious inference is drawn by which the reader will have something of instruction, if he pleases to make use of it.

All the exploits of this lady of fame in her depredations upon mankind stand as so many warnings to honest people to beware of 'em, intimating to 'em by what methods innocent people are drawn in, plundered, and robb'd, and by consequence how to avoid them. Her robbing a little child, dress'd fine by the vanity of the mother to go to the dancing school, is a good memento to such people hereafter; as is likewise her picking the gold-watch from the young ladie's side in the park.

Her getting a parcel from a hairbrain'd wench at the coaches in St. John's-street; her booty at the fire, and also at Harwich;

all give us excellent warning in such cases to be more present to ourselves in sudden surprises of every sort.

Her application to a sober life and industrious management at last in Virginia, with her transported spouse, is a story fruitful of instruction to all the unfortunate creatures who are oblig'd to seek their re-establishment abroad; whether by the misery of transportation, or other disaster; letting them know that diligence and application have their due encouragement, even in the remotest part of the world, and that no case can be so low, so despicable, or so empty of prospect, but that an unwearied industry will go a great way to deliver us from it, will in time raise the meanest creature to appear again in the world, and give him a new cast [1] for his life.

These are a few of the serious inferences which we are led by the hand to in this book, and these are fully sufficient to justify any man in recommending it to the world, and much more to justify the publication of it.

There are two of the most beautiful parts still behind which this story gives some idea of, and lets us into the parts of them, but they are either of them too long to be brought into the same volume; and indeed are, as I may call them, whole volumes of themselves, viz., 1. the life of her governess, as she calls her, who had run thro', it seems in a few years, all the eminent degrees of a gentlewoman, a whore, and a bawd, a midwife, and a midwife keeper, as they are call'd, a pawnbroker, a child-taker, a receiver of thieves, and of stolen goods; and in a word, herself a thief, a breeder up of thieves and the like, and yet at last a penitent.

The second is the life of her transported husband, a highwayman; who it seems liv'd a twelve years' life of successful villany upon the road, and even at last came off so well as to be a voluntier transport, not a convict; and in whose life there is an incredible variety.

But, as I said, these are things too long to bring in here, so neither can I make a promise of their coming out by themselves.

We cannot say, indeed, that this history is carried on quite to the end of the life of this famous Moll Flanders, for no body can write their own life to the full end of it, unless they can

[1] chance, opportunity.

write it after they are dead: but her husband's life being written by a third hand, gives a full account of them both, how long they lived together in that country, and how they came both to England again, after about eight years, in which time they were grown very rich, and where she liv'd, it seems, to be very old; but was not so extraordinary a penitent as she was at first; it seems only that indeed she always spoke with abhorrence of her former life, and of every part of it.

In her last scene at Maryland and Virginia, many pleasant things happen'd, which makes that part of her life very agreeable, but they are not told with the same elegancy as those accounted for by herself; so it is still to be the more advantage that we break off here.

THE FORTUNES
AND MISFORTUNES
OF THE FAMOUS
MOLL FLANDERS

MY true name is so well known in the records or registers
at Newgate, and in the Old Bailey, and there are some
things of such consequence still depending there, relating to
my particular conduct, that it is not to be expected I should
set my name or the account of my family to this work. Perhaps, after my death, it may be better known; at present it
would not be proper, no, not tho' a general pardon should be
issued, even without exceptions of persons or crimes.

It is enough to tell you, that as some of my worst comrades,
who are out of the way of doing me harm, having gone out of the
world by the steps and the string [1] as I often expected to go,
knew me by the name of Moll Flanders; so you may give me
leave to go under that name till I dare own who I have been, as
well as who I am.

I have been told that in one of our neighbour nations, whether
it be in France or where else, I know not, they have an order
from the king that when any criminal is condemn'd, either to
dye, or to the gallies, or to be transported, if they leave any children, as such are generally unprovided for by the forfeiture of
their parents, so they are immediately taken into the care of
the government, and put into an hospital call'd the House of
Orphans, where they are bred up, cloath'd, fed, taught, and
when fit to go out, are placed to trades, or to services, so as to
be well able to provide for themselves by an honest industrious
behaviour.

Had this been the custom in our country, I had not been

[1] the ladder underneath the gallows and the hangman's rope.

left a poor desolate girl without friends, without cloaths, without help or helper, as was my fate; and by which I was not only expos'd to very great distresses, even before I was capable, either of understanding my case, or how to amend it, but brought into a course of life, scandalous in itself, and which in its ordinary course tended to the swift destruction both of soul and body.

But the case was otherwise here; my mother was convicted of felony for a petty theft, scarce worth naming, *viz.* borrowing [1] three pieces of fine holland [2] of a certain draper in Cheapside. The circumstances are too long to repeat, and I have heard them related so many ways, that I can scarce tell which is the right account.

However it was, they all agree in this, that my mother pleaded her belly, [3] and being found quick with child, she was respited for about seven months; after which she was call'd down, as they term it, to her former judgment, but obtain'd the favour afterward of being transported to the plantations, and left me about half a year old, and in bad hands you may be sure.

This is too near the first hours of my life for me to relate anything of my self but by hearsay; 'tis enough to mention that as I was born in such an unhappy place, I had no parish to have recourse to for my nourishment in my infancy, nor can I give the least account how I was kept alive; other than that, as I have been told, some relation of my mother took me away, but at whose expence, or by whose direction I know nothing at all of it.

The first account that I can recollect, or could ever learn of myself, was that I had wander'd among a crew of those people they call Gypsies, or Egyptians; but I believe it was but a little while that I had been among them, for I had not had my skin discoloured, as they do to all children they carry about with them, nor can I tell how I came among them, or how I got from them.

It was at Colchester, in Essex, that those people left me; and I have a notion in my head that I left them there, (that is, that I hid my self and would not go any farther with them) but I am

---

[1] stealing.   [2] linen.
[3] Female criminals who proved to be pregnant had their sentences deferred until the birth of the child.

not able to be particular in that account; only this I remember, that being taken up by some of the parish officers of Colchester, I gave an account that I came into the town with the Gypsies, but that I would not go any farther with them, and that so they had left me, but whither they were gone that I knew not, for tho' they sent round the country to enquire after them, it seems, they could not be found.

I was now in a way to be provided for; for tho' I was not a parish charge upon this or that part of the town by law, yet as my case came to be known, and that I was too young to do any work, being not above three years old, compassion mov'd the magistrates of the town to take care of me, and I became one of their own as much as if I had been born in the place.

In the provision they made for me, it was my good hap to be put to nurse, as they call it, to a woman who was indeed poor, but had been in better circumstances, and who got a little livelihood by taking such as I was suppos'd to be, and keeping them with all necessaries, till they were at a certain age in which it might be suppos'd they might go to service, or get their own bread.

This woman had also a little school, which she kept to teach children to read and to work; and having, I say, liv'd before that in good fashion, she bred up the children with a great deal of art, as well as with a great deal of care.

But which was worth all the rest, she bred them up very religiously also, being herself a very sober, pious woman. (2.) Very housewifely and clean, and (3.) Very mannerly, and with good behaviour: so that excepting a plain diet, coarse lodging, and mean cloaths, we were brought up as mannerly as if we had been at the dancing school.

I was continu'd here till I was eight years old, when I was terrified with news that the magistrates (as I think they call'd them) had ordered that I should go to service; I was able to do but very little wherever I was to go, except it was to run of errands, and be a drudge to some cook-maid, and this they told me of often, which put me into a great fright; for I had a thorough aversion to going to service, as they call'd it, tho' I was so young; and I told my nurse that I believ'd I could get my living without going to service if she pleased to let me; for she had taught me to work with my needle, and spin worsted, which is the chief trade of that city, and I told her that if she would keep me, I would work for her, and I would work very hard.

I talk'd to her almost every day of working hard; and in short I did nothing but work and cry all day, which grieved the good kind woman so much that at last she began to be concern'd for me, for she lov'd me very well.

One day after this, as she came into the room where all the poor children were at work, she sat down just over against me, not in her usual place as mistress, but as if she had set herself on purpose to observe me, and see me work; I was doing something she had set me to, as I remember it was marking some shirts, which she had taken to make, and after a while she began to talk to me. Thou foolish child, says she, thou art always crying, (for I was crying then) prithee, what do'st cry for? Because they will take me away, says I, and put me to service, and I can't work house-work. Well, child, says she, but tho' you can't work house-work you will learn it in time, and they won't put you to hard things at first. Yes they will, says I, and if I can't do it, they will beat me, and the maids will beat me to make me do great work, and I am but a little girl, and I can't do it; and then I cry'd again, till I could not speak any more.

This mov'd my good motherly nurse, so that she resolv'd I should not go to service yet, so she bid me not cry, and she would speak to Mr. Mayor, and I should not go to service till I was bigger.

Well, this did not satisfy me, for to think of going to service at all was such a frightful thing to me, that if she had assured me I should not have gone till I was 20 years old, it would have been the same to me, I should have cry'd all the time, with the very apprehension of its being to be so at last.

When she saw that I was not pacified yet, she began to be angry with me, and What would you have? says she, don't I tell you that you shall not go to service till you are bigger? Ay, says I, but then I must go at last. Why, what, says she, is the girl mad? what, would you be a gentlewoman? Yes, says I, and cry'd heartily till I roar'd out again.

This set the old gentlewoman a laughing at me, as you may

be sure it would. Well, madam, forsooth, says she, gibing at me, you would be a gentlewoman, and how will you come to be a gentlewoman? What, will you do it by your fingers ends?

Yes, says I again, very innocently.

Why, what can you earn, says she, what can you get a day at your work?

Three pence, said I, when I spin, and four pence when I work plain work.

Alas! Poor gentlewoman, said she again, laughing, what will that do for thee?

It will keep me, says I, if you will let me live with you; and this I said in such a poor petitioning tone, that it made the poor woman's heart yearn to me, as she told me afterwards.

But, says she, that will not keep you and buy you cloaths too; and who must buy the little gentlewoman cloaths? says she, and smil'd all the while at me.

I will work harder then, says I, and you shall have it all.

Poor child! It won't keep you, said she, it will hardly find you in victuals.

Then I would have no victuals, says I again, very innocently, let me but live with you.

Why, can you live without victuals? says she. Yes, again says I, very much like a child, you may be sure, and still I cry'd heartily.

I had no policy in all this, you may easily see it was all nature, but it was joined with so much innocence, and so much passion, that, in short, it set the good motherly creature a weeping too, and at last she cry'd as fast as I did, and then took me, and led me out of the teaching room. Come, says she, you shan't go to service, you shall live with me; and this pacify'd me for the present.

After this, she going to wait on the Mayor, my story came up, and my good nurse told Mr. Mayor the whole tale. He was so pleased with it, that he would call his lady and his two daughters to hear it, and it made mirth enough among them, you may be sure.

However, not a week had passed over, but on a sudden comes Mrs. Mayoress and her two daughters to the house to see my old nurse, and to see her school and the children. When they had

looked about them a little: Well, Mrs. ——, says the Mayoress
to my nurse; and pray which is the little lass that is to be a
gentlewoman? I heard her, and I was terrible frighted,
tho' I did not know why neither; but Mrs. Mayoress comes up
to me: Well, miss, says she, and what are you at work upon?
The word 'miss' was a language that had hardly been heard of
in our school, and I wonder'd what sad name it was she call'd
me; however, I stood up, made a court'sy, and she took my
work out of my hand, look'd on it, and said it was very well;
then she look'd upon one of my hands. Nay, she may come to
be a gentlewoman, says she, for ought I know; she has a lady's
hand, I assure you. This pleased me mightily; but Mrs. Mayoress
did not stop there, but put her hand in her pocket, gave me a
shilling, and bid me mind my work, and learn to work well, and
I might be a gentlewoman for ought she knew.

All this while, my good old nurse, Mrs. Mayoress, and all the
rest of them, did not understand me at all, for they meant one
sort of thing by the word 'gentlewoman', and I meant quite
another: for alas, all I understood by being a gentlewoman, was
to be able to work for myself, and get enough to keep me without going to service, whereas they meant to live great and high,
and I know not what.

Well, after Mrs. Mayoress was gone, her two daughters came
in, and they call'd for the gentlewoman too, and they talk'd a
long while to me, and I answered them in my innocent way;
but always if they ask'd me whether I resolved to be a gentlewoman, I answer'd, Yes. At last they ask'd me what a gentlewoman was. That puzzel'd me much; however, I explain'd my
self negatively, that it was one that did not go to service, to do
house-work; they were mightily pleased, and lik'd my little prat-
tle to them, which it seems was agreeable enough to them, and
they gave me money too.

As for my money, I gave it all to my Mistress Nurse, as I call'd
her, and told her, she should have all I got when I was a gentlewoman, as well as now; by this and some other of my talk my
old tutoress began to understand what I meant by being a gentlewoman; and that it was no more than to be able to get my bread
by my own work, and at last she ask'd me whether it was not so.

I told her, Yes, and insisted on it, that to do so was to be a gentlewoman; for, says I, there is such a one, naming a woman that mended lace, and wash'd the ladies lac'd-heads; she, says I, is a gentlewoman, and they call her 'madam'.

Poor child, says my good old nurse, you may soon be such a gentlewoman as that, for she is a person of ill fame, and has had two bastards.

I did not understand anything of that; but I answered, I am sure they call her 'madam', and she does not go to service nor do house-work, and therefore I insisted that she was a gentlewoman, and I would be such a gentlewoman as that.

The ladies were told all this again, and they made themselves merry with it, and every now and then Mr. Mayor's daughters would come and see me, and ask where the little gentlewoman was, which made me not a little proud of my self besides. I was often visited by these young ladies, and sometimes they brought others with them; so that I was known by it, almost all over the town.

I was now about ten years old, and began to look a little womanish, for I was mighty grave, very mannerly, and as I had often heard the ladies say I was pretty, and would be very handsome, you may be sure it made me not a little proud. However, that pride had no ill effect upon me yet, only as they often gave me money, and I gave it to my old nurse, she, honest woman, was so just as to lay it out again for me, and gave me head-dresses, and linnen, and gloves, and I went very neat, for if I had rags on, I would always be clean, or else I would dabble them in water my self; but, I say, my good nurse, when I had money given me, very honestly laid it out for me, and would always tell the ladies this, or that, was bought with their money; and this made them give me more, till at last I was indeed call'd upon by the magistrates to go out to service; but then I was become so good a workwoman my self, and the ladies were so kind to me, that I was past it; for I could earn as much for my nurse as was enough to keep me; so she told them that if they would give her leave, she would keep the gentlewoman, as she call'd me, to be her assist-ant, and teach the children, which I was very well able to do; for I was very nimble at my work, tho' I was yet very young.

But the kindness of the ladies did not end here, for when they understood that I was no more maintain'd by the town as before, they gave me money oftener; and as I grew up, they brought me work to do for them; such as linnen to make, laces to mend, and heads [1] to dress up, and not only paid me for doing them, but even taught me how to do them; so that I was a gentle-woman indeed, as I understood that word; for before I was twelve years old, I not only found myself cloaths, and paid my nurse for my keeping, but got money in my pocket too.

The ladies also gave me cloaths frequently of their own or their children's; some stockings, some petticoats, some gowns, some one thing, some another, and these my old woman man-aged for me like a mother, and kept them for me, obliged me to mend them, and turn them to the best advantage, for she was a rare house-wife.

At last one of the ladies took such a fancy to me, that she would have me home to her house, for a month, she said, to be among her daughters.

Now tho' this was exceedingly kind in her, yet as my good woman said to her, unless she resolv'd to keep me for good and all, she would do the little gentlewoman more harm than good. Well, says the lady, that's true, I'll only take her home for a week then, that I may see how my daughters and she agree, and how I like her temper, and then I'll tell you more; and in the mean time, if any body comes to see her as they used to do, you may only tell them, you have sent her out to my house.

This was prudently managed enough, and I went to the lady's house, but I was so pleased there with the young ladies, and they so pleased with me, that I had enough to do to come away, and they were as unwilling to part with me.

However, I did come away, and liv'd almost a year more with my honest old woman, and began now to be very helpful to her; for I was almost fourteen years old, was tall of my age, and look'd a little womanish; but I had such a taste of genteel living at the lady's house, that I was not so easy in my old quarters as I us'd to be, and I thought it was fine to be a gentlewoman indeed, for I had quite other notions of a gentlewoman now than I had before; and as I thought that it was fine to be a gen-tlewoman, so I lov'd to be among gentlewomen, and therefore I long'd to be there again.

[1] In the early eighteenth century artificial heads of hair were worn by ladies, usually trimmed with ribbon, lace, etc.

When I was about fourteen years and a quarter old, my good old nurse, mother I ought to call her, fell sick and dy'd; I was then in a sad condition indeed, for as there is no great bustle in putting an end to a poor body's family, when once they are carried to the grave, so the poor good woman being buried, the parish children were immediately remov'd by the church-wardens; the school was at an end, and the day-children of it had no more to do but just stay at home, till they were sent some where else. As for what she left, a daughter, a married woman, came and swept it all away, and removing the goods, they had no more to say to me than to jest with me, and tell me that the little gentlewoman might set up for herself, if she pleased.

I was frighted out of my wits almost, and knew not what to do; for I was, as it were, turn'd out of doors to the wide world, and that which was still worse, the old honest woman had two and twenty shillings of mine in her hand, which was all the estate the little gentlewoman had in the world; and when I ask'd the daughter for it, she huft me, and told me she had nothing to do with it.

It was true the good poor woman had told her daughter of it, and that it lay in such a place, that it was the child's money, and had call'd once or twice for me to give it me, but I was unhappily out of the way, and when I came back she was past being in a condition to speak of it. However, the daughter was so honest afterwards as to give it me, tho' at first she us'd me cruelly about it.

Now was I a poor gentlewoman indeed, and I was just that very night to be turn'd into the wide world; for the daughter remov'd all the goods, and I had not so much as a lodging to go to, or a bit of bread to eat. But it seems some of the neighbours took so much compassion of me as to acquaint the lady in whose family I had been; and immediately she sent her maid to fetch me; and away I went with them bag and baggage, and with a glad heart you may be sure. The fright of my condition had made such an impression upon me, that I did not want now to be a gentlewoman, but was very willing to be a servant, and that any kind of servant they thought fit to have me be.

But my new generous mistress had better thoughts for me. I call her generous, for she exceeded the good woman I was with before in every thing, as in estate; I say, in every thing except honesty; and for that, tho' this was a lady most exactly just, yet I must not forget to say on all occasions, that the first, tho' poor, was as uprightly honest as it was possible.

I was no sooner carried away as I have said by this good gentlewoman, but the first lady, that is to say, the Mayoress that was, sent her daughters to take care of me; and another family which had taken notice of me when I was the little gentlewoman sent for me after her, so that I was mightily made of; nay, and they were not a little angry, especially the Mayoress, that her friend had taken me away from her; for as she said, I was hers by right, she having been the first that took any notice of me; but they that had me would not part with me; and as for me I could not be better than where I was.

Here I continued till I was between 17 and 18 years old, and here I had all the advantages for my education that could be imagined; the lady had masters home to teach her daughters to dance, and to speak French, and to write, and others to teach them musick; and as I was always with them, I learn'd as fast as they; and tho' the masters were not appointed to teach me, yet I learn'd by imitation and enquiry all that they learn'd by instruction and direction. So that in short, I learned to dance and speak French as well as any of them, and to sing much better, for I had a better voice than any of them; I could not so readily come at playing the harpsicord or spinnet, because I had no instrument of my own to practise on, and could only come at theirs in the intervals when they left it; but yet I learned tolerably well, and the young ladies at length got two instruments, that is to say, a harpsicord and a spinnet too, and then they taught me themselves; but as to dancing they could hardly help my learning country dances, because they always wanted me to make up even number; and on the other hand, they were as heartily willing to learn me everything that they had been taught themselves, as I could be to take the learning.

By this means I had, as I have said, all the advantages of education that I could have had if I had been as much a gentlewoman as they were with whom I liv'd; and in some things I had the advantage of my ladies, tho' they were my superiors, *viz.* that mine were all the gifts of nature, and which all their fortunes could not furnish. First, I was apparently handsomer than any of them, secondly, I was better shap'd, and thirdly, I sung better, by which I mean, I had a better voice; in all which you will, I hope, allow me to say I do not speak my own conceit, but the opinion of all that knew the family.

I had with all these the common vanity of my sex, *viz.* that being really taken for very handsome, or if you please for a great beauty, I very well knew it, and had as good an opinion of my self as any body else could have of me, and particularly I loved to hear any body speak of it, which happened often, and was a great satisfaction to me.

Thus far I have had a smooth story to tell of my self, and in all this part of my life, I not only had the reputation of living in a very good family, and a family noted and respected every where for vertue and sobriety, and for every valuable thing; but I had the character too of a very sober, modest, and vertuous young woman, and such I had always been; neither had I yet any occasion to think of any thing else, or to know what a temptation to wickedness meant.

But that which I was too vain of was my ruin, or rather my vanity was the cause of it. The lady in the house where I was had two sons, young gentlemen of extraordinary parts and behaviour; and it was my misfortune to be very well with them both, but they managed themselves with me in a quite different manner.

The eldest, a gay gentleman that knew the town, as well as the country, and tho' he had levity enough to do an ill-natured thing, yet had too much judgment of things to pay too dear for his pleasures; he began with that unhappy snare to all women, *viz.* taking notice upon all occasions how pretty I was, as he call'd it, how agreeable, how well carriaged, and the like; and this he contriv'd so subtilly, as if he had known as well how to catch a woman in his net as a partridge when he went a setting; for he would contrive to be talking this to his sisters, when, tho' I was not by, yet when he knew I was not so far off but that I should be sure to hear him. His sisters would return softly to him, Hush, brother, she will hear you, she is but in the next room. Then he would put it off, and talk softlier as if he had not known it, and begin to acknowledge he was wrong; and then as if he had forgot himself, he would speak aloud again, and I that was so well pleased to hear it was sure to listen for it upon all occasions.

After he had thus baited his hook, and found easily enough the method how to lay it in my way, he play'd an open game; and one day going by his sister's chamber when I was there, he comes in with an air of gaiety. O! Mrs. Betty, said he to me, how do you do, Mrs. Betty? don't your cheeks burn, Mrs. Betty? I made a court'sy, and blush'd, but said nothing. What makes you talk so, brother? says the lady. Why, says he, we have been talking of her below stairs this half hour. Well, says his sister, you can say no harm of her, that I am sure, so 'tis no matter what you have been talking about. Nay, says he, 'tis so far from talking harm of her that we have been talking a great deal of good, and a great many fine things have been said of Mrs. Betty, I assure you; and particularly that she is the handsomest young woman in Colchester, and, in short, they begin to toast her health in the town.

I wonder at you, brother, says the sister; Betty wants but one thing, but she had as good want every thing, for the market is against our sex just now; and if a young woman has beauty, birth, breeding, wit, sense, manners, modesty, and all to an ex-tream, yet if she has not money, she's no body, she had as good want them all; nothing but money now recommends a woman; the men play the game all into their own hands.

Her younger brother, who was by, cry'd, Hold, sister, you run too fast, I am an exception to your rule: I assure you, if I find a woman so accomplish'd as you talk of, I won't trouble myself about the money. O, says the sister, but you will take care not to fancy one, then, without the money.

You don't know that neither, says the brother.

But why, sister, says the elder brother, why do you exclaim so about the fortune? you are none of them that want a for-tune, what ever else you want.

I understand you, brother, replies the lady very smartly, you suppose I have the money and want the beauty; but as times go now, the first will do, so I have the better of my neighbours.

Well, says the younger brother, but your neighbours may be even with you; for beauty will steal a husband sometimes in spight of money; and when the maid chances to be handsomer than the mistress, she oftentimes makes as good a market, and rides in a coach before her.

I thought it was time for me to withdraw, and I did so; but not so far but that I heard all their discourse, in which I heard abundance of fine things said of my self, which prompted my vanity, but, as I soon found, was not the way to encrease my interest in the family, for the sister and the younger brother fell grievously out about it; and as he said some very disobliging things to her upon my account, so I could easily see that she resented them by her future conduct to me, which indeed was very unjust; for I had never had the least thought of what she suspected as to her younger brother. Indeed the elder brother in his distant remote way had said a great many things as in jest, which I had the folly to believe were in earnest, or to flatter my self with the hopes of what I ought to have suppos'd he never intended.

It happened one day that he came running up stairs, towards the room where his sister us'd to sit and work, as he often us'd to do; and calling to them before he came in, as was his way too, I being there alone, step'd to the door, and said, Sir, the ladies are not here, they are walk'd down the garden. As I step'd forward to say this, he was just got to the door, and clasping me in his arms, as if it had been by chance, O! Mrs. Betty, says he, are you here? that's better still, I want to speak with you, more than I do with them; and then having me in his arms he kiss'd me three or four times.

I struggled to get away, and yet did it but faintly neither, and he held me fast, and still kiss'd me, till he was out of breath, and, sitting down, says he, Dear Betty, I am in love with you.

His words, I must confess, fir'd my blood; all my spirits flew about my heart, and put me into disorder enough. He repeated it afterwards several times, that he was in love with me, and my heart spoke as plain as a voice that I lik'd it; nay, whenever he said, I am in love with you, my blushes plainly reply'd, Wou'd you were, sir. However, nothing else pass'd at that time; it was but a surprize, and I soon recover'd my self. He had stay'd longer with me, but he happen'd to look out at the window and see his sisters coming up the garden, so he took his leave, kiss'd me again, told me he was very serious, and I should hear more of him very quickly, and away he went infinitely pleas'd, and had there not been one misfortune in it, I had been in the right, but the mistake lay here, that Mrs. Betty was in earnest, and the gentleman was not.

From this time my head run upon strange things, and I may truly say I was not myself; to have such a gentleman talk to me of being in love with me, and of my being such a charming creature, as he told me I was, these were things I knew not how to bear, my vanity was elevated to the last degree. It is true, I had my head full of pride, but knowing nothing of the wickedness of the times, I had not one thought of my virtue about me; and had my young master offer'd it at first sight, he might have taken any liberty he thought fit with me; but he did not see his advantage, which was my happiness for that time.

It was not long, but he found an opportunity to catch me again, and almost in the same posture, indeed it had more of design in it on his part, tho' not on my part. It was thus: the young ladies were gone a visiting with their mother; his brother was out of town, and as for his father he had been at London for a week before; he had so well watch'd me that he knew where I was, tho' I did not so much as know that he was in the house, and he briskly comes up the stairs, and seeing me at work, comes into the room to me directly, and began just as he did before, with taking me in his arms, and kissing me for almost a quarter of an hour together.

It was his younger sister's chamber that I was in, and as there was no body in the house but the maid below stairs, he was, it may be, the ruder. In short, he began to be in earnest with me indeed; perhaps he found me a little too easy, for I made no resistance to him while he only held me in his arms and kiss'd me; indeed, I was too well pleased with it to resist him much.

Well, tir'd with that kind of work, we sat down, and there he talk'd with me a great while. He said he was charm'd with me, and that he could not rest till he had told me how he was in love with me, and if I could love him again, and would make him happy, I should be the saving of his life; and many such fine things. I said little to him again, but easily discovered [1] that I was a fool, and that I did not in the least perceive what he meant.

[1] showed.

Then he walked about the room, and taking me by the hand, I walk'd with him; and by and by taking his advantage, he threw me down upon the bed, and kissed me there most violently; but to give him his due, offered no manner of rudeness to me, only kiss'd me a great while; after this he thought he had heard some body come up stairs, so he got off from the bed, lifted me up, professing a great deal of love for me, but told me it was all an honest affection, and that he meant no ill to me, and with that put five guineas into my hand, and went down stairs.

I was more confounded with the money than I was before with the love; and began to be so elevated, that I scarce knew the ground I stood on: I am the more particular in this, that if it comes to be read by any innocent young body, they may learn from it to guard themselves against the mischiefs which attend an early knowledge of their own beauty; if a young woman once thinks herself handsome, she never doubts the truth of any man that tells her he is in love with her; for if she believes herself charming enough to captivate him, 'tis natural to expect the effects of it.

This gentleman had now fir'd his inclination, as much as he had my vanity, and as if he had found that he had an opportunity, and was sorry he did not take hold of it, he comes up again in about half an hour, and falls to work with me again just as he did before, only with a little less introduction.

And first, when he entered the room, he turn'd about, and shut the door. Mrs. Betty, said he, I fancy'd before, some body was coming up stairs, but it was not so; however, adds he, if they find me in the room with you, they shan't catch me a kissing of you. I told him I did not know who should be coming up stairs, for I believed there was no body in the house but the cook, and the other maid, and they never came up those stairs. Well, my dear, says he, 'tis good to be sure however; and so he sits down and we began to talk; and now, tho' I was still on fire with his first visit, and said little, he did as it were put words in my mouth, telling me how passionately he lov'd me, and that tho' he could not till he came to his estate, yet he was resolv'd to make me happy then, and himself too; that is to say, to marry me, and abundance of such things, which I, poor fool, did not understand the drift of, but acted as if there was no kind of love but that which tended to matrimony; and if he had spoken of that, I had no room, as well as no power, to have said no; but we were not come to that length yet.

We had not sat long, but he got up, and stopping my very breath with kisses, threw me upon the bed again; but then he went further with me than decency permits me to mention, nor had it been in my power to have deny'd him at that moment, had he offered much more than he did.

However, tho' he took these freedoms with me, it did not go to that which they call the last favour, which, to do him justice, he did not attempt; and he made that self-denial of his a plea for all his freedoms with me upon other occasions after this. When this was over, he stay'd but a little while, but he put almost a handful of gold in my hand, and left me a thousand protestations of his passion for me, and of his loving me above all the women in the world.

It will not be strange if I now began to think; but alas! it was but with very little solid reflections: I had a most unbounded stock of vanity and pride, and but a very little stock of virtue. I did indeed cast [1] something with my self what my young master aim'd at, but thought of nothing but the fine words and the gold; whether he intended to marry me, or not, seem'd a matter of no great consequence to me; nor did I so much as think of making any capitulation for my self 'till he made a kind of formal proposal to me, as you shall hear presently.

Thus I gave up my self to ruin without the least concern, and am a fair memento to all young women whose vanity prevails over their virtue. Nothing was ever so stupid on both sides; had I acted as became me, and resisted as virtue and honour requir'd, he had either desisted his attacks, finding no room to expect the end of his design, or had made fair and honourable proposals of marriage; in which case, whoever blam'd him, no body could have blam'd me. In short, if he had known me, and how easy the trifle he aim'd at was to be had, he would have troubled his head no farther, but have given me four or five guineas and have lain with me the next time he had come at me. On the other hand, if I had known his thoughts, and how hard he supposed I would be to be gain'd, I might have made my own terms, and if

[1] ponder.

I had not capitulated for an immediate marriage, I might for a maintainance till marriage, and might have had what I would; for he was rich to excess, besides what he had in expectation. But I had wholly abandoned all such thoughts, and was taken up only with the pride of my beauty, and of being belov'd by such a gentleman: as for the gold, I spent whole hours in looking upon it; I told the guineas over a thousand times a day. Never poor vain creature was so wrapt up with every part of the story as I was, not considering what was before me, and how near my ruin was at the door; and indeed I think I rather wished for that ruin than studied to avoid it.

In the mean time, however, I was cunning enough not to give the least room to any in the family to imagine that I had the least correspondence with him; I scarce ever look'd towards him in publick, or answer'd if he spoke to me; when, but for all that, we had every now and then a little encounter, where we had room for a word or two, and now and then a kiss, but no fair opportunity for the mischief intended; and especially considering that he made more circumlocution than he had occasion for, and the work appearing difficult to him, he really made it so.

But as the devil is an unwearied tempter, so he never fails to find an opportunity for the wickedness he invites to. It was one evening that I was in the garden, with his two younger sisters, and himself, when he found means to convey a note into my hand, by which he told me that he would to-morrow desire me publickly to go of an errand for him, and that I should see him somewhere by the way.

Accordingly after dinner, he very gravely says to me, his sisters being all by, Mrs. Betty, I must ask a favour of you. What's that? says the second sister. Nay, sister, says he, very gravely, if you can't spare Mrs. Betty to-day, any other time will do. Yes, they said, they could spare her well enough, and the sister beg'd pardon for asking. Well, but, says the eldest sister, you must tell Mrs. Betty what it is; if it be any private business that we must not hear, you may call her out, there she is. Why, sister, says the gentleman very gravely, what do you mean? I only desire her to go into the High-street (and then he pulls out a turn-over),[1] to such a shop; and then he tells them a long story

[1] a linen band worn round the neck and turned down.

of two fine neckcloths [1] he had bid money for, and he wanted to have me go and make an errand to buy a neck to that turn-over that he showed, and if they would not take my money for the neckcloths to bid a shilling more, and haggle with them; and then he made more errands, and so continued to have such petty business to do, that I should be sure to stay a good while.

When he had given me my errands, he told them a long story of a visit he was going to make to a family they all knew, and where was to be such and such gentlemen, and very formally ask'd his sisters to go with him, and they as formally excus'd themselves, because of company that they had notice was to come and visit them that afternoon, all which by the way he had contriv'd on purpose.

He had scarce done speaking, but his man came up to tell him that Sir W—— H——'s coach stop'd at the door; so he runs down, and comes up again immediately. Alas! says he aloud, there's all my mirth spoil'd at once; Sir W—— has sent his coach for me, and desires to speak with me. It seems this Sir W—— was a gentleman who liv'd about three miles off, to whom he had spoke on purpose to lend him his charriot for a particular occasion, and had appointed it to call for him, as it did, about three a clock.

Immediately he calls for his best wig, hat, and sword, and ordering his man to go to the other place to make his excuse, that was to say, he made an excuse to send his man away, he prepares to go into the coach. As he was going, he stop'd a while, and speaks mightily earnestly to me about his business, and finds an opportunity to say very softly, Come away, my dear, as soon as ever you can. I said nothing, but made a court'sy, as if I had done so to what he said in publick; in about a quarter of an hour I went out too; I had no dress, other than before, except that I had a hood, a mask, a fan, and a pair of gloves in my pocket; so that there was not the least suspicion in the house. He waited for me in a back lane which he knew I must pass by, and the coachman knew whither to go, which was to a certain place called Mile-End, where liv'd a confident of his, where we went in, and where was all the convenience in the world to be as wicked as we pleas'd.

When we were together, he began to talk very gravely to me,

[1] cravats.

and tell me, he did not bring me there to betray me; that his passion for me would not suffer him to abuse me; that he resolved to marry me as soon as he came to his estate; that in the mean time, if I would grant his request, he would maintain me very honourably, and made me a thousand protestations of his sincerity, and of his affection to me; and that he would never abandon me, and, as I may say, made a thousand more preambles than he need to have done.

However, as he press'd me to speak, I told him I had no reason to question the sincerity of his love to me, after so many protestations, But — and there I stop'd, as if I left him to guess the rest. But what? my dear, says he; I guess what you mean, what if you should be with child, is not that it? Why then, says he, I'll take care of you, and provide for you, and the child too, and that you may see I am not in jest, says he, here's an earnest for you; and with that he pulls out a silk purse with an hundred guineas in it, and gave it me; and I'll give you such another, says he, every year till I marry you.

My colour came and went at the sight of the purse, and with the fire of his proposal together, so that I could not say a word, and he easily perceiv'd it; so putting the purse into my bosom, I made no more resistance to him, but let him do just what he pleas'd, and as often as he pleas'd; and thus I finish'd my own destruction at once, for from this day, being forsaken of my virtue, and my modesty, I had nothing of value left to recommend me, either to God's blessing, or man's assistance.

But things did not end here; I went back to the town, did the business he directed me to, and was at home before any body thought me long; as for my gentleman, he stay'd out till late at night, and there was not the least suspicion in the family, either on his account or on mine.

We had after this frequent opportunities to repeat our crime, and especially at home when his mother and the young ladies went abroad a visiting, which he watch'd so narrowly as never to miss; knowing always before-hand when they went out, and then fail'd not to catch me all alone, and securely enough; so that we took our fill of our wicked pleasures for near half a year; and yet, which was the most to my satisfaction, I was not with child.

But before this half year was expir'd, his younger brother, of whom I have made some mention in the beginning of the story, falls to work with me; and he finding me alone in the garden one evening, begins a story of the same kind to me, made good honest professions of being in love with me; and, in short, proposes fairly and honourably to marry me.

I was now confounded, and driven to such an extremity as the like was never known to me; I resisted the proposal with obstinacy, and began to arm my self with arguments: I laid before him the inequality of the match, the treatment I should meet with in the family, the ingratitude it would be to his good father and mother, who had taken me into their house upon such generous principles, and when I was in such a low condition; and in short, I said everything to disswade him that I could imagine except telling him the truth, which wou'd indeed have put an end to it all, but that I durst not think of mentioning.

But here happened a circumstance that I did not expect indeed, which put me to my shifts; for this young gentleman, as he was plain and honest, so he pretended to nothing but what was so too; and knowing his own innocence, he was not so careful to make his having a kindness for Mrs. Betty a secret in the house as his brother was; and tho' he did not let them know that he had talk'd to me about it, yet he said enough to let his sisters perceive he lov'd me, and his mother saw it too, which tho' they took no notice of to me, yet they did to him, and immediately I found their carriage to me alter'd more than ever before.

I saw the cloud, though I did not foresee the storm; it was easy, I say, to see their carriage was alter'd, and that it grew worse and worse every day, 'till at last I got information that I should in a very little while be desired to remove.

I was not alarm'd at the news, having a full satisfaction that I should be provided for; and especially considering that I had reason every day to expect I should be with child, and that then I should be obliged to remove without any pretences for it.

After some time, the younger gentleman took an opportunity to tell me that the kindness he had for me had got vent in the family; he did not charge me with it, he said, for he knew well enough which way it came out; he told me his way of talking had been the occasion of it, for that he did not make his respect for me so much a secret as he might have done, and the reason was, that he was at a point that if I would consent to have him, he would tell them all openly that he lov'd me, and that he intended to marry me: that it was true his father and mother might resent it, and be unkind, but he was now in a way to live, being bred to the law, and he did not fear maintaining me, and that, in short, as he believ'd I would not be asham'd of him, so he was resolv'd not to be ashamed of me, and that he scorn'd to be afraid to own me now, who he resolv'd to own after I was his wife, and therefore I had nothing to do but to give him my hand, and he would answer for all the rest.

I was now in a dreadful condition indeed, and now I repented heartily my easiness with the eldest brother, not from any reflection of conscience, for I was a stranger to those things, but I could not think of being a whore to one brother, and a wife to the other; it came also into my thoughts that the first brother had promis'd to make me his wife when he came to his estate; but I presently remember'd, what I had often thought of, that he had never spoken a word of having me for a wife after he had conquer'd me for a mistress; and indeed till now, tho' I said I thought of it often, yet it gave no disturbance at all, for as he did not seem in the least to lessen his affection to me, so neither did he lessen his bounty, tho' he had the discretion himself to desire me not to lay out a penny in cloaths, or to make the least show extraordinary, because it would necessarily give jealousy [1] in the family, since every body knew I could come at such things no manner of ordinary way, but by some private friendship, which they would presently have suspected.

I was now in a great strait, and knew not what to do; the main difficulty was this, the younger brother not only laid close siege to me, but suffered it to be seen; he would come into his sister's room, and his mother's room, and sit down, and talk a thousand kind things to me, even before their faces; so that the whole house talk'd of it, and his mother reprov'd him for it, and their carriage to me appeared quite altered. In short, his mother had let fall some speeches, as if she intended to put me out of the family, that is in English, to turn me out of doors. Now, I was sure this could not be a secret to his brother, only that he might think, as indeed no body else yet did, that the

[1] arouse suspicion.

youngest brother had made any proposal to me about it; but as I easily could see that it would go farther, so I saw likewise there was an absolute necessity to speak of it to him, or that he would speak of it to me, but knew not whether I should break it to him, or let it alone till he should break it to me.

Upon serious consideration, for indeed now I began to consider things very seriously, and never till now, I resolv'd to tell him of it first, and it was not long before I had an opportunity, for the very next day his brother went to London upon some business, and the family being out a visiting, just as it happened before, and as indeed was often the case, he came according to his custom to spend an hour or two with Mrs. Betty.

When he had sate down a while, he easily perceived there was an alteration in my countenance, that I was not so free and pleasant with him as I used to be, and particularly, that I had been a crying; he was not long before he took notice of it, and ask'd me in very kind terms what was the matter, and if anything troubled me. I would have put it off if I could, but it was not to be conceal'd; so after suffering many importunities to draw that out of me which I long'd as much as possible to disclose, I told him that it was true, something did trouble me, and something of such a nature that I could hardly conceal from him, and yet that I could not tell how to tell him of it neither; that it was a thing that not only surpriz'd me, but greatly perplext me, and that I knew not what course to take, unless he would direct me. He told me with great tenderness that, let it be what it would, I should not let it trouble me, for he would protect me from all the world.

I then began at a distance, and told him I was afraid the ladies had got some secret information of our correspondence [1]; for that it was easy to see that their conduct was very much chang'd towards me, and that now it was come to pass that they frequently found fault with me, and sometimes fell quite out with me, tho' I never gave them the least occasion: that whereas I us'd always to lye with the eldest sister, I was lately put to lye by my self, or with one of the maids; and that I had over-heard them several times talking very unkindly about me; but that which confirm'd it all was that one of the servants had told me

[1] intercourse.

that she had heard I was to be turn'd out, and that it was not safe for the family that I should be any longer in the house.

He smil'd when he heard of this, and I ask'd him how he could make so light of it, when he must need know that if there was any discovery I was undone, and that it would hurt him, tho' not ruin him, as it would me. I upbraided him, that he was like the rest of his sex, that, when they had the character of a woman at their mercy, oftentimes made it their jest, and at least look'd upon it as a trifle, and counted the ruin of those they had had their will of, as a thing of no value.

He saw me warm and serious, and he chang'd his stile immediately; he told me he was sorry I should have such a thought of him: that he had never given me the least occasion for it, but had been as tender of my reputation as he could be of his own; that he was sure our correspondence had been managed with so much address that not one creature in the family had so much as a suspicion of it; that if he smil'd when I told him my thoughts, it was at the assurance he lately receiv'd that our understanding one another was not so much as guess'd at, and that when he had told me how much reason he had to be easy, I should smile as he did, for he was very certain it would give me a full satisfaction.

This is a mistery I cannot understand, says I, or how it should be to my satisfaction that I am to be turn'd out of doors; for if our correspondence is not discover'd, I know not what else I have done to change the faces of the whole family to me, who formerly used me with so much tenderness, as if I had been one of their own children.

Why, look you, child, says he; that they are uneasy about you, that is true, but that they have the least suspicion of the case as it is, and as it respects you and I, is so far from being true that they suspect my brother Robin, and, in short, they are fully perswaded he makes love to you: nay, the fool has put it into their heads too himself, for he is continually bantring them about it, and making a jest of himself; I confess I think he is wrong to do so, because he cannot but see it vexes them, and makes them unkind to you; but 'tis a satisfaction to me because of the assurance it gives me that they do not suspect me in the least, and I hope this will be to your satisfaction too.

So it is, says I, one way, but this does not reach my case at all, nor is this the chief thing that troubles me, tho' I have been concern'd about that too. What is it then? says he. With which, I fell into tears, and could say nothing to him at all. He strove to pacifie me all he could, but began at last to be very pressing upon me, to tell what it was. At last I answer'd that I thought I ought to tell him too, and that he had some right to know it; besides, that I wanted his direction in the case, for I was in such perplexity that I knew not what course to take; and then I related the whole affair to him. I told him how imprudently his brother had manag'd himself, in making himself so publick; for that if he had kept it a secret, I could but have denied him positively, without giving any reason for it, and he would in time have ceased his sollicitations; but that he had the vanity, first, to depend upon it that I would not deny him, and then had taken the freedom to tell his design to the whole house.

I told him how far I had resisted him, and how sincere and honourable his offers were; but, says I, my case will be doubly hard; for as they carry it ill to me now, because he desires to have me, they'll carry it worse when they shall find I have deny'd him; and they will presently say there's something else in it, and that I am marry'd already to somebody else, or that I would never refuse a match so much above me as this was.

This discourse surpriz'd him indeed very much. He told me that it was a critical point indeed for me to manage, and he did not see which way I should get out of it; but he would consider of it, and let me know next time we met what resolution he was come to about it; and in the mean time desir'd I would not give my consent to his brother, nor yet give him a flat denial, but that I would hold him in suspence a while.

I seem'd to start at his saying I should not give him my consent; I told him he knew very well, I had no consent to give; that he had ingag'd himself to marry me, and that I was thereby ingag'd to him; that he had all along told me I was his wife, and I look'd upon my self as effectually so as if the ceremony had pass'd; and that it was from his own mouth that I did so, he having all along persuaded me to call my self his wife.

Well, my dear, says he, don't be concern'd at that now; if I am not your husband, I'll be as good as a husband to you, and do not let those things trouble you now, but let me look a little farther into this affair, and I shall be able to say more next time we meet.

He pacify'd me as well as he could with this, but I found he was very thoughtful, and that tho' he was very kind to me, and kiss'd me a thousand times and more, I believe, and gave me money too, yet he offer'd no more all the while we were together, which was above two hours, and which I much wonder'd at, considering how it us'd to be, and what opportunity we had.

His brother did not come from London for five or six days, and it was two days more before he got an opportunity to talk with him; but then, getting him by himself, he talk'd very close to him about it; and the same evening found means (for we had a long conference together) to repeat all their discourse to me, which as near as I can remember was to the purpose following. He told him he heard strange news of him since he went, (*viz.*) that he made love to Mrs. Betty. Well, says his brother, a little angrily, and what then? What has anybody to do with that? Nay, says his brother, don't be angry, Robin, I don't pretend to have any thing to do with it; but I find they do concern themselves about it, and that they have used the poor girl ill about it, which I should take as done to my self. Who do you mean by 'they'? says Robin. I mean my mother and the girls, says the elder brother.

But hark ye, says his brother, are you in earnest, do you really love the girl? Why then, says Robin, I will be free with you, I do love her above all the women in the world, and I will have her; let them say and do what they will, I believe the girl will not deny me.

It struck me to the heart when he told me this, for tho' it was most rational to think I would not deny him, yet I knew in my own conscience I must, and I saw my ruin in my being oblig'd to do so; but I knew it was my business to talk otherwise then, so I interrupted him in his story thus: Ay! said I, does he think I cannot deny him? but he shall find I can deny him for all that. Well, my dear, says he, but let me give you the whole story as it went on between us, and then say what you will.

Then he went on and told me that he reply'd thus: But,

brother, you know she has nothing, and you may have several ladies with good fortunes. 'Tis no matter for that, said Robin, I love the girl; and I will never please my pocket in marrying, and not please my fancy. And so my dear, adds he, there is no opposing him.

Yes, yes, says I, I can oppose him, I have learnt to say no now, tho' I had not learnt it before; if the best lord in the land offer'd me marriage now, I could very chearfully say no to him.

Well, but my dear, says he, what can you say to him? You know, as you said before, he will ask you many questions about it, and all the house will wonder what the meaning of it should be.

Why, says I, smiling, I can stop all their mouths at one clap, by telling him, and them too, that I am married already to his elder brother.

He smil'd a little too at the word, but I could see it startled him, and he could not hide the disorder it put him into: however, he return'd, Why, tho' that may be true, in some sense, yet I suppose you are but in jest; when you talk of giving such an answer as that, it may not be convenient on many accounts.

No, no, says I pleasantly, I am not so fond of letting that secret come out, without your consent.

But what then can you say to them, says he, when they find you possitive against a match which would be apparently so much to your advantage? Why, says I, should I be at a loss? First, I am not oblig'd to give them any reason: on the other hand, I may tell them I am married already, and stop there, and that will be a full stop too to him, for he can have no reason to ask one question after it.

Ay, says he, but the whole house will teize you about that, and if you deny them possitively, they will be disoblig'd at you, and suspicious besides.

Why, says I, what can I do? What would you have me do? I was in strait enough before, as I told you, and acquainted you with the circumstances that I might have your advice.

My dear, says he, I have been considering very much upon it, you may be sure, and tho' the advice has many mortifications in it to me, and may at first seem strange to you, yet all things consider'd, I see no better way for you than to let him go on; and if you find him hearty and in earnest, marry him.

I gave him a look full of horror at those words, and turning pale as death, was at the very point of sinking down out of the chair I sat in, when giving a start, My dear, says he aloud, what's the matter with you? Where are you agoing? and a great many such things; and with jogging and calling to me, fetch'd me a little to my self, tho' it was a good while before I fully recover'd my senses, and was not able to speak for several minutes.

When I was fully recover'd, he began again. My dear, says he, I would have you consider seriously of it: you may see plainly how the family stand in this case, and they would be stark mad if it was my case, as it is my brother's, and, for ought I see, it would be my ruin and yours too.

Ay! says I, still speaking angrily, are all your protestations and vows to be shaken by the dislike of the family? Did I not always object that to you, and you made a light thing of it, as what you were above, and would not value; and is it come to this now? Is this your faith and honour, your love, and the solidity of your promises?

He continued perfectly calm, notwithstanding all my reproaches, and I was not sparing of them at all; but he reply'd at last, My dear, I have not broken one promise with you yet; I did tell you I would marry you when I was come to my estate; but you see my father is a hail, healthy man, and may live these thirty years still, and not be older than several are round us in the town; and you never propos'd my marrying you sooner, because you know it might be my ruin; and as to the rest, I have not fail'd you in any thing.

I could not deny a word of this. But why then, says I, can you perswade me to such a horrid step as leaving you, since you have not left me? Will you allow no affection, no love on my side, where there has been so much on your side? Have I made you no returns? Have I given no testimony of my sincerity, and of my passion? Are the sacrifices I have made of honour and modesty to you no proof of my being ty'd to you in bonds too strong to be broken?

But here, my dear, says he, you may come into a safe station, and appear with honour, and the remembrance of what we have done may be wrapt up in an eternal silence, as if it had never happen'd; you shall always have my sincere affection, only then it shall be honest, and perfectly just to my brother; you shall be my dear sister, as now you are my dear — and there he stop'd.

Your dear whore, says I, you would have said, and you might as well have said it; but I understand you. However, I desire you to remember the long discourses you have had with me, and the many hours' pains you have taken to perswade me to believe my self an honest woman; that I was your wife intentionally, and that it was as effectual a marriage that had pass'd between us as if we had been publickly wedded by the parson of the parish; you know these have been your own words to me.

I found this was a little too close upon him, but I made it up in what follows; he stood stock still for a while, and said nothing, and I went on thus: You cannot, says I, without the highest injustice believe that I yielded upon all these perswasions without a love not to be questioned, not to be shaken again by any thing that could happen afterward. If you have such dishonourable thoughts of me, I must ask you what foundation have I given for such a suggestion.

If, then, I have yielded to the importunities of my affection, and if I have been perswaded to believe that I am really your wife, shall I now give the lye to all those arguments, and call my self your whore, or mistress, which is the same thing? And will you transfer me to your brother? Can you transfer my affection? Can you bid me cease loving you, and bid me love him? Is it in my power, think you, to make such a change at demand? No, sir, said I, depend upon it, 'tis imposible, and whatever the change on your side may be, I will ever be true; and I had much rather, since it is come that unhappy length, be your whore than your brother's wife.

He appear'd pleas'd, and touch'd with the impression of this last discourse, and told me that he stood where he did before; that he had not been unfaithful to me in any one promise he had ever made yet, but that there were so many terrible things presented themselves to his view in the affair before me, that he had thought of the other as a remedy, only that he thought this would not be an entire parting us, but we might love as friends all our days, and perhaps with more satisfaction than we should in the station we were now in: that he durst say I could not apprehend any thing from him, as to betraying a secret, which could not but be the destruction of us both if it came out: that he had but one question to ask of me, that could lye in the way of it, and if that question was answer'd, he could not but think still it was the only step I could take.

I guess'd at his question presently, *viz.*, whether I was not with child? As to that, I told him he need not be concern'd about it, for I was not with child. Why then, my dear, says he, we have no time to talk farther now; consider of it, I cannot but be of the opinion still that it will be the best course you can take. And with this, he took his leave, and the more hastily too, his mother and sisters ringing at the gate, just at the moment he had risen up to go.

He left me in the utmost confusion of thought; and he easily perceiv'd it the next day, and all the rest of the week, but he had no opportunity to come at me all that week, till the Sunday after, when I being indispos'd did not go to church, and he making some excuse stay'd at home.

And now he had me an hour and half again by my self, and we fell into the same arguments all over again; at last, I ask'd him warmly what opinion he must have of my modesty, that he could suppose I should so much as entertain a thought of lying with two brothers, and assur'd him it could never be. I added, if he was to tell me that he would never see me more, than which nothing but death could be more terrible, yet I could never entertain a thought so dishonourable to my self, and so base to him; and therefore I entreated him, if he had one grain of respect or affection left for me, that he would speak no more of it to me, or that he would pull his sword out and kill me. He appear'd surpriz'd at my obstinacy, as he call'd it, told me I was unkind to my self, and unkind to him in it; that it was a crisis unlook'd for upon us both, but that he did not see any other way to save us both from ruin, and therefore he thought it the more unkind; but that if he must say no more of it to me, he added with an unusual coldness that he did not know any thing else we had to talk of; and so he rose up to take his leave. I rose up too, as if with the same indifference, but when he came to give me as it were a parting kiss, I burst out into such a passion of crying, that tho' I would have spoke, I could not, and only pressing his hand, seem'd to give him the adieu, but cry'd vehemently.

He was sensibly mov'd with this; so he sat down again, and said a great many kind things to me, but still urg'd the necessity of what he had proposed; all the while insisting that if I did refuse he would notwithstanding provide for me; but letting me plainly see that he would decline me in the main point; nay, even as a mistress; making it a point of honour not to lye with the woman that, for ought he knew, might one time or other come to be his brother's wife.

The bare loss of him as a gallant was not so much my affliction as the loss of his person, whom indeed I lov'd to distraction; and the loss of all the expectations I had, and which I always built my hopes upon, of having him one day for my husband. These things oppress'd my mind so much that, in short, the agonies of my mind threw me into a high fever, and long it was that none in the family expected my life.

I was reduc'd very low indeed, and was often delirious; but nothing lay so near me as the fear that, when I was light headed, I should say something or other to his prejudice; I was distress'd in my mind also to see him, and so he was to see me, for he really lov'd me most passionately; but it could not be; there was not the least room to desire it on one side, or other.

It was near five weeks that I kept my bed, and tho' the violence of my fever abated in three weeks, yet it several times return'd; and the physicians said two or three times they could do no more for me, but that they must leave nature and the distemper to fight it out. After the end of five weeks I grew better, but was so weak, so alter'd, and recover'd so slowly, that the physicians apprehended I should go into a consumption; and which vex'd me most, they gave their opinion that my mind was oppress'd, that something troubl'd me, and, in short, that I was in love; upon this, the whole house set upon me to press me to tell whether I was in love or not, and with who; but as I well might, I deny'd my being in love at all.

They had on this occasion a squabble one day about me at table that had like to put the whole family in an uproar; they happen'd to be all at table but the father; as for me, I was ill, and in my chamber. At the beginning of the talk, the old gentlewoman, who had sent me somewhat to eat, bid her maid go up and ask me if I would have any more; but the maid brought down word I had not eaten half what she had sent me already. Alas, says the old lady, that poor girl; I am afraid she will never be well. Well! says the elder brother, how should Mrs. Betty be well? they say she is in love. I believe nothing of it, says the old gentlewoman. I don't know, says the eldest sister, what to say to it, they have made such a rout about her being so handsome, and so charming, and I know not what, and that in her hearing too, that has turn'd the creature's head, I believe, and who knows what possessions may follow such doings? For my part I don't know what to make of it.

Why, sister, you must acknowledge she is very handsome, says the elder brother. Ay, and a great deal handsomer than you, sister, says Robin, and that's your mortification. Well, well, that is not the question, says his sister, the girl is well enough, and she knows it, she need not be told of it to make her vain.

We don't talk of her being vain, says the elder brother, but of her being in love; may be she is in love with herself; it seems my sisters think so.

I would she was in love with me, says Robin, I'd quickly put her out of her pain. What d'ye mean by that, son? says the old lady, how can you talk so? Why, madam, says Robin again, very honestly, do you think I'd let the poor girl die for love, and of me too, that is so near at hand to be had? Fye, brother, says the second sister, how can you talk so? Would you take a creature that has not a groat in the world? Prithee, child, says Robin, beauty's a portion, and good humour with it is a double portion; I wish thou hadst half her stock of both for thy portion. So there was her mouth stop'd.

I find, says the eldest sister, if Betty is not in love, my brother is; I wonder he has not broke his mind to Betty, I warrant she won't say no. They that yield when they are ask'd, says Robin, are one step before them that were never ask'd to yield, and two steps before them that yield before they are ask'd; and that's an answer to you, sister.

This fir'd the sister, and she flew into a passion, and said things were come to that pass that it was time the wench (meaning me) was out of the family; and but that she was not fit to be turn'd out, she hop'd her father and mother would consider of it, as soon as she could be remov'd.

Robin reply'd, that was for the master and mistress of the family, who were not to be taught by one that had so little judgment as his eldest sister.

It run up a great deal farther; the sister scolded, Robin rally'd and banter'd, but poor Betty lost ground by it extreamly in the family. I heard of it, and cry'd heartily, and the old lady came up to me, some body having told her that I was so much concern'd about it: I complain'd to her that it was very hard the doctors should pass such a censure [1] upon me, for which they had no ground; and that it was still harder, considering the circumstances I was under in the family; that I hop'd I had done nothing to lessen her esteem for me, or given any occasion for the bickering between her sons and daughters; and I had more need to think of a coffin than of being in love, and beg'd she would not let me suffer in her opinion for anybody's mistakes but my own.

She was sensible of the justice of what I said, but told me, since there had been such a clamour among them, and that her younger son talk'd after such a rattling way as he did, she desir'd I would be so faithful to her as to answer her but one question sincerely; I told her I would, and with the utmost plainness and sincerity. Why then, the question was, whether there was any thing between her son Robert and me? I told her with all the protestations of sincerity that I was able to make, and as I might well do, that there was not, nor ever had been; I told her that Mr. Robert had rattled and jested, as she knew it was his way, and that I took it always as I suppos'd he meant it, to be a wild airy way of discourse that had no signification in it; and assured her that there was not the least tittle of what she understood by it between us; and that those who had suggested it had done me a great deal of wrong, and Mr. Robert no service at all.

The old lady was fully satisfy'd, and kiss'd me, spoke chearfully to me, and bid me take care of my health, and want for nothing, and so took her leave. But when she came down,

1 judgment, opinion.

she found the brother and all his sisters together by the ears; they were angry, even to passion, at his upbraiding them with their being homely, and having never had any sweethearts, never having been ask'd the question, their being so forward as almost to ask first, and the like. He rallied them with Mrs. Betty; how pretty, how good humour'd, how she sung better than they did, and danc'd better, and how much handsomer she was; and in doing this, he omitted no ill-natur'd thing that could vex them. The old lady came down in the height of it, and, to stop it, told them the discourse she had had with me, and how I answer'd that there was nothing between Mr. Robert and I.

She's wrong there, says Robin, for if there was not a great deal between us, we should be closer together than we are: I told her I loved her hugely, says he, but I could never make the jade believe I was in earnest. I do not know how you should, says his mother; no body in their senses could believe you were in earnest, to talk so to a poor girl whose circumstances you know so well.

But prithee, son, adds she, since you tell us you could not make her believe you were in earnest, what must we believe about it? for you ramble so in your discourse, that no body knows whether you are in earnest or in jest. But as I find the girl by your own confession has answer'd truly, I wish you would do so too, and tell me seriously, so that I may depend upon it: Is there any thing in it or no? Are you in earnest or no? Are you distracted indeed, or are you not? 'Tis a weighty question; I wish you would make us easy about it.

By my faith, madam, says Robin, 'tis in vain to mince the matter, or tell any more lyes about it; I am in earnest, as much as a man is that's going to be hang'd. If Mrs. Betty would say she lov'd me, and that she would marry me, I'd have her to-morrow morning fasting; and say, *To have, and to hold,* instead of eating my breakfast.

Well, says the mother, then there's one son lost; and she said it in a very mournful tone, as one greatly concern'd at it. I hope not, madam, says Robin; no man is lost when a good wife has found him. Why, but, child, says the old lady, she is a beggar. Why then, madam, she has the more need of charity, says Robin; I'll take her off the hands of the parish, and she and I'll beg together. It's bad jesting with such things, says the mother. I don't jest, madam, says Robin. We'll come and beg your pardon, madam, and your blessing, madam, and my father's. This is all out of the way, son, says the mother; if you are in earnest you are undone. I am afraid not, says he, for I am really afraid she won't have me; after all my sister's huffing, I believe I shall never be able to persuade her to it.

That's a fine tale, indeed; she is not so far gone neither, Mrs. Betty is no fool, says the youngest sister; do you think she has learn'd to say no, any more than other people? No, Mrs. Mirth-Wit, says Robin, Mrs. Betty's no fool, but Mrs. Betty may be engaged some other way, and what then? Nay, says the eldest sister, we can say nothing to that; who must it be to then? She is never out of the doors; it must be between you. I have nothing to say to that, says Robin, I have been examined enough; there's my brother; if it must be between us, go to work with him.

This stung the elder brother to the quick, and he concluded that Robin had discover'd something; however, he kept himself from appearing disturb'd. Prithee, says he, don't go to sham your stories off upon me; I tell you, I deal in no such ware, I have nothing to say to no Mrs. Betty's in the parish; and with that he rose up, and brush'd off. No, says the eldest sister, I dare answer for my brother; he knows the world better.

Thus the discourse ended; but it left the eldest brother quite confounded. He concluded his brother had made a full discovery, and he began to doubt whether I had been concern'd in it, or not; but with all his management, he could not bring it about to get at me. At last he was so perplex'd that he was quite desperate, and resolv'd he would see me whatever came of it. In order to this, he contriv'd it so that one day after dinner, watching his eldest sister, till he could see her go up stairs, he runs after her. Hark ye, sister, says he, where is this sick woman? may not a body see her? Yes, says the sister, I believe you may, but let me go in first a little, and I'll tell you. So she run up to the door, and gave me notice, and presently

call'd to him again. Brother, says she, you may come in if
you please. So in he came, just in the same kind of rant. Well,
says he, at the door as he came in, where's this sick body that's
in love? How do ye do, Mrs. Betty? I would have got up
out of my chair, but was so weak I could not for a good while;
and he saw it, and his sister too, and she said, Come, do not
strive to stand up; my brother desires no ceremony, especially
now you are so weak. No, no, Mrs. Betty, pray sit still, says he,
and so sits himself down in a chair over against me, and appear'd
as if he was mighty merry.

He talk'd a deal of rambling stuff to his sister, and to me,
sometimes of one thing, sometimes another, on purpose to amuse [1]
her, and every now and then would turn it upon the old
story. Poor Mrs. Betty, says he, it is a sad thing to be in love;
why, it has reduced you sadly. At last I spoke a little: I am
glad to see you so merry, sir, says I, but I think the doctor
might have found something better to do than to make his
game of his patients. If I had been ill of no other distemper, I
know the proverb too well to have let him come to me. What
proverb? says he. What,

> Where love is the case,
> The *doctor's* an ass.

Is that not it, Mrs. Betty? I smil'd, and said nothing. Nay, says
he, I think the effect has prov'd it to be love; for it seems the
doctor has done you little service; you mend very slowly,
they say; I doubt there's somewhat in it, Mrs. Betty, I doubt
you are sick of the incurables. I smil'd and said, No, indeed,
sir, that's none of my distemper.

We had a deal of such discourse, and sometimes others that
signified as little. By and by he ask'd me to sing them a
song; at which I smil'd, and said my singing days were over.
At last he ask'd me, if he should play upon his flute to me.
His sister said she believ'd my head could not bear it; I bow'd
and said, Pray, madam, do not hinder it, I love the flute very
much. Then his sister said, Well, do then, brother. With that
he pull'd out the key of his closet: Dear sister, says he, I am

[1] divert her attention, delude her.

very lazy, do step and fetch my flute, it lies in such a drawer, naming a place where he was sure it was not, that she might be a little while a looking for it.

As soon as she was gone, he related the whole story to me of the discourse his brother had about me, and his concern about it, which was the reason of his contriving this visit. I assured him I had never opened my mouth, either to his brother, or to any body else: I told him the dreadful exigence I was in; that my love to him, and his offering to have me forget that affection, and remove it to another, had thrown me down; and that I had a thousand times wish'd I might dye rather than recover, and to have the same circumstances to struggle with as I had before. I added that I foresaw that, as soon as I was well, I must quit the family, and that as for marrying his brother, I abhor'd the thoughts of it, after what had been my case with him, and that he might depend upon it I would never see his brother again upon that subject; that if he would break all his vows and oaths and engagements with me, be that between his conscience and himself, but he should never be able to say that I who he had perswaded to call my self his wife, and who had given him the liberty to use me as a wife, was not as faithful to him as a wife ought to be, whatever he might be to me.

He was going to reply, and had said that he was sorry I could not be perswaded, and was a going to say more, but he heard his sister a coming, and so did I; and yet I forced out these few words as a reply, that I could never be perswaded to love one brother and marry the other. He shook his head, and said, Then I am ruin'd, meaning himself; and that moment his sister enter'd the room, and told him she could not find the flute. Well, says he merrily, this laziness won't do; so he gets up and goes himself to look for it, but comes back without it too, not but that he could have found it, but he had no mind to play; and, besides, the errand he sent his sister on was answer'd another way; for he only wanted to speak to me, which he had done, tho' not much to his satisfaction.

I had however a great deal of satisfaction in having spoken my mind to him in freedom, and with such an honest plainness, as I have related; and tho' it did not at all work the way

I desired, that is to say, to oblige the person to me the more, yet it took from him all possibility of quitting me but by a downright breach of honour, and giving up all the faith of a gentleman which he had so often engaged by, never to abandon me, but to make me his wife as soon as he came to his estate.

It was not many weeks after this before I was about the house again, and began to grow well; but I continued melancholly and retir'd, which amaz'd the whole family, except he that knew the reason of it; yet it was a great while before he took any notice of it, and I, as backward to speak as he, carried [1] as respectfully to him, but never offer'd to speak a word that was particular of any kind whatsoever; and this continued for sixteen or seventeen weeks, so that as I expected every day to be dismiss'd the family, on account of what distaste they had taken another way, in which I had no guilt, I expected to hear no more of this gentleman, after all his solemn vows, but to be ruin'd and abandon'd.

At last I broke the way my self in the family for my removing; for being talking seriously with the old lady one day about my own circumstances, and how my distemper had left a heaviness upon my spirits, the old lady said, I am afraid, Betty, what I have said to you about my son has had some influence upon you, and that you are melancholly on his account; pray will you let me know how the matter stands with you both, if it may not be improper? For as for Robin, he does nothing but rally and banter when I speak of it to him. Why, truly, madam, said I, that matter stands as I wish it did not, and I shall be very sincere with you in it, whatever befalls me. Mr. Robert has several times propos'd marriage to me, which is what I had no reason to expect, my poor circumstances consider'd; but I have always resisted him, and that perhaps in terms more possitive than became me, considering the regard that I ought to have for every branch of your family. But, said I, madam, I could never so far forget my obligations to you, and all your house, to offer to consent to a thing which I knew must needs be disobliging to you, and have possitively told him that I would never entertain a thought of

[1] behaved.

that kind, unless I had your consent, and his father's also, to whom I was bound by so many invincible obligations.

And is this possible, Mrs. Betty? says the old lady. Then you have been much juster to us than we have been to you; for we have all look'd upon you as a kind of a snare to my son; and I had a proposal to make you for your removing for fear of it; but I had not yet mention'd it to you, because I was afraid of grieving you too much, least it should throw you down again, for we have a respect for you still, tho' not so much as to have it be the ruin of my son. But if it be as you say, we have all wrong'd you very much.

As to the truth of what I say, madam, said I, I refer to your son himself; if he will do me any justice, he must tell you the story just as I have told it.

Away goes the old lady to her daughters, and tells them the whole story, just as I had told it her, and they were surpris'd at it, you may be sure, as I believ'd they would be; one said she could never have thought it, another said Robin was a fool; a third said she would not believe a word of it, and she would warrant that Robin would tell the story another way. But the old lady, who was resolv'd to go to the bottom of it, before I could have the least opportunity of acquainting her son with what had pass'd, resolv'd too that she would talk with her son immediately, and to that purpose sent for him, for he was gone but to a lawyer's house in the town, and upon her sending he returned immediately.

Upon his coming up to them, for they were all together, Sit down, Robin, says the old lady, I must have some talk with you. With all my heart, madam, says Robin, looking very merry, I hope it is about a good wife, for I am at a great loss in that affair. How can that be? says his mother, did you not say you resolv'd to have Mrs. Betty? Ay, madam, says Robin, but there is one that has forbid the banns. Forbid the banns? who can that be? Even Mrs. Betty herself, says Robin. How so? says his mother; have you ask'd her the question then? Yes indeed, madam, says Robin, I have attack'd her in form five times since she was sick, and am beaten off: the jade is so stout, she won't capitulate, nor yield upon any terms, except such as I can't effectually grant. Explain your self, says the mother, for I am surpris'd; I do not understand you, I hope you are not in earnest.

Why, madam, says he, the case is plain enough upon me, it explains itself; she won't have me, she says. Is not that plain enough? I think 'tis plain, and pretty rough too. Well, but, says the mother, you talk of conditions that you cannot grant; what, does she want a settlement? Her joynter[1] ought to be according to her portion; what does she bring? Nay, as to fortune, says Robin, she is rich enough; I am satisfied in that point; but 'tis I that am not able to come up to her terms, and she is possitive she will not have me without.

Here the sisters put in: Madam, says the second sister, 'tis impossible to be serious with him, he will never give a direct answer to anything; you had better let him alone, and talk no more of it, you know how to dispose of her out of his way. Robin was a little warm'd with his sister's rudeness, but he was even with her presently. There are two sorts of people, madam, says he, turning to his mother, that there is no contending with, that is, a wise body and a fool; 'tis a little hard I should engage with both of them together.

The younger sister then put in: We must be fools indeed, says she, in my brother's opinion, that he should make us believe he has seriously ask'd Mrs. Betty to marry him, and she has refus'd him.

Answer, and answer not, says Solomon, reply'd her brother. When your brother had said that he had ask'd her no less than five times, and that she possitively denied him, methinks a younger sister need not question the truth of it, when her mother did not. My mother, you see, did not understand it, says the second sister. There's some difference, says Robin, between desiring me to explain it, and telling me she did not believe it.

Well, but, son, says the old lady, if you are disposed to let us into the mystery of it, what were these hard conditions? Yes, madam, says Robin, I had done it before now, if the teazers here had not worried me by way of interruption. The conditions are, that I bring my father and you to consent to it, and without that she protests she will never see me more upon

[1] the amount settled by a husband on his wife.

that head; and the conditions, as I said, I suppose I shall never be able to grant. I hope my warm sisters will be answer'd now, and blush a little.

This answer was surprising to them all, tho' less to the mother, because of what I had said to her. As to the daughters, they stood mute a great while; but the mother said with some passion, Well, I heard this before, but I could not believe it, but if it is so, then we have all done Betty wrong, and she has behav'd better than I expect'd. Nay, says the eldest sister, if it is so, she has acted handsomely indeed. I confess, says the mother, it was none of her fault if he was enough fool to take a fancy to her; but to give such an answer to him shews more respect to us than I can tell how to express; I shall value the girl the better for it, as long as I know her. But I shall not, says Robin, unless you will give your consent. I'll consider of that a while, says the mother; I assure you, if there were not some other objections, this conduct of hers would go a great way to bring me to consent. I wish it would go quite thro' with it, says Robin; if you had as much thought about making me easy as you have about making me rich, you would soon consent to it.

Why, Robin, says the mother again, are you really in earnest? Would you fain have her? Really, madam, says Robin, I think 'tis hard you should question me again upon that head; I won't say that I will have her; how can I resolve that point, when you see I cannot have her without your consent? But this I will say, I am earnest that I will never have any body else, if I can help it; Betty or no body is the word, and the question which of the two shall be in your breast to decide, madam, provided only that my good humour'd sisters here may have no vote in it.

All this was dreadful to me, for the mother began to yield, and Robin press'd her home in it. On the other hand, she advised with the eldest son, and he used all the arguments in the world to perswade her to consent; alledging his brother's passionate love for me, and my generous regard to the family in refusing my own advantages upon such a nice point of honour, and a thousand such things. And as to the father, he was a man in a hurry of publick affairs and getting money, seldom at home, thoughtful of the main chance, but left all those things to his wife.

You may easily believe that when the plot was thus, as they thought, broke out, it was not so difficult, or so dangerous, for the elder brother, who no body suspected of anything, to have a freer access than before. Nay, the mother, which was just as he wished, propos'd it to him to talk with Mrs. Betty. It may be, son, said she, you may see farther into the thing than I; and see if she has been so possitive as Robin says she has been, or no. This was as well as he could wish, and he, as it were, yielding to talk with me at his mother's request, she brought me to him into her own chamber, told me her son had some business with me at her request, and then she left us together, and he shut the door after her.

He came back to me, and took me in his arms and kiss'd me very tenderly; but told me it was now come to that crisis, that I should make my self happy or miserable as long as I liv'd; that if I could not comply to his desire, we should both be ruin'd. Then he told me the whole story between Robin, as he call'd him, and his mother, and his sisters, and himself, as above. And now dear child, says he, consider what it will be to marry a gentleman of a good family, in good circumstances, and with the consent of the whole house, and to enjoy all that the world can give you; and what, on the other hand, to be sunk into the dark circumstances of a woman that has lost her reputation; and that tho' I shall be a private friend to you while I live, yet as I shall be suspected always, so you will be afraid to see me, and I shall be afraid to own you.

He gave me no time to reply, but went on with me thus: What has happened between us, child, so long as we both agree to do so, may be buried and forgotten: I shall always be your sincere friend, without any inclination to nearer intimacy, when you become my sister; and we shall have all the honest part of conversation without any reproaches between us of having done amiss. I beg of you to consider it, and do not stand in the way of your own safety and prosperity. And to satisfy you that I am sincere, added he, I here offer you five hundred pounds to make you some amends for the freedoms I have taken with you, which we shall look upon as some of the follies of our lives, which 'tis hoped we may repent of.

He spoke this in so much more moving terms than it is possible for me to express that you may suppose, as he held me above an hour and half in that discourse, so he answer'd all my objections, and fortified his discourse with all the arguments that human wit and art could devise.

I cannot say, however, that any thing he said made impression enough upon me, so as to give me any thought of the matter, till he told me at last very plainly that if I refus'd, he was sorry to add that he could never go on with me in that station as we stood before; that tho' he lov'd me as well as ever, and that I was as agreeable to him, yet the sense of virtue had not so forsaken him as to suffer him to lye with a woman that his brother courted to make his wife; that if he took his leave of me, with a denial from me in this affair, whatever he might do for me in the point of support, grounded on his first engagement of maintaining me, yet he would not have me be surpris'd that he was obliged to tell me he could not allow himself to see me any more; and that indeed I could not expect it of him.

I received this last part with some tokens of surprize and disorder, and had much ado to avoid sinking down, for indeed I lov'd him to an extravagance not easy to imagine; but he perceiv'd my disorder, and entreated me to consider seriously of it, assured me that it was the only way to preserve our mutual affection; that in this station we might love as friends, with the utmost passion, and with a love of relation untainted, free from our own just reproaches, and free from other people's suspicions; that he should ever acknowledge his happiness owing to me; that he would be debtor to me as long as he liv'd, and would be paying that debt as long as he had breath. Thus he wrought me up, in short, to a kind of hesitation in the matter; having the dangers on one side represented in lively figures, and indeed heighten'd by my imagination of being turn'd out to the wide world, a meer cast-off whore, for it was no less, and perhaps expos'd as such; with little to provide for myself, with no friend, no acquaintance in the whole world out of that town, and there I could not pretend to stay; all this terrify'd me to to the last degree, and he took care upon all occasions to lay it home to me in the worst colours; on the other hand, he fail'd not to set forth the easy prosperous life which I was going to live.

He answer'd all that I could object from affection, and from former engagements, with telling me the necessity that was before us of taking other measures now; and as to his promises of marriage, the nature of things, he said, had put an end to that, by the probability of my being his brother's wife before the time to which his promises all referr'd.

Thus in a word, I may say, he reason'd me out of my reason; he conquer'd all my arguments, and I began to see a danger that I was in which I had not considered of before; and that was, of being drop'd by both of them, and left alone in the world to shift for my self.

This, and his perswasion, at length prevail'd with me to consent, tho' with so much reluctance that it was easy to see I should go to church like a bear to the stake; I had some little apprehensions about me too, lest my new spouse, who, by the way, I had not the least affection for, should be skilful enough to challenge me on another account upon our first coming to bed together; but whether he did it with design or not, I know not, but his elder brother took care to make him very much fuddled before he went to bed, so that I had the satisfaction of a drunken bedfellow the first night. How he did it I know not, but I concluded that he certainly contriv'd it, that his brother might be able to make no judgment of the difference between a maid and a married woman, nor did he ever entertain any notions of it, or disturb his thoughts about it.

I should go back a little here to where I left off. The elder brother having thus managed me, his next business was to manage his mother, and he never left till he had brought her to acquiesce, and be passive even without acquainting the father, other than by post letters, so that she consented to our marrying privately, leaving her to manage the father afterwards.

Then he cajol'd with his brother, and perswaded him what service he had done him, and how he had brought his mother to consent, which, tho' true, was not indeed done to serve him, but to serve himself; but thus diligently did he cheat him, and had the thanks of a faithful friend for shifting off his whore into his brother's arms for a wife. So naturally do men give up honour and justice, and even Christianity, to secure themselves.

I must now come back to Brother Robin, as we always call'd him, who, having got his mother's consent, as above, came big with the news to me, and told me the whole story of it, with a sincerity so visible, that I must confess it griev'd me that I must be the instrument to abuse so honest a gentleman; but there was no remedy, he would have me, and I was not oblig'd to tell him that I was his brother's whore, tho' I had no other way to put him off; so I came gradually into it, and behold we were married.

Modesty forbids me to reveal the secrets of the marriage bed, but nothing could have happen'd more suitable to my circumstances than that, as above, my husband was so fuddled when he came to bed that he could not remember in the morning whether he had had any conversation with me or no, and I was obliged to tell him he had, tho' in reality he had not, that I might be sure he could make no enquiry about any thing else.

It concerns the story in hand very little to enter into the farther particulars of the family, or of my self, for the five years that I liv'd with this husband, only to observe that I had two children by him, and that at the end of the five years he died. He had been really a very good husband to me, and we liv'd very agreeably together; but as he had not received much from them, and had in the little time he liv'd acquir'd no great matters, so my circumstances were not great, nor was I much mended by the match. Indeed I had preserv'd the elder brother's bonds to me to pay me 500*l.* which he offered me for my consent to marry his brother; and this, with what I had saved of the money he formerly gave me, and about as much more by my husband, left me a widow with about 1200*l.* in my pocket.

My two children were indeed taken happily off my hands by my husband's father and mother, and that was all they got by Mrs. Betty.

I confess I was not suitably affected with the loss of my husband; nor can I say that I ever lov'd him as I ought to have done, or was suitable to [1] the good usage I had from him, for he was a tender, kind, good-humour'd man as any woman could desire; but his brother being so always in my sight, at

[1] accordant with.

least while we were in the country, was a continual snare to
me; and I never was in bed with my husband but I wish'd my
self in the arms of his brother; and tho' his brother never offer'd
me the least kindness that way after our marriage, but carried
it just as a brother ought to do, yet it was impossible for me to
do so to him. In short, I committed adultery and incest with
him every day in my desires, which without doubt was as effectually criminal.

Before my husband dy'd, his elder brother was married,
and we being then remov'd to London, were written to by the
old lady to come and be at the wedding; my husband went,
but I pretended indisposition, so I staid behind; for in short,
I could not bear the sight of his being given to another woman,
tho' I knew I was never to have him my self.

I was now, as above, left loose to the world, and being still
young and handsome, as every body said of me, and I assure
you I thought my self so, and with a tolerable fortune in my
pocket, I put no small value upon my self. I was courted by
several very considerable tradesmen, and particularly very
warmly by one, a linnen-draper, at whose house, after my husband's death, I took a lodging, his sister being my acquaintance; here I had all the liberty and opportunity to be gay, and
appear in company that I could desire, my landlord's sister
being one of the maddest, gayest things alive, and not so much
mistress of her vertue as I thought at first she had been. She
brought me into a world of wild company, and even brought
home several persons, such as she lik'd well enough to gratify,
to see her pretty widow. Now as fame and fools make an
assembly, I was here wonderfully caress'd; had abundance of
admirers, and such as call'd themselves lovers; but I found not
one fair proposal among them all; as for their common design,
that I understood too well to be drawn into any more snares
of that kind. The case was alter'd with me, I had money in my
pocket, and had nothing to say to them: I had been trick'd
once by that cheat call'd love, but the game was over, I was
resolv'd now to be married or nothing, and to be well married
or not at all.

I lov'd the company indeed of men of mirth and wit, and
was often entertain'd with such, as I was also with others;

but I found by just observation that the brightest men came
upon the dullest errand, that is to say, the dullest as to what
I aim'd at; on the other hand, those who came with the best
proposals were the dullest and most disagreeable part of the
world. I was not averse to a tradesman, but then I would have
a tradesman, forsooth, that was something of a gentleman too;
that when my husband had a mind to carry me to the Court,
or to the play, he might become a sword, and look as like a
gentleman as another man, and not like one that had the mark
of his apron-strings upon his coat, or the mark of his hat upon
his perriwig; that should look as if he was set on to his sword
when his sword was put on to him, and that carried his trade in
his countenance.

Well, at last I found this amphibious creature, this land-water-
thing call'd a gentleman-tradesman, and as a just plague upon
my folly I was catch'd in the very snare which, as I might say,
I laid for my self.

This was a draper, too, for tho' my comrade would have
bargain'd for me with her brother, yet when they came to the
point, it was, it seems, for a mistress, and I kept true to this
notion, that a woman should never be kept for a mistress that
had money to make her self a wife.

Thus my pride, not my principle, my money, not my vertue,
kept me honest; tho', as it prov'd, I found I had much better
have been sold by my she comrade to her brother than have
sold my self as I did to a tradesman that was rake, gentleman,
shop-keeper, and beggar all together.

But I was hurried on (by my fancy to a gentleman) to ruin
my self in the grossest manner that ever woman did; for my
new husband coming to a lump of money at once, fell into such
a profusion of expence that all I had, and all he had, would not
have held it out above one year.

He was very fond of me for about a quarter of a year, and
what I got by that was that I had the pleasure of seeing a great
deal of my money spent upon my self. Come, my dear, says he
to me one day, shall we go and take a turn into the country for
a week? Ay, my dear, says I, whither would you go? I care
not whither, says he, but I have a mind to look like quality
for a week; we'll go to Oxford, says he. How, says I, shall

we go? I am no horse-woman, and 'tis too far for a coach. Too far? says he; no place is too far for a coach and six. If I carry you out, you shall travel like a dutchess. Hum, says I, my dear, 'tis a frolick, but if you have a mind to it, I don't care. Well, the time was appointed, we had a rich coach, very good horses, a coachman, postillion, and two footmen in very good liveries; a gentleman on horseback, and a page with a feather in his hat upon another horse; the servants all call'd him my lord, and I was her honour, the countess, and thus we travel'd to Oxford, and a pleasant journey we had; for, give him his due, not a beggar alive knew better how to be a lord than my husband. We saw all the rarities at Oxford, talk'd with two or three fellows of colleges about putting a nephew that was left to his lordship's care to the University, and of their being his tutors; we diverted our selves with bantering several other poor scholars with the hopes of being at least his lordship's chaplain and putting on a scarf;[1] and thus having liv'd like quality indeed as to expence, we went away for Northampton, and in a word, in about twelve days' ramble came home again, to the tune of about 93*l.* expence.

Vanity is the perfection of a fop; my husband had this excellence, that he valued nothing of expence; as his history, you may be sure, has very little weight in it, 'tis enough to tell you that in about two years and a quarter he broke, got into a spunging-house,[2] being arrested in an action too heavy for him to give bail to, so he sent for me to come to him.

It was no surprise to me, for I had foreseen something before that all was going to wreck, and had been taking care to reserve something if I could for my self. But when he sent for me, he behav'd much better than I expected. He told me plainly he had plaid the fool, and suffer'd himself to be surpriz'd, which he might have prevented; that now he foresaw he could not stand it, and therefore he would have me go home, and in the night take away every thing I had in the house of any value, and secure it; and after that, he told me that if I could get away 100*l.* or 200*l.* in goods out of the shop, I should do it. Only, says he, let me know nothing of it, neither

[1] a band of silk worn by a nobleman's chaplain.
[2] a house kept by a bailiff for the preliminary confinement of debtors.

what you take, or whither you carry it; for as for me, says he, I am resolv'd to get out of this house and be gone; and if you never hear of me more, my dear, says he, I wish you well; I am only sorry for the injury I have done you. He said some very handsome things to me indeed at parting; for I told you he was a gentleman, and that was all the benefit I had of his being so, that he used me very handsomely, even to the last, only spent all I had, and left me to rob the creditors for something to subsist on.

However, I did as he bad me, that you may be sure, and having thus taken my leave of him I never saw him more; for he found means to break out of the bailiff's house that night, or the next. How, I knew not, for I could come at no knowledge of anything, more than this, that he came home about three a clock in the morning, caus'd the rest of his goods to be remov'd into the Mint,[1] and the shop to be shut up; and having rais'd what money he could, he got over to France, from whence I had one or two letters from him, and no more.

I did not see him when he came home, for he having given me such instructions as above, and I having made the best of my time, I had no more business back again at the house, not knowing but I might have been stop'd there by the creditors; for a commission of bankrupt being soon after issued, they might have stop'd me by orders from the commissioners. But my husband having desperately got out from the bailiff's by letting himself down from almost the top of the house to the top of another building, and leaping from thence, which was almost two stories, and which was enough indeed to have broken his neck, he came home and got away his goods before the creditors could come to seize, that is to say, before they could get out the commission, and be ready to send their officers to take possession.

My husband was so civil to me, for still I say he was much of a gentleman, that in the first letter he wrote me he let me know where he had pawn'd 20 pieces of fine holland for 30*l.* which were worth above 90*l.*, and enclos'd me the token for the taking them up, paying the money, which I did, and made

[1] a sanctuary for insolvent debtors in Southwark.

in time above 100*l*. of them, having leisure to cut them, and sell them to private families, as opportunity offer'd.

However, with all this, and all that I had secur'd before, I found upon casting things up my case was very much alter'd, and my fortune much lessen'd; for including the hollands, and a parcel of fine muslins which I carry'd off before, and some plate, and other things, I found I could hardly muster up 500*l*. and my condition was very odd, for tho' I had no child (I had had one by my gentleman draper, but it was buried), yet I was a widow bewitch'd, I had a husband, and no husband, and I could not pretend to marry again, though I knew well enough my husband would never see England any more, if he liv'd fifty years. Thus, I say, I was limited from marriage, what offer soever might be made me; and I had not one friend to advise with in the condition I was in, at least not one who I could trust the secret of my circumstances to, for if the commissioners were to have been inform'd where I was, I should have been fetch'd up, and all I had sav'd be taken away.

Upon these apprehensions, the first thing I did was to go quite out of my knowledge, and go by another name. This I did effectually, for I went into the Mint too, took lodgings in a very private place, dress'd me up in the habit of a widow, and call'd my self Mrs. Flanders.

Here, however, I conceal'd my self, and tho' my new acquaintance knew nothing of me, yet I soon got a great deal of company about me; and whether it be that women are scarce among the people that generally are to be found there, or that some consolations in the miseries of that place are more requisite than on other occasions, I soon found that an agreeable woman was exceedingly valuable among the sons of affliction there; and that those that cou'd not pay half a crown in the pound to their creditors, and run in debt at the sign of the *Bull* for their dinners, would yet find money for a supper, if they lik'd the woman.

However, I kept myself safe yet, tho' I began like my Lord Rochester's mistress, that lov'd his company but would not admit him farther, to have the scandal of a whore without the joy; and upon this score, tir'd with the place, and with the company too, I began to think of removing.

It was indeed a subject of strange reflection to me to see men in the most perplex'd circumstances, who were reduc'd some degrees below being ruin'd, whose families were objects of their own terror and other people's charity, yet while a penny lasted, nay, even beyond it, endeavouring to drown their sorrow in their wickedness; heaping up more guilt upon themselves, labouring to forget former things which now it was the proper time to remember, making more work for repentance, and sinning on, as a remedy for sin past.

But it is none of my talent to preach; these men were too wicked, even for me; there was something horrid and absurd in their way of sinning, for it was all a force even upon themselves;[1] they did not only act against conscience, but against nature, and nothing was more easy than to see how sighs would interrupt their songs, and paleness and anguish sit upon their brows, in spight of the forc'd smiles they put on; nay, sometimes it would break out at their very mouths, when they had parted with their money for a lewd treat, or a wicked embrace; I have heard them, turning about, fetch a deep sigh, and cry, What a dog am I! Well, Betty, my dear, I'll drink thy health, tho', (meaning the honest wife that perhaps had not a half crown for herself, and three or four children). The next morning they were at their penitentials again, and perhaps the poor weeping wife comes over to him, either brings him some account of what his creditors are doing, and how she and the children are turn'd out of doors, or some other dreadful news; and this adds to his self reproaches; but when he has thought and por'd on it till he is almost mad, having no principles to support him, nothing within him, or above him, to comfort him, but finding it all darkness on every side, he flies to the same relief again, *viz.* to drink it away, debauch it away, and falling into company of men in just the same condition with himself, he repeats the crime, and thus he goes every day one step onward of his way to destruction.

I was not wicked enough for such fellows as these yet; on the contrary, I began to consider here very seriously what I had to do; how things stood with me, and what course I ought to take. I knew I had no friends, no, not one friend or rela-

[1] i.e., they acted against their natural impulses.

tion in the world; and that little I had left apparently wasted, which, when it was gone, I saw nothing but misery and starving was before me. Upon these considerations, I say, and fill'd with horror at the place I was in, I resolv'd to be gone.

I had made an acquaintance with a sober good sort of a woman, who was a widow too like me, but in better circumstances; her husband had been a captain of a ship, and having had the misfortune to be cast away coming home from the West Indies, was so reduc'd by the loss that tho' he had saved his life then, it broke his heart, and kill'd him afterwards, and his widow being persued by the creditors, was forc'd to take shelter in the Mint. She soon made things up with the help of friends, and was at liberty again; and finding that I rather was there to be conceal'd than by any particular prosecutions, and finding also that I agreed with her, or rather she with me, in a just abhorrence of the place and of the company, she invited me to go home with her, till I could put myself in some posture of settling in the world to my mind; withal telling me that it was ten to one but some good captain of a ship might take a fancy to me, and court me, in that part of the town where she liv'd.

I accepted of her offer, and was with her half a year, and should have been longer, but in that interval what she propos'd to me happen'd to herself, and she marry'd very much to her advantage; but whose fortune soever was upon the increase, mine seem'd to be upon the wane, and I found nothing present except two or three boatswains, or such fellows, but as for the commanders they were generally of two sorts. 1. Such as having good business, that is to say, a good ship, resolv'd not to marry, but with advantage. 2. Such as being out of employ, wanted a wife to help them to a ship; I mean, (1) A wife who, having some money, could enable them to hold a good part of a ship themselves, so to encourage owners to come in; or (2) A wife who, if she had not money, had friends who were concern'd in shipping, and so could help to put the young man into a good ship, and neither of these was my case; so I look'd like one that was to lie on hand.

This knowledge I soon learnt by experience, *viz.*, that the state of things was altered as to matrimony, that marriages were

here the consequences of politick schemes for forming interests, carrying on business, and that love had no share, or but
very little in the matter.

That, as my sister in law at Colchester had said, beauty,
wit, manners, sense, good humour, good behaviour, education, vertue, piety, or any other qualification, whether of body
or mind, had no power to recommend; that money only made a
woman agreeable; that men chose mistresses indeed by the gust
of their affection, and it was requisite for a whore to be handsome, well shap'd, have a good mein, and a graceful behaviour,
but that for a wife, no deformity would shock the fancy, no
ill qualities the judgment; the money was the thing; the portion
was neither crooked, or monstrous, but the money was always
agreeable, whatever the wife was.

On the other hand, as the market run all on the men's side,
I found the women had lost the privilege of saying no; that it
was a favour now for a woman to have the question ask'd, and
if any young lady had so much arrogance as to counterfeit a
negative, she never had the opportunity of denying twice;
much less of recovering that false step, and accepting what she
had seem'd to decline. The men had such choice every where
that the case of the women was very unhappy; for they seem'd
to ply at every door, and if the man was by great chance refus'd
at one house, he was sure to be receiv'd at the next.

Besides this, I observ'd that the men made no scruple to set
themselves out, and to go a fortune-hunting, as they call it, when
they had really no fortune themselves to demand it, or merit to
deserve it; and they carry'd it so high that a woman was scarce
allow'd to enquire after the character or estate of the person
that pretended to her. This I had an example of in a young
lady at the next house to me, and with whom I had contracted
an intimacy; she was courted by a young captain, and tho' she
had near 2000*l.* to her fortune, she did but enquire of some of
his neighbours about his character, his morals, or substance, and
he took occasion at the next visit to let her know, truly, that
he took it very ill, and that he should not give her the trouble
of his visits any more. I heard of it, and I had begun my acquaintance with her; I went to see her upon it. She enter'd into
a close conversation with me about it, and unbosom'd herself

very freely; I perceiv'd presently that tho' she thought herself very ill us'd, yet she had no power to resent it; that she was exceedingly piqu'd she had lost him, and particularly that another of less fortune had gain'd him.

I fortify'd her mind against such a meanness, as I call'd it; I told her, that as low as I was in the world, I would have despis'd a man that should think I ought to take him upon his own recommendation only; also I told her that as she had a good fortune she had no need to stoop to the disaster of the times; that it was enough that the men could insult us that had but little money, but if she suffer'd such an affront to pass upon her without resenting it, she would be render'd low-priz'd upon all occasions; that a woman can never want an opportunity to be reveng'd of a man that has us'd her ill, and that there were ways enough to humble such a fellow as that, or else certainly women were the most unhappy creatures in the world.

She was very well pleas'd with the discourse, and told me seriously that she would be very glad to make him sensible of her resentment, and either to bring him on again, or have the satisfaction of her revenge being as publick as possible.

I told her that if she would take my advice, I would tell her how she should obtain her wishes in both those things; and that I would engage I would bring the man to her door again, and make him beg to be let in. She smil'd at that, and soon let me see that if he came to her door her resentment was not so great to let him stand long there.

However, she listened very willingly to my offer of advice; so I told her that the first thing she ought to do, was a piece of justice to herself; namely, that whereas he had reported among the ladies that he had left her, and pretended to give the advantage of the negative to himself, she should take care to have it well spread among the women, which she could not fail of an opportunity to do, that she had enquired into his circumstances, and found he was not the man he pretended to be. Let them be told too, madam, said I, that you found he was not the man you expected, and that you thought it was not safe to meddle with him, that you heard he was of an ill temper, and that he boasted how he had us'd the women ill upon many occasions, and that particularly he was debauch'd in his morals, etc. The last of which indeed had some truth in it; but I did not find that she seem'd to like him much the worse for that part.

She came most readily into all this, and immediately she went to work to find instruments. She had very little difficulty in the search; for telling her story in general to a couple of her gossips, it was the chat of the tea table all over that part of the town, and I met with it wherever I visited. Also, as it was known that I was acquainted with the young lady her self, my opinion was ask'd very often, and I confirm'd it with all the necessary aggravations, and set out his character in the blackest colours; and as a piece of secret intelligence I added what the gossips knew nothing of, *viz.* that I had heard he was in very bad circumstances; that he was under a necessity of a fortune to support his interest with the owners of the ship he commanded; that his own part was not paid for, and if it was not paid quickly, his owners would put him out of the ship, and his chief mate was likely to command it, who offer'd to buy that part which the captain had promis'd to take.

I added, for I was heartily piqu'd at the rogue, as I call'd him, that I had heard a rumour too, that he had a wife alive at Plymouth, and another in the West Indies, a thing which they all knew was not very uncommon for such kind of gentlemen.

This work'd as we both desir'd it, for presently the young lady at the next door, who had a father and mother that govern'd both her and her fortune, was shut up, and her father forbid him the house. Also in one place more the woman had the courage, however strange it was, to say no; and he could try no where but he was reproached with his pride, and that he pretended not to give the women leave to enquire into his character, and the like.

By this time he began to be sensible of his mistake; and seeing all the women on that side the water alarm'd, he went over to Ratcliff, and got access to some of the ladies there; but tho' the young women there too were, according to the fate of the day, pretty willing to be ask'd, yet such was his ill luck, that his character follow'd him over the water; so that tho' he might have had wives enough, yet it did not happen among the women that had good fortunes, which was what he wanted.

But this was not all; she very ingeniously manag'd another thing for herself, for she got a young gentleman, who was a relation, to come and visit her two or three times a week in a very fine chariot and good liveries, and her two agents and I also presently spread a report all over that this gentleman came to court her; that he was a gentleman of a thousand pounds a year, and that he was fallen in love with her, and that she was going to her aunt's in the city, because it was inconvenient for the gentleman to come to her with his coach to Rotherhith, the streets being so narrow and difficult.

This took immediately; the captain was laugh'd at in all companies, and was ready to hang himself; he tried all the ways possible to come at her again, and wrote the most passionate letters to her in the world, and in short, by great application, obtained leave to wait on her again, as he said, only to clear his reputation.

At this meeting she had her full revenge of him; for she told him she wonder'd what he took her to be, that she should admit any man to a treaty of so much consequence as that of marriage, without enquiring into his circumstances; that if he thought she was to be huff'd into wedlock, and that she was in the same circumstances which her neighbours might be in, *viz.* to take up with the first good Christian that came, he was mistaken; that, in a word, his character was really bad, or he was very ill beholden to his neighbours; and that unless he could clear up some points in which she had justly been prejudiced, she had no more to say to him, but give him the satisfaction of knowing that she was not afraid to say no, either to him, or any man else.

With that she told him what she had heard, or rather rais'd herself by my means, of his character; his not having paid for the part he pretended to own of the ship he commanded; of the resolution of his owners to put him out of the command, and to put his mate in his stead; and of the scandal rais'd on his morals; his having been reproach'd with such and such women, and his having a wife at Plymouth, and another in the West-Indies, and the like; and she ask'd him whether she had not good reason, if these things were not clear'd up, to refuse him and to insist upon having satisfaction in points so significant as they were?

He was so confounded at her discourse that he could not answer a word, and she began to believe that all was true, by his disorder, tho' she knew that she had been the raiser of these reports herself.

After some time he recovered a little, and from that time was the most humble, modest, and importunate man alive in his courtship.

She ask'd him if he thought she was so at her last shift that she could or ought to bear such treatment, and if he did not see that she did not want [1] those who thought it worth their while to come farther to her than he did, meaning the gentleman whom she had brought to visit her by way of sham.

She brought him by these tricks to submit to all possible measures to satisfy her, as well of his circumstances as of his behaviour. He brought her undeniable evidence of his having paid for his part of the ship; he brought her certificates from his owners that the report of their intending to remove him from the command of the ship was false and groundless; in short, he was quite the reverse of what he was before.

Thus I convinced her that if the men made their advantage of our sex in the affair of marriage, upon the supposition of there being such a choice to be had, and of the women being so easy, it was only owing to this, that the women wanted courage to maintain their ground, and that, according to my Lord Rochester,

> *A woman's ne'er so ruin'd but she can*
> *Revenge herself on her undoer, man.*

After these things this young lady plaid her part so well that tho' she resolv'd to have him, and that indeed having him was the main bent of her design, yet she made his obtaining her to be to him the most difficult thing in the world; and this she did, not by a haughty reserv'd carriage, but by a just policy, playing back upon him his own game; for as he pretended by a kind of lofty carriage to place himself above the occasion of a character, she broke with him upon that subject, and at the same time that she made him submit to all possible enquiry after his affairs, she apparently shut the door against his looking into her own.

It was enough to him to obtain her for a wife: as to what she had, she told him plainly that, as he knew her circumstances,

[1] lack.

it was but just she should know his; and tho' at the same time he had only known her circumstances by common fame, yet he had made so many protestations of his passion for her that he could ask no more but her hand to his grand request, and the like ramble according to the custom of lovers. In short, he left himself no room to ask any more questions about her estate, and she took the advantage of it; for she placed part of her fortune so in trustees, without letting him know anything of it, that it was quite out of his reach, and made him be very well contented with the rest.

It is true she was pretty well besides, that is to say, she had about 1400*l.* in money, which she gave him, and the other, after some time, she brought to light, as a perquisite to herself, which he was to accept as a mighty favour, seeing, though it was not to be his, it might ease him in the article of her particular expences; and I must add that by this conduct the gentleman himself became not only more humble in his applications to her to obtain her, but also was much the more an obliging husband when he had her: I cannot but remind the ladies how much they place themselves below the common station of a wife, which, if I may be allow'd not to be partial, is low enough already; I say, they place themselves below their common station, and prepare their own mortifications by their submitting so to be insulted by the men before-hand, which I confess I see no necessity of.

This relation may serve therefore to let the ladies see that the advantage is not so much on the other side as the men think it is; and that tho' it may be true the men have but too much choice among us, and that some women may be found who will dishonour themselves, be cheap, and too easy to come at; yet if they will have women worth having, they may find them as uncomeatable as ever; and that those that are otherwise have often such deficiencies, when had, as rather recommend the ladies that are difficult than encourage the men to go on with their easy courtship, and expect wives equally valuable that will come at first call.

Nothing is more certain than that the ladies always gain of the men by keeping their ground, and letting their pretended lovers see they can resent being slighted, and that they are not afraid of saying no. They insult us mightily with telling us of the number of women; that the wars, and the sea, and trade, and other incidents have carried the men so much away that there is no proportion between the numbers of the sexes; but I am far from granting that the number of the women is so great, or the number of the men so small; but if they will have me tell the truth, the disadvantage of the women is a terrible scandal upon the men, and it lies here only: namely, that the age is so wicked, and the sex so debauch'd, that in short the number of such men as an honest woman ought to meddle with is small indeed; and it is but here and there that a man is to be found who is fit for an honest woman to venture upon.

But the consequence even of that too amounts to no more than this, that women ought to be the more nice; for how do we know the just character of the man that makes the offer? To say that the woman should be the more easy on this occasion is to say we should be the forwarder to venture because of the greatness of the danger, which is very absurd.

On the contrary, the women have ten thousand times the more reason to be wary and backward, by how much the hazard of being betray'd is the greater, and would the ladies act the wary part, they would discover every cheat that offer'd; for, in short, the lives of very few men now-a-days will bear a character; and if the ladies do but make a little enquiry, they would soon be able to distinguish the men, and deliver themselves. As for women that do not think their own safety worth their own thought, that impatient of their present state run into matrimony, as a horse rushes into the battle; I can say nothing to them but this, that they are a sort of ladies that are to be pray'd for among the rest of distemper'd people, and they look like people that venture their estates in a lottery where there is a hundred thousand blanks to one prize.

No man of common sense will value a woman the less for not giving up herself at the first attack, or for not accepting his proposal without enquiring into his person or character; on the contrary, he must think her the weakest of all creatures, as the rate of men now goes. In short, he must have a very contemptible opinion of her capacities that, having but one cast for her life, shall cast that life away at once, and make matrimony, like death, be a leap in the dark.

I would fain have the conduct of my sex a little regulated in this particular, which is the same thing in which of all the parts of life I think at this time we suffer most in. 'Tis nothing but lack of courage, the fear of not being married at all, and of that frightful state of life call'd *an old maid*. This, I say, is the woman's snare; but would the ladies once but get above that fear, and manage rightly, they would more certainly avoid it by standing their ground, in a case so absolutely necessary to their felicity, than by exposing themselves as they do; and if they did not marry so soon, they would make themselves amends by marrying safer; she is always married too soon who gets a bad husband, and she is never married too late who gets a good one. In a word, there is no woman, deformity or lost reputation excepted, but if she manages well may be married safely one time or other; but if she precipitates herself, it is ten thousand to one but she is undone.

But I come now to my own case, in which there was at this time no little nicety. The circumstances I was in made the offer of a good husband the most necessary thing in the world to me; but I found soon that to be made cheap and easy was not the way. It soon began to be found that the widow had no fortune, and to say this was to say all that was ill for me. Being well bred, handsome, witty, modest, and agreeable (all which I had allow'd to my character, whether justly, or no), is not to the purpose: I say, all these would not do without the dross. In short, the widow, they said, had no money!

I resolv'd therefore that it was necessary to change my station, and make a new appearance in some other place, and even to pass by another name if I found occasion.

I communicated my thoughts to my intimate friend, the captain's lady, who I had so faithfully served in her case with the captain; and who was as ready to serve me in the same kind as I could desire. I made no scruple to lay my circumstances open to her; my stock was but low, for I had made but about 540*l.* at the close of my last affair, and I had wasted some of that. However, I had about 460*l.* left, a great many very rich cloaths, a gold watch, and some jewels, tho' of no extraordinary value, and about 30*l.* or 40*l.* left in linnen not dispos'd of.

My dear and faithful friend, the captain's wife, was so sensible of the service I had done her in the affair above that she was not only a steddy friend to me, but knowing my circumstances, she frequently made me presents as money came into her hands, such as fully amounted to a maintainance; so that I spent none of my own; and at last she made this unhappy proposal to me, *viz.* that as we had observ'd, as above, how the men made no scruple to set themselves out as persons meriting a woman of fortune of their own, it was but just to deal with them in their own way, and, if it was possible, to deceive the deceiver.

The captain's lady, in short, put this project into my head, and told me if I would be rul'd by her I should certainly get a husband of fortune, without leaving him any room to reproach me with want of my own. I told her that I would give up my self wholly to her directions, and that I would have neither tongue to speak, or feet to step in that affair but as she should direct me; depending that she would extricate me out of every difficulty that she brought me into, which she said she would answer for.

The first step she put me upon was to call her cousin, and go to a relation's house of hers in the country, where she directed me, and where she brought her husband to visit me; and calling me cousin, she work'd matters so about that her husband and she together invited me most passionately to come to town and live with them, for they now liv'd in a quite different place from where they were before. In the next place, she tells her husband that I had at least 1500*l.* fortune, and that I was like to have a great deal more.

It was enough to tell her husband this, there needed nothing on my side; I was but to sit still and wait the event, for it presently went all over the neighbourhood that the young widow at Captain ——'s was a fortune, that she had at least 1500*l.*, and perhaps a great deal more, and that the captain said so; and if the captain was ask'd at any time about me, he made no scruple to affirm it, tho' he knew not one word of the matter, other than that his wife had told him so; and in this he thought no harm, for he really believ'd it to be so. With the reputation of this fortune, I presently found myself bless'd with admirers enough, and that I had my choice of men, as they said they were, which by the way confirms what I was saying before. This being my case, I, who had a subtil game to play, had nothing now to do but to single out from them all the properest man that might be for my purpose; that is to say, the man who was most likely to depend upon the hear-say of fortune, and not enquire too far into the particulars; and unless I did this, I did nothing, for my case would not bear much enquiry.

I pick'd out my man without difficulty by the judgment I made of his way of courting me. I had let him run on with his protestations that he lov'd me above all the world; that if I would make him happy, that was enough; all which I knew was upon supposition that I was very rich, tho' I never told him a word of it my self.

This was my man, but I was to try him to the bottom, and indeed in that consisted my safety, for if he baulked, I knew I was undone, as surely as he was undone if he took me; and if I did not make some scruple about his fortune, it was the way to lead him to raise some about mine; and first, therefore, I pretended on all occasions to doubt his sincerity, and told him, perhaps he only courted me for my fortune; he stop'd my mouth in that part, with the thunder of his protestations, as above, but still I pretended to doubt.

One morning he pulls off his diamond ring, and writes upon the glass of the sash [1] in my chamber this line:

You I love, and you alone.

I read it and ask'd him to lend me the ring, with which I wrote under it thus:

And so in love says every one.

He takes his ring again, and writes another line thus:

Virtue alone is an estate.

I borrowed it again and I wrote under it:

But money's virtue, gold is fate.

He colour'd as red as fire to see me turn so quick upon him, and

[1] window.

in a kind of rage told me he would conquer me, and wrote again thus:

> *I scorn your gold, and yet I love.*

I ventur'd all upon the last cast of poetry, as you'll see, for I wrote boldly under his last:

> *I'm poor: let's see how kind you'll prove.*

This was a sad truth to me; whether he believ'd me or no, I could not tell; I supposed then that he did not. However, he flew to me, took me in his arms, and kissing me very eagerly, and with the greatest passion imaginable, he held me fast till he call'd for a pen and ink, and told me he could not wait the tedious writing on a glass, but pulling out a piece of paper, he began and wrote again:

> *Be mine with all your poverty.*

I took his pen, and follow'd immediately thus:

> *Yet secretly you hope I lye.*

He told me that was unkind, because it was not just, and that I put him upon contradicting me, which did not consist with good manners, and therefore since I had insensibly drawn him into this poetical scribble, he beg'd I would not oblige him to break it off; so he writes again:

> *Let love alone be our debate.*

I wrote again:

> *She loves enough that does not hate.*

This he took for a favour, and so laid down the cudgels, that is to say, the pen; I say, he took it for a favour, and a mighty one it was, if he had known all. However, he took it as I meant it, that is, to let him think I was inclin'd to go on with him, as indeed I had reason to do, for he was the best humour'd merry sort of a fellow that I ever met with; and I often reflected how doubly criminal it was to deceive such a man; but that necessity which press'd me to a settlement suitable to my condition was my authority for it, and certainly his affection to me, and the goodness of his temper, however they might argue against using him ill, yet they strongly argued to me that he would better take the disappointment than some fiery temper'd wretch who might have nothing to recommend him but those passions which would serve only to make a woman miserable.

Besides, though I had jested with him (as he suppos'd it) so often about my poverty, yet when he found it to be true, he had fore-closed all manner of objection, seeing, whether he was in jest or in earnest, he had declar'd he took me without any regard to my portion, and, whether I was in jest or in earnest, I had declar'd myself to be very poor, so that, in a word, I had him fast both ways; and tho' he might say afterwards he was cheated, yet he could never say that I had cheated him.

He pursued me close after this, and, as I saw there was no need to fear losing him, I play'd the indifferent part with him longer than prudence might otherwise have dictated to me. But I consider'd how much this caution and indifference would give me the advantage over him when I should come to own my circumstances to him; and I managed it the more warily, because I found he infer'd from thence that I had either the more money, or the more judgment, and would not venture at all.

I took the freedom one day to tell him that it was true I had receiv'd the compliment of a lover from him, namely, that he would take me without enquiring into my fortune, and I would make him a suitable return in this, *viz.* that I would make as little enquiry into his as consisted with reason, but I hoped he would allow me to ask some questions, which he should answer or not as he thought fit; one of these questions related to our manner of living, and the place where, because I had heard he had a great plantation in Virginia, and I told him I did not care to be transported.

He began from this discourse to let me voluntarily into all his affairs, and to tell me in a frank open way all his circumstances, by which I found he was very well to pass in the world; but that great part of his estate consisted of three plantations which he had in Virginia, which brought him in a very good income of about 300*l.* a year; but that, if he was to live upon them, would bring him in four times as much. Very well, thought I, you shall carry me thither then as soon as you please, tho' I won't tell you so before hand.

I jested with him about the figure he would make in Virginia, but found he would do any thing I desired; so I turn'd my tale. I told him I had good reason not to desire to go there to live, because if his plantations were worth so much there, I had not a fortune suitable to a gentleman of 1200*l.* a year, as he said his estate would be.

He reply'd he did not ask what my fortune was, he had told me from the beginning he would not, and he would be as good as his word; but whatever it was, he assured me he would never desire me to go to Virginia with him, or go thither himself without me, unless I made it my choice.

All this, you may be sure, was as I wish'd, and indeed nothing could have happen'd more perfectly agreeable; I carried it on as far as this with a sort of indifferency that he often wonder'd at, and I mention it the rather to intimate again to the ladies that nothing but want of courage for such an indifferency makes our sex so cheap, and prepares them to be ill us'd as they are; would they venture the loss of a pretending fop now and then who carries it high upon the point of his own merit, they would certainly be slighted less, and courted more; had I discovered really what my great fortune was, and that in all I had not full 500*l.* when he expected 1500*l.* yet I hook'd him so fast, and play'd him so long, that I was satisfied he would have had me in my worst circumstances; and indeed it was less a surprize to him when he learnt the truth than it would have been, because having not the least blame to lay on me, who had carried it with an air of indifference to the last, he could not say one word, except that indeed he thought it had been more, but that, if it had been less, he did not repent his bargain; only that he should not be able to maintain me so well as he intended.

In short, we were married, and very happily married on my side, I assure you, as to the man; for he was the best humour'd man that ever woman had, but his circumstances were not so good as I imagined, as on the other hand he had not better'd himself so much as he expected.

When we were married, I was shrewdly put to it to bring him that little stock I had, and to let him see it was no more; but there was a necessity for it, so I took my opportunity one day when we were alone, to enter into a short dialogue with him about it. My dear, said I, we have been married a fortnight; is it not time to let you know whether you have got a wife with something or with nothing? Your own time for that, my dear, says he; I am satisfied I have got the wife I love; I have not troubled you much, says he, with my enquiry after it.

That's true, said I, but I have great difficulty about it, which I scarce know how to manage. What's that, my dear? says he. Why, says I, 'tis a little hard upon me, and 'tis harder upon you; I am told that Captain —— (meaning my friend's husband) has told you I had a great deal more than ever I pretended to have, and I am sure I never employ'd him so to do.

Well, says he, Captain —— may have told me, but what then? If you have not so much, that may lye at his door, but you never told me what you had, so I have no reason to blame you if you have nothing at all.

That is so just, said I, and so generous, that it makes my having but a little a double affliction to me.

The less you have, my dear, says he, the worse for us both; but I hope your affliction is not caus'd for fear I shall be unkind to you for want of a portion; no, no, if you have nothing, tell me plainly; I may perhaps tell the captain he has cheated me, but I can never say you have, for did not you give it under your hand that you was poor, and so I ought to expect you to be.

Well, said I, my dear, I am glad I have not been concern'd in deceiving you before marriage; if I deceive you since, 'tis ne'er the worse. That I am poor, 'tis too true, but not so poor as to have nothing neither; so I pull'd out some bank bills, and gave him about a hundred and sixty pounds; there is something, my dear, says I, and not quite all neither.

I had brought him so near to expecting nothing, by what I had said before, that the money, tho' the sum was small in it self, was doubly welcome; he own'd it was more than he look'd for, and that he did not question by my discourse to him but that my fine cloaths, gold watch, and a diamond ring or two, had been all my fortune.

I let him please himself with that 160*l.* two or three days, and then having been abroad that day, and as if I had been to fetch it, I brought him a hundred pounds more home in gold, and told him there was a little more portion for him; and in short, in about a week more, I brought him 180*l.* more, and about 60*l.* in linnen, which I made him believe I had been obliged to take with the 100*l.* which I gave him in gold, as a composition for a debt of 600*l.*, being little more than five shillings in the pound, and over-valued too.

And now, my dear, says I to him, I am very sorry to tell you that I have given you my whole fortune; I added, that if the person who had my 600*l.* had not abus'd me, I had been worth a thousand pound to him, but that as it was, I had been faithful, and reserv'd nothing to my self, but if it had been more he should have had it.

He was so obliged by the manner, and so pleas'd with the sum, for he had been in a terrible fright least it had been nothing at all, that he accepted it very thankfully; and thus I got over the fraud of passing for a fortune without money, and cheating a man into marrying me on pretence of it; which, by the way, I take to be one of the most dangerous steps a woman can take, and in which she runs the most hazzards of being ill used after-wards.

My husband, to give him his due, was a man of infinite good nature, but he was no fool; and finding his income not suited to the manner of living which he had intended, if I had brought him what he expected, and being under a disappointment in his return [1] of his plantations in Virginia, he discovered many times his inclination of going over to Virginia to live upon his own; and often would be magnifying the way of living there, how cheap, how plentiful, how pleasant, and the like.

I began presently to understand his meaning, and I took him up very plainly one morning, and told him that I did so; that I found his estate turn'd to no account at this distance, compar'd to what it would do if he liv'd upon the spot, and that I found he had a mind to go and live there; that I was sensible he had been disappointed in a wife, and that finding his expectations not an-swer'd that way, I could do no less, to make him amends, than tell him, that I was very willing to go to Virginia with him and live there.

He said a thousand kind things to me upon the subject of my making such a proposal to him. He told me that tho' he was dis-

[1] profits.

appointed in his expectations of a fortune, he was not disappointed in a wife, and that I was all to him that a wife could be, but that this offer was so kind that it was more than he could express.

To bring the story short, we agreed to go. He told me that he had a very good house there well furnish'd, that his mother liv'd in it, and one sister, which was all the relations he had; that as soon as he came there, they would remove to another house which was her own for life, and his after her decease; so that I should have all the house to my self; and I found it all exactly as he said.

We put on board the ship which we went in a large quantity of good furniture for our house, with stores of linnen and other necessaries, and a good cargoe for sale, and away we went.

To give an account of the manner of our voyage, which was long and full of dangers, is out of my way, I kept no journal, neither did my husband; all that I can say is that after a terrible passage, frighted twice with dreadful storms, and once with what was still more terrible, I mean a pyrate, who came on board and took away almost all our provisions; and, which would have been beyond all to me, they had once taken my husband, but by intreaties were prevail'd with to leave him: I say, after all these terrible things, we arriv'd in York River in Virginia, and coming to our plantation, we were received with all the tenderness and affection (by my husband's mother) that could be express'd.

We liv'd here all together, my mother-in-law, at my entreaty, continuing in the house, for she was too kind a mother to be parted with; my husband likewise continued the same at first, and I thought myself the happiest creature alive; when an odd and surprizing event put an end to all that felicity in a moment, and rendered my condition the most uncomfortable in the world.

My mother was a mighty chearful good humour'd old woman; I may call her so, for her son was above thirty: I say, she was very pleasant good company and us'd to entertain me in particular with abundance of stories to divert me, as well of the country we were in as of the people.

Among the rest, she often told me how the greatest part of

the inhabitants of that colony came thither in very indifferent circumstances from England; that, generally speaking, they were of two sorts; either (1.) such as were brought over by masters of ships to be sold as servants; or (2.) such as are transported after having been found guilty of crimes punishable with death.

When they come here, says she, we make no difference; the planters buy them, and they work together in the field till their time is out; when 'tis expir'd, said she, they have encouragement given them to plant for themselves; for they have a certain number of acres of land allotted them by the country, and they go to work to clear and cure [1] the land, and then to plant it with tobacco and corn for their own use; and as the merchants will trust them with tools and necessaries upon the credit of their crop before it is grown, so they again plant every year a little more than the year before, and so buy whatever they want with the crop that is before them. Hence, child, says she, many a Newgate-bird becomes a great man, and we have, continued she, several justices of the peace, officers of the train'd bands, and magistrates of the towns they live in, that have been burnt in the hand.

She was going on with that part of the story, when her own part in it interrupted her, and with a great deal of good humour'd confidence she told me she was one of the second sort of inhabitants herself; that she came away openly, having ventur'd too far in a particular case, so that she was become a criminal. And here's the mark of it, child, says she, and shewed me a very fine white arm and hand, but branded in the in-side of the hand, as in such cases it must be.

This story was very moving to me, but my mother (smiling) said, You need not think such a thing strange, daughter, for some of the best men in the country are burnt in the hand, and they are not asham'd to own it; there's Major ——, says she, he was an eminent pickpocket; there's Justice Ba——r was a shoplifter, and both of them were burnt in the hand, and I could name you several such as they are.

We had frequent discourses of this kind, and abundance of instances she gave me of the like. After some time, as she was ʒelling some stories of one that was transported but a few weeks

---

[1] = clear, free from timber.

ago, I began in an intimate kind of way to ask her to tell me
something of her own story, which she did with the utmost
plainness and sincerity; how she had fallen into very ill company
in London in her young days, occasion'd by her mother sending her frequently to carry victuals to a kinswoman of hers who
was a prisoner in Newgate in a miserable starving condition,
who was afterwards condemn'd to dye, but having got respite
by pleading her belly, perish'd afterwards in the prison.

Here my mother-in-law ran out in a long account of the
wicked practices in that dreadful place. And, child, says my
mother, perhaps you may know little of it, or it may be have
heard nothing about it; but depend upon it, says she, we all
know here that there are more thieves and rogues made by
that one prison of Newgate than by all the clubs and societies
of villains in the nation; 'tis that cursed place, says my mother,
that half peoples this colony.

Here she went on with her own story so long, and in so
particular a manner, that I began to be very uneasy, but coming
to one particular that requir'd telling her name, I thought I
should have sunk down in the place; she perceiv'd I was out
of order, and ask'd me if I was not well, and what ail'd me? I
told her I was so affected with the melancholly story she had
told that it had overcome me, and I beg'd of her to talk no more
of it. Why, my dear, says she very kindly, what need these
things trouble you? These passages were long before your
time, and they give me no trouble at all now, nay, I look back
on them with a particular satisfaction, as they have been a means
to bring me to this place. Then she went on to tell me how she
fell into a good family, where behaving herself well, and her
mistress dying, her master married her, by whom she had my
husband and his sister, and that by her diligence and good management after her husband's death she had improved the plantations to such a degree as they then were, so that most of the
estate was of her getting, not of her husband's, for she had been
a widow upwards of sixteen years.

I heard this part of the story with very little attention, because I wanted much to retire and give vent to my passions,
and let any one judge what must be the anguish of my mind,
when I came to reflect that this was certainly no more or less

than my own mother, and that I had now had two children, and was big with another by my own brother, and lay with him still every night.

I was now the most unhappy of all women in the world. O! had the story never been told me, all had been well; it had been no crime to have lain with my husband, if I had known nothing of it.

I had now such a load on my mind that it kept me perpetually waking; to reveal it I could not find would be to any purpose, and yet to conceal it would be next to impossible; nay, I did not doubt but I should talk in my sleep, and tell my husband of it whether I would or no. If I discover'd it, the least thing I could expect was to lose my husband, for he was too nice and too honest a man to have continu'd my husband after he had known I had been his sister, so that I was perplex'd to the last degree.

I leave it to any man to judge what difficulties presented to my view. I was away from my native country at a distance prodigious, and the return to me unpassable; I liv'd very well, but in a circumstance unsufferable in itself; if I had discover'd my self to my mother, it might be difficult to convince her of the particulars, and I had no way to prove them. On the other hand, if she had question'd or doubted me, I had been undone, for the bare suggestion would have immediately separated me from my husband, without gaining my mother or him, so that between the surprize on one hand, and the uncertainty on the other, I had been sure to be undone.

In the mean time, as I was but too sure of the fact, I liv'd therefore in open avowed incest and whoredom, and all under the appearance of an honest wife; and tho' I was not much touched with the crime of it, yet the action had something in it shocking to nature, and made my husband even nauseous to me. However, upon the most sedate consideration, I resolv'd that it was absolutely necessary to conceal it all, and not make the least discovery of it either to mother or husband; and thus I liv'd with the greatest pressure imaginable for three years more.

During this time my mother used to be frequently telling me old stories of her former adventures, which however were no ways pleasant to me; for by it, tho' she did not tell it me in plain terms, yet I could understand, joyn'd with what I heard my self of my first tutors, that in her younger days she had been whore and thief; but I verily believe she had liv'd to repent sincerely of both, and that she was then a very pious, sober, and religious woman.

Well, let her life have been what it would then, it was certain that my life was very uneasy to me; for I liv'd, as I have said, but in the worst sort of whoredom, and as I could expect no good of it, so really no good issue came of it, and all my seeming prosperity wore off and ended in misery and destruction. It was some time indeed before it came to this, for every thing went wrong with us afterwards, and that which was worse, my husband grew strangely alter'd, froward, jealous, and unkind, and I was as impatient of bearing his carriage, as the carriage was unreasonable and unjust. These things proceeded so far, and we came at last to be in such ill terms with one another that I claim'd a promise of him which he enter'd willingly into with me, when I consented to come from England with him, *viz.* that if I did not like to live there, I should come away to England again when I pleas'd, giving him a year's warning to settle his affairs.

I say, I now claim'd this promise of him, and I must confess I did it not in the most obliging terms that could be neither; but I insisted that he treated me ill, that I was remote from my friends, and could do my self no justice, and that he was jealous without cause, my conversation having been unblameable, and he having no pretence for it, and that to remove to England would take away all occasion from him.

I insisted so peremptorily upon it that he could not avoid coming to a point, either to keep his word with me, or to break it; and this, notwithstanding he used all the skill he was master of, and employ'd his mother and other agents to prevail with me to alter my resolutions; indeed the bottom [1] of the thing lay at my heart, and that made all his endeavours fruitless, for my heart was alienated from him. I loathed the thoughts of bedding with him, and used a thousand pretences of illness and humour to prevent his touching me, fearing nothing more than to be with child again, which to be sure would have prevented, or at least delay'd my going over to England.

However, at last I put him so out of humour that he took

[1] reality.

up a rash and fatal resolution, that in short I should not go to England; that tho' he had promis'd me, yet it was an unreasonable thing, that it would be ruinous to his affairs, would unhinge his whole family, and be next to an undoing him in the world; that therefore I ought not to desire it of him, and that no wife in the world that valued her family and her husband's prosperity would insist upon such a thing.

This plung'd [1] me again, for when I considered the thing calmly, and took my husband as he really was, a diligent careful man in the main, and that he knew nothing of the dreadful circumstances that he was in, I could not but confess to my self that my proposal was very unreasonable, and what no wife that had the good of her family at heart wou'd have desir'd.

But my discontents were of another nature; I look'd upon him no longer as a husband, but as a near relation, the son of my own mother, and I resolv'd somehow or other to be clear of him, but which way I did not know.

It is said by the ill-natur'd world of our sex that if we are set on a thing, it is impossible to turn us from our resolutions. In short, I never ceas'd poring upon the means to bring to pass my voyage, and came that length with my husband at last, as to propose going without him. This provok'd him to the last degree, and he call'd me not only an unkind wife, but an unnatural mother, and ask'd me how I could entertain such a thought without horror as that of leaving my two children (for one was dead) without a mother, and never to see them more. It was true, had things been right, I should not have done it, but now it was my real desire never to see them, or him either, any more; and as to the charge of unnatural, I could easily answer it to my self, while I knew that the whole relation was unnatural in the highest degree.

However, there was no bringing my husband to any thing; he would neither go with me, or let me go without him, and it was out of my power to stir without his consent, as any one that is acquainted with the constitution of that country knows very well.

We had many family quarrels about it, and they began to grow up to a dangerous height; for as I was quite estrang'd from

[1] overwhelmed.

him in affection, so I took no heed to my words, but sometimes gave him language that was provoking. In short, I strove all I could to bring him to a parting with me, which was what above all things I desir'd most.

He took my carriage very ill, and indeed he might well do so, for at last I refus'd to bed with him, and carrying on the breach upon all occasions to extremity, he told me once he thought I was mad, and if I did not alter my conduct, he would put me under cure; that is to say, into a mad-house. I told him he should find I was far enough from mad, and that it was not in his power, or any other villain's, to murther me; I confess at the same time I was heartily frighted at his thoughts of putting me into a mad-house, which would at once have destroy'd all the possibility of bringing the truth out; for that [1] then no one would have given credit to a word of it.

This therefore brought me to a resolution, whatever came of it, to lay open my whole case; but which way to do it, or to whom, was an inextricable difficulty; when another quarrel with my husband happen'd, which came up to such an extream as almost push'd me on to tell it him all to his face; but tho' I kept it in so as not to come to the particulars, I spoke so much as put him into the utmost confusion, and in the end brought out the whole story.

He began with a calm expostulation upon my being so resolute to go to England; I defended it, and one hard word bringing on another, as is usual in all family strife, he told me I did not treat him as if he was my husband, or talk of my children as if I was a mother; and, in short, that I did not deserve to be us'd as a wife; that he had us'd all the fair means possible with me; that he had argu'd with all the kindness and calmness that a husband or a Christian ought to do, and that I made him such a vile return that I treated him rather like a dog than a man, and rather like the most contemptible stranger than a husband; that he was very loth to use violence with me, but that, in short, he saw a necessity of it now, and that for the future he should be oblig'd to take such measures as should reduce me to my duty.

My blood was now fir'd to the utmost, and nothing could

[1] because.

appear more provok'd; I told him, for his fair means and his foul, they were equally contemn'd by me; that for my going to England, I was resolv'd on it, come what would; and that as to treating him not like a husband, and not showing my self a mother to my children, there might be something more in it than he understood at present; but I thought fit to tell him thus much, that he neither was my lawful husband, nor they lawful children, and that I had reason to regard neither of them more than I did.

I confess I was mov'd to pity him when I spoke it, for he turn'd pale as death, and stood mute as one thunderstruck, and once or twice I thought he would have fainted; in short, it put him in a fit something like an apoplex; he trembl'd, a sweat or dew ran off his face, and yet he was cold as a clod, so that I was forced to fetch something to keep life in him; when he recover'd of that, he grew sick and vomited, and in a little after was put to bed, and the next morning was in a violent fever.

However, it went off again, and he recovered, tho' but slowly, and when he came to be a little better, he told me I had given him a mortal wound with my tongue, and he had only one thing to ask before he desir'd an explanation; I interrupted him, and told him I was sorry I had gone so far, since I saw what disorder it put him into, but I desir'd him not to talk to me of explanations, for that would but make things worse.

This heighten'd his impatience, and indeed perplex'd him beyond all bearing; for now he began to suspect that there was some mystery yet unfolded, but could not make the least guess at it; all that run in his brain was that I had another husband alive, but I assur'd him there was not the least of that in it; indeed, as to my other husband, he was effectually dead to me, and had told me I should look on him as such, so I had not the least uneasiness on that score.

But now I found the thing too far gone to conceal it much longer, and my husband himself gave me an opportunity to ease my self of the secret much to my satisfaction. He had laboured with me three or four weeks, but to no purpose, only to tell him, whether I had spoken those words only to put him in a passion, or whether there was any thing of truth in the bottom of them. But I continued inflexible, and would explain nothing, unless he would first consent to my going to England, which he would never do, he said, while he liv'd; on the other hand, I said it was in my power to make him willing when I pleas'd, nay, to make him entreat me to go; and this increas'd his curiosity, and made him importunate to the highest degree.

At length he tells all this story to his mother, and sets her upon me to get it out of me, and she us'd her utmost skill indeed; but I put her to a full stop at once by telling her that the mystery of the whole matter lay in herself; that it was my respect to her had made me conceal it, and that, in short, I could go no farther, and therefore conjur'd her not to insist upon it.

She was struck dumb at this suggestion, and could not tell what to say or to think; but laying aside the supposition as a policy of mine, continued her importunity on account of her son, and, if possible, to make up the breach between us two. As to that, I told her that it was indeed a good design in her, but that it was impossible to be done; and that if I should reveal to her the truth of what she desir'd, she would grant it to be impossible, and cease to desire it. At last I seem'd to be prevail'd on by her importunity, and told her I dare trust her with a secret of the greatest importance, and she would soon see that this was so, and that I would consent to lodge it in her breast, if she would engage solemnly not to acquaint her son with it without my consent.

She was long in promising this part, but rather than not come at the main secret she agreed to that too, and after a great many other preliminaries, I began and told her the whole story. First I told her how much she was concern'd in all the unhappy breach which had happen'd between her son and me, by telling me her own story, and her London name; and that the surprize she could see I was in was upon that occasion. Then I told her my own story, and my name, and assur'd her by such other tokens as she could not deny, that I was no other, nor more or less than her own child, her daughter born of her body in Newgate; the same that had sav'd her from the gallows by being in her belly, and that she left in such and such hands when she was transported.

It is impossible to express the astonishment she was in; she was not inclin'd to believe the story, or to remember the particulars; for she immediately foresaw the confusion that must follow in the family upon it; but every thing concurr'd so exactly with the stories she had told me of herself (and which, if she had not told me, she would perhaps have been content to have denied), that she had stop'd her own mouth, and she had nothing to do but take me about the neck and kiss me, and cry most vehemently over me, without speaking one word for a long time together. At last she broke out: Unhappy child! says she, what miserable chance could bring thee hither? and in the arms of my son too! Dreadful girl! says she, why, we are all undone! Married to thy own brother! Three children, and two alive, all of the same flesh and blood! My son and my daughter lying together as husband and wife! All confusion and distraction, miserable family! What will become of us? What is to be said? What is to be done? And thus she run on a great while, nor had I any power to speak, or if I had, did I know what to say, for every word wounded me to the soul. With this kind of amazement we parted for the first time, tho' my mother was more surpriz'd than I was, because it was more news to her than to me. However, she promis'd again that she would say nothing of it to her son, till we had talk'd of it again.

It was not long, you may be sure, before we had a second conference upon the same subject; when, as if she had been willing to forget the story she had told me of herself, or to suppose that I had forgot some of the particulars, she began to tell them with alterations and omissions; but I refresh'd her memory in many things which I supposed she had forgot, and then came in so opportunely with the whole history that it was impossible for her to go from it; and then she fell into her rhapsodies again, and exclamations at the severity of her misfortunes. When these things were a little over with her, we fell into a close debate about what should be first done before we gave an account of the matter to my husband. But to what purpose could be all our consultations? We could neither of us see our way thro' it, or how it could be safe to open such a scene to him; it was impossible to make any judgment, or give any guess at what temper he would receive it in, or what measures he would take upon it; and if he should have so little government of himself as to make it publick, we easily foresaw that it would be the ruin of the whole family, and if at last he should take the advantage the law would give him, he might put me away with disdain, and leave me to sue for the little portion that I had, and perhaps waste it all in the suit, and then be a beggar; and thus I should see him perhaps in the arms of another wife in a few months, and be my self the most miserable creature alive.

My mother was as sensible of this as I; and upon the whole we knew not what to do; after some time, we came to more sober resolutions, but then it was with this misfortune too, that my mother's opinion and mine were quite different from one another, and indeed inconsistent with one another; for my mother's opinion was that I should bury the whole thing entirely, and continue to live with him as my husband till some other event should make the discovery of it more convenient; and that in the mean time she would endeavour to reconcile us together again, and restore our mutual comfort and family peace; that we might lie as we us'd to do together, and so let the whole matter remain a secret as close as death. For, child, says she, we are both undone if it comes out.

To encourage me to this, she promis'd to make me easy in my circumstances, and to leave me what she could at her death, secur'd for me separately from my husband; so that if it should come out afterwards, I should be able to stand on my own feet, and procure justice too from him.

This proposal did not agree with my judgment, tho' it was very fair and kind in my mother, but my thoughts run quite another way.

As to keeping the thing in our own breasts, and letting it all remain as it was, I told her it was impossible; and I ask'd her how she could think I could bear the thoughts of lying with my own brother? In the next place I told her that her being alive was the only support of the discovery, and that while she own'd me for her child, and saw reason to be satisfied that I was so, no body else would doubt it; but that if she should die before the discovery, I should be taken for an impudent creature that had forg'd such a thing to go away from my husband, or should be counted craz'd and distracted. Then I told her how he had threaten'd already to put me into a mad-house, and what concern I had been in about it, and how that was the thing that drove me to the necessity of discovering it to her as I had done.

From all which I told her that I had, on the most serious reflections I was able to make in the case, come to this resolution, which I hop'd she would like, as a medium between both, *viz.* that she should use her endeavours with her son to give me leave to go for England, as I had desired, and to furnish me with a sufficient sum of money, either in goods along with me, or in bills for my support there, all along suggesting that he might one time or other think it proper to come over to me.

That when I was gone she should then in cold blood discover the case to him gradually, and as her own discretion should guide; so that he might not be surpriz'd with it, and fly out into any passions and excesses; and that she should concern herself to prevent his slighting the children, or marrying again, unless he had a certain account of my being dead.

This was my scheme, and my reasons were good; I was really alienated from him in the consequence of these things; indeed, I mortally hated him as a husband, and it was impossible to remove that riveted aversion I had to him; at the same time, it being an unlawful incestuous living, added to that aversion, and every thing added to make cohabiting with him the most nauseous thing to me in the world; and I think verily it was come to such a height that I could almost as willingly have embrac'd a dog as have let him offer any thing of that kind to me, for which reason I could not bear the thoughts of coming between the sheets with him. I cannot say that I was right in carrying it such a length while at the same time I did not resolve to discover the thing to him; but I am giving an account of what was, not of what ought or ought not to be.

In this directly opposite opinion to one another my mother and I continued a long time, and it was impossible to reconcile our judgments; many disputes we had about it, but we could never either of us yield our own, or bring over the other.

I insisted on my aversion to lying with my own brother; and she insisted upon its being impossible to bring him to consent to my going to England; and in this uncertainty we continued, not differing so as to quarrel, or any thing like it, but so as not to be able to resolve what we should do to make up that terrible breach.

At last I resolv'd on a desperate course, and told my mother my resolution, *viz.* that, in short, I wou'd tell him of it my self. My mother was frighted to the last degree at the very thoughts of it; but I bid her be easy, told her I would do it gradually and softly, and with all the art and good humour I was mistress of, and time it also as well as I could, taking him in good humour too. I told her I did not question but if I cou'd be hypocrite enough to feign more affection to him than I really had, I should succeed in all my design, and we might part by consent, and with a good agreement, for I might love him well enough for a brother, tho' I could not for a husband.

All this while he lay at my mother to find out, if possible, what was the meaning of that dreadful expression of mine, as he call'd it, which I mention'd before; namely, that I was not his lawful wife, nor my children his legal children. My mother put him off, told him she could bring me to no explanations, but found there was something that disturb'd me very much, and she hop'd she should get it out of me in time, and in the mean time recommended to him earnestly to use me more tenderly, and win me with his usual good carriage; told him of his terrifying and affrighting me with his threats of sending me to a mad-house and the like, and advis'd him not to make a woman desperate on any account whatever.

He promis'd her to soften his behaviour, and bid her assure me that he lov'd me as well as ever, and that he had no such design as that of sending me to a mad-house, whatever he might say in his passion; also he desir'd my mother to use the same perswasions to me too, and we might live together as we us'd to do.

I found the effects of this treaty presently; my husband's conduct was immediately alter'd, and he was quite another man to me; nothing could be kinder and more obliging than he was to me upon all occasions; and I could do no less than make some return to it, which I did as well as I could, but it was but in an awkward manner at best, for nothing was more frightful to me than his caresses, and the apprehensions of being with child again by him was ready to throw me into fits; and this made me see that there was an absolute necessity of breaking the case to him without any more delay, which, however, I did with all the caution and reserve imaginable.

He had continued his alter'd carriage to me near a month, and we began to live a new kind of life with one another; and could I have satisfied my self to have gone on with it, I believe it might have continued as long as we had continu'd alive together. One evening, as we were sitting and talking together under a little awning which serv'd as an arbour at the entrance into the garden, he was in a very pleasant agreeable humour, and said abundance of kind things to me, relating to the pleasure of our present good agreement, and the disorders of our past breach, and what a satisfaction it was to him that we had room to hope we should never have any more of it.

I fetch'd a deep sigh, and told him there was no body in the world could be more delighted than I was in the good agreement we had always kept up, or more afflicted with the breach of it, but I was sorry to tell him that there was an unhappy circumstance in our case, which lay too close to my heart, and which I knew not how to break to him, that rendered my part of it very miserable, and took from me all the comfort of the rest.

He importun'd me to tell him what it was. I told him I could not tell how to do it; that while it was conceal'd from him I alone was unhappy, but if he knew it also, we should be both so; and that therefore to keep him in the dark about it was the kindest thing that I could do, and it was on that account alone that I kept a secret from him, the very keeping of which I thought would first or last be my destruction.

It is impossible to express his surprize at this relation, and the double importunity which he used with me to discover it to him. He told me I could not be call'd kind to him, nay, I could not be faithful to him, if I conceal'd it from him; I told him I thought so too, and yet I could not do it. He went back to what I had said before to him, and told me he hoped it did not relate to what I said in my passion; and that he had resolv'd to forget all that, as the effect of a rash provok'd spirit. I told him I wish'd I could forget it all too, but that it was not to be done; the impression was too deep, and it was impossible.

He then told me he was resolv'd not to differ with me in any thing, and that therefore he would importune me no more about it, resolving to acquiesce in whatever I did or said; only begg'd I would then agree that whatever it was it should no more interrupt our quiet and our mutual kindness.

This was the most provoking thing he could have said to me, for I really wanted his farther importunities, that I might be prevail'd with to bring out that which indeed was like death to me to conceal; so I answer'd him plainly that I could not say I was glad not to be importuned, tho' I could not tell how to comply. But come, my dear, said I, what conditions will you make with me upon the opening this affair to you?

Any conditions in the world, said he, that you can in reason desire of me. Well, said I, come, give it me under your hand that if you do not find I am in any fault, or that I am willingly concern'd in the causes of the misfortunes that is to follow, you will not blame me, use me the worse, do me any injury, or make me be the sufferer for that which is not my fault.

That, says he, is the most reasonable demand in the world, not to blame you for that which is not your fault; give me a pen and ink, says he. So I ran in and fetch'd pen, ink, and paper, and he wrote the condition down in the very words I had proposed it, and sign'd it with his name. Well, says he, what is next, my dear? Why, says I, the next is that you will not blame me for not discovering the secret to you before I knew it. Very just again, says he, with all my heart; so he wrote down that also and sign'd it.

Well, my dear, says I, then I have but one condition more to make with you, and that is, that as there is no body concern'd in it but you and I, you shall not discover it to any person in the world, except your own mother; and that in all the measures you shall take upon the discovery, as I am equally concern'd in it with you, tho' as innocent as your self, you shall do nothing in a passion, nothing to my prejudice, or to your mother's prejudice, without my knowledge and consent.

This a little amaz'd him, and he wrote down the words distinctly, but read them over and over before he sign'd them,

hesitating at them several times and repeating them: *My mother's
prejudice! and your prejudice!* What mysterious thing can this
be? However, at last he sign'd it.

Well, says I, my dear, I'll ask you no more under your hand,
but as you are to hear the most unexpected and surprizing thing
that perhaps ever befel any family in the world, I beg you to
promise me you will receive it with composure and a presence
of mind suitable to a man of sense.

I'll do my utmost, says he, upon condition you will keep me
no longer in suspense, for you terrify me with all these preliminaries.

Well then, says I, it is this; as I told you before in a heat that
I was not your lawful wife, and that our children were not
legal children, so I must let you know now in calmness, and
in kindness, but with affliction enough, that *I am your own
sister*, and you *my own brother*, and that we are both the children of our mother now alive and in the house, who is convinc'd of the truth of it, in a manner not to be denied or
contradicted.

I saw him turn pale, and look wild, and I said, Now remember your promise, and receive it with presence of mind; for
who cou'd have said more to prepare you for it than I have
done? However, I call'd a servant, and got him a little glass
of rum, which is the usual dram of the country, for he was
fainting away.

When he was a little recover'd, I said to him, This story,
you may be sure, requires a long explanation, and therefore
have patience and compose your mind to hear it out, and I'll
make it as short as I can; and with this I told him what I thought
was needful of the fact, and particularly how my mother came
to discover it to me, as above. And now, my dear, says I, you
will see reason for my capitulations, and that I neither have
been the cause of this matter, nor could be so, and that I
could know nothing of it before now.

I am fully satisfied of that, says he, but 'tis a dreadful surprize to me; however, I know a remedy for it all, and a remedy
that shall put an end to all your difficulties without your going
to England. That would be strange, said I, as all the rest. No,
no, says he, I'll make it easy; there's no body in the way of

it all but my self. He look'd a little disorder'd when he said this, but I did not apprehend any thing from it at that time, believing, as it us'd to be said, *that they who do those things never talk of them; or that they who talk of such things never do them.*

But things were now come to their height with him, and I observ'd he became pensive and melancholly; and in a word, as I thought, a little distemper'd in his head. I endeavour'd to talk him into temper, and into a kind of scheme for our government in the affair, and sometimes he would be well, and talk with some courage about it; but the weight of it lay too heavy upon his thoughts, and went so far that he made two attempts upon himself, and in one of them had actually strangled himself, and had not his mother come into the room in the very moment, he had died; but with the help of a Negro servant, she cut him down and recover'd him.

Things were now come to a lamentable height. My pity for him now began to revive that affection which at first I really had for him, and I endeavour'd sincerely, by all the kind carriage I could, to make up the breach; but in short, it had gotten too great a head, it prey'd upon his spirits, and it threw him into a ling'ring consumption, tho' it happen'd not to be mortal. In this distress I did not know what to do, as his life was apparently declining, and I might perhaps have marry'd again there, very much to my advantage, had it been my business to have staid in the country; but my mind was restless too, I hanker'd after coming to England, and nothing would satisfy me without it.

In short, by an unwearied importunity, my husband, who was apparently decaying, as I observ'd, was at last prevail'd with; and so, my fate pushing me on, the way was made clear for me, and my mother concurring, I obtain'd a very good cargo for my coming to England.

When I parted with my brother, for such I am now to call him, we agreed that after I arriv'd, he should pretend to have an account that I was dead in England, and so might marry again when he wou'd; he promis'd, and engag'd to me, to correspond with me as a sister, and to assist and support me as long as I liv'd; and that if he dy'd before me, he would leave sufficient to his mother to take care of me still in the name of a sister, and he was in some respects just to this; but it was so oddly manag'd that I felt the disappointments very sensibly afterwards, as you shall hear in its time.

I came away in the month of August, after I had been eight years in that country, and now a new scene of misfortunes attended me, which perhaps few women have gone thro' the like.

We had an indifferent good voyage till we came just upon the coast of England, and where we arriv'd in two and thirty days, but were then ruffled with two or three storms, one of which drove us away to the coast of Ireland, and we put in at Kinsale. We remain'd there about thirteen days, got some refreshment on shore, and put to sea again, tho' we met with very bad weather again, in which the ship sprung her main-mast, as they call'd it. But we got at last into Milford Haven in Wales, where, tho' it was remote from our port, yet having my foot safe upon the firm ground of the isle of Britain, I resolv'd to venture it no more upon the waters, which had been so terrible to me; so getting my cloaths and money on shore, with my bills of loading and other papers, I resolv'd to come for London, and leave the ship to get to her port as she could. The port whither she was bound was to Bristol, where my brother's chief correspondent liv'd.

I got to London in about three weeks, where I heard, a little while after, that the ship was arriv'd at Bristol, but at the same time had the misfortune to know that by the violent weather she had been in, and the breaking of her main-mast, she had great damage on board, and that a great part of her cargoe was spoil'd.

I had now a new scene of life upon my hands, and a dreadful appearance it had; I was come away with a kind of final farewel; what I brought with me was indeed considerable, had it come safe, and by the help of it I might have married again tollerably well; but as it was, I was reduc'd to between two or three hundred pounds in the whole, and this without any hope of recruit. I was entirely without friends, nay, even so much as without acquaintances, for I found it was absolutely necessary not to revive former acquaintance; and as for my subtle friend that set me up formerly for a fortune, she was dead and her husband also.

The looking after my cargoe of goods soon after obliged me to take a journey to Bristol, and during my attendance upon that affair, I took the diversion of going to the Bath,[1] for as I was still far from being old, so my humour, which was always gay, continu'd so to an extream; and being now, as it were, a woman of fortune, tho' I was a woman without a fortune, I expected something or other might happen in the way that might mend my circumstances, as had been my case before.

The Bath is a place of gallantry enough; expensive, and full of snares; I went thither indeed in the view of taking what might offer; but I must do myself justice, as to protest I meant nothing but in an honest way, nor had any thoughts about me at first that look'd the way which afterwards I suffered them to be guided.

Here I stay'd the whole latter season, as it is call'd there, and contracted some unhappy acquaintance, which rather prompted the follies I fell afterwards into than fortify'd me against them. I liv'd pleasantly enough, kept good company, that is to say, gay fine company; but had the discouragement to find this way of living sunk me exceedingly, and that as I had no settled income, so spending upon the main stock was but a certain kind of bleeding to death; and this gave me many sad reflections. However, I shook them off, and still flatter'd myself that something or other might offer for my advantage.

But I was in the wrong place for it; I was not now at Redriff, where, if I had set my self tollerably up, some honest sea captain or other might have talk'd with me upon the honourable terms of matrimony; but I was at the Bath, where men find a mistress sometimes, but very rarely look for a wife; and consequently all the particular acquaintances a woman can expect there must have some tendency that way.

I had spent the first season well enough, for tho' I had contracted some acquaintance with a gentleman who came to the Bath for his diversion, yet I had enter'd into no felonious treaty. I had resisted some casual offers of gallantry, and had manag'd that way well enough; I was not wicked enough to come into

[1] The ancient city of Bath is about twelve miles from Bristol.

the crime for the meer vice of it, and I had no extraordinary offers that tempted me with the main thing which I wanted.

However, I went this length the first season, (*viz.*) I contracted an acquaintance with a woman in whose house I lodg'd, who, tho' she did not keep an ill house, yet had none of the best principles in her self. I had on all occasions behav'd my self so well as not to get the least slur upon my reputation, and all the men that I had convers'd with were of so good reputation that I had not gotten the least reflection by conversing with them; nor did any of them seem to think there was room for a wicked correspondence, if they had offered it; yet there was one gentleman, as above, who always singled me out for the diversion of my company, as he call'd it, which, as he was pleased to say, was very agreeable to him, but at that time there was no more in it.

I had many melancholly hours at the Bath after all the company was gone, for tho' I went to Bristol sometimes for the disposing my effects, and for recruits of money, yet I chose to come back to the Bath for my residence, because being on good terms with the woman in whose house I lodg'd in the summer, I found that during the winter I liv'd rather cheaper there than I could do any where else; here, I say, I pass'd the winter as heavily as I had pass'd the autumn chearfully; but having contracted a nearer intimacy with the said woman in whose house I lodg'd, I could not avoid communicating something of what lay hardest upon my mind, and particularly the narrowness of my circumstances. I told her also that I had a mother and a brother in Virginia in good circumstances, and as I had really written back to my mother in particular to represent my condition, and the great loss I had receiv'd, so I did not fail to let my new friend know that I expected a supply from thence, and so indeed I did; and as the ships went from Bristol to York-River, in Virginia, and back again generally in less time than from London, and that my brother corresponded chiefly at Bristol, I thought it was much better for me to wait here for my returns than to go to London.

My new friend appear'd sensibly affected with my condition, and indeed was so very kind as to reduce the rate of my living with her to so low a price during the winter that she convinc'd me she got nothing by me; and as for lodging, during the winter I paid nothing at all.

When the spring season came on, she continu'd to be as kind to me as she could, and I lodg'd with her for a time, till it was found necessary to do otherwise; she had some persons of character that frequently lodg'd in her house, and in particular the gentleman who, as I said, singled me out for his companion in the winter before; and he came down again with another gentleman in his company and two servants, and lodg'd in the same house. I suspected that my landlady had invited him thither, letting him know that I was still with her, but she deny'd it.

In a word, this gentleman came down and continu'd to single me out for his peculiar confidence; he was a compleat gentleman, that must be confess'd, and his company was agreeable to me, as mine, if I might believe him, was to him; he made no professions to me but of an extraordinary respect, and he had such an opinion of my virtue that, as he often profess'd, he believ'd, if he should offer any thing else, I should reject him with contempt. He soon understood from me that I was a widow, that I had arriv'd at Bristol from Virginia by the last ships, and that I waited at the Bath till the next Virginia fleet should arrive, by which I expected considerable effects; I understood by him that he had a wife, but that the lady was distemper'd in her head, and was under the conduct of her own relations, which he consented to, to avoid any reflection that might be cast upon him for mismanaging her cure; and in the mean time he came to the Bath to divert his thoughts under such a melancholly circumstance.

My landlady, who of her own accord encourag'd the correspondence on all occasions, gave me an advantageous character of him, as a man of honour and of virtue, as well as of a great estate; and indeed I had reason to say so of him too, for tho' we lodg'd both on a floor, and he had frequently come into my chamber, even when I was in bed, and I also into his, yet he never offered any thing to me farther than a kiss, or so much as solicited me to any thing till long after, as you shall hear.

I frequently took notice to my landlady of his exceeding modesty, and she again used to tell me she believ'd it was so from the beginning; however, she used to tell me that she thought I ought to expect some gratifications from him for my company, for indeed he did as it were engross me. I told her I had not given him the least occasion to think I wanted it, or that I would accept of it from him. She told me she would take that part upon her, and she manag'd it so dextrously that the first time we were together alone, after she had talk'd with him, he began to enquire a little into my circumstances, as how I had subsisted my self since I came on shore, and whether I did not want money? I stood off very boldly, I told him that tho' my cargoe of tobacco was damag'd, yet that it was not quite lost; that the merchant that I had been consigned to had so honestly managed for me that I had not wanted, and that I hop'd, with frugal management, I should make it hold out till more would come, which I expected by the next fleet; that in the mean time I had retrench'd my expences, and whereas I kept a maid last season, now I liv'd without; and whereas I had a chamber and a dining room then on the first floor, I now had but one room two pair of stairs,[1] and the like. But I live, said I, as well satisfy'd now as then; adding that his company had made me live much more chearfully than otherwise I should have done, for which I was much oblig'd to him; and so I put off all room for any offer at the present. It was not long before he attack'd me again, and told me he found that I was backward to trust him with the secret of my circumstances, which he was sorry for; assuring me that he enquir'd into it with no design to satisfy his own curiosity, but meerly to assist me if there was any occasion; but since I would not own my self to stand in need of any assistance, he had but one thing more to desire of me, and that was, that I would promise him that when I was any way streighten'd I would frankly tell him of it, and that I would make use of him with the same freedom that he made the offer; adding that I should always find I had a true friend, tho' perhaps I was afraid to trust him.

I omitted nothing that was fit to be said by one infinitely oblig'd, to let him know that I had a due sense of his kindness; and indeed from that time I did not appear so much reserv'd to him as I had done before, tho' still within the bounds of the strictest virtue on both sides; but how free soever our conversation was, I could not arrive to that freedom which he desir'd,

[1] on the third floor.

viz. to tell him I wanted money, tho' I was secretly very glad of his offer.

Some weeks pass'd after this, and still I never ask'd him for money; when my landlady, a cunning creature, who had often press'd me to it, but found that I could not do it, makes a story of her own inventing, and comes in bluntly to me when we were together, O! widow, says she, I have bad news to tell you this morning. What is that? said I; is the Virginia ships taken by the French? (for that was my fear). No, no, says she, but the man you sent to Bristol yesterday for money is come back, and says he has brought none.

I could by no means like her project; I thought it look'd too much like prompting him, which he did not want, and I saw that I should lose nothing by being backward, so took her up short. I can't imagine why he should say so, said I, for I assure you he brought me all the money I sent him for, and here it is, said I (pulling out my purse with about 12 guineas in it), and added, I intend you shall have most of it by and by.

He seem'd distasted [1] a little at her talking as she did, as well as I, taking it, as I fancy'd he would, as something forward of her; but when he saw me give such an answer, he came immediately to himself, The next morning we talk'd of it again, when I found he was fully satisfied; and, smiling, said he hop'd I would not want money, and not tell him of it, and that I had promis'd him otherwise. I told him I had been very much dissatisfied at my landlady's talking so publickly the day before of what she had nothing to do with; but I suppos'd she wanted what I ow'd her, which was about eight guineas, which I had resolv'd to give her, and had given it her the same night.

He was in a mighty good humour when he heard me say I had paid her, and it went off into some other discourse at that time; but the next morning, he having heard me up before him, he call'd to me, and I answer'd. He ask'd me to come into his chamber; he was in bed when I came in, and he made me come and sit down on his bed side, for he said he had something to say to me. After some very kind expressions, he ask'd me if I would be very honest to him, and give a sincere answer to one thing he would desire of me. After some little cavil with him at the word

[1] offended.

sincere, and asking him if I had ever given him any answers which were not sincere, I promis'd him I would. Why, then, his request was, he said, to let him see my purse; I immediately put my hand into my pocket, and laughing at him, pull'd it out, and there was in it three guineas and a half. Then he ask'd me, if there was all the money I had. I told him, no, laughing again, not by a great deal.

Well, then, he said, he would have me promise to go and fetch him all the money I had, every farthing. I told him I would, and I went into my chamber, and fetch'd him a little private drawer, where I had about six guineas more, and some silver, and threw it all down upon the bed, and told him there was all my wealth, honestly to a shilling. He look'd a little at it, but did not tell it, and huddled it all into the drawer again, and then reaching his pocket, pull'd out a key, and bad me open a little walnut-tree box he had upon the table, and bring him such a drawer, which I did: in this drawer, there was a great deal of money in gold, I believe near 200 guineas, but I knew not how much. He took the drawer, and taking me by the hand, made me put it in, and take a whole handful; I was backward at that, but he held my hand hard in his hand, and put it into the drawer, and made me take out as many guineas almost as I could well take up at once.

When I had done so, he made me put them into my lap, and took my little drawer, and pour'd out all my own money among his, and bad me get me gone, and carry it all into my own chamber.

I relate this story the more particularly, because of the good humour of it, and to show the temper with which we convers'd. It was not long after this but he began every day to find fault with my cloaths, with my laces, and head-dresses; and in a word, press'd me to buy better, which by the way I was willing enough to do, tho' I did not seem to be so; I lov'd nothing in the world better than fine cloaths, but I told him I must house-wife the money he had lent me, or else I should not be able to pay him again. He then told me in a few words that as he had a sincere respect for me, and knew my circumstances, he had not lent me that money, but given it me, and that he thought I had merited it from him, by giving him my company so intirely as I had done. After this, he made me take a maid, and keep house, and his friend being gone, he obliged me to dyet him, which I did very willingly, believing, as it appear'd, that I should lose nothing by it, nor did the woman of the house fail to find her account in it too.

We had liv'd thus near three months, when the company beginning to wear away at the Bath, he talk'd of going away, and fain he would have me to go to London with him. I was not very easy in that proposal, not knowing what posture I was to live in there, or how he might use me. But while this was in debate, he fell very sick; he had gone out to a place in Somersetshire call'd Shepton, and was there taken very ill, and so ill that he could not travel; so he sent his man back to the Bath, to beg me that I would hire a coach and come over to him. Before he went, he had left his money and other things of value with me, and what to do with them I did not know, but I secur'd them as well as I could, and lock'd up the lodgings and went to him, where I found him very ill indeed, so I perswaded him to be carry'd in a litter to Bath, where was more help and better advice to be had.

He consented, and I brought him to the Bath, which was about fifteen miles, as I remember. Here he continued very ill of a fever, and kept his bed five weeks, all which time I nurs'd him and tended him as carefully as if I had been his wife; indeed, if I had been his wife I could not have done more; I sat up with him so much and so often, that at last, indeed, he would not let me sit up any longer, and then I got a pallet bed into his room, and lay in it just at his bed's feet.

I was indeed sensibly affected with his condition, and with the apprehensions of losing such a friend as he was, and was like to be to me, and I us'd to sit and cry by him many hours together. At last he grew better, and gave hopes that he would recover, as indeed he did, tho' very slowly.

Were it otherwise than what I am going to say, I should not be backward to disclose it, as it is apparent I have done in other cases; but I affirm, through all this conversation, abating the coming into the chamber when I or he was in bed, and the necessary offices of attending him night and day when he was sick, there had not pass'd the least immodest word or action between us. O! that it had been so to the last.

After some time he gathered strength and grew well apace, and I would have remov'd my pallet bed, but he would not let me till he was able to venture himself without any body to sit up with him, when I remov'd to my own chamber.

He took many occasions to express his sense of my tenderness for him; and when he grew well he made me a present of fifty guineas for my care, and, as he call'd it, hazarding my life to save his.

And now he made deep protestations of a sincere inviolable affection for me, but with the utmost reserve for my virtue, and his own. I told him I was fully satisfy'd of it; he carried it that length that he protested to me, that if he was naked in bed with me he would as sacredly preserve my virtue as he would defend it if I was assaulted by a ravisher. I believ'd him, and told him I did so; but this did not satisfy him; he would, he said, wait for some opportunity to give me an undoubted testimony of it.

It was a great while after this that I had occasion, on my business, to go to Bristol, upon which he hir'd me a coach, and would go with me; and now indeed our intimacy increas'd. From Bristol he carry'd me to Gloucester, which was meerly a journey of pleasure to take the air; and here it was our hap to have no lodgings in the inn, but in one large chamber with two beds in it. The master of the house going with us to show his rooms, and coming into that room, said very frankly to him, Sir, it is none of my business to enquire whether the lady be your spouse or no, but if not, you may lye as honestly in these two beds, as if you were in two chambers; and with that he pulls a great curtain which drew quite across the room, and effectually divided the beds. Well, says my friend, very readily, these beds will do, and as for the rest, we are too near a kin to lye together, tho' we may lodge near one another; and this put an honest face on the thing too. When we came to go to bed, he decently went out of the room till I was in bed, and then went to bed in the other bed, but lay there talking to me a great while.

At last, repeating his usual saying, that he could lye naked in the bed with me, and not offer me the least injury, he starts out of his bed. And now, my dear, says he, you shall see how just I will be to you, and that I can keep my word; and away he comes to my bed.

I resisted a little, but I must confess I should not have resisted him much, if he had not made those promises at all; so after a little struggle, I lay still and let him come to bed. When he was there he took me in his arms, and so I lay all night with him, but he had no more to do with me, or offer'd anything to me, other than embracing me, as I say, in his arms, no, not the whole night, but rose up and dress'd him in the morning, and left me as innocent for him as I was the day I was born.

This was a surprising thing to me, and perhaps may be so to others who know how the laws of nature work, for he was a vigorous brisk person; nor did he act thus on a principle of religion at all, but of meer affection; insisting on it, that tho' I was to him the most agreeable woman in the world, yet because he lov'd me he could not injure me.

I own it was a noble principle, but as it was what I never saw before, so it was perfectly amazing. We travell'd the rest of the journey as we did before, and came back to the Bath, where, as he had opportunity to come to me when he would, he often repeated the same moderation, and I frequently lay with him, and altho' all the familiarities of man and wife were common to us, yet he never once offered to go any farther, and he valu'd himself much upon it; I do not say that I was so wholly pleas'd with it as he thought I was; for I own I was much wickeder than he.

We liv'd thus near two years, only with this exception, that he went three times to London in that time, and once he continu'd there four months, but to do him justice, he always supply'd me with money to subsist on very handsomely.

Had we continu'd thus, I confess we had had much to boast of; but as wise men say, it is ill venturing too near the brink of a command,[1] so we found it; and here again I must do him the justice to own that the first breach was not on his part. It was one night that we were in bed together warm and merry, and having drank, I think, a little more both of us than usual, tho' not in the least to disorder us, when after some other follies which I cannot name, and being clasp'd close in his arms, I told him, (I repeat it with shame and horror of soul) that I could find in my heart to discharge him of his engagement for one night and no more.

He took me at my word immediately, and after that there was

[1] commandment.

no resisting him; neither indeed had I any mind to resist him any more.

Thus the government of our virtue was broken, and I exchang'd the place of friend for that unmusical harsh sounding title of whore. In the morning we were both at our penitentials; I cried very heartily, he express'd himself very sorry; but that was all either of us could do at that time, and the way being thus clear'd, and the bars of virtue and conscience thus remov'd, we had the less to struggle with.

It was but a dull kind of conversation that we had together for all the rest of that week. I look'd on him with blushes; and every now and then started that melancholly objection, *What if I should be with child now? What will become of me then?* He encouraged me by telling me that as long as I was true to him he would be so to me; and since it was gone such a length (which indeed he never intended), yet if I was with child, he would take care of that and me too. This harden'd us both; I assured him if I was with child, I would die for want of a midwife rather than name him as the father of it; and he assured me I should never want if I should be with child. These mutual assurances harden'd us in the thing, and after this we repeated the crime as often as we pleased, till at length, as I fear'd, so it came to pass, and I was indeed with child.

After I was sure it was so, and I had satisfied him of it too, we began to think of taking measures for the managing it, and I propos'd trusting the secret to my landlady, and asking her advice, which he agreed to. My landlady, a woman (as I found) us'd to such things, made light of it; she said she knew it would come to that at last, and made us very merry about it. As I said above, we found her an experienced old lady at such work; she undertook everything, engag'd to procure a midwife and a nurse, to satisfy all enquiries, and bring us off with reputation, and she did so very dexterously indeed.

When I grew near my time, she desir'd my gentleman to go away to London, or make as if he did so; when he was gone, she acquainted the parish officers that there was a lady ready to lye in at her house, but that she knew her husband very well, and gave them, as she pretended, an account of his name, which she call'd Sir Walter Cleave; telling them he was a worthy gentleman, and that he would answer for all enquiries, and the like. This satisfied the parish officers presently, and I lay in, in as much credit as I could have done if I had really been my Lady Cleave; and was assisted in my travail by three or four of the best citizens' wives of Bath, which, however, made me a little the more expensive to him; I often expressed my concern to him about that part, but he bid me not be concerned at it.

As he had furnish'd me very sufficiently with money for the extraordinary expenses of my lying in, I had every thing very handsome about me; but did not affect to be so gay or extravagant neither; besides, knowing the world, as I had done, and that such kind of things do not often last long, I took care to lay up as much money as I could for a wet day, as I call'd it; making him believe it was all spent upon the extraordinary appearance of things in my lying in.

By this means, with what he had given me as above, I had at the end of my lying in 200 guineas by me, including also what was left of my own.

I was brought to bed of a fine boy indeed, and a charming child it was; and when he heard of it, he wrote me a very kind obliging letter about it, and then told me he thought it would look better for me to come away for London as soon as I was up and well, that he had provided apartments for me at Hammersmith, as if I came only from London, and that after a while I should go back to the Bath, and he would go with me.

I lik'd his offer very well, and hir'd a coach on purpose, and taking my child, and a wet-nurse to tend and suckle it, and a maid servant with me, away I went for London.

He met me at Reading in his own charriot, and taking me into that, left the servant and the child in the hir'd coach, and so he brought me to my new lodgings at Hammersmith; with which I had abundance of reason to be very well pleas'd, for they were very handsome rooms.

And now I was indeed in the height of what I might call prosperity, and I wanted nothing but to be a wife, which however could not be in this case, and therefore on all occasions I studied to save what I could, as I said above, against the time of scarcity; knowing well enough that such things as these do not always continue, that men that keep mistresses often change them, grow weary of them, or jealous of them, or something or other; and sometimes the ladies that are thus well us'd are not careful by a prudent conduct to preserve the esteem of their persons, or the nice article of their fidelity, and then they are justly cast off with contempt.

But I was secur'd in this point, for as I had no inclination to change, so I had no manner of acquaintance, so no temptation to look any farther; I kept no company but in the family where I lodg'd, and with a clergyman's lady at next door; so that when he was absent I visited no body, nor did he ever find me out of my chamber or parlour whenever he came down; if I went any where to take the air it was always with him.

The living in this manner with him, and his with me, was certainly the most undesigned thing in the world; he often protested to me that when he became first acquainted with me, and even to the very night when we first broke in upon our rules, he never had the least design of lying with me; that he always had a sincere affection for me, but not the least real inclination to do what he had done; I assured him I never suspected him, that if I had, I should not so easily have yielded to the freedoms which brought it on, but that it was all a surprize, and was owing to our having yielded too far to our mutual inclinations that night; and indeed I have often observ'd since, and leave it as a caution to the readers of this story, that we ought to be cautious of gratifying our inclinations in loose and lewd freedoms, lest we find our resolutions of virtue fail us in the juncture when their assistance should be most necessary.

It is true that from the first hour I began to converse with him I resolv'd to let him lye with me, if he offered it; but it was because I wanted his help, and knew of no other way of securing him. But when we were that night together, and, as I have said, had gone such a length, I found my weakness; the inclination was not to be resisted, but I was obliged to yield up all even before he ask'd it.

However, he was so just to me that he never upbraided me with that; nor did he ever express the least dislike of my conduct on any other occasion, but always protested he was as much delighted with my company as he was the first hour we came together.

It is true that he had no wife, that is to say, she was no wife to him, but the reflections of conscience oftentimes snatch a man, especially a man of sense, from the arms of a mistress, as it did him at last, tho' on another occasion.

On the other hand, tho' I was not without secret reproaches of my own conscience for the life I led, and that even in the greatest height of the satisfaction I ever took, yet I had the terrible prospect of poverty and starving, which lay on me as a frightful spectre, so that there was no looking behind me. But as poverty brought me into it, so fear of poverty kept me in it, and I frequently resolv'd to leave it quite off, if I could but come to lay up money enough to maintain me. But these were thoughts of no weight, and whenever he came to me they vanish'd; for his company was so delightful that there was no being melancholly when he was there; the reflections were all the subject of those hours when I was alone.

I liv'd six years in this happy, but unhappy condition, in which time I brought him three children, but only the first of them liv'd; and tho' I remov'd twice in that six years, yet I came back the sixth year to my first lodgings at Hammersmith. Here it was that I was one morning surpris'd with a kind but melancholly letter from my gentleman; intimating that he was very ill, and was afraid he should have another fit of sickness, but that his wife's relations being in the house with him, it would not be practicable to have me with him, which, however, he express'd his great dissatisfaction in, and that he wish'd I could be allow'd to tend and nurse him as I did before.

I was very much concern'd at this account, and was very impatient to know how it was with him; I waited a fortnight or thereabouts, and heard nothing, which surpriz'd me, and I began to be very uneasy indeed; I think I may say that for the next fortnight I was near to distracted. It was my particular difficulty that I did not know directly where he was; for I understood at first he was in the lodgings of his wife's mother; but having remov'd my self to London, I soon found, by the help of the direction I had for writing my letters to him, how to enquire after him, and there I found that he was at a house in Bloomsbury, whither he had remov'd his whole family; and that his wife and wife's mother were in the same house, tho' the wife was not suffer'd to know that she was in the same house with her husband.

Here I also soon understood that he was at the last extremity, which made me almost at the last extremity too, to have a true account. One night I had the curiosity to disguise my self like a servant maid in a round cap and straw hat, and went to the door, as sent by a lady of his neighbourhood where he liv'd before, and giving master and mistress's service, I said I was sent to know how Mr. —— did, and how he had rested that night. In delivering this message I got the opportunity I desir'd for speaking with one of the maids; I held a long gossip's tale with her, and had all the particulars of his illness, which I found was a pluresy, attended with a cough and fever. She told me also who was in the house, and how his wife was, who, by her relation, they were in some hopes might recover her understanding; but as to the gentleman himself, the doctors said there was very little hopes of him, that in the morning they thought he had been dying, and that he was but little better then, for they did not expect that he could live over the next night.

This was heavy news for me, and I began now to see an end of my prosperity, and to see that it was well I had plaid the good housewife, and sav'd something while he was alive, for now I had no view of my own living before me.

It lay very heavy upon my mind, too, that I had a son, a fine lovely boy, about five years old, and no provision made for it, at least that I knew of; with these considerations, and a sad heart, I went home that evening, and began to cast with my self how I should live, and in what manner to bestow my self for the residue of my life.

You may be sure I could not rest without enquiring again very quickly what was become of him; and not venturing to go my self, I sent several sham messengers, till after a fortnight's waiting longer, I found that there was hopes of his life, tho' he was still very ill; then I abated my sending to the house, and in some time after I learnt in the neighbourhood that he was about house, and then that he was abroad [1] again.

I made no doubt then but that I should soon hear of him, and began to comfort my self with my circumstances, being, as I

---

[1] able to go out.

thought, recovered; I waited a week, and two weeks, and with much surprize near two months, and heard nothing but that being recovered he was gone into the country for the air, after his distemper; after this it was yet two months more, and then I understood he was come to his city-house again, but still I heard nothing from him.

I had written several letters for him, and directed them as usual, and found two or three of them had been call'd for, but not the rest. I wrote again in a more pressing manner than ever, and in one of them let him know that I must be forc'd to wait on him my self, representing my circumstances, the rent of lodgings to pay, and the provision for the child wanting, and my own deplorable condition, destitute of subsistance after his most solemn engagement to take care of, and provide for me; I took a copy of this letter, and finding it lay at the house near a month, and was not call'd for, I found means to have the copy of it put into his hands at a coffee-house, where I found he had us'd to go.

This letter forc'd an answer from him, by which, tho' I found I was to be abandon'd, yet I found he had sent a letter to me some time before, desiring me to go down to the Bath again; its contents I shall come to presently.

It is true that sick beds are the times when such correspondences as this are look'd on with different countenances, and seen with other eyes, than we saw them with before. My lover had been at the gates of death, and at the very brink of eternity; and, it seems, struck with a due remorse, and with sad reflections upon his past life of gallantry and levity; and among the rest, his criminal correspondence with me, which was indeed neither more or less than a long continu'd life of adultery, had represented itself as it really was, not as it had been formerly thought by him to be, and he look'd upon it now with a just abhorence.

I cannot but observe also, and leave it for the direction of my sex in such cases of pleasure, that whenever sincere repentance succeeds such a crime as this, there never fails to attend a hatred of the object; and the more the affection might seem to be before, the hatred will be more in proportion. It will always be so, indeed it cannot be otherwise; for there cannot be a true and sincere abhorence of the offence, and the love to the cause of it

remain; there will with an abhorence of the sin be found a detestation of the fellow-sinner; you can expect no other.

I found it so here, tho' good manners and justice in this gentleman kept him from carrying it on to any extream; but the short
history of his part in this affair was thus: he perceived by my
last letter, and by the rest, which he went for after, that I was
not gone to the Bath, and that his first letter had not come to my
hand; upon which he writes me this following:

Madam,

*I am surpris'd that my letter dated the 8th of last month did
not come to your hand; I give you my word it was deliver'd at
your lodgings, and to the hands of your maid.*

*I need not acquaint you with what has been my condition for
some time past; and how having been at the edge of the grave,
I am by the unexpected and undeserved mercy of heaven restor'd
again. In the condition I have been in, it cannot be strange to
you that our unhappy correspondence has not been the least of
the burthens which lay upon my conscience; I need say no more;
those things that must be repented of, must be also reform'd.*

*I wish you would think of going back to the Bath; I enclose
you here a bill for 50l. for clearing your self at your lodgings,
and carrying you down, and hope it will be no surprize to you to
add that on this account only, and not for any offence given me
on your side, I can see you no more. I will take due care of the
child; leave him where he is, or take him with you, as you please.
I wish you the like reflections, and that they may be to your advantage; I am, &c.*

I was struck with this letter as with a thousand wounds; the
reproaches of my own conscience were such as I cannot express,
for I was not blind to my own crime; and I reflected that I might
with less offence have continued with my brother, since there
was no crime in our marriage on that score, neither of us knowing it.

But I never once reflected that I was all this while a marry'd
woman, a wife to Mr. —— the linnen-draper, who, tho' he had
left me by the necessity of his circumstances, had no power to
discharge me from the marriage contract which was between
us, or to give me a legal liberty to marry again; so that I had been

no less than a whore and an adulteress all this while. I then re-proach'd my self with the liberties I had taken, and how I had been a snare to this gentleman, and that indeed I was principal in the crime; that now he was mercifully snatch'd out of the gulph by a convincing work upon his mind, but that I was left as if I was abandon'd by heaven to a continuing in my wickedness.

Under these reflections I continu'd very pensive and sad for near a month, and did not go down to the Bath, having no inclina-tion to be with the woman who I was with before, lest, as I thought, she should prompt me to some wicked course of life again, as she had done; and besides, I was loth she should know I was cast off, as above.

And now I was greatly perplex'd about my little boy; it was death to me to part with the child, and yet when I consider'd the danger of being one time or other left with him to keep without being able to support him, I then resolv'd to leave him; but then I concluded to be near him my self too, that I might have the satisfaction of seeing him, without the care of providing for him. So I sent my gentleman a short letter that I had obey'd his orders in all things, but that of going back to the Bath; that, however, parting from him was a wound to me that I could never recover, yet that I was fully satisfied his reflections were just, and would be very far from desiring to obstruct his reformation.

Then I represented my own circumstances to him in the most moving terms: I told him that those unhappy distresses which first mov'd him to a generous friendship for me would, I hope, move him to a little concern for me now; tho' the criminal part of our correspondence, which I believ'd neither of us intended to fall into at that time, was broken off; that I desir'd to repent as sincerely as he had done, but intreated him to put me in some condition that I might not be expos'd to temptations from the frightful prospect of poverty and distress; and if he had the least apprehensions of my being troublesome to him, I beg'd he would put me in a posture to go back to my mother in Virginia, from whence he knew I came, and that would put an end to all his fears on that account; I concluded, that if he would send me 50*l.* more to facilitate my going away, I would send him back a gen-eral release, and would promise never to disturb him more with any importunities; unless it were to hear of the welldoing of the child, who, if I found my mother living, and my circumstances able, I would send for and take him also off of his hands.

This was inded all a cheat thus far, *viz.* that I had no intention to go to Virginia, as the account of my former affairs there may convince any body of; but the business was to get this last fifty pounds of him, if possible, knowing well enough it would be the last penny I was ever to expect.

However, the argument I us'd, namely, of giving him a general release, and never troubling him any more, prevail'd effectually, and he sent me a bill for the money by a person who brought with him a general release for me to sign, and which I frankly sign'd; and thus, tho' full sore against my will, a final end was put to this affair.

And here I cannot but reflect upon the unhappy consequence of too great freedoms between persons stated [1] as we were, upon the pretence of innocent intentions, love of friendship, and the like; for the flesh has generally so great a share in those friendships that it is great odds but inclination prevails at last over the most solemn resolutions; and that vice breaks in at the breaches of decency, which really innocent friendship ought to preserve with the greatest strictness. But I leave the readers of these things to their own just reflections, which they will be more able to make effectual than I, who so soon forgot my self, and am therefore but a very indifferent monitor.

I was now a single person again, as I may call my self; I was loos'd from all the obligations either of wedlock or mistressship in the world; except my husband the linnen draper, who, I having not now heard from in almost fifteen years, no body could blame me for thinking my self entirely freed from; seeing also he had at his going away told me that if I did not hear frequently from him, I should conclude he was dead, and I might freely marry again to whom I pleas'd.

I now began to cast up my accounts; I had by many letters, and much importunity, and with the intercession of my mother too, had a second return of some goods from my brother, as I now call him, in Virginia, to make up the damage of the cargo I brought away with me, and this too was upon the condition of my sealing a general release to him, which, though, I thought

[1] placed.

hard, but yet I was oblig'd to promise. I manag'd so well in this case that I got my goods away before the release was sign'd, and then I always found something or other to say to evade the thing, and to put off the signing it at all; till at length I pretended I must write to my brother, before I could do it.

Including this recruit, and before I got the last 50*l*., I found my strength to amount, put all together, to about 400*l*., so that with that I had above 450*l*. I had sav'd 100*l*. more, but I met with a disaster with that, which was this; that a goldsmith in whose hands I had trusted it broke, so I lost 70*l*. of my money, the man's composition not making above 30*l*. out of his 100*l*. I had a little plate, but not much, and was well enough stock'd with cloaths and linnen.

With this stock I had the world to begin again; but you are to consider that I was not now the same woman as when I liv'd at Rotherhith; for first of all I was near 20 years older, and did not look the better for my age, nor for my rambles to Virginia and back again; and tho' I omitted nothing that might set me out to advantage, except painting, for that I never stoop'd to, yet there would always be some difference seen between five-and-twenty and two-and-forty.

I cast about innumerable ways for my future state of life, and began to consider very seriously what I should do, but noth- ing offer'd; I took care to make the world take me for some- thing more than I was, and had it given out that I was a fortune, and that my estate was in my own hands, the last of which was very true, the first of it was as above. I had no acquaintance, which was one of my worst misfortunes, and the consequence of that was, I had no adviser, and, above all, I had no body to whom I could in confidence commit the secret of my circumstances to; and I found by experience that to be friendless is the worst con- dition, next to being in want, that a woman can be reduc'd to: I say a woman, because 'tis evident men can be their own advis- ers, and their own directors, and know how to work themselves out of difficulties and into business better than women; but if a woman has no friend to communicate her affairs to, and to advise and assist her, 'tis ten to one but she is undone; nay, and the more money she has, the more danger she is in of being wrong'd and deceiv'd; and this was my case in the affair of the hundred pound which I left in the hand of the goldsmith, as above, whose credit, it seems, was upon the ebb before, but I, that had no body to consult with, knew nothing of it, and so lost my money.

When a woman is thus left desolate and void of council, she is just like a bag of money, or a jewel dropt on the highway, which is a prey to the next comer; if a man of virtue and upright principles happens to find it, he will have it cried, and the owner may come to hear of it again; but how many times shall such a thing fall into hands that will make no scruple of seizing it for their own, to once that it shall come into good hands.

This was evidently my case, for I was now a loose unguided creature, and had no help, no assistance, no guide for my conduct. I knew what I aim'd at, and what I wanted, but knew nothing how to pursue the end by direct means; I wanted to be plac'd in a settled state of living, and had I happen'd to meet with a sober good husband, I should have been as true a wife to him as virtue it self could have form'd. If I had been otherwise, the vice came in always at the door of necessity, not at the door of inclination; and I understood too well, by the want of it, what the value of a settl'd life was, to do any thing to forfeit the felicity of it; nay, I should have made the better wife for all the difficulties I had pass'd thro', by a great deal; nor did I, in any of the times that I had been a wife, give my husbands the least uneasiness on account of my behaviour.

But all this was nothing; I found no incouraging prospect; I waited, I liv'd regularly, and with as much frugality as became my circumstances, but nothing offer'd, nothing presented, and the main stock wasted apace. What to do I knew not; the terror of approaching poverty lay hard upon my spirits. I had some money, but where to place it I knew not, nor would the interest of it maintain me, at least not in London.

At length a new scene opened. There was in the house where I lodg'd a North Country gentlewoman, and nothing was more frequent in her discourse than her account of the cheapness of provisions and the easy way of living in her country; how plentiful and how cheap everything was, what good company they kept, and the like; till at last I told her she almost tempted me to go and live in her country; for I that was a widow, tho' I had sufficient to live on, yet had no way of increasing it, and that

London was an extravagant place; that I found I could not live here under one hundred pound a year, unless I kept no company, no servant, made no appearance, and buried my self in privacy, as if I was oblig'd to it by necessity.

I should have observ'd that she was always made to believe, as every body else was, that I was a great fortune, or at least that I had three or four thousand pounds, if not more, and all in my own hands; and she was mighty sweet upon me when she thought me inclin'd in the least to go into her country. She said she had a sister liv'd near Liverpool, that her brother was a considerable gentleman there, and had a great estate also in Ireland; that she wou'd go down there in about two months, and if I would give her my company thither, I should be as welcome as her self for a month or more as I pleas'd, till I should see how I lik'd the country; and if I thought fit to live there, she would undertake they would take care, tho' they did not entertain lodgers themselves, they would recommend me to some agreeable family, where I should be plac'd to my content.

If this woman had known my real circumstances, she would never have laid so many snares, and taken so many weary steps to catch a poor desolate creature that was good for little when it was caught; and indeed I, whose case was almost desperate, and thought I cou'd not be much worse, was not very anxious about what might befall me, provided they did me no personal injury; so I suffered my self, tho' not without a great deal of invitation, and great professions of sincere friendship and real kindness, I say, I suffer'd my self to be prevail'd upon to go with her, and accordingly I put my self in a posture for a journey, tho' I did not absolutely know whither I was to go.

And now I found my self in great distress. What little I had in the world was all in money, except, as before, a little plate, some linnen, and my cloaths; as for houshold stuff I had little or none, for I had liv'd always in lodgings; but I had not one friend in the world with whom to trust that little I had, or to direct me how to dispose of it; I thought of the bank, and of the other companies in London, but I had no friend to commit the management of it to; and to keep and carry about me bank bills, talleys,[1] orders, and such things, I look'd upon as unsafe; that if they were

[1] accounts.

lost my money was lost, and then I was undone; and on the other hand I might be robb'd, and perhaps murder'd in a strange place for them; and what to do I knew not.

It came into my thoughts one morning that I would go to the bank my self, where I had often been to receive the interest of some bills I had, and where I had found the clark to whom I apply'd my self very honest to me, and particularly so fair one time, that when I had misstold my money, and taken less than my due, and was coming away, he set me to rights and gave me the rest, which he might have put into his own pocket.

I went to him and ask'd if he would trouble himself to be my adviser, who was a poor friendless widow, and knew not what to do. He told me if I desir'd his opinion of any thing within the reach of his business, he would do his endeavour that I should not be wrong'd, but that he would also help me to a good sober person of his acquaintance, who was a clark in such business too, tho' not in their house, whose judgment was good, and whose honesty I might depend upon; for, added he, I will answer for him, and for every step he takes; if he wrongs you, madam, of one farthing, it shall lye at my door; and he delights to assist people in such cases, he does it as an act of charity.

I was a little at a stand at this discourse, but after some pause I told him I had rather have depended upon him, because I had found him honest, but if that cou'd not be, I would take his recommendation sooner than any one's else. I dare say, madam, says he, that you will be as well satisfied with my friend as with me, and he is thoroughly able to assist you, which I am not. It seems he had his hands full of the business of the bank, and had engag'd to meddle with no other business than that of his office. He added that his friend should take nothing of me for his advice or assistance, and this indeed encourag'd me.

He appointed the same evening, after the bank was shut, for me to meet him and his friend. As soon as I saw his friend, and he began but to talk of the affair, I was fully satisfied I had a very honest man to deal with; his countenance spoke it, and his character, as I heard afterwards, was every where so good that I had no room for any more doubts upon me.

After the first meeting, in which I only said what I had said before, he appointed me to come the next day, telling me I might

in the mean time satisfy my self of him by enquiry, which however I knew not how to do, having no acquaintance my self.

Accordingly I met him the next day, when I entered more
freely with him into my case; I told him my circumstances at
large, that I was a widow come over from America, perfectly
desolate and friendless; that I had a little money, and but a little,
and was almost distracted for fear of losing it, having no friend
in the world to trust with the management of it; that I was going
into the North of England to live cheap that my stock might not
waste; that I would willingly lodge my money in the bank, but
that I durst not carry the bills about me; and how to correspond
about it, or with who, I knew not.

He told me I might lodge the money in the bank as an account,
and its being entred in the books would entitle me to the money
at any time, and if I was in the north I might draw bills on the
cashier, and receive it when I would; but that then it wou'd be
esteem'd as running cash, and the bank would give no interest
for it; that I might buy stock with it, and so it would lie in store
for me, but that then, if I wanted to dispose of it, I must come
up to town to transfer it, and even it would be with some difficulty I should receive the half yearly dividend, unless I was here
in person, or had some friend I could trust with having the stock
in his name to do it for me, and that would have the same difficulty in it as before; and with that he look'd hard at me and smil'd
a little. At last, says he, Why do you not get a head steward,
madam, that may take you and your money together, and then
you would have the trouble taken off of your hands? Ay, sir, and
the money too, it may be, said I, for truly I find the hazard that
way is as much as 'tis t'other way. But I remember I said,
secretly to my self, I wish you would ask me the question fairly,
I would consider very seriously on it before I said no.

He went on a good way with me, and I thought once or twice
he was in earnest, but to my real affliction I found at last he had
a wife; but when he own'd he had a wife he shook his head, and
said with some concern that indeed he had a wife, and no wife.
I began to think he had been in the condition of my late lover,
and that his wife had been lunatick, or some such thing. However, we had not much more discourse at that time, but he told
me he was in too much hurry of business then, but that if I

would come home to his house after their business was over, he would consider what might be done for me, to put my affairs in a posture of security. I told him I would come, and desir'd to know where he liv'd. He gave me a direction in writing, and, when he gave it me, he read it to me, and said, There 'tis, madam, if you dare trust yourself with me. Yes, sir, said I, I believe I may venture to trust you with myself, for you have a wife, you say, and I don't want a husband; besides, I dare trust you with my money, which is all I have in the world, and if that were gone, I may trust my self any where.

He said some things in jest that were very handsome and mannerly, and would have pleas'd me very well if they had been in earnest; but that pass'd over, I took the directions, and appointed to be at his house at seven o'clock the same evening.

When I came he made several proposals for my placing my money in the bank, in order to my having interest for it; but still some difficulty or other came in the way, which he objected as not safe; and I found such a sincere disinterested honesty in him, that I began to think I had certainly found the honest man I wanted; and that I could never put my self into better hands; so I told him with a great deal of frankness that I had never met with a man or woman yet that I could trust, or in whom I could think my self safe, but that I saw he was so disinterestedly concern'd for my safety that I would freely trust him with the management of that little I had, if he would accept to be steward for a poor widow that could give him no salary.

He smil'd, and standing up, with great respect saluted me; he told me he could not but take it very kindly that I had so good an opinion of him; that he would not deceive me, that he would do any thing in his power to serve me and expect no salary; but that he could not by any means accept of a trust that might bring him to be suspected of self-interest, and that if I should die he might have disputes with my executors, which he should be very loth to encumber himself with.

I told him if those were all his objections I would soon remove them, and convince him that there was not the least room for any difficulty; for that first, as for suspecting him, if ever, *now* was the time to suspect him and not to put the trust into his hands, and whenever I did suspect him, he could but throw it up then and refuse to go on. Then, as to executors, I assur'd him I had no heirs, nor any relations in England, and I would have neither heirs or executors but himself, unless I should alter my condition, and then his trust and trouble should cease together, which however I had no prospect of yet; but I told him if I died as I was, it should be all his own, and he would deserve it by being so faithful to me, as I was satisfied he would be.

He chang'd his countenance at this discourse, and ask'd me how I came to have so much good-will for him, and looking very much pleas'd said he might very lawfully wish he was single for my sake; I smil'd and told him that as he was not, my offer could have no design upon him, and to wish was not to be allow'd; 'twas criminal to his wife.

He told me I was wrong; for, says he, as I said before, I have a wife and no wife, and 'twould be no sin to wish her hang'd. I know nothing of your circumstances that way, sir, said I; but it cannot be innocent to wish your wife dead. I tell you, says he again, she is a wife and no wife; you don't know what I am, or what she is.

That's true, said I, sir, I don't know what you are, but I believe you to be an honest man, and that's the cause of all my confidence in you.

Well, well, says he, and so I am, but I am something else too, madam; for, says he, to be plain with you, I am a cuckold, and she is a whore. He spoke it in a kind of jest, but it was with such an awkward smile that I perceiv'd it stuck very close to him, and he look'd dismally when he said it.

That alters the case indeed, sir, said I, as to that part you were speaking of; but a cuckold, you know, may be an honest man, it does not alter that case at all; besides, I think, said I, since your wife is so dishonest to you, you are too honest to her to own her for your wife; but that, said I, is what I have nothing to do with. Nay, says he, I do think to clear my hands of her, for to be plain with you, madam, added he, I am no contented cuckold neither. On the other hand, I assure you it provokes me to the highest degree, but I can't help my self; she that will be a whore, will be a whore.

I waiv'd the discourse, and began to talk of my business, but I found he could not have done with it, so I let him alone, and he went on to tell me all the circumstances of his case, too long to relate here; particularly, that having been out of England some time before he came to the post he was in, she had had two children in the mean time by an officer of the army; and that when he came to England, and, upon her submission, took her again, and maintain'd her very well, yet she run away from him with a linnen-draper's apprentice, robb'd him of what she could come at, and continu'd to live from him still. So that, madam, says he, she is a whore not by necessity, which is the common bait, but by inclination, and for the sake of the vice.

Well, I pitied him, and wish'd him well rid of her, and still would have talk'd of my business, but it would not do. At last he looked steadily at me: Look you, madam, says he, you came to ask advice of me, and I will serve you as faithfully as if you were my own sister; but I must turn the tables, since you oblige me to do it, and are so friendly to me, and I think I must ask advice of you; tell me, what must a poor abus'd fellow do with a whore? What can I do to do myself justice upon her?

Alas, sir, says I, 'tis a case too nice for me to advise in, but it seems she has run away from you, so you are rid of her fairly; what can you desire more? Ay, she is gone indeed, said he, but I am not clear of her for all that. That's true, says I, she may indeed run you into debt, but the law has furnish'd you with methods to prevent that also; you may cry her down,[1] as they call it.

No, no, says he, that is not the case, I have taken care of all that; 'tis not that part that I speak of, but I would be rid of her that I might marry again.

Well, sir, says I, then you must divorce her; if you can prove what you say, you may certainly get that done, and then you are free.

That's very tedious and expensive, says he.

Why, says I, if you can get any woman you like to take your word, I suppose your wife would not dispute the liberty with you that she takes herself.

Ay, says he, but 'twou'd be hard to bring an honest woman to do that; and for the other sort, says he, I have had enough of her to meddle with any more whores.

It occur'd to me presently: I would have taken your word with

[1] publicly disclaim responsibility for her.

all my heart, if you had but ask'd me the question, but that was
to my self. To him I reply'd, Why, you shut the door against any
honest woman accepting you, for you condemn all that should
venture upon you, and conclude that a woman that takes you
now can't be honest.

Why, says he, I wish you would satisfy me that an honest
woman would take me, I'd venture it; and then turns short upon
me: Will you take me, madam?

That's not a fair question, says I, after what you have said;
however, least you shou'd think I wait only a recantation of it,
I shall answer you plainly, no, not I; my business is of another
kind with you, and I did not expect you would have turn'd my
serious application to you in my distracted case into a comedy.

Why, madam, says he, my case is as distracted as yours can be,
and I stand in as much need of advice as you do, for I think if I
have not relief some where, I shall be mad my self, and I know
not what course to take, I protest to you.

Why, sir, says I, 'tis easier to give advice in your case than
mine. Speak then, says he, I beg of you, for now you encourage
me.

Why, says I, if your case is so plain, you may be legally divorc'd, and then you may find honest women enough to ask the
question of fairly; the sex is not so scarce that you can want a
wife.

Well then, said he, I am in earnest, I'll take your advice; but
shall I ask you one question seriously before hand?

Any question, said I, but that you did before.

No, that answer will not do, said he, for in short, that is the
question I shall ask.

You may ask what questions you please, but you have my
answer to that already, said I; besides, sir, said I, can you think
so ill of me, as that I wou'd give any answer to such a question
beforehand? Can any woman alive believe you in earnest, or think
you design any thing but to banter her?

Well, well, says he, I do not banter you, I am in earnest; consider of it.

But, sir, says I, a little gravely, I came to you about my own
business; I beg of you to let me know what you will advise me
to do.

I will be prepar'd, says he, against you come again.

Nay, says I, you have forbid my coming any more.

Why so? said he, and look'd a little surpriz'd.

Because, said I, you can't expect I should visit you on the account you talk of.

Well, says he, you shall promise to come again, however, and I will not say any more of it till I have the divorce, but I desire you'll prepare to be better condition'd [1] when that's done, for you shall be the woman, or I will not be divorc'd at all: I owe it to your unlooked for kindness, if to nothing else, but I have other reasons too.

He could not have said anything in the world that pleas'd me better; however, I knew that the way to secure him was to stand off while the thing was so remote, as it appear'd to be, and that it was time enough to accept of it when he was able to perform it; so I said very respectfully to him, it was time enough to consider of these things when he was in a condition to talk of them; in the mean time, I told him, I was going a great way from him, and he would find objects enough to please him better. We broke off here for the present, and he made me promise him to come again the next day, for my own business, which after some pressing I did; tho' had he seen farther into me, I wanted no pressing on that account.

I came the next evening accordingly, and brought my maid with me, to let him see that I kept a maid. He would have had me let the maid have staid, but I would not, but order'd her aloud to come for me again about nine a clock, but he forbid that, and told me he would see me safe home, which I was not very well pleased with, supposing he might do that to know where I liv'd, and enquire into my character and circumstances. However, I ventur'd that, for all the people there knew of me was to my advantage; and all the character he had of me was that I was a woman of fortune, and that I was a very modest sober body; which, whether true or not in the main, yet you may see how necessary it is for all women who expect any thing in the world to preserve the character of their virtue, even when perhaps they may have sacrifiz'd the thing itself.

I found, and was not a little pleas'd with it, that he had provided a supper for me: I found also he liv'd very handsomely,

[1] disposed.

and had a house very handsomely furnish'd, and which I was re-
joic'd at indeed, for I look'd upon it all as my own.

We had now a second conference upon the subject matter of
the last. He laid his business very home indeed; he protested his
affection to me, and indeed I had no room to doubt it; he declared
that it began from the first moment I talk'd with him, and long
before I had mentioned leaving my effects with him. 'Tis no
matter when it began, thought I; if it will but hold, 'twill be well
enough. He then told me how much the offer I had made of
trusting him with my effects had engag'd him. So I intended
it should, thought I, but then I thought you had been a single
man too. After we had supp'd, I observ'd he press'd me very
hard to drink two or three glasses of wine, which, however, I
declin'd, but drank one glass or two. He then told me he had
a proposal to make to me, which I should promise him I would
not take ill, if I should not grant it; I told him I hop'd he would
make no dishonourable proposal to me, especially in his own
house, and that if it was such, I desir'd he would not mention it,
that I might not be obliged to offer any resentment to him that
did not become the respect I profess'd for him, and the trust
I had plac'd in him, in coming to this house; and beg'd of him he
would give me leave to go away, and accordingly began to put
on my gloves, and prepare to be gone, tho' at the same time I no
more intended it than he intended to let me.

Well, he importun'd me not to talk of going; he assured me
he was very far from offering any such thing to me that was
dishonourable, and if I thought so, he would chuse to say no
more of it.

That part I did not relish at all; I told him I was ready to hear
anything that he had to say, depending that he would say nothing
unworthy of himself, or unfit for me to hear. Upon this,
he told me his proposal was this: that I would marry him, tho'
he had not yet obtain'd the divorce from the whore his wife; and
to satisfy me that he meant honourably, he would promise not
to desire me to live with him, or go to bed to him till the divorce
was obtain'd. My heart said yes to this offer at first word, but it
was necessary to play the hypocrite a little more with him; so I
seem'd to decline the motion with some warmth as unfair, told
him that such a proposal could be of no signification, but to en-

tangle us both in great difficulties; for if he should not at last obtain the divorce, yet we could not dissolve the marriage, neither could we proceed in it; so that if he was disappointed in the divorce, I left him to consider what a condition we should both be in.

In short, I carried on the argument against this so far that I convinc'd him it was not a proposal that had any sense in it; then he went from it to another, *viz.* that I would sign and seal a contract with him, conditioning [1] to marry him as soon as the divorce was obtain'd, and to be void if he could not get it.

I told him that was more rational than the other; but as this was the first time that ever I could imagine him weak enough to be in earnest, I did not use to say yes at first asking; I would consider of it. I plaid with this lover, as an angler does with a trout: I found I had him fast on the hook, so I jested with his new proposal, and put him off. I told him he knew little of me, and bad him enquire about me; I let him also go home with me to my lodging, tho' I would not ask him to go in, for I told him it was not decent.

In short, I ventur'd to avoid signing a contract, and the reason why I did it was because the lady that had invited me to go with her into Lancashire insisted so positively upon it, and promised me such great fortunes and fine things there that I was tempted to go and try; perhaps, said I, I may mend [2] myself very much, and then I made no scruple of quitting my honest citizen, whom I was not so much in love with as not to leave him for a richer.

In a word, I avoided a contract; but told him I would go into the north, that he would know where to write to me by the business I had entrusted with him, that I would give him a sufficient pledge of my respect for him, for I would leave almost all I had in the world in his hands; and I would thus far give him my word that as soon as he had sued out the divorce, if he would send me an account of it, I would come up to London, and that then we would talk seriously of the matter.

It was a base design I went with, that I must confess, tho' I was invited thither with a design much worse, as the sequel will discover. Well, I went with my friend, as I call'd her, into Lan-

[1] stipulating.
[2] improve my circumstances.

cashire; all the way we went she caressed me with the utmost appearance of a sincere undissembled affection; treated [1] me, except my coach-hire, all the way; and her brother brought a gentleman's coach to Warrington to receive us, and we were carried from thence to Liverpool with as much ceremony as I could desire.

We were also entertain'd at a merchant's house in Liverpool three or four days very handsomely: I forbear to tell his name because of what follow'd. Then she told me she would carry me to an uncle's house of hers where we should be nobly entertain'd; and her uncle, as she call'd him, sent a coach and four horses for us, and we were carried near forty miles I know not whither.

We came however to a gentleman's seat, where was a numerous family, a large park, extraordinary company indeed, and where she was call'd cousin; I told her if she had resolv'd to bring me into such company as this, she should have let me have furnish'd my self with better cloaths; the ladies took notice of that, and told me very genteely, they did not value people in their own country so much by their cloaths as they did in London; that their cousin had fully inform'd them of my quality, and that I did not want cloaths to set me off; in short, they entertain'd me not like what I was, but like what they thought I had been, namely, a widow lady of a great fortune.

The first discovery I made here was that the family were all Roman Catholicks, and the cousin too; nobody in the world could behave better to me; and I had all the civility shown that I could have had, if I had been of their opinion. The truth is, I had not so much principle of any kind as to be nice in point of religion; and I presently learn'd to speak favourably of the Romish Church; particularly I told them I saw little but the prejudice of education in all the differences that were among Christians about religion, and if it had so happen'd that my father had been a Roman Catholick, I doubted not but I should have been as well pleas'd with their religion as my own.

This obliged them in the highest degree, and as I was besieg'd day and night with good company and pleasant discourse, so I had two or three old ladies that lay at me upon the subject of religion too; I was so complaisant that I made no scruple to be

[1] paid for.

present at their mass, and to conform to all their gestures as they shew'd me the pattern, but I would not come too cheap; so that I only in the main encouraged them to expect that I would turn Roman Catholick, if I was instructed in the Catholick doctrine, as they call'd it, and so the matter rested.

I stay'd here about six weeks; and then my conductor led me back to a country village, about six miles from Liverpool, where her brother (as she call'd him) came to visit me in his own charriot, with two footmen in a good livery; and the next thing was to make love to me. As it happen'd to me, one would think I could not have been cheated, and indeed I thought so my self, having a safe card at home, which I resolv'd not to quit unless I could mend my self very much. However, in all appearance this brother was a match worth my listening to, and the least his estate was valu'd at, was a 1000*l.* a year, but the sister said it was worth 1500*l.* a year, and lay most of it in Ireland.

I that was a great fortune, and pass'd for such, was above being ask'd how much my estate was; and my false friend taking it upon a foolish hearsay had rais'd it from 500*l.* to 5000*l.*, and by the time she came into the country she call'd it 15,000*l.* The Irishman, for such I understood him to be, was stark mad at this bait. In short, he courted me, made me presents, and run in debt like a mad man for the expences of his courtship. He had, to give him his due, the appearance of an extraordinary fine gentleman; he was tall, well-shap'd, and had an extraordinary address; talk'd as naturally of his park, and his stables, or his horses, his game-keepers, his woods, his tenants, and his servants, as if he had been in a mansion house, and I had seen them all about me.

He never so much as ask'd me about my fortune or estate; but assur'd me that when we came to Dublin he would joynture me in 600*l.* a year in good land; and that he would enter into a deed of settlement, or contract here, for the performance of it.

This was such language indeed as I had not been us'd to, and I was here beaten out of all my measures;[1] I had a she devil in my bosom, every hour telling me how great her brother liv'd. One time she would come for my orders, how I would have my coach painted, and how lin'd; and another time what cloaths my

[1] plan of action (or, possibly, moderation).

page should wear. In short, my eyes were dazled, I had now lost my power of saying no, and to cut the story short, I consented to be married; but to be more private we were carried farther into the country, and married by a priest, which I was assur'd woud marry us as effectually as a Church of England parson.

I cannot say but I had some reflections in this affair, upon the dishonourable forsaking my faithful citizen, who lov'd me sincerely, and who was endeavouring to quit himself of a scandalous whore by whom he had been barbarously us'd, and promis'd himself infinite happiness in his new choice; which choice was now giving up her self to another in a manner almost as scandalous as hers could be.

But the glittering show of a great estate and of fine things, which the deceived creature that was now my deceiver represented every hour to my imagination, hurried me away, and gave me no time to think of London, or of any thing there, much less of the obligation I had to a person of infinitely more real merit than what was now before me.

But the thing was done, I was now in the arms of my new spouse, who appear'd still the same as before; great even to magnificence, and nothing less than a thousand pounds a year could support the ordinary equipage he appear'd in.

After we had been married about a month, he began to talk of my going to Westchester in order to embark for Ireland. However, he did not hurry me, for we stay'd near three weeks longer, and then he sent to Chester for a coach to meet us at the Black-Rock, as they call it, over against Liverpool. Thither we went in a fine boat they call a pinnace with six oars, his servants and horses and baggage going in a ferry-boat. He made his excuse to me that he had not acquaintance at Chester, but he would go before and get some handsome appartment for me at a private house. I ask'd him how long we should stay at Chester. He said, not at all any longer than one night or two, but he would immediately hire a coach to go to Holyhead; then I told him he should by no means give himself the trouble to get private lodgings for one night or two, for that Chester being a great place, I made no doubt but there would be very good inns and accommodation enough; so we lodg'd at an inn not far from the cathedral, I forgot what sign it was at.

Here my spouse, talking of my going to Ireland, ask'd me if I had no affairs to settle at London before we went off. I told him, no, not of any great consequence, but what might be done as well by letter from Dublin. Madam, says he very respectfully, I suppose the greatest part of your estate, which my sister tells me is most of it in money in the Bank of England, lies secure enough, but in case it requir'd transferring, or any way altering its property, it might be necessary to go up to London, and settle those things before we went over.

I seem'd to look strange at it, and told him I knew not what he meant; that I had no effects in the Bank of England that I knew of; and I hope he could not say that I had ever told him I had. No, he said, I had not told him so, but his sister had said the greatest part of my estate lay there. And I only mention'd it, my dear, said he, that if there was any occasion to settle it, or order any thing about it, we might not be oblig'd to the hazard and trouble of another voyage back again; for, he added, that [1] he did not care to venture me too much upon the sea.

I was surpris'd at this talk, and began to consider what the meaning of it must be, and it presently occurr'd to me that my friend, who call'd him brother, had represented me in colours which were not my due; and I thought that I would know the bottom of it before I went out of England, and before I should put my self into I knew not whose hands in a strange country.

Upon this I call'd his sister into my chamber the next morning, and letting her know the discourse her brother and I had been upon, I conjur'd her to tell me what she had said to him, and upon what foot it was that she had made this marriage. She own'd that she had told him that I was a great fortune, and said that she was told so at London. Told so! says I warmly, did I ever tell you so? No, she said, it was true I never did tell her so, but I had said several times that what I had was in my own disposal. I did so, return'd I very quick, but I never told you I had any-thing call'd a fortune; no, that I had one hundred pounds, or the value of an hundred pounds in the world; and how did it consist with my being a fortune, said I, that I should come here into the north of England with you, only upon the account of living cheap? At these words, which I spoke warm and high, my hus-

[1] for . . . that = because.

band came into the room, and I desir'd him to come in and sit down, for I had something of moment to say before them both, which it was absolutely necessary he should hear.

He look'd a little disturb'd at the assurance with which I seem'd to speak it, and came and sat down by me, having first shut the door; upon which I began, for I was very much provok'd, and turning my self to him, I am afraid, says I, my dear, for I spoke with kindness on his side, that you have a very great abuse put upon you, and an injury done you never to be repair'd in your marrying me, which, however, as I have had no hand in it, I desire I may be fairly acquitted of it, and that the blame may lye where it ought and no where else, for I wash my hands of every part of it.

What injury can be done me, my dear, says he, in marrying you? I hope it is to my honour and advantage every way. I will soon explain it to you, says I, and I fear there will be no reason to think yourself well us'd, but I will convince you, my dear, says I again, that I have had no hand in it.

He look'd now scar'd and wild, and began, I believed, to suspect what follow'd; however, looking towards me, and saying only, Go on, he sat silent, as if to hear what I had more to say; so I went on. I ask'd you last night, said I, speaking to him, if ever I made any boast to you of my estate, or ever told you I had any estate in the Bank of England, or anywhere else, and you own'd I had not, as is most true; and I desire you will tell me here, before your sister, if ever I gave you any reason from me to think so, or that ever we had any discourse about it; and he own'd again I had not, but said I had appeared always as a woman of fortune, and he depended on it that I was so, and hoped he was not deceiv'd. I am not enquiring whether you have been deceiv'd, said I, I fear you have, and I too; but I am clearing myself from being concern'd in deceiving you.

I have been now asking your sister if ever I told her of any fortune or estate I had, or gave her any particulars of it; and she owns I never did. And pray, madam, said I, be so just to me to charge me, if you can, if ever I pretended to you that I had an estate; and why, if I had, should I ever come down into this country with you on purpose to spare that little I had, and live cheap? She could not deny one word, but said she had been told in London that I had a very great fortune, and that it lay in the Bank of England.

And now, dear sir, said I, turning my self to my new spouse again, be so just to me as to tell me who has abus'd both you and me so much, as to make you believe I was a fortune, and prompt you to court me to this marriage? He could not speak a word, but pointed to her; and after some more pause, flew out in the most furious passion that ever I saw a man in my life; cursing her, and calling her all the whores and hard names he could think of; and that she had ruin'd him, declaring that she had told him I had fifteen thousand pounds, and that she was to have five hundred pounds of him for procuring this match for him. He then added, directing his speech to me, that she was none of his sister, but had been his whore for two years before, that she had had one hundred pounds of him in part of this bargain, and that he was utterly undone if things were as I said; and in his raving he swore he would let her heart's blood out immediately, which frightened her and me too. She cried, said she had been told so in the house where I lodg'd; but this aggravated him more than before that she should put so far upon him, and run things such a length upon no other authority than a hear-say; and then, turning to me again, said very honestly he was afraid we were both undone. For to be plain, my dear, I have no estate, says he; what little I had this devil has made me run out in putting me into this equipage; she took the opportunity of his being earnest in talking with me, and got out of the room, and I never saw her more.

I was confounded now as much as he, and knew not what to say: I thought many ways that I had the worst of it, but his saying he was undone, and that he had no estate neither put me into a meer distraction. Why, says I to him, this has been a hellish juggle, for we are married here upon the foot of a double fraud; you are undone by the disappointment, it seems, and if I had had a fortune I had been cheated too, for you say you have nothing.

You would indeed have been cheated, my dear, says he, but you would not have been undone, for fifteen thousand pounds would have maintain'd us both very handsomely in this country; and I had resolv'd to have dedicated every groat of it to you; I would not have wrong'd you of a shilling, and the rest I would have made up in my affection to you, and tenderness of you as long as I liv'd.

This was very honest indeed, and I really believe he spoke as he intended, and that he was a man that was as well qualified to make me happy, as to his temper and behaviour, as any man ever was; but his having no estate, and being run into debt on this ridiculous account in the country, made all the prospect dismal and dreadful, and I knew not what to say, or what to think.

I told him it was very unhappy that so much love and so much good nature as I discovered in him should be thus precipitated into misery; that I saw nothing before us but ruin, for as to me, it was my unhappiness that what little I had was not able to relieve us a week, and with that I pull'd out a bank bill of 20*l.* and eleven guineas, which I told him I had saved out of my little income; and that by the account that creature had given me of the way of living in that country, I expected it would maintain me three or four years; that if it was taken from me, I was left destitute, and he knew what the condition of a woman must be if she had no money in her pocket; however, I told him, if he would take it, there it was.

He told me with great concern, and I thought I saw tears in his eyes, that he would not touch it, that he abhor'd the thoughts of stripping me, and making me miserable; that he had fifty guineas left, which was all he had in the world, and he pull'd it out and threw it down on the table, bidding me take it, tho' he were to starve for want of it.

I returned, with the same concern for him, that I could not bear to hear him talk so; that on the contrary, if he could propose any probable method of living, I would do any thing that became me, and that I would live as narrow as he could desire.

He beg'd of me to talk no more at that rate, for it would make him distracted; he said he was bred a gentleman, tho' he was reduc'd to a low fortune, and that there was but one way left which he could think of, and that would not do unless I cou'd answer him one question, which, however, he said he would not press me to; I told him I would answer it honestly; whether it would be to his satisfaction or no, that I could not tell.

Why then, my dear, tell me plainly, says he, will the little you have keep us together in any figure, or in any station or place, or will it not?

It was my happiness that I had not discover'd my self or my circumstances at all, no, not so much as my name; and seeing there was nothing to be expected from him, however good humour'd, and however honest he seem'd to be, but to live on what I knew would soon be wasted, I resolv'd to conceal every thing but the bank-bill and eleven guineas, and I would have been very glad to have lost that, and have been set down where he took me up. I had indeed another bank-bill about me of 30*l*., which was the whole of what I brought with me, as well to subsist on in the country, as not knowing what might offer; because this creature, the go-between that had thus betray'd us both, had made me believe strange things of marrying to my advantage, and I was not willing to be without money whatever might happen. This bill I conceal'd, and that made me the freer of the rest, in consideration of his circumstances, for I really pitied him heartily.

But to return to this question, I told him I never willingly deceiv'd him, and I never would: I was very sorry to tell him that the little I had would not subsist us; that it was not sufficient to subsist me alone in the south country, and that this was the reason that made me put my self into the hands of that woman who call'd him brother, she having assured me that I might board very handsomely at a town call'd Manchester, where I had not yet been, for about six pounds a year, and my whole income not being above 15*l*. a year, I thought I might live easy upon it, and wait for better things.

He shook his head, and remain'd silent, and a very melancholly evening we had; however, we supp'd together, and lay together that night, and when we had almost supp'd he look'd a little better, and more chearful, and call'd for a bottle of wine. Come, my dear, says he, tho' the case is bad, it is to no purpose to be dejected; come, be as easy as you can, I will endeavour to find out some way or other to live; if you can but subsist your self, that is better than nothing, I must try the world again; a man ought to think like a man. To be discouraged is to yield to the misfortune. With this he fill'd a glass, and drank to me, holding my hand all the while the wine went down, and protesting his main concern was for me.

It was really a true gallant spirit he was of, and it was the more grievous to me. 'Tis something of relief even to be undone by a man of honour rather than by a scoundrel; but here the greatest disappointment was on his side, for he had really spent a great deal of money, and it was very remarkable on what poor terms she proceeded; first, the baseness of the creature herself is to be observ'd, who for the getting one hundred pounds herself could be content to let him spend three or four more, tho' perhaps it was all he had in the world, and more than all; when she had not the least ground, more than a little tea-table chat, to say that I had any estate, or was a fortune, or the like. It is true the design of deluding a woman of fortune, if I had been so, was base enough; the putting the face of great things upon poor circumstances was a fraud, and bad enough; but the case a little differ'd too, and that in his favour, for he was not a rake that made a trade to delude women, and as some have done, get six or seven fortunes after one another, and then rifle and run away from them; but he was already a gentleman, unfortunate and low, but had liv'd well; and tho' if I had had a fortune, I should have been enrag'd at the slut for betraying me, yet really, for the man, a fortune would not have been ill bestow'd on him, for he was a lovely person indeed; of generous principles, good sense, and of abundance of good humour.

We had a great deal of close conversation that night, for we neither of us slept much; he was as penitent for having put all those cheats upon me as if it had been fellony, and that he was going to execution; he offered me again every shilling of the money he had about him, and said he would go into the army and seek for more.

I ask'd him why he would be so unkind to carry me into Ireland, when I might suppose he could not have subsisted me there? He took me in his arms. My dear, said he, I never design'd to go to Ireland at all, much less to have carried you thither; but came hither to be out of the observation of the people who had heard what I pretended to, and that no body might ask me for money before I was furnish'd to supply them.

But where, then, said I, were we to have gone next?

Why, my dear, said he, I'll confess the whole scheme to you, as I had laid it; I purposed here to ask you something about your estate, as you see I did, and when you, as I expected you would, had enter'd into some account of the particulars, I would have made an excuse to have put off your voyage to Ireland for some time, and so have gone for London.

Then, my dear, says he, I resolv'd to have confess'd all the circumstances of my own affairs to you, and let you know I had indeed made use of these artifices to obtain your consent to marry me, but had now nothing to do but to ask your pardon, and to tell you how abundantly I would endeavour to make you forget what was past, by the felicity of the days to come.

Truly, said I to him, I find you would soon have conquer'd me; and it is my affliction now that I am not in a condition to let you see how easily I should have been reconcil'd to you, and have pass'd by all the tricks you had put upon me, in recompence of so much good humour; but, my dear, said I, what can we do now? We are both undone, and what better are we for our being reconcil'd, seeing we have nothing to live on?

We propos'd a great many things, but nothing could offer, where there was nothing to begin with. He beg'd me at last to talk no more of it, for he said I would break his heart; so we talk'd of other things a little, till at last he took a husband's leave of me, and so went to sleep.

He rose before me in the morning, and indeed, having lain awake almost all night, I was very sleepy, and lay till near eleven o'clock; in this time he took his horses, and three servants, and all his linnen and baggage, and away he went, leaving a short but moving letter for me on the table, as follows:

My Dear,

I am a dog; I have abus'd you; but I have been drawn in to do it by a base creature, contrary to my principle, and the general practice of my life. Forgive me, my dear! I ask your pardon with the greatest sincerity; I am the most miserable of men, in having deluded you: I have been so happy to possess you, and am now so wretched as to be forc'd to fly from you. Forgive me, my dear, once more I say forgive me! I am not able to see you ruin'd by me, and my self unable to support you. Our marriage is nothing, I shall never be able to see you again; I here discharge you from it; if you can marry to your advantage do not decline it on my account; I here swear to you on my faith, and on the word of a man of honour, I will never disturb your repose if I should know of it, which however is not likely. On the other hand, if you should not marry, and if good fortune should befall me, it shall be all yours wherever you are.

I have put some of the stock of money I have left into your pocket; take places for your self and your maid in the stage coach, and go for London; I hope it will bear your charges thither, without breaking into your own. Again I sincerely ask your pardon, and will do so, as often as I shall ever think of you.

> *Adieu, my dear, for ever,*
> *I am yours most affectionately,*
> *J. E.*

Nothing that ever befel me in my life sunk so deep into my heart as this farewel. I reproach'd him a thousand times in my thoughts for leaving me, for I would have gone with him thro' the world, if I had beg'd my bread. I felt in my pocket, and there I found ten guineas, his gold watch, and two little rings, one a small diamond ring, worth only about six pound, and the other a plain gold ring.

I sat down and look'd upon these things two hours together, and scarce spoke a word, till my maid interrupted me by telling me my dinner was ready. I eat but little, and after dinner I fell into a violent fit of crying, every now and then calling him by his name, which was James. O Jemy! said I, come back, come back, I'll give you all I have; I'll beg, I'll starve with you. And thus I run raving about the room several times, and then sat down between whiles, and then walking about again, call'd upon him to come back, and then cry'd again; and thus I pass'd the afternoon, till about seven o'clock, when it was near dusk in the evening, being August, when to my unspeakable surprise he comes back into the inn, and comes directly up into my chamber.

I was in the greatest confusion imaginable, and so was he too. I could not imagine what should be the occasion of it; and began to be at odds with myself whether to be glad or sorry; but my affection byass'd all the rest, and it was impossible to conceal my joy, which was too great for smiles, for it burst out into tears. He was no sooner enter'd the room, but he run to me and took me in his arms, holding me fast and almost stopping my breath with his kisses, but spoke not a word. At length I began: My dear, said I, how could you go away from me? To which he gave no answer, for it was impossible for him to speak.

When our extasies were a little over, he told me he was gone above 15 miles, but it was not in his power to go any farther without coming back to see me again, and to take his leave of me once more.

I told him how I had pass'd my time, and how loud I had call'd him to come back again; he told me he heard me very plain upon Delamere Forest, at a place about 12 miles off. I smil'd; Nay, says he, do not think I am in jest, for if ever I heard your voice in my life, I heard you call me aloud, and sometimes I thought I saw you running after me. Why, said I, what did I say? for I had not nam'd the words to him. You call'd aloud, says he, and said, *O Jemy! O Jemy! come back, come back.*

I laugh'd at him. My dear, says he, do not laugh, for depend upon it, I heard your voice as plain as you hear mine now; if you please, I'll go before a magistrate and make oath of it. I then began to be amaz'd and surpriz'd, and indeed frighted, and told him what I had really done, and how I had call'd after him, as above. When we had amus'd ourselves [1] awhile about this, I said to him, Well, you shall go away from me no more, I'll go all over the world with you rather. He told me it would be a very difficult thing for him to leave me, but since it must be, he hoped I would make it as easy to me as I could; but as for him, it would be his destruction, that he foresaw.

However, he told me that he had consider'd he had left me to travel to London alone, which was a long journey; and that as he might as well go that way as any way else, he was resolv'd to see me thither, or near it; and if he did go away then without taking his leave, I should not take it ill of him, and this he made me promise.

He told me how he had dismiss'd his three servants, sold their horses, and sent the fellows away to seek their fortunes, and all in a little time, at a town on the road, I know not where. And, says he, it cost me some tears all alone by myself, to think how much happier they were than their master, for they could go to the next gentleman's house to see for a service; whereas, said he, I knew not whither to go, or what to do with myself.

I told him, I was so compleatly miserable in parting with him that I could not be worse; and that now he was come again I would not go from him, if he would take me with him, let him

[1] engaged our attention.

go whither he would; and in the mean time I agreed that we would go together to London; but I could not be brought to consent he should go away at last, and not take his leave of me; but told him, jesting, that if he did, I would call him back again as loud as I did before. Then I pull'd out his watch and gave it him back, and his two rings, and his ten guineas; but he would not take them, which made me very much suspect that he resolv'd to go off upon the road, and leave me.

The truth is, the circumstances he was in, the passionate expressions of his letter, the kind gentlemanly treatment I had from him in all the affair, with the concern he show'd for me in it, his manner of parting with that large share which he gave me of his little stock left, all these had join'd to make such impressions on me that I could not bear the thoughts of parting with him.

Two days after this we quitted Chester, I in the stage coach, and he on horseback; I dismiss'd my maid at Chester; he was very much against my being without a maid, but she being hired in the country, keeping no servant at London, I told him it would have been barbarous to have taken the poor wench, and have turn'd her away as soon as I came to town; and it would also have been a needless charge on the road; so I satisfy'd him, and he was easy on that score.

He came with me as far as Dunstable, within 30 miles of London, and then he told me fate and his own misfortunes oblig'd him to leave me, and that it was not convenient for him to go to London, for reasons which it was of no value to me to know, and I saw him preparing to go. This stage coach we were in did not usually stop at Dunstable, but I desiring it for a quarter of an hour, they were content to stand at an inn-door a while, and we went into the house.

Being in the inn, I told him I had but one favour more to ask him, and that was, that since he could not go any farther, he would give me leave to stay a week or two in the town with him, that we might in that time think of something to prevent such a ruinous thing to us both as a final separation would be; and that I had something of moment to offer to him, which perhaps he might find practicable to our advantage.

This was too reasonable a proposal to be denied, so he call'd the landlady of the house, and told her his wife was taken ill,

and so ill that she cou'd not think of going any farther in the
stage coach, which had tir'd her almost to death, and ask'd if
she cou'd not get us a lodging for two or three days in a private
house where I might rest me a little, for the journey had been
too much for me. The landlady, a good sort of a woman, well
bred, and very obliging, came immediately to see me; told me
she had two or three very good rooms in a part of the house
quite out of the noise, and if I saw them, she did not doubt but
I would like them, and I should have one of her maids, that
should do nothing else but wait on me. This was so very kind
that I could not but accept of it; so I went to look on the rooms,
and lik'd them very well, and indeed they were extraordinarily
furnish'd, and very pleasant lodgings; so we paid the stage
coach, took out our baggage, and resolv'd to stay here a while.

Here I told him I would live with him now till all my money
was spent, but would not let him spend a shilling of his own.
We had some kind squabble about that, but I told him it was
the last time I was like to enjoy his company, and I desir'd he
would let me be master in that thing only, and he should govern in every thing else; so he acquiesc'd.

Here one evening, taking a walk into the fields, I told him
I would now make the proposal to him I had told him of; accordingly I related to him how I had liv'd in Virginia, that I
had a mother, I believ'd, was alive there still, tho' my husband
was dead some years; I told him that had not my effects miscarry'd, which by the way I magnify'd pretty much, I might
have been fortune good enough to him to have kept us from
being parted in this manner. Then I enter'd into the manner
of people's settling in those countries, how they had a quantity of land given them by the constitution of the place; and if
not, that it might be purchased at so easy a rate that it was not
worth naming.

I then gave him a full and distinct account of the nature of
planting, how with carrying over but two or three hundred
pounds value in English goods, with some servants and tools,
a man of application wou'd presently lay a foundation for a family, and in a few years would raise an estate.

I let him into the nature of the product of the earth, how the
ground was cur'd and prepar'd, and what the usual increase of

it was; and demonstrated to him that in a very few years, with such a beginning, we should be as certain of being rich as we were now certain of being poor.

He was surpriz'd at my discourse; for we made it the whole subject of our conversation for near a week together, in which time I laid it down in black and white, as we say, that it was morally impossible, with a supposition of any reasonable good conduct, but that we must thrive there and do very well.

Then I told him what measures I would take to raise such a sum as 300*l.* or thereabouts; and I argued with him how good a method it would be to put an end to our misfortunes, and restore our circumstances in the world to what we had both expected; and I added that after seven years, we might be in a posture to leave our plantation in good hands, and come over again and receive the income of it, and live here and enjoy it; and I gave him examples of some that had done so, and liv'd now in very good figure in London.

In short, I press'd him so to it, that he almost agreed to it, but still something or other broke it off; till at last he turn'd the tables, and began to talk almost to the same purpose of Ireland.

He told me that a man that could confine himself to a country life, and that cou'd find stock to enter upon any land, should have farms there for 50*l.* a year, as good as were let here for 200*l.* a year; that the produce was such, and so rich the land, that if much was not laid up, we were sure to live as handsomely upon it as a gentleman of 3000*l.* a year could do in England; and that he had laid a scheme to leave me in London, and go over and try; and if he found he could lay a handsome foundation of living suitable to the respect he had for me, as he doubted not he should do, he would come over and fetch me.

I was dreadfully afraid that upon such a proposal he would have taken me at my word, *viz.* to turn my little income into money, and let him carry it over into Ireland and try his experiment with it; but he was too just to desire it, or to have accepted it if I had offer'd it; and he anticipated me in that, for he added that he would go and try his fortune that way, and if he found he cou'd do any thing at it to live, then by adding mine to it when I went over, we should live like our selves; but that he would not hazard a shilling of mine till he had made the experiment with a little, and he assur'd me that if he found nothing to be done in Ireland, he would then come to me and join in my project for Virginia.

He was so earnest upon his project being to be try'd first that I cou'd not withstand him; however, he promis'd to let me hear from him in a very little time after his arriving there, to let me know whether his prospect answer'd his design, that if there was not a probability of success, I might take the occasion to prepare for our other voyage, and then, he assur'd me, he would go with me to America with all his heart.

I could bring him to nothing farther than this, and which entertain'd us near a month, during which I enjoy'd his company, which was the most entertaining that ever I met with in my life before. In this time he let me into part of the story of his own life, which was indeed surprizing, and full of infinite variety, sufficient to fill up a much brighter history for its adventures and incidents than any I ever saw in print. But I shall have occasion to say more of him hereafter.

We parted at last, tho' with the utmost reluctance on my side, and indeed he took his leave very unwillingly too, but necessity oblig'd him, for his reasons were very good why he would not come to London, as I understood more fully afterwards.

I gave him a direction how to write to me, tho' still I reserv'd the grand secret, which was not to let him ever know my true name, who I was, or where to be found; he likewise let me know how to write a letter to him, so that he said he would be sure to receive it.

I came to London the next day after we parted, but did not go directly to my old lodgings; but for another nameless reason took a private lodging in St. John's-street, or as it is vulgarly call'd St. Jones's, near Clarkenwell; and here being perfectly alone, I had leisure to sit down and reflect seriously upon the last seven months' ramble I had made, for I had been abroad no less; the pleasant hours I had with my last husband I look'd back on with an infinite deal of pleasure; but that pleasure was very much lessen'd when I found some time after that I was really with child.

This was a perplexing thing because of the difficulty which

was before me, where I should get leave to lye-in; it being one of the nicest [1] things in the world at that time of day for a woman that was a stranger, and had no friends, to be entertain'd in that circumstance without security, which I had not, neither could I procure any.

I had taken care all this while to preserve a correspondence with my friend at the bank, or rather he took care to correspond with me, for he wrote to me once a week; and tho' I had not spent my money so fast as to want any from him, yet I often wrote also to let him know I was alive. I had left directions in Lancashire, so that I had these letters convey'd to me; and during my recess at St. Jones's I received a very obliging letter from him, assuring me that his process for a divorce went on with success, tho' he met with some difficulties in it that he did not expect.

I was not displeas'd with the news that his process was more tedious than he expected; for tho' I was in no condition to have had him yet, not being so foolish to marry him when I knew my self to be with child by another man, as some I know have ventur'd to do; yet I was not willing to lose him, and in a word, resolv'd to have him if he continu'd in the same mind, as soon as I was up again; for I saw apparently I should hear no more from my other husband; and as he had all along press'd me to marry, and had assur'd me he would not be at all disgusted at it, or ever offer to claim me again, so I made no scruple to resolve to do it if I could, and if my other friend stood to his bargain; and I had a great deal of reason to be assur'd that he would by the letters he wrote to me, which were the kindest and most obliging that could be.

I now grew big, and the people where I lodg'd perceiv'd it, and began to take notice of it to me, and as far as civility would allow, intimated that I must think of removing. This put me to extreme perplexity, and I grew very melancholly, for indeed I knew not what course to take; I had money, but no friends, and was like now to have a child upon my hands to keep, which was a difficulty I had never had upon me yet, as my story hitherto makes appear.

In the course of this affair I fell very ill, and my melancholly

---

[1] most delicate, or difficult.

really encreas'd my distemper; my illness prov'd at length to be only an ague, but my apprehensions were really that I should miscarry; I should not say apprehensions, for indeed I would have been glad to miscarry, but I cou'd never entertain so much as a thought of taking any thing to make me miscarry, I abhorr'd, I say, so much as the thought of it.

However, speaking of it, the gentlewoman who kept the house propos'd to me to send for a midwife; I scrupled it at first, but after some time consented, but told her I had no acquaintance with any midwife, and so left it to her.

It seems the mistress of the house was not so great a stranger to such cases as mine was as I thought at first she had been, as will appear presently, and she sent for a midwife of the right sort, that is to say, the right sort for me.

The woman appear'd to be an experienced woman in her business, I mean as a midwife, but she had another calling too, in which she was as expert as most women, if not more. My landlady had told her I was very melancholly, and that she believ'd that had done me harm; and once, before me, said to her, Mrs. B——, I believe this lady's trouble is of a kind that is pretty much in your way, and therefore if you can do anything for her, pray do, for she is a very civil gentlewoman, and so she went out of the room.

I really did not understand her, but my Mother Midnight began very seriously to explain what she meant, as soon as she was gone. Madam, says she, you seem not to understand what your landlady means, and when you do, you need not let her know at all that you do so.

She means that you are under some circumstances that may render your lying-in difficult to you, and that you are not willing to be expos'd; I need say no more but to tell you that if you think fit to communicate so much of your case to me as is necessary, for I do not desire to pry into those things, I perhaps may be in a condition to assist you, and to make you easy, and remove all your dull thoughts upon that subject.

Every word this creature said was a cordial to me, and put new life and new spirit into my very heart; my blood began to circulate immediately, and I was quite another body; I eat my victuals again, and grew better presently after it. She said a great the *Famous* MOLL FLANDERS   141

deal more to the same purpose, and then having press'd me to be
free with her, and promis'd in the solemnest manner to be secret,
she stop'd a little, as if waiting to see what impression it made
on me, and what I would say.

I was too sensible of the want I was in of such a woman, not
to accept her offer; I told her my case was partly as she guess'd,
and partly not, for I was really married, and had a husband, tho'
he was so remote at that time as that he cou'd not appear publickly.

She took me short, and told me, that was none of her business;
all the ladies that came under her care were married women to
her. Every woman, says she, that is with child has a father for
it, and whether that father was a husband or no husband was no
business of hers; her business was to assist me in my present circumstances, whether I had a husband or no. For, madam, says
she, to have a husband that cannot appear, is to have no husband,
and therefore whether you are a wife or a mistress is all one
to me.

I found presently that whether I was a whore or a wife, I was
to pass for a whore here, so I let that go; I told her it was true as
she said, but that, however, if I must tell her my case, I must
tell it her as it was. So I related it as a short as I could, and I concluded it to her. I trouble you with this, madam, said I, not that,
as you said before, it is much to the purpose in your affair; but
this is to the purpose, namely, that I am not in any pain about
being seen, or being conceal'd, for 'tis perfectly indifferent to
me; but my difficulty is that I have no acquaintance in this
part of the nation.

I understand you, madam, says she, you have no security to
bring to prevent the parish impertinences usual in such cases;
and perhaps, says she, do not know very well how to dispose of
the child when it comes. The last, says I, is not so much my
concern as the first. Well, madam, answers the midwife, dare
you put your self into my hands? I live in such a place; tho' I
do not enquire after you, you may enquire after me; my name is
B——, I live in such a street (naming the street), at the Sign
of the Cradle, my profession is a midwife, and I have many
ladies that come to my house to lye-in. I have given security to
the parish in general to secure them from any charge from what

shall come into the world under my roof; I have but one question to ask in the whole affair, madam, says she, and if that be answer'd, you shall be entirely easy of the rest.

I presently understood what she meant, and told her, Madam, I believe I understand you; I thank God, tho' I want friends in this part of the world, I do not want money, so far as may be necessary, tho' I do not abound in that neither. This I added, because I would not make her expect great things. Well, madam, says she, that is the thing indeed, without which nothing can be done in these cases; and yet, says she, you shall see that I will not impose upon you, or offer anything that is unkind to you, and you shall know every thing before hand, that you may suit yourself to the occasion, and be either costly or sparing as you see fit.

I told her she seem'd to be so perfectly sensible of my condition, that I had nothing to ask of her but this, that as I had money sufficient, but not a great quantity, she would order it so, that I might be at as little superfluous charge as possible.

She reply'd that she should bring in an account of the expences of it in two or three shapes, I should chuse as I pleas'd; and I desir'd her to do so.

The next day she brought it, and the copy of her three bills was as follows.

		l.	*s.*	*d.*
1.	For three months' lodging in her house, including my dyet at 10*s.* a week	06	00	0
2.	For a nurse for the month, and use of child-bed linnen			
3.	For a minister to christen the child, and to the godfathers and clark	01	10	0
4.	For a supper at the christening if I had five friends at it	01	00	0
	For her fees as a midwife, and for taking off the trouble of the parish	03	03	0
	To her maid servant attending	00	10	0
		13	13	0

This was the first bill; the second was in the same terms.

	l.	*s.*	*d.*
1. For three months' lodging and dyet &c., at 20s. per week	12	00	0
2. For a nurse for the month, and the use of linnen and lace	02	10	0
3. For the minister to christen the child, &c. as above	02	00	0
4. For a supper, and for sweatmeats	03	03	0
For her fees, as above	05	05	0
For a servant-maid	01	00	0
	26	18	0

This was the second rate bill; the third, she said, was for a degree higher, and when the father or friends appeared.

	l.	*s.*	*d.*
1. For three months' lodging and diet having two rooms and a garret for a servant	30	00	0
2. For a nurse for the month, and the finest suit of child-bed linnen	04	04	0
3. For the minister to christen the child, &c.	02	10	0
4. For a supper, the gentleman to send in the wine	06	00	0
For my fees, &c.	10	10	0
The maid besides their own maid only	00	10	0
	53	14	0

I look'd upon all the three bills, and smil'd, and told her I did not see but that she was very reasonable in her demands and things consider'd, and I did not doubt but her accommodations were good.

She told me I should be a judge of that, when I saw them. I told her I was sorry to tell her that I fear'd I must be her lowest-rated customer. And perhaps, madam, said I, you will make me the less wellcome upon that account. No, not at all, said she, for where I have one of the third sort, I have two of the second, and four of the first, and I get as much by them in proportion as by any; but if you doubt my care of you, I will allow any friend you have to see if you are well waited on, or no.

Then she explain'd the particulars of her bill. In the first place, madam, said she, I would have you observe that here is three

months' keeping you at but 10s. a week; I undertake to say you
will not complain of my table. I suppose, says she, you do not
live cheaper where you are now. No, indeed, said I, nor so cheap,
for I give six shillings *per* week for my chamber, and find my
own dyet, which costs me a great deal more.

Then, madam, says she, if the child should not live, as it sometimes happens, there is the minister's article saved; and if you
have no friends to come, you may save the expence of a supper;
so that, take those articles out, madam, says she, your lying-in
will not cost you above 5l. 3s. more than your ordinary charge
of living.

This was the most reasonable thing that I ever heard of; so
I smil'd, and told her I would come and be a customer; but I
told her also that as I had two months and more to go, I might
perhaps be obliged to stay longer with her than three months,
and desir'd to know if she would not be oblig'd to remove me
before it was proper. No, she said, her house was large, and besides, she never put any body to remove that had lain-in 'till they
were willing to go; and if she had more ladies offer'd, she was
not so ill belov'd among her neighbours but she could provide
accommodation for twenty, if there was occasion.

I found she was an eminent lady in her way, and in short, I
agreed to put my self into her hands. She then talk'd of other
things, look'd about into my accommodations, where I was,
found fault with my wanting attendance, and conveniences, and
that I should not be us'd so at her house. I told her I was shy of
speaking, for the woman of the house look'd stranger, or at least
I thought so, since I had been ill, because I was with child; and
I was afraid she would put some affront or other upon me, supposing that I had been able to give but a slight account of
my self.

O dear, says she, her ladyship is no stranger to these things;
she has try'd to entertain ladies in your condition, but could
not secure the parish; and besides, such a nice [1] lady as you take
her to be; however, since you are agoing you shall not meddle
with her, but I'll see you are a little better look'd after while you
are here, and it shall not cost you the more neither.

I did not understand her: however, I thank'd her, so we

[1] scrupulous.

parted. The next morning she sent me a chicken roasted and
hot, and a bottle of sherry, and ordered the maid to tell me that
she was to wait on me every day as long as I staid there.

This was surprisingly good and kind, and I accepted it very
willingly. At night she sent to me again to know if I wanted
any thing, and to order the maid to come to her in the morning
for dinner; the maid had orders to make me some chocolate in
the morning before she came away, and at noon she brought
me the sweetbread of a breast of veal whole, and a dish of soup
for my dinner, and after this manner she nurs'd me up at a distance, so that I was mightily well pleased, and quickly well, for
indeed my dejections before were the principal part of my
illness.

I expected, as is usually the case among such people, that the
servant she sent me would have been some impudent brazen
wench of Drury Lane [1] breeding, and I was very uneasy upon
that account, so I would not let her lye in the house the first
night, but had my eyes about me as narrowly as if she had been
a publick thief.

My gentlewoman guess'd presently what was the matter,
and sent her back with a short note that I might depend upon
the honesty of her maid; that she would be answerable for her
upon all accounts; and that she took no servants without very
good security. I was then perfectly easy, and indeed the
maid's behaviour spoke for it self, for a modester, quieter, soberer girl never came into any body's family, and I found her
so afterwards.

As soon as I was well enough to go abroad, I went with the
maid to see the house, and to see the appartment I was to have,
and every thing was so handsome and so clean, that, in short,
I had nothing to say, but was wonderfully pleased with what
I had met with, which, considering the melancholly circumstances I was in, was beyond what I looked for.

It might be expected that I should give some account of the
nature of the wicked practices of this woman in whose hands
I was now fallen; but it would be but too much encouragement
to the vice to let the world see what easy measures were here
taken to rid the women's burthen of a child clandestinely gotten.

[1] This quarter was much frequented by street-walkers.

This grave matron had several sorts of practice, and this was one, that if a child was born, tho' not in her house, for she had the occasion to be call'd to many private labours, she had people always ready who for a piece of money would take the child off their hands, and off from the hands of the parish too; and those children, as she said, were honestly taken care of. What should become of them all, considering so many as by her account she was concern'd with, I cannot conceive.

I had many times discourses upon that subject with her; but she was full of this argument, that she sav'd the life of many an innocent lamb, as she call'd them, which would perhaps have been murder'd; and of many a woman, who, made desperate by the misfortune, would otherwise be tempted to destroy their children. I granted her that this was true, and a very commendable thing, provided the poor children fell into good hands afterwards, and were not abus'd and neglected by the nurses; she answered that she always took care of that, and had no nurses in her business but what were very good people, and such as might be depended upon.

I could say nothing to the contrary, and so was oblig'd to say, Madam, I do not question but you do your part, but what those people do is the main question; and she stop'd my mouth again with saying she took the utmost care about it.

The only thing I found in all her conversation on these subjects that gave me any distaste was, that one time in discoursing about my being so far gone with child, she said something that look'd as if she could help me off with my burthen sooner, if I was willing; or in English, that she could give me something to make me miscarry, if I had a desire to put an end to my troubles that way; but I soon let her see that I abhor'd the thoughts of it; and to do her justice, she put it off so cleverly, that I could not say she really intended it, or whether she only mentioned the practice as a horrible thing; for she couch'd her words so well, and took my meaning so quickly, that she gave her negative before I could explain my self.

To bring this part into so narrow a compass as possible, I quitted my lodging at St. Jones's, and went to my new governess, for so they call'd her in the house, and there I was indeed treated with so much courtesy, so carefully look'd to, and every thing so well, that I was surpris'd at it, and could not at first see what advantage my governess made of it; but I found afterwards that she profess'd to make no profit of the lodger's dyet, nor indeed cou'd she get much by it, but that her profit lay in the other articles of her management, and she made enough that way, I assure you; for 'tis scarce credible what practice she had, as well abroad as at home, and yet all upon the private account, or in plain English, the whoring account.

While I was at her house, which was near four months, she had no less than twelve ladies of pleasure brought to bed within doors, and I think she had two and thirty or thereabouts under her conduct without doors, whereof one, as nice as she was with me, was lodg'd with my old landlady at St. Jones's.

This was a strange testimony of the growing vice of the age, and, as bad as I had been my self, it shock'd my very senses; I began to nauseate the place I was in, and, above all, the practice; and yet I must say that I never saw, or do I believe there was to be seen, the least indecency in the house the whole time I was there.

Not a man was ever seen to come up stairs, except to visit the lying-in ladies within their month, nor then without the old lady with them, who made it a piece of the honour of her management that no man should touch a woman, no, not his own wife, within the month; nor would she permit any man to lye in the house upon any pretence whatever, no, not tho' it was with his own wife, and her saying for it was, that she car'd not how many children was born in her house, but she would have none got there if she could help it.

It might perhaps be carried farther than was needful, but it was an error of the right hand if it was an error, for by this she kept up the reputation, such as it was, of her business, and obtain'd this character, that tho' she did take care of the women when they were debauch'd, yet she was not instrumental to their being debauch'd at all, and yet it was a wicked trade she drove too.

While I was here, and before I was brought to bed, I receiv'd a letter from my trustee at the bank full of kind obliging things, and earnestly pressing me to return to London. It was near a fortnight old when it came to me, because it had first been sent into

Lancashire, and then return'd to me; he concludes with telling me that he had obtain'd a decree against his wife, and that he would be ready to make good his engagement to me, if I would accept of him, adding a great many protestations of kindness and affection, such as he would have been far from offering if he had known the circumstances I had been in, and which, as it was, I had been very far from deserving.

I return'd an answer to this letter, and dated it at Liverpool, but sent it by a messenger, alledging that it came in cover to a friend in town; I gave him joy of his deliverance, but rais'd some scruples at the lawfulness of his marrying again, and told him I suppos'd he would consider very seriously upon that point before he resolv'd on it, the consequence being too great for a man of his judgment to venture rashly upon; so concluded, wishing him very well in whatever he resolv'd, without letting him into any thing of my own mind, or giving any answer to his proposal of my coming to London to him, but mention'd at a distance my intention to return the latter end of the year, this being dated in April.

I was brought to bed about the middle of May, and had another brave boy, and my self in as good condition as usual on such occasions. My governess did her part as a midwife with the greatest art and dexterity imaginable, and far beyond all that ever I had had any experience of before.

Her care of me in my travail, and after in my lying-in, was such that if she had been my own mother it could not have been better; let none be encouraged in their loose practices from this dexterous lady's management, for she is gone to her place, and I dare say has left nothing behind her that can or will come up to it.

I think I had been brought to bed about twenty days when I receiv'd another letter from my friend at the bank, with the surprising news that he had obtain'd a final sentence of divorce against his wife, and had serv'd her with it on such a day, and that he had such an answer to give to all my scruples about his marrying again as I could not expect, and as he had no desire of; for that his wife, who had been under some remorse before for her usage of him, as soon as she heard that he had gain'd his point, had very unhappily destroy'd herself that same evening.

He express'd himself very handsomly as to his being concern'd at her disaster, but clear'd himself of having any hand in
it, and that he had only done himself justice in a case in which
he was notoriously injur'd and abus'd. However, he said that he
was extremely afflicted at it, and had no view of any satisfaction
left in this world but only in the hope that I would come and
relieve him by my company; and then he press'd me violently
indeed to give him some hopes, that I would at least come up to
town and let him see me, when he would farther enter into discourse about it.

I was exceedingly surpriz'd at the news, and began now seriously to reflect on my circumstances, and the inexpressible misfortune it was to have a child upon my hands, and what to do
in it I knew not. At last I open'd my case at a distance to my
governess; I appear'd melancholy for several days, and she lay at
me continually to know what troubled me; I could not for my
life tell her that I had an offer of marriage, after I had so often
told her that I had a husband, so that I really knew not what to
say to her. I own'd I had something which very much troubl'd
me, but at the same time told her I cou'd not speak of it to any
one alive.

She continued importuning me several days, but it was impossible, I told her, for me to commit the secret to any body.
This, instead of being an answer to her, encreas'd her importunities; she urg'd her having been trusted with the greatest secrets
of this nature, that it was her business to conceal every thing, and
that to discover things of that nature would be her ruin; she
ask'd me if ever I had found her tatling of other people's affairs,
and how could I suspect her? She told me, to unfold myself to
her was telling it to no body; that she was silent as death, that
it must be a very strange case indeed that she could not help me
out of; but to conceal it was to deprive myself of all possible help,
or means of help, and to deprive her of the opportunity of serv-
ing me. In short, she had such a bewitching eloquence, and so
great a power of perswasion, that there was no concealing any
thing from her.

So I resolv'd to unbosom myself to her; I told her the history
of my Lancashire marriage, and how both of us had been disappointed; how we came together, and how we parted; how he

discharg'd me, as far as lay in him, and gave me free liberty to marry again, protesting that if he knew it he would never claim me, or disturb, or expose me; that I thought I was free, but was dreadfully afraid to venture, for fear of the consequences that might follow in case of a discovery.

Then I told her what a good offer I had; show'd her my friend's letters, inviting me to London, and with what affection they were written, but blotted out the name, and also the story about the disaster of his wife, only that she was dead.

She fell a laughing at my scruples about marrying, and told me the other was no marriage, but a cheat on both sides; and that as we were parted by mutual consent, the nature of the contract was destroy'd, and the obligation was mutually discharg'd. She had arguments for this at the tip of her tongue; and, in short, reason'd me out of my reason; not but that it was too by the help of my own inclination.

But then came the great and main difficulty, and that was the child; this she told me must be remov'd, and that so as that it should never be possible for any one to discover it. I knew there was no marrying without concealing that I had had a child, for he would soon have discover'd by the age of it that it was born, nay, and gotten too, since my parly with him, and that would have destroy'd all the affair.

But it touch'd my heart so forcibly to think of parting entirely with the child, and, for ought I knew, of having it murther'd, or starv'd by neglect and ill-usage, which was much the same, that I could not think of it without horror. I wish all those women who consent to the disposing their children out of the way, as it is call'd, for decency sake, would consider that 'tis only a contriv'd method of murther; that is to say, killing their children with safety.

It is manifest to all that understand any thing of children that we are born into the world helpless, and uncapable either to supply our own wants, or so much as make them known; and that without help we must perish; and this help requires not only an assisting hand, whether of the mother, or some body else, but there are two things necessary in that assisting hand, that is, care and skill; without both which, half the children that are born would die; nay, tho' they were not to be deny'd food; and one half more of those that remain'd would be cripples or fools, lose their limbs, and perhaps their sense. I question not but that these are partly the reasons why affection was plac'd by nature in the hearts of mothers to their children; without which they would never be able to give themselves up, as 'tis necessary they should, to the care and waking pains needful to the support of children.

Since this care is needful to the life of children, to neglect them is to murther them; again, to give them up to be manag'd by those people who have none of that needful affection plac'd by nature in them, is to neglect them in the highest degree; nay, in some it goes farther, and is in order to their being lost; so that 'tis an intentional murther, whether the child lives or dies.

All those things represented themselves to my view, and that in the blackest and most frightful form; and as I was very free with my governess, who I had now learn'd to call mother, I represented to her all the dark thoughts which I had about it, and told her what distress I was in. She seem'd graver by much at this part then at the other; but as she was harden'd in these things beyond all possibility of being touch'd with the religious part, and the scruples about the murther, so she was equally impenetrable in that part which related to affection. She ask'd me if she had not been careful and tender of me in my lying-inn, as if I had been her own child? I told her I own'd she had. Well, my dear, says she, and when you are gone, what are you to me? and what would it be to me if you were to he hang'd? Do you think there are not women, who, as it is their trade, and they get their bread by it, value themselves upon their being as careful of children as their own mothers? Yes, yes, child, says she, fear it not; how were we nurs'd ourselves? Are you sure you was nurs'd up by your own mother? and yet you look fat and fair, child, says the old beldam; and with that she stroak'd me over the face. Never be concern'd, child, says she, going on in her drolling way: I have no murtherers about me, I employ the best nurses that can be had; and have as few children miscarry under their hands as there would if they were all nurs'd by mothers; we want neither care nor skill.

She touch'd me to the quick when she ask'd if I was sure that I was nurs'd by my own mother; on the contrary, I was sure

I was not; and I trembled and look'd pale at the very expression. Sure, said I to my self, this creature cannot be a witch, or have any conversation with a spirit that can inform her what I was before I was able to know it my self? and I look'd at her as if I had been frighted; but reflecting that it could not be possible for her to know any thing about me, that went off, and I began to be easy, but it was not presently.[1]

She perceiv'd the disorder I was in, but did not know the meaning of it; so she run on in her wild talk upon the weakness of my supposing that children were murder'd because they were not all nurs'd by the mother; and to perswade me that the children she disposed of were as well used as if the mothers had the nursing of them themselves.

It may be true, mother, says I, for ought I know, but my doubts are very strongly grounded. Come then, says she, lets hear some of them. Why first, says I, you give a piece of money to these people to take the child off the parent's hands, and to take care of it as long as it lives; now we know, mother, said I, that those are poor people, and their gain consists in being quit of the charge as soon as they can; how can I doubt but that, as it is best for them to have the child die, they are not over solicitous about its life?

This is all vapours and fancy, says she; I tell you their credit depends upon the child's life, and they are as careful as any mother of you all.

O mother, says I, if I was but sure my little baby would be carefully look'd to, and have justice done it, I should be happy; but it is impossible I can be satisfy'd in that point unless I saw it, and to see it would be ruin and destruction, as my case now stands; so what to do I know not.

A fine story! says the governess; you would see the child, and you would not see the child; you would be conceal'd and discover'd both together; these are things impossible, my dear, and so you must e'en do as other conscientious mothers have done before you; and be contented with things as they must be, tho' not as you wish them to be.

I understood what she meant by conscientious mothers; she would have said conscientious whores. But she was not willing

[1] immediately.

to disoblige me, for really in this case I was not a whore, because legally marry'd, the force of my former marriage excepted.

However, let me be what I would, I was not come up to that pitch of hardness common to the profession, I mean, to be unnatural, and regardless of the safety of my child; and I preserv'd this honest affection so long that I was upon the point of giving up my friend at the bank, who lay so hard at me to come to him, and marry him, that there was hardly any room to deny him.

At last my old governess came to me, with her usual assurance. Come, my dear, says she, I have found out a way how you shall be at a certainty that your child shall be used well, and yet the people that take care of it shall never know you.

O mother, say I, if you can do so, you will engage me to you for ever. Well, says she, are you willing to be at some small annual expence, more than what we usually give to the people we contract with? Ay, says I, with all my heart, provided I may be concealed. As to that, says she, you shall be secure, for the nurse shall never dare to enquire about you, and you shall once or twice a year go with me and see your child, and see how 'tis used, and be satisfy'd that it is in good hands, no body knowing who you are.

Why, said I, do you think that when I come to see my child I shall be able to conceal my being the mother of it? Do you think that possible?

Well, says she, if you discover it, the nurse shall be never the wiser. She shall be forbid to take any notice; if she offers it, she shall lose the money which you are to be suppos'd to give her, and the child be taken from her too.

I was very well pleas'd with this; so the next week a country woman was brought from Hertford, or thereabouts, who was to take the child off our hands entirely, for 10*l.* in money; but if I would allow 5*l.* a year more to her, she would be oblig'd to bring the child to my governesses house as often as we desir'd, or we should come down and look at it, and see how well she used it.

The woman was a very wholesome-look'd likely woman, a cottager's wife, but she had very good cloaths and linnen, and every thing well about her, and with a heavy heart and many a tear I let her have my child. I had been down at Hertford and

look'd at her, and at her dwelling, which I lik'd well enough;
and I promised her great things if she would be kind to the
child, so she knew at first word that I was the child's mother;
but she seem'd to be so much out of the way, and to have no
room to enquire after me, that I thought I was safe enough, so in
short, I consented to let her have the child, and I gave her 10*l*.,
that is to say I gave it to my governess, who gave it the poor
woman before my face, she agreeing never to return the child
back to me, or to claim any thing more for its keeping or bringing up; only that I promised, if she took a great deal of care of
it, I would give her something more as often as I came to see it;
so that I was not bound to pay the 5*l*., only that I promis'd my
governess I would do it. And thus my great care was over, after
a manner, which, tho' it did not at all satisfy my mind, yet was
the most convenient for me, as my affairs then stood, of any that
could be thought of at that time.

I then began to write to my friend at the bank in a more kindly
style; and particularly about the beginning of July I sent him a
letter that I purpos'd to be in town sometime in August. He
return'd me an answer in the most passionate terms imaginable,
and desir'd me to let him have timely notice, and he would
come and meet me two days journey. This puzzl'd me scurvily,
and I did not know what answer to make to it; once I was resolv'd
to take the stage coach to West Chester, on purpose only to have
the satisfaction of coming back, that he might see me really
come in the same coach; for I had a jealous [1] thought, tho I had no
ground for it at all, least he should think I was not really in the
country.

I endeavour'd to reason my self out of it, but it was in vain;
the impression lay so strong on my mind, that it was not to be
resisted. At last it came as an addition to my new design of going
into the country that it would be an excellent blind to my old
governess, and would cover entirely all my other affairs, for she
did not know in the least whether my new lover liv'd in London
or in Lancashire, and when I told her my resolution, she was fully
perswaded it was in Lancashire.

Having taken my measures for this journey, I let her know it,
and sent the maid that tended me from the beginning to take

[1] apprehensive.

a place for me in the coach; she would have had me let the maid have waited on me down to the last stage, and come up again in the waggon, but I convinc'd her it would not be convenient. When I went away, she told me she would enter into no measures for correspondence, for she saw evidently that my affection to my child would cause me to write to her, and to visit her too, when I came to town again; I assur'd her it would and so took my leave, well satisfy'd to have been freed from such a house, however good my accommodations there had been.

I took the place in the coach not to its full extent, but to a place called Stone, in Cheshire, where I not only had no manner of business, but not the least acquaintance with any person in the town. But I knew that with money in the pocket one is at home any where; so I lodg'd there two or three days, 'till, watching my opportunity, I found room in another stage coach, and took passage back again for London, sending a letter to my gentleman, that I should be such a certain day at Stony-Stratford,[1] where the coachman told me he was to lodge.

It happen'd to be a chance coach that I had taken up, which, having been hired on purpose to carry some gentlemen to West-Chester, who were going for Ireland, was now returning, and did not tye it self up to exact times or places as the stages did; so that having been oblig'd to lye still on Sunday, he had time to get himself ready to come out, which otherwise he could not have done.

His warning was so short that he could not reach Stony-Stratford time enough to be with me at night, but he met me at a place called Brickhill the next morning, just as we were coming into the town.

I confess I was very glad to see him, for I thought my self a little disappointed over night. He pleas'd me doubly too by the figure he came in, for he brought a very handsome (gentleman's) coach, and four horses, with a servant to attend him.

He took me out of the stage coach immediately, which stop'd at an inn in Brickhill, and putting into the same inn, he set up his own coach, and bespoke his dinner. I ask'd him what he meant by that, for I was for going forward with the journey. He said, no, I had need of a little rest upon the road, and that was a

[1] In Buckinghamshire, about 50 miles from London.

very good sort of a house, tho' it was but a little town; so we would go no farther that night, whatever came of it.

I did not press him much, for since he had come so far to meet me, and put himself to so much expence, it was but reasonable I should oblige him a little too, so I was easy as to that point.

After dinner we walk'd to see the town, to see the church, and to view the fields and the country, as is usual for strangers to do, and our landlord was our guide in going to see the church. I observ'd my gentleman enquir'd pretty much about the parson, and I took the hint immediately that he certainly would propose to be married; and it follow'd presently, that, in short, I would not refuse him; for to be plain with my circumstances, I was in no condition now to say no, I had no reason now to run any more such hazards.

But while these thoughts run round in my head, which was the work but of a few moments, I observ'd my landlord took him aside and whisper'd to him, tho' not very softly neither, for so much I over-heard: Sir, if you shall have occasion — The rest I could not hear, but it seems it was to this purpose: Sir, if you shall have occasion for a minister, I have a friend a little way off that will serve you, and be as private as you please. My gentleman answer'd loud enough for me to hear, Very well, I believe I shall.

I was no sooner come back to the inn but he fell upon me with irresistible words; that since he had had the good fortune to meet me, and everything concurr'd, it would be hastening his felicity if I would put an end to the matter just there. What do you mean, says I, colouring a little; what, in an inn, and on the road! Bless us all, said I, how can you talk so! O, I can talk so very well, says he, I came on purpose to talk so, and I'll show you that I did; and with that he pulls out a great bundle of papers. You fright me, said I, what are all these? Don't be frighted, my dear, said he, and kiss'd me (this was the first time that he had been so free to call me *my dear*). Then he repeated it, Don't be frighted, you shall see what it is all; then he laid them all abroad;[1] there was first the deed or sentence of divorce from his wife, and the full evidence of her playing the whore; then there was the certificates of the minister and church-wardens of the parish where she liv'd,

[1] at large.

proving that she was buried, and intimating the manner of her death; the copy of the coroner's warrant for a jury to sit upon her, and the verdict of the jury, who brought it in *non compos mentis:* all this was to give me satisfaction, tho', by the way, I was not so scrupulous, had he known all, but that I might have taken him without it. However, I look'd them all over as well as I cou'd, and told him that this was all very clear indeed, but that he need not have brought them out with him, for it was time enough. Well, he said, it might be time enough for me, but no time but the present time was time enough for him.

There were other papers roll'd up, and I ask'd him what they were? Why, ay, says he, that's the question I wanted to have you ask me; so he takes out a little chagreen case, and gives me out of it a very fine diamond ring. I could not refuse it, if I had a mind to do so, for he put it upon my finger; so I only made him a curtsy. Then he takes out another ring. And this, says he, is for another occasion, and puts that into his pocket. Well, but let me see it tho', says I, and smil'd; I guess what it is, I think you are mad. I should have been mad if I had done less, says he; and still he did not show it me, and I had a great mind to see it; so I says, Well, but let me see it. Hold, says he, first look here. Then he took up the roll again, and read it, and behold! it was a license for us to be married. Why, says I, are you distracted? you were fully satisfy'd, sure, that I would yield at first word, or resolv'd to take no denial. The last is certainly the case, said he. But you may be mistaken, said I. No, no, says he, I must not be denied, I can't be denied; and with that he fell to kissing me so violently, I could not get rid of him.

There was a bed in the room, and we were walking to and again, eager in the discourse; at last, he takes me by surprize in his arms, and threw me on the bed and himself with me, and holding me still fast in his arms, but without the least offer of any undecency, courted me to consent with such repeated entreaties and arguments; protesting his affection, and vowing he would no let me go till I had promised him, that at last I said, Why, you resolve not to be deny'd, indeed, I think. No, no, says he, I must not be deny'd, I won't be deny'd, I can't be deny'd. Well, well, said I, and giving him a slight kiss; then you shan't be deny'd, let me get up.

He was so transported with my consent, and the kind manner

of it, that I began to think once he took it for a marriage, and would not stay for the form; but I wrong'd him, for he took me by the hand, pull'd me up again, and then giving me two or three kisses, thank'd me for my kind yielding to him; and was so overcome with the satisfaction of it that I saw tears stand in his eyes.

I turned from him, for it fill'd my eyes with tears too; and ask'd him leave to retire a little to my chamber. If I had a grain of true repentance for an abominable life of 24 years past, it was then. Oh! what a felicity is it to mankind, said I to myself, that they cannot see into the hearts of one another! How happy had it been if I had been wife to a man of so much honesty and so much affection from the beginning!

Then it occurr'd to me, What an abominable creature am I! and how is this innocent gentleman going to be abus'd by me! How little does he think that having divorc'd a whore he is throwing himself into the arms of another! that he is going to marry one that has lain with two brothers, and has had three children by her own brother! one that was born in Newgate, whose mother was a whore, and is now a transported thief; one that has lain with thirteen men, and has had a child since he saw me! Poor gentleman! said I, what he is going to do! After this reproaching myself was over, it followed thus: Well, if I must be his wife, if it please God to give me grace, I'll be a true wife to him, and love him suitably to the strange excess of his passion for me; I will make him amends, by what he shall see, for the abuses I put upon him, which he does not see.

He was impatient for my coming out of my chamber, but finding me long, he went down stairs, and talk'd with my landlord about the parson.

My landlord, an officious, tho' well-meaning fellow, had sent away for the clergyman; and when my gentleman began to speak to him of sending for him, Sir, says he to him, my friend is in the house; so without any more words he brought them together. When he came to the minister, he ask'd him if he would venture to marry a couple of strangers that were both willing. The parson said that Mr. —— had said something to him of it; that he hop'd it was no clandestine business; that he seem'd to be a grave gentleman, and he suppos'd madam was not a girl, so that the consent of friends should be wanted. To put you out of doubt of that, says my gentleman, read this paper; and out he pulls the license. I am satisfy'd, says the minister; where is the lady? You shall see her presently, says my gentleman.

When he had said thus, he comes up stairs, and I was by that time come out of my room. So he tells me the minister was below, and that upon showing him the license, he was free to marry us with all his heart, but he asks to see you; so he ask'd if I would let him come up.

'Tis time enough, said I, in the morning, is it not? Why, said he, my dear, he seem'd to scruple whether it was not some young girl stolen from her parents, and I assur'd him we were both of age to command our own consent; and that made him ask to see you. Well, said I, do as you please. So up they brings the parson, and a merry good sort of gentleman he was: he had been told, it seems, that we had met there by accident, that I came in a Chester coach, and my gentleman in his own coach to meet me; that we were to have met last night at Stony-Stratford, but that he could not reach so far. Well, sir, says the parson, every ill turn has some good in it; the disappointment, sir, says he to my gentleman, was yours, and the good turn is mine, for if you had met at Stony-Stratford I had not had the honour to marry you. Landlord, have you a Common Prayer Book?

I started as if I had been frighted. Sir, says I, what do you mean? What, to marry in an inn, and at night too! Madam, says the minister, if you will have it be in the church you shall; but I assure you your marriage will be as firm here as in the church; we are not tyed by the canons to marry no where but in the church; and as for the time of day, it does not at all weigh in this case; our princes are married in their chambers, and at eight or ten a clock at night.

I was a great while before I could be perswaded, and pretended not to be willing at all to be married but in the church; but it was all grimace;[1] so I seem'd at last to be prevail'd on, and my landlord, and his wife and daughter, were call'd up. My landlord was father and clark and all together, and we were married, and very merry we were; tho' I confess the self-reproaches

[1] sham.

which I had upon me before lay close to me, and extorted every now and then a deep sigh from me, which my bridegroom took notice of, and endeavour'd to encourage me, thinking, poor man, that I had some little hesitations at the step I had taken so hastily.

We enjoy'd our selves that evening compleatly, and yet all was kept so private in the inn that not a servant in the house knew of it, for my landlady and her daughter waited on me, and would not let any of the maids come up stairs. My landlady's daughter I call'd my bride maid; and sending for a shopkeeper the next morning, I gave the young woman a good suit of knots,[1] as good as the town would afford, and finding it was a lacemaking town, I gave her mother a piece of bone-lace for a head.[2]

One reason that my landlord was so close was that he was unwilling the minister of the parish should hear of it; but, for all that, somebody heard of it, so as that we had the bells set a ringing the next morning early, and the musick, such as the town would afford, under our window; but my landlord brazen'd it out that we were marry'd before we came thither, only that being his former guests, we would have our wedding-supper at his house.

We could not find in our hearts to stir the next day; for, in short, having been disturb'd by the bells in the morning, and having perhaps not slept over much before, we were so sleepy afterwards that we lay in bed till almost twelve a clock.

I beg'd my landlady, that we might have no more musick in the town, nor ringing of bells, and she manag'd it so well that we were very quiet. But an odd passage interrupted all my mirth for a good while; the great room of the house look'd into the street, and I had walk'd to the end of the room, and it being a pleasant warm day, I had open'd the window, and was standing at it for some air, when I saw three gentlemen ride by, and go into an inn just against[3] us.

It was not to be conceal'd, nor did it leave me any room to question it but[4] the second of the three was my Lancashire husband. I was frighted to death, I never was in such a consternation in my life, I thought I should have sunk into the ground, my blood run chill in my veins, and I trembl'd as if I had been in a cold fit of an ague: I say, there was no room to question the

---

[1] a good set of ribbons.   [2] head dress.
[3] opposite.   [4] but that.

truth of it, I knew his cloaths, I knew his horse, and I knew his face.

The first reflection I made was that my husband was not by to see my disorder, and that I was very glad of. The gentlemen had not been long in the house but they came to the window of their room, as is usual; but my window was shut, you may be sure. However, I could not keep from peeping at them, and there I saw him again, heard him call to one of the servants for something he wanted, and receiv'd all the terrifying confirmations of its being the same person that were possible to be had.

My next concern was to know what was his business there, but that was impossible; sometimes my imagination form'd an idea of one frightful thing, sometimes of another; sometimes I thought he had discover'd me, and was come to upbraid me with ingratitude and breach of honour; then I fancied he was coming up stairs to insult me; and innumerable thoughts came into my head of what was never in his head, nor ever could be, unless the devil had reveal'd it to him.

I remain'd in the fright near two hours, and scarce ever kept my eye from the window or door of the inn where they were. At last hearing a great clutter in the passage of their inn, I run to the window, and, to my great satisfaction, I saw them all three go out again and travel on westward; had they gone towards London, I should have been still in a fright, least I should meet him again, and that he should know me; but he went the contrary way, and so I was eas'd of that disorder.

We resolv'd to be going the next day, but about six a clock at night we were alarm'd with a great uproar in the street, and people riding as if they had been out of their wits, and what was it but a hue and cry after three highway men that had rob'd two coaches and some travellers near Dunstable Hill, and notice had, it seems, been given that they had been seen at Brickhill at such a house, meaning the house where those gentlemen had been.

The house was immediately beset and search'd, but there were witnesses enough that the gentlemen had been gone above three hours; the crowd having gathered about, we had the news presently; and I was heartily concern'd now another way. I presently told the people of the house that I durst say those were honest persons, for that I knew one of the gentlemen to be a very honest person, and of a good estate in Lancashire.

The constable who came with the hue and cry was immediately inform'd of this, and came over to me to be satisfy'd from my own mouth, and I assur'd him that I saw the three gentlemen as I was at the window, that I saw them afterwards at the windows of the room they din'd in; that I saw them take horse, and I would assure him I knew one of them to be such a man that he was a gentleman of a very good estate and an undoubted character in Lancashire, from whence I was just now upon my journey.

The assurance with which I deliver'd this gave the mob gentry a check, and gave the constable such satisfaction that he immediately sounded a retreat, told his people these were not the men, but that he had an account they were very honest gentlemen, and so they went all back again. What the truth of the matter was I knew not, but certain it was that the coaches were rob'd at Dunstable Hill, and 56ol. in money taken, besides some of the lace merchants that always travel that way had been visited too; as to the three gentlemen, that remains to be explain'd hereafter.

Well, this allarm stop'd us another day, tho' my spouse told me it was always safest travelling after a robbery, for that the thieves were sure to be gone far enough off when they had allarm'd the country; but I was uneasy, and indeed principally least my old acquaintance should be upon the road still, and should chance to see me.

I never liv'd four pleasanter days together in my life; I was a meer bride all this while, and my new spouse strove to make me easie in every thing. O could this state of life have continu'd! how had all my past troubles been forgot, and my future sorrows been avoided! but I had a past life of a most wretched kind to account for, some of it in this world as well as in another.

We came away the fifth day; and my landlord, because he saw me uneasie, mounted himself, his son, and three honest country fellows, with good fire-arms, and, without telling us of it, follow'd the coach, and would see us safe into Dunstable; we could do no less than treat them very handsomely at Dunstable, which cost my spouse about ten or twelve shillings, and something he gave the men for their time too, but my landlord would take nothing for himself.

This was the most happy contrivance for me that could have fallen out, for had I come to London unmarried, I must either have come to him for the first night's entertainment, or have discovered to him that I had not one acquaintance in the whole city of London that could receive a poor bride for the first night's lodging with her spouse. But now I made no scruple of going directly home with him, and there I took possession at once of a house well furnished, and a husband in very good circumstances, so that I had a prospect of a very happy life, if I knew how to manage it; and I had leisure to consider of the real value of the life I was likely to live; how different it was to be from the loose part I had acted before, and how much happier a life of virtue and sobriety is than that which we call a life of pleasure.

O, had this particular scene of life lasted, or had I learnt from that time I enjoy'd it to have tasted the true sweetness of it, and had I not fallen into that poverty which is the sure bane of virtue, how happy had I been, not only here, but perhaps for ever! For while I liv'd thus, I was really a penitent for all my life pass'd, I look'd back on it with abhorrence, and might truly be said to hate my self for it. I often reflected how my lover at Bath, strook by the hand of God, repented and abandon'd me, and refus'd to see me any more, tho' he lov'd me to an extreme; but I, prompted by that worst of devils, poverty, return'd to the vile practice, and made the advantage of what they call a handsome face be the relief to my necessities, and beauty be a pimp to vice.

Now I seem'd landed in a safe harbour, after the stormy voyage of life past was at an end; and I began to be thankful for my deliverance. I sat many an hour by myself, and wept over the remembrance of past follies, and the dreadful extravagances of a wicked life, and sometimes I flatter'd myself that I had sincerely repented.

But there are temptations which it is not in the power of human nature to resist, and few know what would be their case, if driven to the same exigences. As covetousness is the root

of all evil, so poverty is the worst of all snares. But I waive that
discourse till I come to the experiment.[1]

I liv'd with this husband in the utmost tranquility; he was
a quiet, sensible, sober man, virtuous, modest, sincere, and in his
business diligent and just. His business was in a narrow compass,
and his income sufficient to a plentiful way of living in the ordinary way; I do not say to keep an equipage, and make a figure
as the world calls it, nor did I expect it, or desire it; for as I ab-
horred the levity and extravagance of my former life, so I chose
now to live retir'd, frugal, and within ourselves; I kept no company, made no visits; minded my family, and obliged my husband; and this kind of life became a pleasure to me.

We liv'd in an uninterrupted course of ease and content for
five years, when a sudden blow from an almost invisible hand
blasted all my happiness, and turn'd me out into the world in
a condition the reverse of all that had been before it.

My husband having trusted one of his fellow clarks with
a sum of money, too much for our fortunes to bear the loss
of, the clark fail'd, and the loss fell very heavy on my husband,
yet it was not so great but that if he had had courage to
have look'd his misfortunes in the face, his credit was so good,
that, as I told him, he would easily recover it; for to sink
under trouble is to double the weight, and he that will die in
it, shall die in it.

It was in vain to speak comfortably to him; the wound had
sunk too deep, it was a stab that touch'd the vitals; he grew
melancholy and disconsolate, and from thence lethargick, and
died; I foresaw the blow, and was extremely oppress'd in my
mind, for I saw evidently that if he died I was undone.

I had had two children by him and no more, for it began
to be time for me to leave bearing children, for I was now
eight and forty, and I suppose if he had liv'd I should have had no
more.

I was now left in a dismal and disconsolate case indeed, and
in several things worse than ever. First, it was past the flourishing time with me when I might expect to be courted for a
mistress; that agreeable part had declin'd some time, and the
ruins only appear'd of what had been; and that which was

[1] experience.

worse than all was this, that I was the most dejected, disconsolate creature alive; I that had encourag'd my husband, and endeavour'd to support his spirits under his trouble, could not support my own; I wanted that spirit in trouble which I told him was so necessary for bearing the burthen.

But my case was indeed deplorable, for I was left perfectly friendless and helpless, and the loss my husband had sustain'd had reduc'd his circumstances so low, that tho' indeed I was not in debt, yet I could easily foresee that what was left would not support me long; that it wasted daily for subsistence, so that it would be soon all spent, and then I saw nothing before me but the utmost distress, and this represented it self so lively to my thoughts that it seem'd as if it was come before it was really very near; also my very apprehensions doubl'd the misery, for I fancied every sixpence that I paid for a loaf of bread was the last I had in the world, and that to-morrow I was to fast, and be starv'd to death.

In this distress I had no assistant, no friend to comfort or advise me, I sat and cried and tormented myself night and day; wringing my hands, and sometimes raving like a distracted woman; and indeed I have often wonder'd it had not affected my reason, for I had the vapours to such a degree that my understanding was sometimes quite lost in fancies and imaginations.

I liv'd two years in this dismal condition, wasting that little I had, weeping continually over my dismal circumstances, and as it were only bleeding to death, without the least hope or prospect of help; and now I had cried so long, and so often, that tears were exhausted, and I began to be desperate, for I grew poor apace.

For a little relief, I had put off my house and took lodgings; and as I was reducing my living, so I sold off most of my goods, which put a little money in my pocket, and I liv'd near a year upon that, spending very sparingly, and eeking things out to the utmost; but still when I look'd before me, my heart would sink within me at the inevitable approach of misery and want. O, let none read this part without seriously reflecting on the circumstances of a desolate state, and how they would grapple with want of friends and want of bread; it will certainly make them think not of sparing what they have only, but of looking up to Heaven for support, and of the wise man's prayer, *Give me not poverty lest I steal.*

Let 'em remember that a time of distress is a time of dreadful temptation, and all the strength to resist is taken away; poverty presses, the soul is made desperate by distress, and what can be done? It was one evening, when, being brought, as I may say, to the last gasp, I think I may truly say I was distracted and raving, when prompted by I know not what spirit, and, as it were, doing I did not know what, or why, I dress'd me, for I had still pretty good cloaths, and went out. I am very sure I had no manner of design in my head when I went out, I neither knew or consider'd where to go, or on what business; but as the Devil carried me out, and laid his bait for me, so he brought me to be sure to the place, for I knew not whither I was going or what I did.

Wandring thus about I knew not whither, I pass'd by an apothecary's shop in Leadenhall-street, where I saw lye on a stool just before the compter a little bundle wrapt in a white cloth; beyond it stood a maid servant with her back to it, looking up towards the top of the shop, where the apothecary's apprentice, as I suppose, was standing upon the compter, with his back also to the door, and a candle in his hand, looking and reaching up to the upper shelf for something he wanted, so that both were engag'd, and no body else in the shop.

This was the bait; and the Devil who laid the snare prompted me, as if he had spoke, for I remember, and shall never forget it, 'twas like a voice spoken over my shoulder, Take the bundle; be quick; do it this moment. It was no sooner said but I step'd into the shop, and with my back to the wench, as if I had stood up for a cart that was going by, I put my hand behind me and took the bundle, and went off with it, the maid or fellow not perceiving me, or any one else.

It is impossible to express the horror of my soul all the while I did it. When I went away I had no heart to run, or scarce to mend my pace; I cross'd the street indeed, and went down the first turning I came to, and I think it was a street that went thro' into Fenchurch-street; from thence I crossed and turn'd thro' so many ways and turnings that I could never tell which way it was, nor where I went, I felt not the ground I stept on, and the farther I was out of danger, the faster I went, till tyr'd and out of breath, I was forc'd to sit down on a little bench at a door, and then found I was got into Thames-street, near Billingsgate. I rested me a little and went on; my blood was all in a fire, my heart beat as if I was in a sudden fright: in short, I was under such a surprize that I knew not whither I was a going, or what to do.

After I had tyr'd my self thus with walking a long way about, and so eagerly, I began to consider and make home to my lodging, where I came about nine a clock at night.

What the bundle was made up for, or on what occasion laid where I found it, I knew not, but when I came to open it, I found there was a suit of child-bed linnen in it, very good and almost new, the lace very fine; there was a silver porringer of a pint, a small silver mug and six spoons, with some other linnen, a good smock, and three silk handkerchiefs, and in the mug, in a paper, eighteen shillings and six-pence in money.

All the while I was opening these things I was under such dreadful impressions of fear, and in such terror of mind, tho' I was perfectly safe, that I cannot express the manner of it; I sat me down and cried most vehemently. Lord, said I, what am I now? a thief! why, I shall be taken next time and be carried to Newgate and be try'd for my life! and with that I cry'd again a long time, and I am sure, as poor as I was, if I had durst for fear, I would certainly have carried the things back again; but that went off after a while. Well, I went to bed for that night, but slept little; the horror of the fact was upon my mind, and I knew not what I said or did all night, and all the next day. Then I was impatient to hear some news of the loss; and would fain know how it was, whether they were a poor bodie's goods, or a rich; perhaps, said I, it may be some poor widow like me that had pack'd up these goods to go and sell them for a little bread for herself and a poor child, and are now starving and breaking their hearts, for want of that little they would have fetch'd; and this thought tormented me worse than all the rest, for three or four days.

But my own distresses silenc'd all these reflections, and the prospect of my own starving, which grew every day more

frightful to me, harden'd my heart by degrees; it was then particularly heavy upon my mind that I had been reform'd and had,
as I hop'd, repented of all my pass'd wickednesses; that I had
liv'd a sober, grave, retir'd life for several years, but now I
should be driven by the dreadful necessity of my circumstances
to the gates of destruction, soul and body; and two or three
times I fell upon my knees, praying to God, as well as I could,
for deliverance; but I cannot but say my prayers had no hope in
them; I knew not what to do, it was all fear without, and dark
within; and I reflected on my pass'd life as not repented of, that
Heaven was now beginning to punish me, and would make me
as miserable as I had been wicked.

Had I gone on here I had perhaps been a true penitent; but
I had an evil counsellor within, and he was continually prompting to relieve my self by the worst means; so one evening
he tempted me again by the same wicked impulse that had said,
Take that bundle, to go out again and seek for what might
happen.

I went out now by day-light, and wandred about I knew not
whither, and in search of I knew not what, when the Devil put
a snare in my way of a dreadful nature indeed, and such a one
as I have never had before or since; going thro' Aldersgate-street,
there was a pretty little child had been at a dancing-school, and
was a going home all alone, and my prompter, like a true devil,
set me upon this innocent creature; I talk'd to it, and it prattl'd
to me again, and I took it by the hand and led it a long till I
came to a pav'd alley that goes into Bartholomew-Close, and
I led it in there. The child said that was not its way home; I
said, Yes, my dear, it is, I'll show you the way home. The child
had a little necklace on of gold beads, and I had my eye upon
that, and in the dark of the alley I stoop'd, pretending to mend
the child's clog that was loose, and took off her necklace, and the
child never felt it, and so led the child on again. Here, I say,
the Devil put me upon killing the child in the dark alley, that it
might not cry, but the very thought frighted me so that I
was ready to drop down, but I turn'd the child about and bad
it go back again, for that was not its way home; the child
said so she would, and I went thro' into Bartholomew-Close,
and then turn'd round to another passage that goes into Long-

lane, so away into Charterhouse-Yard, and out into St. John's-street; then crossing into Smithfield, went down Chick-lane, and into Field-lane, to Holbourn-bridge, when, mixing with the crowd of people usually passing there, it was not possible to have been found out; and thus I made my second sally into the world.

The thoughts of this booty put out all the thoughts of the first, and the reflections I had made wore quickly off; poverty harden'd my heart, and my own necessities made me regardless of anything. The last affair left no great concern upon me, for as I did the poor child no harm, I only thought I had given the parents a just reproof for their negligence, in leaving the poor lamb to come home by it self, and it would teach them to take more care another time.

This string of beads was worth about twelve or fourteen pounds, I suppose it might have been formerly the mother's, for it was too big for the child's wear, but that, perhaps, the vanity of the mother to have her child look fine at the dancing school had made her let the child wear it, and no doubt the child had a maid sent to take care of it, but she, like a careless jade, was taken up perhaps with some fellow that had met her, and so the poor baby wandred till it fell into my hands.

However, I did the child no harm, I did not so much as fright it, for I had a great many tender thoughts about me yet, and did nothing but what, as I may say, meer necessity drove me to.

I had a great many adventures after this, but I was young in the business, and did not know how to manage, otherwise than as the Devil put things into my head; and indeed he was seldom backward to me. One adventure I had which was very lucky to me; I was going thro' Lombard-street in the dusk of the evening, just by the end of Three King Court, when on a sudden comes a fellow running by me as swift as lightning, and throws a bundle that was in his hand just behind me, as I stood up against the corner of the house at the turning into the alley; just as he threw it in, he said, God bless you, mistress, let it lie there a little, and away he runs. After him comes two more, and immediately a young fellow without his hat, crying Stop thief! they persued the two last fellows so close that they were forc'd to drop what they had got, and one of them was taken into the bargain, the other got off free.

I stood stock still all this while till they came back, dragging the poor fellow they had taken, and lugging the things they had found, extremely well satisfied that they had recovered the booty, and taken the thief; and thus they pass'd by me, for I look'd only like one who stood up while the crowd was gone.

Once or twice I ask'd what was the matter, but the people neglected answering me, and I was not very importunate; but after the crowd was wholly pass'd, I took my opportunity to turn about and take up what was behind me and walk away. This indeed I did with less disturbance than I had done formerly, for these things I did not steal, but they were stolen to my hand. I got safe to my lodgings with this cargo, which was a peice of fine black lustring [1] silk, and a peice of velvet; the latter was but part of a peice of about 11 yards; the former was a whole peice of near 50 yards; it seems it was a mercer's shop that they had rifl'd; I say, rifled, because the goods were so considerable that they had lost; for the goods that they recover'd were pretty many, and I believe came to about six or seven several peices of silk. How they came to get so many I could not tell; but as I had only robb'd the thief, I made no scruple at taking these goods, and being very glad of them too.

I had pretty good luck thus far, and I made several adventures more, tho' with but small purchase,[2] yet with good success, but I went in daily dread that some mischief would befal me, and that I should certainly come to be hang'd at last. The impression this made on me was too strong to be slighted, and it kept me from making attempts that, for ought I knew, might have been very safely perform'd; but one thing I cannot omit, which was a bait to me many a day. I walked frequently out into the villages round the town to see if nothing would fall in my way there; and going by a house near Stepney, I saw on the window-board two rings, one a small diamond ring, and the other a plain gold ring, to be sure, laid there by some thoughtless lady that had more money than forecast,[3] perhaps only till she wash'd her hands.

I walk'd several times by the window to observe if I could

---

[1] a glossy silk fabric.   [2] booty, gains.   [3] prudence.

see whether there was any body in the room or no, and I could see no body, but still I was not sure; it came presently into my thoughts to rap at the glass, as if I wanted to speak with some body, and if any body was there they would be sure to come to the window, and then I would tell them to remove those rings, for that I had seen two suspicious fellows take notice of them. This was a ready thought; I rapt once or twice and nobody came, when I thrust hard against the square of glass, and broke it with little noise, and took out the two rings, and walk'd away; the diamond ring was worth about 3*l.*, and the other about 9*s.*

I was now at a loss for a market for my goods, and especially for my two peices of silk, I was very loth to dispose of them for a trifle; as the poor unhappy thieves in general do, who, after they have ventur'd their lives for perhaps a thing of value, are forc'd to sell it for a song when they have done; but I was resolv'd I would not do thus, whatever shift I made; however, I did not well know what course to take. At last I resolv'd to go to my old governess, and acquaint my self with her again; I had punctually supply'd the 5*l.* a year to her for my little boy as long as I was able; but at last was oblig'd to put a stop to it. However, I had written a letter to her, wherein I had told her that my circumstances were reduc'd; that I had lost my husband, and that I was not able to do it any longer, and beg'd the poor child might not suffer too much for its mother's misfortunes.

I now made her a visit, and I found that she drove something of the old trade still, but that she was not in such flourishing circumstances as before; for she had been sued by a certain gentleman who had had his daughter stolen from him; and who it seems she had helped to convey away; and it was very narrowly that she escap'd the gallows; the expence also had ravag'd her, so that her house was but meanly furnished, and she was not in such repute for her practice as before; however, she stood upon her legs, as they say, and as she was a bustling woman, and had some stock left, she was turn'd pawn-broker, and liv'd pretty well.

She receiv'd me very civilly, and with her usual obliging manner told me she would not have the less respect for me, for my being reduc'd; that she had taken care my boy was very well look'd after, tho' I could not pay for him, and that the woman that had him was easie, so that I needed not to trouble my self about him, till I might be better able to do it effectually.

I told her I had not much money left, but that I had some things that were monie's worth, if she could tell me how I might turn them into money; she ask'd what it was I had. I pull'd out the string of gold beads, and told her it was one of my husband's presents to me; then I show'd her the two parcels of silk which I told her I had from Ireland, and brought up to town with me, and the little diamond ring; as to the small parcel of plate and spoons, I had found means to dispose of them my self before; and as for the childbed linnen I had, she offer'd me to take it her self, believing it to have been my own; she told me that she was turn'd pawn-broker, and that she would sell those things for me as pawn'd to her, and so she sent presently for proper agents that bought them, being in her hands, without any scruple, and gave good prizes [1] too.

I now began to think this necessary woman might help me a little in my low condition to some business; for I would gladly have turn'd my hand to any honest employment if I could have got it; but honest business did not come within her reach; if I had been younger, perhaps she might have helped me, but my thoughts were off of that kind of livelihood, as being quite out of the way after 50, which was my case, and so I told her.

She invited me at last to come, and be at her house till I could find something to do, and it should cost me very little, and this I gladly accepted of; and now living a little easier, I enter'd into some measures to have my little son by my last husband taken off; and this she made easie too, reserving a payment only of 5*l.* a year, if I could pay it. This was such a help to me that for a good while I left off the wicked trade that I had so newly taken up; and gladly I would have got work, but that was very hard to do for one that had no acquaintance.

However, at last I got some quilting work for ladies' beds, petticoats, and the like; and this I lik'd very well and work'd very hard, and with this I began to live; but the diligent devil who resolv'd I should continue in his service continually

----

[1] prices.

prompted me to go out and take a walk, that is to say, to see if any thing would offer in the old way.

One evening I blindly obeyed his summons, and fetch'd a long circuit thro' the streets, but met with no purchase; but not content with that, I went out the next evening too, when going by an alehouse I saw the door of a little room open, next the very street, and on the table a silver tankard, things much in use in publick houses at that time; it seems some company had been drinking there, and the careless boys had forgot to take it away.

I went into the box frankly, and setting the silver tankard on the corner of the bench, I sat down before it, and knock'd with my foot; a boy came presently, and I bad him fetch me a pint of warm ale, for it was cold weather; the boy run, and I heard him go down the cellar to draw the ale; while the boy was gone, another boy come, and cried, D'ye call? I spoke with a melancholly air, and said, No, the boy is gone for a pint of ale for me.

While I sat here, I heard the woman in the bar say, Are they all gone in the Five? which was the box I sat in, and the boy said, Yes. Who fetch'd the tankard away? says the woman. I did, says another boy; that's it — pointing, it seems, to another tankard, which he had fetch'd from another box by mistake; or else it must be that the rogue forgot that he had not brought it in, which certainly he had not.

I heard all this, much to my satisfaction, for I found plainly that the tankard was not mist, and yet they concluded it was fetch'd away; so I drank my ale, call'd to pay, and as I went away, I said, Take care of your plate, child, meaning a silver pint mug which he brought me to drink in; the boy said, Yes, madam, very welcome, and away I came.

I came home to my governess, and now I thought it was a time to try her, that if I might be put to the necessity of being expos'd she might offer me some assistance; when I had been at home some time, and had an opportunity of talking to her, I told her I had a secret of the greatest consequence in the world to commit to her, if she had respect enough for me to keep it a secret: she told me she had kept one of my secrets faithfully; why should I doubt her keeping another? I told her the strangest thing in the world had befallen me, even without any design; and so told her the whole story of the tankard.

And have you brought it away with you, my dear? says she. To be sure I have, says I, and shew'd it her. But what shall I do now, says I, must not I carry it again?

Carry it again! says she. Ay, if you want to go to Newgate. Why, says I, they can't be so base to stop me, when I carry it to them again? You don't know those sort of people, child, says she, they'll not only carry you to Newgate, but hang you too without any regard to the honesty of returning it; or bring in an account of all the other tankards as they have lost for you to pay for. What must I do then? says I. Nay, says she, as you have plaid the cunning part and stole it, you must e'en keep it, there's no going back now; besides child, says she, don't you want it more than they do? I wish you could light of such a bargain once a week.

This gave me a new notion of my governess, and that since she was turn'd pawn-broker, she had a sort of people about her that were none of the honest ones that I had met with there before.

I had not been long there but I discover'd it more plainly than before, for every now and then I saw hilts of swords, spoons, forks, tankards, and all such kind of ware brought in, not to be pawn'd, but to be sold down right; and she bought them all without asking any questions, but had good bargains as I found by her discourse.

I found also that in following this trade she always melted down the plate she bought, that it might not be challeng'd; and she came to me and told me one morning that she was going to melt, and if I would, she would put my tankard in, that it might not be seen by any body; I told her with all my heart; so she weigh'd it, and allow'd me the full value in silver again; but I found she did not do so to the rest of her customers.

Sometime after this, as I was at work, and very melancholly, she begins to ask me what the matter was? I told her my heart was very heavy, I had little work, and nothing to live on, and knew not what course to take; she laugh'd and told me I must go out again and try my fortune; it might be that I might meet with another peice of plate. O, mother! says I, that is a trade that I have no skill in, and if I should be taken I am undone at once. Says she, I could help you to a school-mistress that

shall make you as dexterous as her self. I trembled at that proposal, for hitherto I had had no confederates, nor any acquaintance among that tribe; but she conquer'd all my modesty,
and all my fears; and in a little time, by the help of this
confederate, I grew as impudent a thief, and as dexterous, as ever
Moll Cut-Purse [1] was, tho' if fame does not belie her, not half
so handsome.

The comrade she helped me to dealt in three sorts of craft,
(*viz.*) shop-lifting, stealing of shop-books and pocket-books, and
taking off gold watches from the ladies' sides; and this last she
did so dexterously that no woman ever arriv'd to the perfection
of that art like her. I lik'd the first and the last of these things
very well, and I attended her some time in the practice, just as
a deputy attends a midwife without any pay.

At length she put me to practice; she had shewn me her art,
and I had several times unhook'd a watch from her own side
with great dexterity; at last she show'd me a prize, and this was
a young lady with child who had a charming watch; the thing
was to be done as she came out of the church; she goes on one
side of the lady, and pretends, just as she came to the steps,
to fall, and fell against the lady with so much violence as put
her into a great fright, and both cry'd out terribly: in the very
moment that she jostl'd the lady, I had hold of the watch, and
holding it the right way, the start she gave drew the hook out
and she never felt it; I made off immediately, and left my
school-mistress to come out of her fright gradually, and the
lady too; and presently the watch was miss'd. Ay, says my comrade, then it was those rogues that thrust me down, I warrant
ye; I wonder the gentle-woman did not miss her watch before,
then we might have taken them.

She humour'd the thing so well that no body suspected her,
and I was got home a full hour before her. This was my first
adventure in company; the watch was indeed a very fine one, and
had many trinkets about it, and my governess allow'd us 20*l.* for
it, of which I had half, and thus I was enter'd a compleat thief,
harden'd to a pitch above all the reflections of conscience or
modesty, and to a degree which I never thought possible in me.

Thus the devil who began, by the help of an irresistible

---

[1] Mary Frith (d. 1649), a celebrated pickpocket.

poverty, to push me into this wickedness, brought me on to a height beyond the common rate, even when my necessities were not so terrifying; for I had now got into a little vein of work, and as I was not at a loss to handle my needle, it was very probable I might have got my bread honestly enough.

I must say that if such a prospect of work had presented it self at first, when I began to feel the approach of my miserable circumstances; I say, had such a prospect of getting bread by working presented it self then, I had never fallen into this wicked trade, or into such a wicked gang as I was now embark'd with; but practice had hardened me, and I grew audacious to the last degree; and the more so, because I had carried it on so long, and had never been taken; for in a word, my new partner in wickedness and I went on together so long, without being ever detected, that we not only grew bold, but we grew rich, and we had at one time one and twenty gold watches in our hands.

I remember that one day being a little more serious than ordinary, and finding I had so good a stock beforehand as I had, for I had near 200*l.* in money for my share, it came strongly into my mind, no doubt from some kind spirit, if such there be, that as at first poverty excited me, and my distresses drove me to these dreadful shifts; so seeing those distresses were now relieved, and I could also get something towards a mainte-nance by working, and had so good a bank to support me, why should I not now leave off, while I was well; that I could not expect to go always free; and if I was once surpris'd, I was undone.

This was doubtless the happy minute, when, if I had hearken'd to the blessed hint from whatsoever hand it came, I had still a cast[1] for an easie life; but my fate was otherwise de-termin'd, the busie devil that drew me in had too fast hold of me to let me go back; but as poverty brought me in, so avarice kept me in, till there was no going back; as to the arguments which my reason dictated for perswading me to lay down, avarice stept in and said, Go on, you have had very good luck, go on till you have gotten four or five hundred pound, and then you shall leave off, and then you may live easie without working at all.

[1] chance.

Thus I that was once in the Devil's clutches was held fast there as with a charm, and had no power to go without the circle, till I was ingulph'd in labyrinths of trouble too great to get out at all.

However, these thoughts left some impression upon me, and made me act with some more caution than before, and more than my directors us'd for themselves. My comrade, as I called her, she should have been called my teacher, with another of her scholars, was the first in the misfortune; for happening to be upon the hunt for purchase, they made an attempt upon a linnen-draper in Cheapside, but were snap'd by a hawk's-ey'd journey-man, and seiz'd with two pieces of cambrick, which were taken also upon them.

This was enough to lodge them both in Newgate, where they had the misfortune to have some of their former sins brought to remembrance; two other indictments being brought against them, and the facts being prov'd upon them, they were both con-demn'd to die; they both pleaded their bellies and were both voted quick with child; tho' my tutress was no more with child than I was.

I went frequently to see them, and condole with them, ex-pecting that it would be my turn next; but the place gave me so much horror, reflecting that it was the place of my unhappy birth, and of my mother's misfortunes, that I could not bear it, so I left off going to see them.

And O! cou'd I but have taken warning by their disasters, I had been happy still, for I was yet free, and had nothing brought against me; but it could not be, my measure was not yet fill'd up.

My comrade, having the brand of an old offender, was exe-cuted; the young offender was spar'd, having obtained a reprieve; but lay starving a long while in prison, till at last she got her name into what they call a circuit pardon, and so came off.

This terrible example of my comrade frighted me heartily, and for a good while I made no excursions; but one night, in the neighbourhood of my governess's house, they cry'd, Fire; my governess look'd out, for we were all up, and cry'd immedi-ately that such a gentlewoman's house was all of a light fire a top, and so indeed it was. Here she gives me a jog. Now, child, says she, there is a rare opportunity, the fire being so near that you may go to it before the street is block'd up with the crowd. She presently gave me my cue: Go, child, says she, to the house, and run in and tell the lady, or any body you see, that you come to help them, and that you came from such a gentlewoman (that is, one of her acquaintance farther up the street).

Away I went, and coming to the house I found them all in confusion, you may be sure; I run in, and finding one of the maids, Alas! sweetheart, said I, how came this dismal accident? where is your mistress? Is she safe? And where are the children? I come from Madam —— to help you. Away runs the maid; Madam, madam, says she, screaming as loud as she cou'd yell, here is a gentlewoman come from Madam —— to help us. The poor woman half out of her wits, with a bundle under her arm, and two little children, comes towards me. Madam, says I, let me carry the poor children to Madam —— , she desires you to send them; she'll take care of the poor lambs; and so I takes one of them out of her hand, and she lifts the tother up into my arms. Ay, do, for God sake, says she, carry them; O thank her for her kindness. Have you anything else to secure, madam? says I, she will take care of it. O dear! says she, God bless her, take this bundle of plate and carry it to her too; O, she is a good woman; O, we are utterly ruin'd, undone; and away she runs from me out of her wits, and the maids after her, and away comes I with the two children and the bundle.

I was no sooner got into the street, but I saw another woman come to me. O! says she, mistress, in a piteous tone, you will let fall the child; come, come, this is a sad time, let me help you, and immediately lays hold of my bundle to carry it for me. No, says I, if you will help me, take the child by the hand, and lead it for me but to the upper end of the street, I'll go with you and satisfie you for your pains.

She could not avoid going, after what I said, but the creature, in short, was one of the same business with me, and wanted nothing but the bundle; however, she went with me to the door, for she could not help it; when we were come there I whisper'd her, Go child, said I, I understand your trade, you may meet with purchase enough.

She understood me and walk'd off; I thundered at the door

with the children, and as the people were rais'd before by the noise of the fire, I was soon let in, and I said, Is Madam awake? pray tell her Mrs. —— desires the favour of her to take the two children in; poor lady, she will be undone, their house is all of a flame. They took the children in very civily, pitied the family in distress, and away came I with my bundle; one of the maids ask'd me if I was not to leave the bundle too; I said, No, sweetheart, 'tis to go to another place, it does not belong to them.

I was a great way out of the hurry now, and so I went on, and brought the bundle of plate, which was very considerable, strait home to my old governess; she told me she would not look into it, but bad me go again and look for more.

She gave me the like cue to the gentlewoman of the next house to that which was on fire, and I did my endeavour to go, but by this time the allarm of fire was so great, and so many engines playing and the street so throng'd with people, that I cou'd not get near the house, whatever I cou'd do; so I came back again to my governesses, and taking the bundle up into my chamber, I began to examine it. It is with horror that I tell what a treasure I found there; 'tis enough to say, that besides most of the family plate, which was considerable, I found a gold chain, an old-fashion'd thing, the locket of which was broken, so that I suppose it had not been us'd some years, but the gold was not the worse for that; also a little box of burying rings, the lady's wedding-ring, and some broken bits of old lockets of gold, a gold watch, and a purse with about 24*l.* value in old pieces of gold coin, and several other things of value.

This was the greatest and the worst prize that ever I was concern'd in, for indeed, tho', as I have said above, I was harden'd now beyond the power of all reflection in other cases, yet it really touch'd me to the very soul when I look'd into this treasure, to think of the poor disconsolate gentlewoman who had lost so much besides, and who would think to be sure that she had sav'd her plate and best things; how she wou'd be surpriz'd when she should find that she had been deceiv'd, and that the person that took her children and her goods had not come, as was pretended, from the gentlewoman in next

street, but that the children had been put upon her without her
own knowledge.

I say, I confess the inhumanity of this action mov'd me very
much, and made me relent exceedingly, and tears stood in my
eyes upon that subject, But with all my sense of its being cruel
and inhuman, I cou'd never find in my heart to make any
restitution: the reflection wore off, and I quickly forgot the
circumstances that attended it.

Nor was this all, for tho' by this jobb I was become con-
siderably richer than before, yet the resolution I had formerly
taken of leaving off this horrid trade, when I had gotten a little
more, did not return; but I must still get more; and the avarice
had such success, that I had no more thoughts of coming to a
timely alteration of life; tho' without it I cou'd expect no safety,
no tranquility in the possession of what I had gain'd; a little more,
and a little more, was the case still.

At length yielding to the importunities of my crime, I cast off
all remorse, and all the reflections on that head turn'd to no more
than this, that I might perhaps come to have one booty more
that might compleat all; but tho' I certainly had that one booty,
yet every hit look'd towards another, and was so encouraging
to me to go on with the trade that I had no gust [1] to the laying
it down.

In this condition, harden'd by success, and resolving to go
on, I fell into the snare in which I was appointed to meet
with my last reward for this kind of life. But even this was
not yet, for I met with several successful adventures more in
this way.

My governess was for awhile really concern'd for this misfortune of my comrade that had been hang'd, for she knew
enough of my governess to have sent her the same way, and
which made her very uneasy; indeed she was in a very great
fright.

It is true, that when she was gone and had not told what
she knew, my governess was easy as to that point, and perhaps
glad she was hang'd; for it was in her power to have obtain'd
a pardon at the expence of her friends; but the loss of her, and
the sense of her kindness in not making her market [2] of what

---

[1] inclination.
[2] doing a deal (i.e., betraying her confederates).

she knew, mov'd my governess to mourn very sincerely for
her. I comforted her as well as I cou'd, and she in return
harden'd me to merit more compleatly the same fate.

However, as I said, it made me the more wary, and par
ticularly I was very shie of shop-lifting, especially among the
mercers and drapers, who are a set of fellows, that have their
eyes very much about them. I made a venture or two among the
lace folks, and the milleners, and particularly at one shop, where
two young women were newly set up, and had not been bred
to trade: there, I carried off a piece of bonelace,[1] worth six or
seven pound, and a paper of thread; but this was but once, it
was a trick that would not serve again.

It was always reckon'd a safe job when we heard of a new
shop, and especially when the people were such as were not bred
to shops; such may depend upon it that they will be visited
once or twice at their beginning, and they must be very sharp
indeed if they can prevent it.

I made another adventure or two after this, but they were
but trifles. Nothing considerable offering for a good while, I
began to think that I must give over trade in earnest; but my
governess, who was not willing to lose me, and expected great
things of me, brought me one day into company with a young
woman and a fellow that went for her husband, tho' as it
appear'd afterwards she was not his wife, but they were partners
in the trade they carried on; and in something else too. In
short, they robb'd together, lay together, were taken together,
and at last were hang'd together.

I came into a kind of league with these two by the help
of my governess, and they carried me out into three or four
adventures, where I rather saw them commit some coarse and
unhandy robberies, in which nothing but a great stock of impudence on their side, and gross negligence on the people's
side who were robb'd, could have made them successful; so
I resolv'd from that time forward to be very cautious how I
adventur'd with them; and indeed when two or three unlucky[2]
projects were propos'd by them, I declin'd the offer, and perswaded them against it. One time they particularly propos'd
robbing a watchmaker of 3 gold watches, which they had ey'd

1 lace knitted upon a pattern marked by pins, with bobbins made of bone
2 likely to fail.

in the day time, and found the place where he laid them; one of them had so many keys of all kinds, that he made no question to open the place where the watchmaker had laid them; and so we made a kind of an appointment; but when I came to look narrowly into the thing, I found they propos'd breaking open the house, and this I would not embark in, so they went without me. They did get into the house by main force, and broke up the lock'd place where the watches were, but found but one of the gold watches, and a silver one, which they took, and got out of the house again very clear; but the family being alarm'd cried out, *Thieves!*, and the man was pursued and taken, the young woman had got off too, but unhappily was stop'd at a distance, and the watches found upon her; and thus I had a second escape, for they were convicted, and both hang'd, being old offenders, tho' but young people; and as I said before that they robb'd together, so now they hang'd together, and there ended my new partnership.

I began now to be very wary, having so narrowly escap'd a scouring,[1] and having such an example before me; but I had a new tempter who prompted me every day, I mean my governess; and now a prize presented, which as it came by her management, so she expected a good share of the booty. There was a good quantity of Flanders-lace lodg'd in a private house, where she had heard of it; and Flanders lace being prohibited, it was a good booty to any custom-house officer that could come at it: I had a full account from my governess, as well of the quantity as of the very place where it was conceal'd, so I went to a customhouse officer, and told him I had a discovery to make to him, if he would assure me that I should have my due share of the reward. This was so just an offer that nothing could be fairer; so he agreed, and taking a constable, and me with him, we beset the house; as I told him I could go directly to the place, he left it to me, and the hole being very dark, I squeez'd myself into it, with a candle in my hand, and so reach'd the peices out to him, taking care, as I gave him some, so to secure as much about myself as I could conveniently dispose of. There was near 300*l.* worth of lace in the whole; and I secur'd about 50*l.* worth of it myself. The people of the house were not owners

---

[1] chastising.

of the lace, but a merchant who had entrusted them with it; so that they were not so surpriz'd as I thought they would be.

I left the officer overjoy'd with his prize, and fully satisfy'd with what he had got, and appointed to meet him at a house of his own directing, where I came after I had dispos'd of the cargo I had about me, of which he had not the least suspicion; when I came, he began to capitulate,[1] believing I did not understand the right I had in the prize, and would fain have put me off with twenty pound, but I let him know that I was not so ignorant as he suppos'd I was; and yet I was glad too that he offer'd to bring me to a certainty; I asked 100*l.* and he rose up to 30*l.*; I fell to 80*l.* and he rose again to 40*l.*; in a word, he offered 50*l.* and I consented, only demanding a piece of lace which I thought came to about 8 or 9 pound, as if it had been for my own wear, and he agreed to it, so I got 50*l.* in money paid me that same night, and made an end of the bargain; nor did he ever know who I was, or where to enquire for me; so that if it had been discover'd that part of the goods were embezzel'd, he could have made no challenge upon me for it.

I very punctually [2] divided this spoil with my governess, and I pass'd with her from this time for a very dexterous manager in the nicest cases; I found that this last was the best and easiest sort of work that was in my way, and I made it my business to enquire out prohibited goods; and after buying some usually betray'd them, but none of these discoveries amounted to any thing considerable, not like that I related just now; but I was cautious of running the great risques which I found others did, and in which they miscarried every day.

The next thing of moment was an attempt at a gentlewoman's gold watch; it happen'd in a crowd, at a meeting-house, where I was in very great danger of being taken; I had full hold of her watch, but giving a great jostle, as if some body had thrust me against her, and in the juncture giving the watch a fair pull, I found it would not come, so I let it go that moment, and cried as if I had been kill'd, that somebody had trod upon my foot, and that there was certainly pick-pockets there; for some body or other had given a pull at my watch, for you are to observe

---

[1] make terms, bargain.   [2] scrupulously.

that on these adventures we always went very well dress'd, and I had very good cloths on, and a gold watch by my side, as like a lady as other folks.

I had no sooner said so, but the other gentlewoman cried out, *A pick-pocket!* too, for some body, she said, had try'd to pull her watch away.

When I touch'd her watch, I was close to her, but when I cry'd out, I stop'd as it were short, and the crowd bearing her forward a little, she made a noise too, but it was at some distance from me, so that she did not in the least suspect me, but when she cried out, *A pick-pocket!* some body cried out, Ay, and here has been another, this gentlewoman has been attempted too.

At that very instant, a little farther in the crowd, and very luckily too, they cried out, *A pick-pocket!* again, and really seiz'd a young fellow in the very fact. This, tho' unhappy for the wretch, was very opportunely for my case, tho' I had carried it handsomely enough before, but now it was out of doubt, and all the loose part of the crowd ran that way, and the poor boy was deliver'd up to the rage of the street, which is a cruelty I need not describe, and which, however, they are always glad of, rather than be sent to Newgate, where they lie often a long time, and sometimes they are hang'd, and the best they can look for, if they are convicted, is to be transported.

This was a narrow escape to me, and I was so frighted that I ventur'd no more at gold watches a great while; there were indeed many circumstances in this adventure which assisted to my escape; but the chief was that the woman whose watch I had pull'd at was a fool; that is to say, she was ignorant of the nature of the attempt, which one would have thought she should not have been, seeing she was wise enough to fasten her watch, so that it could not be slipt up; but she was in such a fright that she had no thought about her; for she, when she felt the pull, scream'd out, and push'd herself forward, and put all the people about her into disorder, but said not a word of her watch, or of a pick-pocket, for at least two minutes; which was time enough for me, and to spare; for as I had cried out behind her, as I have said, and bore myself back in the crowd as she bore forward, there were several people, at least seven or eight, the throng being still moving on, that were got between me and her in that time, and then I crying out *A pick-pocket!* rather sooner than she, she might as well be the person suspected as I, and the people were confus'd in their enquiry; whereas, had she with a presence of mind needful on such an occasion, as soon as she felt the pull, not skream'd out as she did, but turn'd immediately round, and seiz'd the next body that was behind her, she had infallibly taken me.

This is a direction not of the kindest sort to the fraternity; but 'tis certainly a key to the clue of a pick-pocket's motions, and whoever can follow it will as certainly catch the thief as he will be sure to miss if he does not.

I had another adventure, which puts this matter out of doubt, and which may be an instruction for posterity in the case of a pick-pocket; my good old governess, to give a short touch at her history, tho' she had left off the trade, was, as I may say, born a pick-pocket, and, as I understood afterward, had run thro' all the several degrees of that art, and yet had been taken but once; when she was so grossly detected, that she was convicted and order'd to be transported; but being a woman of a rare tongue, and withal having money in her pocket, she found means, the ship putting into Ireland for provisions, to get on shore there, where she practised her old trade some years; when falling into another sort of company she turned midwife and procuress, and play'd a hundred pranks, which she gave me a little history of, in confidence between us as we grew more intimate; and it was to this wicked creature that I ow'd all the dexterity I arriv'd to, in which there were few that ever went beyond me, or that practis'd so long without any misfortune.

It was after those adventures in Ireland, and when she was pretty well known in that country, that she left Dublin, and came over to England, where the time of her transportation being not expir'd, she left her former trade, for fear of falling into bad hands again, for then she was sure to have gone to wreck. Here she set up the same trade she had followed in Ireland, in which she soon, by her admirable management, and a good tongue, arrived to the height which I have already described, and indeed began to be rich, tho' her trade fell again afterwards.

I mention thus much of the history of this woman here, the better to account for the concern she had in the wicked life I was now leading; into all the particulars of which she led me, as it were, by the hand, and gave me such directions, and I so well follow'd them, that I grew the greatest artist of my time, and work'd myself out of every danger with such dexterity, that when several more of my comrades run themselves into Newgate, by that time they had been half a year at the trade, I had now practis'd upwards of five year, and the people at Newgate did not so much as know me; they had heard much of me indeed, and often expected me there; but I always got off, tho' many times in the extreamest danger.

One of the greatest dangers I was now in was that I was too well known among the trade, and some of them whose hatred was owing rather to envy than any injury I had done them began to be angry that I should always escape when they were always catch'd and hurried to Newgate. These were they that gave me the name of *Moll Flanders:* for it was no more of affinity with my real name, or with any of the names I had ever gone by, than black is of kin to white, except that once, as before, I call'd my self Mrs. Flanders, when I sheltered my self in the Mint; but that these rogues never knew, nor could I ever learn how they came to give me the name, or what the occasion of it was.

I was soon inform'd that some of these who were gotten fast into Newgate had vowed to impeach me; and as I knew that two or three of them were but too able to do it, I was under a great concern, and kept within doors for a good while; but my governess, who was partner in my success, and who now plaid a sure game, for she had no share in the hazard, I say, my governess was something impatient of my leading such a useless unprofitable life, as she call'd it; and she laid a new contrivance for my going abroad, and this was to dress me up in men's cloaths, and so put me into a new kind of practice.

I was tall and personable, but a little too smooth fac'd for a man; however, as I seldom went abroad but in the night it did well enough; but it was long before I could behave in my new cloaths; it was impossible to be so nimble, so ready, so dexterous at these things, in a dress contrary to nature; and as I did every thing clumsily, so I had neither the success or easiness of escape that I had before, and I resolv'd to leave it off; but that resolution was confirm'd soon after by the following accident.

As my governess had disguis'd me like a man, so she joyn'd me with a man, a young fellow that was nimble enough at his business, and for about three weeks we did very well together. Our principal trade was watching shop-keepers' compters,[1] and slipping off any kinds of goods we could see carelessly laid any where, and we made several good bargains, as we call'd them, at this work. And as we kept always together, so we grew very intimate, yet he never knew that I was not a man; nay, tho' I several times went home with him to his lodgings, according as our business directed, and four or five times lay with him all night. But our design lay another way, and it was absolutely necessary to me to conceal my sex from him, as appear'd afterwards. The circumstances of our living, coming in late, and having such business to do as requir'd that no body should be trusted with coming into our lodgings, were such as made it impossible to me to refuse lying with him, unless I would have own'd my sex, and as it was I effectually conceal'd my self.

But his ill, and my good fortune, soon put an end to this life, which I must own I was sick of too. We had made several prizes in this new way of business, but the last would have been extraordinary; there was a shop in a certain street which had a warehouse behind it that look'd into another street, the house making the corner.

Through the window of the warehouse we saw lying on the compter or show-board, which was just before it, five peices of silks, besides other stuffs; and tho' it was almost dark, yet the people being busie in the fore shop had not had time to shut up those windows, or else had forgot it.

This the young fellow was so overjoy'd with, that he could not restrain himself; it lay within his reach, he said, and he swore violently to me that he would have it, if he broke down the house for it; I dissuaded him a little, but saw there was no remedy, so he run rashly upon it, slipt out a square out of the sash window dexterously enough, and got four peices of the silks,

[1] counters.

and came with them towards me, but was immediately persued
with a terrible clutter and noise; we were standing together
indeed, but I had not taken any of the goods out of his hand,
when I said to him hastily, You are undone! He run like lightning, and I too, but the pursuit was hotter after him, because
he had the goods; he dropt two of the peices, which stop'd
them a little, but the crowd encreas'd, and pursued us both;
they took him soon after with the other two peices, and then
the rest follow'd me; I run for it and got into my governess's
house, whither some quick-ey'd people follow'd me so warmly
as to fix me there; they did not immediately knock at the door,
by which I got time to throw off my disguise, and dress me in
my own cloaths; besides, when they came there, my governess,
who had her tale ready, kept her door shut, and call'd out to them
and told them there was no man came in there; the people
affirm'd there did a man come in there, and swore they would
break open the door.

My governess, not at all surpriz'd, spoke calmly to them, told
them they should very freely come and search her house, if
they would bring a constable, and let in none but such as the
constable would admit, for it was unreasonable to let in a whole
crowd; this they could not refuse, tho' they were a crowd;
so a constable was fetch'd immediately, and she very freely
open'd the door; the constable kept the door, and the men he
appointed search'd the house, my governess going with them
from room to room; when she came to my room she call'd to
me, and said aloud, Cousin, pray open the door, here's some
gentlemen that must come and look into your room.

I had a little girl with me, which was my governess's grand-
child, as she call'd her; and I bad her open the door, and there
sat I at work with a great litter of things about me, as if I
had been at work all day, being undress'd, with only night-
cloaths on my head, and a loose morning gown about me.
My governess made a kind of excuse for their disturbing me,
telling partly the occasion of it, and that she had no remedy
but to open the doors to them, and let them satisfie themselves,
for all she could say would not satisfie them. I sat still, and bid
them search if they pleas'd, for if there was any body in the
house, I was sure they was not in my room; and for the rest

of the house I had nothing to say to that, I did not understand what they look'd for.

Every thing look'd so innocent and so honest about me, that they treated me civiller than I expected, but it was not till they had search'd the room to a nicety, even under the bed, and in the bed, and every where else, where it was possible any thing cou'd be hid; when they had done and cou'd find nothing, they ask'd my pardon, and went down.

When they had thus searched the house from bottom to top, and then from top to bottom, and cou'd find nothing, they appeas'd the mob pretty well; but they carried my governess before the justice. Two men swore that they see the man who they pursued go into her house. My governess rattled and made a great noise that her house should be insulted, and that she should be used thus for nothing; that if a man did come in, he might go out again presently for ought she knew, for she was ready to make oath that no man had been within her doors all that day as she knew of; *which was very true*; that it might be, that as she was above stairs, any fellow in a fright might find the door open, and run in for shelter when he was pursued, but that she knew nothing of it; and if it had been so, he certainly went out again, perhaps at the other door, for she had another door into an alley, and so had made his escape.

This was indeed probable enough, and the justice satisfied himself with giving her an oath that she had not receiv'd or admitted any man into her house to conceal him, or protect or hide him from justice. This oath she might justly take, and did so, and so she was dismiss'd.

It is easie to judge what a fright I was in upon this occasion, and it was impossible for my governess ever to bring me to dress in that disguise again; for, as I told her, I should certainly betray myself.

My poor partner in this mischief was now in a bad case, for he was carry'd away before my Lord Mayor, and by his Worship committed to Newgate, and the people that took him were so willing, as well as able, to prosecute him, that they offer'd themselves to enter into recognisances to appear at the sessions, and persue the charge against him.

However, he got his indictment deferr'd, upon promise to

discover his accomplices, and particularly the man that was concern'd with him in this robbery, and he fail'd not to do his endeavour, for he gave in my name, who he call'd Gabriel Spencer, which was the name I went by to him, and here appear'd the wisdom of my concealing my self from him, without which I had been undone.

He did all he could to discover this Gabriel Spencer; he describ'd me; he discover'd the place where he said I lodg'd; and in a word, all the particulars that he could of my dwelling; but having conceal'd the main circumstances of my sex from him, I had a vast advantage, and he could never hear of me; he brought two or three families into trouble by his endeavouring to find me out, but they knew nothing of me, any more than that he had a fellow with him that they had seen, but knew nothing of; and as to my governess, tho' she was the means of his coming to me, yet it was done at second hand, and he knew nothing of her neither.

This turn'd to his disadvantage; for having promis'd discoveries, but not being able to make it good, it was look'd upon as trifling, and he was the more fiercely persued by the shop-keeper.

I was however terribly uneasie all this while, and that I might be quite out of the way, I went away from my governess for a while; but not knowing whither to wander, I took a maid servant wth me, and took the stage-coach to Dunstable to my old landlord and landlady, where I lived so handsomely with my Lancashire husband. Here I told her a formal story, that I expected my husband every day from Ireland, and that I had sent a letter to him that I would meet him at Dunstable at her house, and that he would certainly land, if the wind was fair, in a few days; so that I was come to spend a few days with them till he could come, for he would either come post, or in the West-Chester coach, I knew not which, but which soever it was, he would be sure to come to that house to meet me.

My landlady was mighty glad to see me, and my landlord made such a stir with me that if I had been a princess I could not have been better used, and here I might have been welcome a month or two if I had thought fit.

But my business was of another nature; I was very uneasie,

(though so well disguis'd that it was scarce possible to detect me)
least this fellow should find me out; and tho' he could not
charge me with the robbery, having perswaded him not to venture, and having done nothing of it myself, yet he might have
charg'd me with other things, and have bought his own life at
the expence of mine.

This fill'd me with horrible apprehensions: I had no recourse,
no friend, no confident but my old governess, and I knew no
remedy but to put my life into her hands; and so I did, for I
let her know where to send to me, and had several letters from
her while I stay'd here, some of them almost scar'd me out of
my wits; but at last she sent me the joyful news that he was
hang'd, which was the best news to me that I had heard a great
while.

I had stay'd here five weeks, and liv'd very comfortably indeed (the secret anxiety of my mind excepted), but when I
receiv'd this letter I look'd pleasantly again, and told my landlady that I had receiv'd a letter from my spouse in Ireland, that
I had the good news of his being very well, but had the bad
news that his business would not permit him to come away so
soon as he expected, and so I was like to go back again without him.

My landlady complimented me upon the good news, however,
that I had heard he was well, for I have observ'd, Madam, says
she, you han't been so pleasant as you us'd to be; you have been
over head and ears in care for him, I dare say, says the good
woman; 'tis easie to be seen there's an alteration in you for the
better, says she. Well, I am sorry the esquire can't come yet,
says my landlord; I should have been heartily glad to have seen
him; when you have certain news of his coming, you'll take a
step hither again, madam, says he, you shall be very welcome
whenever you please to come.

With all these fine compliments we parted, and I came merry
enough to London, and found my governess as well pleas'd as
I was; and now she told me she would never recommend any
partner to me again, for she always found, she said, that I had
the best luck when I ventur'd by my self; and so indeed I had,
for I was seldom in any danger when I was by my self, or if
I was, I got out of it with more dexterity than when I was

entangled with the dull measures of other people, who had perhaps less forecast,[1] and were more impatient than I; for tho' I had as much courage to venture as any of them, yet I us'd more caution before I undertook a thing, and had more presence of mind to bring my self off.

I have often wondered even at my own hardiness another way, that when all my companions were surpriz'd, and fell so suddenly into the hand of justice, yet I could not all this while enter into one serious resolution to leave off this trade; and especially considering that I was now very far from being poor, that the temptation of necessity, which is the general introduction of all such wickedness, was now removed; that I had near 500*l.* by me in ready money, on which I might have liv'd very well, if I had thought fit to have retir'd; but, I say, I had not so much as the least inclination to leave off; no, not so much as I had before, when I had but 200*l.* beforehand, and when I had no such frightful examples before my eyes as these were. From hence 'tis evident, that when once we are harden'd in crime, no fear can affect us, no example give us any warning.

I had indeed one comrade whose fate went very near me for a good while, tho' I wore it off too in time; that case was indeed very unhappy. I had made a prize of a piece of very good damask in a mercer's shop, and went clear off my self; but had convey'd the piece to this companion of mine, when we went out of the shop; and she went one way, I went another. We had not been long out of the shop, but the mercer mist the piece of stuff, and sent his messengers, one, one way, and one another, and they presently seiz'd her that had the piece, with the damask upon her; as for me, I had very luckily stept into a house where there was a lace chamber, up one pair of stairs, and had the satisfaction, or the terror indeed, of looking out of the window, and seeing the poor creature drag'd away to the justice, who immediately committed her to Newgate.

I was careful to attempt nothing in the lace-chamber, but tumbl'd their goods pretty much to spend time; then bought a few yards of edging, and paid for it, and came away very sad hearted indeed for the poor woman who was in tribulation, for what I only had stolen.

[1] prudence.

Here again my old caution stood me in good stead; tho'
I often robb'd with these people, yet I never let them know
who I was; nor could they ever find out my lodging, tho' they
often endeavour'd to watch me to it. They all knew me by the
name of Moll Flanders, tho' even some of them rather believ'd
I was she than knew me to be so; my name was publick among
them indeed; but how to find me out they knew not, nor so
much as how to guess at my quarters, whether they were at
the east end of the town, or the west; and this wariness was
my safety upon all these occasions.

I kept close a great while upon the occasion of this woman's
disaster; I knew that if I should do any thing that should miscarry, and should be carry'd to prison, she would be there, and
ready to witness against me, and perhaps save her life at my
expence; I consider'd that I began to be very well known by
name at the Old Baily,[1] tho' they did not know my face; and
that if I should fall into their hands, I should be treated as an
old offender; and for this reason I was resolv'd to see what this
poor creature's fate should be before I stirr'd, tho' several times
in her distress I convey'd money to her for her relief.

At length she came to her tryal; she pleaded she did not
steal the things, but that one Mrs. Flanders as she heard her
call'd (for she did not know her) gave the bundle to her after
they came out of the shop, and bad her carry it home. They
ask'd her where this Mrs. Flanders was. But she could not
produce her, neither could she give the least account of me; and
the mercer's men swearing positively that she was in the shop
when the goods were stolen, that they immediately miss'd them,
and pursu'd her, and found them upon her; thereupon the jury
brought her in guilty, but the court considering that she really
was not the person who stole the goods, and that it was very
possible she could not find out this Mrs. Flanders (meaning
me) tho' it would save her life, which indeed was true, they
allow'd her to be transported, which was the utmost favour
she could obtain, only that the court told her, if she could in
the mean time produce the said Mrs. Flanders, they would
intercede for her pardon, that is to say, if she could find me
out, and hang me, she should not be transported. This I took

[1] i.e., the Old Bailey Sessions Court, near Newgate Prison.

care to make impossible to her, and so she was shipp'd off in pursuance of her sentence a little while after.

I must repeat it again, that the fate of this poor woman troubl'd me exceedingly; and I began to be very pensive, knowing that I was really the instrument of her disaster; but my own life, which was so evidently in danger, took off my tenderness; and seeing she was not put to death, I was easie at her transportation, because she was then out of the way of doing me any mischief whatever should happen.

The disaster of this woman was some months before that of the last recited story, and was indeed partly the occasion of my governess proposing to dress me up in men's cloaths, that I might go about unobserv'd; but I was soon tir'd of that disguise, as I have said, for it expos'd me to too many difficulties.

I was now easie, as to all fear of witnesses against me, for all those that had either been concern'd with me, or that knew me by the name of Moll Flanders, were either hang'd or transported; and if I should have had the misfortune to be taken, I might call myself any thing else as well as Moll Flanders, and no old sins could be plac'd to my account; so I began to run a tick [1] again, with the more freedom, and several successful adventures I made tho' not such as I had made before.

We had at that time another fire happen'd not a great way off from the place where my governess liv'd, and I made an attempt there as before, but as I was not soon enough before the crowd of people came in, and could not get to the house I aim'd at, instead of a prize, I got a mischief, which had almost put a period to my life and all my wicked doings together; for the fire being very furious, and the people in a great fright in removing their goods, and throwing them out of window, a wench from out of a window threw a featherbed just upon me; it is true, the bed being soft it broke no bones: but as the weight was great, and made greater by the fall, it beat me down, and laid me dead for a while: nor did the people concern themselves much to deliver me from it, or to recover me at all; but I lay like one dead and neglected a good while, till some body going to remove the bed out of the way helped me up; it was indeed a wonder the people in the house had not thrown other

[1] on credit (i.e., Moll passed as an honest woman).

goods out after it, and which might have fallen upon it, and then I had been inevitably kill'd; but I was reserv'd for further afflictions.

This accident however spoil'd my market for that time, and I came home to my governess very much hurt, and frighted, and it was a good while before she could set me upon my feet again.

It was now a merry time of the year, and Bartholomew Fair [1] was begun; I had never made any walks that way, nor was the fair of much advantage to me; but I took a turn this year into the cloisters, and there I fell into one of the raffling shops. It was a thing of no great consequence to me, but there came a gentleman extreamly well dress'd, and very rich, and as 'tis frequent to talk to every body in those shops he singl'd me out, and was very particular with me; first he told me he would put in for me to raffle, and did so; and some small matter coming to his lot, he presented it to me, I think it was a feather muff. Then he continu'd to keep talking to me with a more than common appearance of respect; but still very civil and much like a gentleman.

He held me in talk so long, till at last he drew me out of the raffling place to the shop-door, and then to take a walk in the cloister, still talking of a thousand things cursorily without any thing to the purpose. At last he told me that he was charm'd with my company, and ask'd me if I durst trust myself in a coach with him; he told me he was a man of honour, and would not offer any thing to me unbecoming him. I seem'd to decline it a while, but suffer'd myself to be importun'd a little, and then yielded.

I was at a loss in my thoughts to conclude at first what this gentleman design'd; but I found afterward he had had some drink in his head, and that he was not very unwilling to have some more. He carried me to the Spring Garden, at Knights-Bridge, where we walk'd in the gardens, and he treated me very handsomely; but I found he drank freely, he pressed me also to drink, but I declin'd it.

Hitherto he kept his word with me, and offer'd me nothing amiss; we came away in the coach again, and he brought me

[1] Held in Smithfield at the end of August.

into the streets, and by this time it was near ten a clock at night, when he stop'd the coach at a house where it seems he was acquainted, and where they made no scruple to show us up stairs into a room with a bed in it; at first I seem'd to be un-willing to go up, but after a few words I yielded to that too, being indeed willing to see the end of it, and in hopes to make something of it at last; as for the bed &c., I was not much con-cern'd about that part.

Here he began to be a little freer with me than he had promis'd; and I by little and little yielded to every thing, so that, in a word, he did what he pleas'd with me; I need say no more. All this while he drank freely too, and about one in the morning we went into the coach again. The air and the shak-ing of the coach made the drink get more up in his head, and he grew uneasy, and was for acting over again what he had been doing before; but as I thought my game now secure, I resisted, and brought him to be a little still, which had not lasted five minutes but he fell fast asleep.

I took this opportunity to search him to a nicety; I took a gold watch, with a silk purse of gold, his fine full bottom perre-wig, and silver fring'd gloves, his sword, and fine snuff-box, and gently opening the coach-door, stood ready to jump out while the coach was going on; but the coach stopping in the narrow street beyond Temple-Bar to let another coach pass, I got softly out, fasten'd the door again, and gave my gentleman and the coach the slip together.

This was an adventure indeed unlook'd for, and perfectly un-design'd by me; tho' I was not so past the merry part of life, as to forget how to behave when a fop so blinded by his appetite should not know an old woman from a young: I did not indeed look so old as I was by ten or twelve year; yet I was not a young wench of seventeen, and it was easie enough to be distinguish'd. There is nothing so absurd, so surfeiting, so ridiculous as a man heated by wine in his head, and a wicked gust [1] in his inclination together; he is in the possession of two devils at once, and can no more govern himself by his reason than a mill can grind without water; vice tramples upon all that was in him that had any good in it; nay, his very sense is

[1] relish.

blinded by its own rage, and he acts absurdities even in his view; such is drinking more, when he is drunk already; picking up a common woman, without any regard to what she is, or who she is, whether sound or rotten, clean or unclean, whether ugly or handsome, old or young, and so blinded, as not really to distinguish; such a man is worse than lunatick; prompted by his vicious head he no more knows what he is doing than this wretch of mine knew when I pick'd his pocket of his watch and his purse of gold.

These are the men of whom Solomon says, *They go like an ox to the slaughter, till a dart strikes through their liver* [1]; an admirable description, by the way, of the foul disease, which is a poisonous deadly contagion mingling with the blood, whose center or foundation is in the liver; from whence, by the swift circulation of the whole mass, that dreadful nauseous plague strikes immediately thro' his liver, and his spirits are infected, his vitals stab'd thro' as with a dart.

It is true this poor unguarded wretch was in no danger from me, tho' I was greatly apprehensive at first what danger I might be in from him; but he was really to be pitied in one respect, that he seem'd to be a good sort of a man in himself; a gentleman that had no harm in his design; a man of sense, and of a fine behaviour; a comely, handsome person, a sober and solid countenance, a charming beautiful face, and every thing that cou'd be agreeable; only had unhappily had some drink the night before; had not been in bed, as he told me when we were together; was hot, and his blood fir'd with wine, and in that condition his reason, as it were asleep, had given him up.

As for me, my business was his money, and what I could make of him, and after that if I could have found out any way to have done it, I would have sent him safe home to his house, and to his family, for 'twas ten to one but he had an honest virtuous wife, and innocent children, that were anxious for his safety, and would have been glad to have gotten him home, and taken care of him, till he was restor'd to himself; and then with what shame and regret would he look back upon himself! how would he reproach himself with associating himself with a whore! pick'd up in the worst of all holes, the cloister, among the dirt and

[1] Proverbs, vii. 22–3.

filth of the town! how would he be trembling for fear he had got the pox, for fear a dart had struck through his liver, and hate himself ever time he look'd back upon the madness and brutality of his debauch! how would he, if he had any principles of honour, abhor the thought of giving any ill distemper, if he had it, as for ought he knew he might, to his modest and virtuous wife, and thereby sowing the contagion in the life-blood of his posterity!

Would such gentlemen but consider the contemptible thoughts which the very women they are concern'd with, in such cases as these, have of them, it wou'd be a surfeit to them. As I said above, they value not the pleasure, they are rais'd by no inclination to the man, the passive jade thinks of no pleasure but the money; and when he is as it were drunk in the extasies of his wicked pleasure, her hands are in his pockets for what she can find there; and of which he can no more be sensible in the moment of his folly than he can fore-think of it when he goes about it.

I knew a woman that was so dexterous with a fellow who indeed deserv'd no better usage, that, while he was busie with her another way, convey'd his purse with twenty guineas in it out of his fob pocket, where he had put it for fear of her, and put another purse with guilded counters in it into the room of it. After he had done, he says to her, Now han't you pick'd my pocket? She jested with him, and told him she suppos'd he had not much to lose; he put his hand to his fob, and with his fingers felt that his purse was there, which fully satisfy'd him, and so she brought off his money; and this was a trade with her, she kept a sham gold watch, and a purse of counters in her pocket to be ready on all such occasions; and I doubt not practis'd it with success.

I came home with this last booty to my governess, and really, when I told her the story, it so affected her that she was hardly able to forbear tears, to think how such a gentleman run a daily risque of being undone, every time a glass of wine got into his head.

But as to the purchase I got, and how entirely I strip'd him, she told me it pleased her wonderfully. Nay, child, says she, the usage may, for ought I know, do more to reform him than all the sermons that ever he will hear in his life, and if the remainder of the story be true, so it did.

I found the next day she was wonderful inquisitive about this gentleman; the description I gave her of him, his dress, his person, his face, all concurr'd to make her think of a gentleman whose character she knew; she mus'd awhile, and I going on in the particulars, says she, I lay a hundred pound I know the man.

I am sorry if you do, says I, for I would not have him expos'd on any account in the world; he has had injury enough already, and I would not be instrumental to do him any more. No, no, says she, I will do him no injury, but you may let me satisfy my curiosity a little, for if it is he, I warrant you I find it out. I was a little startled at that, and I told her, with an apparent concern in my face, that by the same rule he might find me out, and then I was undone. She return'd warmly, Why, do you think I will betray you, child? No, no, says she, not for all he is worth in the world; I have kept your counsel in worse things than these, sure you may trust me in this. So I said no more.

She laid her scheme another way, and without acquainting me with it, but she was resolv'd to find it out; so she goes to a certain friend of hers who was acquainted in the family that she guess'd at, and told her she had some extraordinary business with such a gentleman (who by the way was no less than a baronet, and of a very good family), and that she knew not how to come at him without somebody to introduce her. Her friend promis'd her readily to do it, and accordingly goes to the house to see if the gentleman was in town.

The next day, she comes to my governess and tells her that Sir —— was at home, but that he had met with a disaster and was very ill, and there was no speaking to him. What disaster? says my governess hastily, as if she was surpriz'd at it. Why, says her friend, he had been at Hampstead to visit a gentleman of his acquaintance, and as he came back again he was set upon and robb'd! and having got a little drink too, as they suppose, the rogues abus'd him, and he is very ill. Robb'd! says my governess, and what did they take from him? Why, says her friend, they took his gold watch, and his gold snuff-box, his fine perriwig, and what money he had in his pocket, which was considerable to be sure, for Sir —— never goes without a purse of guineas about him.

Pshaw! says my old governess jeering, I warrant you he has got drunk now and got a whore, and she has pick'd his pocket, and so he comes home to his wife and tells her he has been robb'd; that's an old sham, a thousand such tricks are put upon the poor women every day.

Fye, says her friend, I find you don't know Sir ——, why, he is as civil a gentleman, there is not a finer man, nor a soberer, modester person in the whole city; he abhors such things, there's no body that knows him will think such a thing of him. Well, well, says my governess, that's none of my business, if it was, I warrant I should find there was something of that in it; your modest men in common opinion are sometimes no better than other people, only they keep a better character, or if you please, are the better hypocrites.

No, no, says her friend, I can assure you Sir —— is no hypocrite, he is really an honest, sober gentleman, and he has certainly been robb'd. Nay, says my governess, it may be he has, it is no business of mine I tell you; I only want to speak with him, my business is of another nature. But, says her friend, let your business be of what nature it will, you cannot see him yet, for he is not fit to be seen, for he is very ill, and bruis'd very much. Ay, says my governess, nay then he has fallen into bad hands, to be sure. And then she ask'd gravely, Pray where is he bruised? Why, in his head, says her friend, and one of his hands, and his face, for they us'd him barbarously. Poor gentleman, says my governess, I must wait then till he recovers; and adds, I hope it will not be long.

Away she comes to me and tells me this story. I have found out your fine gentleman, and a fine gentleman he was, says she, but, mercy on him, he is in a sad pickle now, I wonder what the d—l you have done to him; why you have almost kill'd him. I look'd at her with disorder enough. I kill'd him! says I, you must mistake the person, I am sure I did nothing to him, he was very well when I left him, said I, only drunk and fast asleep. I know nothing of that, says she, but he is in a sad pickle now; and so she told me all that her friend had said. Well then, says

I, he fell into bad hands after I left him, for I left him safe enough.

About ten days after, my governess goes again to her friend, to introduce her to this gentleman; she had enquir'd otherways in the mean time, and found that he was about again, so she got leave to speak with him.

She was a woman of an admirable address, and wanted no body to introduce her; she told her tale much better than I shall be able to tell it for her, for she was mistress of her tongue, as I said already. She told him that she came, tho' a stranger, with a single design of doing him a service, and he should find she had no other end in it; that as she came purely on so friendly an account, she beg'd a promise from him, that if he did not accept what she should officiously propose, he would not take it ill that she meddl'd with what was not her business; she assur'd him that as what she had to say was a secret that belong'd to him only, so whether he accepted her offer or not, it should remain a secret to all the world, unless he expos'd it himself; nor should his refusing her service in it make her so little show her respect as to do him the least injury, so that he should be entirely at liberty to act as he thought fit.

He look'd very shy at first, and said he knew nothing that related to him that requir'd much secresie; that he had never done any man any wrong, and car'd not what any body might say of him; that it was no part of his character to be unjust to any body, nor could he imagine in what any man cou'd render him any service; but that if it was as she said, he could not take it ill from any one that should endeavour to serve him; and so, as it were, left her at liberty either to tell him, or not to tell him, as she thought fit.

She found him so perfectly indifferent that she was almost afraid to enter into the point with him; but however, after some other circumlocutions, she told him that by a strange and unaccountable accident she came to have a particular knowledge of the late unhappy adventure he had fallen into; and that in such a manner, that there was nobody in the world but herself and him that were acquainted with it, no, not the very person that was with him.

He look'd a little angrily at first. What adventure? said he.

Why sir, said she, of your being robb'd coming from Knights-br—, Hampstead, sir, I should say, says she: be not surpris'd, sir, says she, that I am able to tell you every step you took that day from the Cloyster in Smithfield, to the Spring-garden at Knightsbridge, and thence to the —— in the Strand, and how you were left asleep in the coach afterwards; I say, let not this surprize you, for sir, I do not come to make a booty [1] of you, I ask nothing of you, and I assure you the woman that was with you knows nothing who you are, and never shall; and yet perhaps I may serve you farther still, for I did not come barely to let you know that I was inform'd of these things, as if I wanted a bribe to conceal them; assure your self, sir, said she, that whatever you think fit to do or say to me, it shall be all a secret as it is, as much as if I were in my grave.

He was astonish'd at her discourse, and said gravely to her, Madam, you are a stranger to me, but it is very unfortunate that you should be let into the secret of the worst action of my life, and a thing that I am justly asham'd of, in which the only satisfaction I had was, that I thought it was known only to God and my own conscience. Pray, sir, says she, do not reckon the discovery of it to me to be any part of your misfortune; it was a thing, I believe, you were surprised into, and perhaps the woman us'd some art to prompt you to it; however, you will never find any just cause, said she, to repent that I came to hear of it; nor can your mouth be more silent in it than I have been, and ever shall be.

Well, says he, but let me do some justice to the woman too, whoever she is, I do assure you she prompted me to nothing, she rather declin'd me; it was my own folly and madness that brought me into it all, ay, and brought her into it too; I must give her her due so far. As to what she took from me, I cou'd expect no less from her in the condition I was in, and to this hour I know not whether she robbed me or the coachman; if she did it I forgive her, I think all gentlemen that do so should be us'd in the same manner; but I am more concern'd for some other things than I am for all that she took from me.

My governess now began to come into the whole matter, and he open'd himself freely to her. First, she said to him, in answer to what he had said about me, I am glad, sir, you

[1] profit.

are so just to the person that you were with; I assure you she is a gentlewoman, and no woman of the town; and however you prevail'd with her as you did, I am sure 'tis not her practice; you run [1] a great venture indeed, sir, but if that be part of your care, you may be perfectly easie, for I do assure you no man has touch'd her, before you, since her husband; and he has been dead now almost eight year.

It appear'd that this was his grievance, and that he was in a very great fright about it; however, when my governess said this to him, he appeared very well pleas'd; and said, Well, madam, to be plain with you, if I was satisfy'd of that, I should not so much value what I lost; for as to that, the temptation was great, and perhaps she was poor and wanted it. If she had not been poor, sir, says she, I assure you she would never have yielded to you; and as her poverty first prevail'd with her to let you do as you did, so the same poverty prevail'd with her to pay her self at last, when she saw you was in such a condition that, if she had not done it, perhaps the next coachman or chair-man might have done it more to your hurt.

Well, says he, much good may it do her; I say again, all the gentlemen that do so ought to be us'd in the same manner, and then they would be cautious of themselves; I have no more concern about it, but on the score which you hinted at before. Here he entred into some freedoms with her on the subject of what pass'd between us, which are not so proper for a woman to write, and the great terror that was upon his mind with relation to his wife, for fear she should have receiv'd any injury from me, and should communicate it farther; and ask'd her at last if she cou'd not procure him an opportunity to speak with me. My governess gave him farther assurances of my being a woman clear from any such thing, and that he was as entirely safe in that respect as he was with his own lady; but as for seeing me, she said it might be of dangerous consequence; but however, that she would talk with me, and let him know; endeavouring at the same time to perswade him not to desire it, and that it cou'd be of no service to him; seeing she hop'd he had no desire to renew the correspondence, and that on my account it was a kind of putting my life in his hands.

He told her, he had a great desire to see me, that he would

[1] ran.

give her any assurances that were in his power, not to take any advantages of me, and that in the first place he would give me a general release from all demands of any kind. She insisted how it might tend to farther divulging the secret, and might be injurious to him, entreating him not to press for it, so at length he desisted.

They had some discourse upon the subject of the things he had lost, and he seem'd to be very desirous of his gold watch, and told her if she cou'd procure that for him, he would willingly give as much for it as it was worth; she told him she would endeavour to procure it for him and leave the valuing it to himself.

Accordingly the next day she carried the watch, and he gave her 30 guineas for it, which was more than I should have been able to make of it, tho' it seems it cost much more; he spoke something of his perriwig, which it seems cost him three-score guineas, and his snuff-box, and in a few days more she carried them too; which oblig'd him very much, and he gave her thirty more; the next day I sent him his fine sword and cane *gratis*, and demanded nothing of him, but had no mind to see him, unless he might be satisfy'd I knew who he was, which he was not willing to.

Then he entered into a long talk with her of the manner how she came to know all this matter; she form'd a long tale of that part; how she had it from one that I had told the whole story to, and that was to help me dispose of the goods; and this confident brought things to her, she being by profession a pawn-broker; and she hearing of his worship's disaster, guess'd at the thing in general; that having gotten the things into her hands, she had resolv'd to come and try as she had done. She then gave him repeated assurances that it should never go out of her mouth, and tho' she knew the woman very well, yet she had not let her know (meaning me) any thing of who the person was, which, by the way, was false; but however it was not to his damage, for I never open'd my mouth of it to any body.

I had a great many thoughts in my head about my seeing him again, and was often sorry that I had refus'd it; I was perswaded that if I had seen him, and let him know that I knew him, I should have made some advantage of him, and perhaps have had some maintenance from him; and tho' it was a life wicked enough, yet it was not so full of danger as this I was in-gag'd in. However those thoughts wore off, and I declin'd seeing him again, for that time; but my governess saw him often, and he was very kind to her, giving her something almost every time he saw her; one time in particular she found him very merry, and, as she thought, he had some wine in his head then, and he press'd her again to let him see that woman, that, as he said, had bewitch'd him so that night; my governess, who was from the beginning for my seeing him, told him, he was so desirous of it that she could almost yield to it, if she could prevail upon me; adding that if he would please to come to her house in the even-ing, she would endeavour it, upon his repeated assurances of forgetting what was past.

Accordingly she came to me and told me all the discourse; in short, she soon byass'd me to consent, in a case which I had some regret in my mind for declining before; so I prepar'd to see him; I dress'd me to all the advantage possible, I assure you, and for the first time us'd a little art, I say for the first time, for I had never yielded to the baseness of paint before, having always had vanity enough to believe I had no need of it.

At the hour appointed he came; and as she observ'd before, so it was plain still, that he had been drinking, tho' very far from what we call being in drink. He appear'd exceeding pleas'd to see me, and enter'd into a long discourse with me upon the old affair; I beg'd his pardon very often, for my share of it, pro-tested I had not any such design when first I met him, that I had not gone out with him, but that I took him for a very civil gentleman, and that he made me so many promises of offering no uncivility to me.

He alledg'd the wine he drank, and that he scarce knew what he did, and that if it had not been so, he should never have taken the freedom with me he had done. He protested to me that he never touch'd any woman but me since he was marry'd to his wife, and it was a surprize upon him; complimented me upon being so particularly agreeable to him, and the like, and talk'd so much of that kind, 'till I found he had talk'd himself almost into a temper to do the thing again. But I took him up short, I protested I had never suffer'd any man to touch me since my husband died, which was near eight year; he said he believ'd it; and added, that Madam had intimated as much to him, and that it was his opinion of that part which made him desire to see me again; and since he had once broken in upon his virtue with me, and found no ill consequences, he could be safe in venturing again; and so in short he went on to what I expected, and to what will not bear relating.

My old governess had foreseen it, as well as I, and therefore led him into a room which had not a bed in it, and yet had a chamber within it which had a bed, whither we withdrew for the rest of the night, and in short, after some time being together, he went to bed, and lay there all night; I withdrew, but came again undress'd before it was day, and lay with him the rest of the time.

Thus, you see, having committed a crime once is a sad handle to the committing of it again; all the reflections wear off when the temptation renews itself. Had I not yielded to see him again, the corrupt desire in him had worn off, and 'tis very probable he had never fallen into it with any body else, as I really believe he had not done before.

When he went away, I told him I hop'd he was satisfy'd he had not been robb'd again. He told me he was fully satisfy'd in that point; and putting his hand in his pocket gave me five guineas, which was the first money I had gain'd that way for many years.

I had several visits of the like kind from him, but he never came into a settled way of maintenance, which was what I would have been best pleas'd with. Once, indeed, he ask'd me how I did to live; I answer'd him pretty quick that I assur'd him I had never taken that course that I took with him; but that indeed I work'd at my needle, and could just maintain my self, that sometimes it was as much as I was able to do, and I shifted [1] hard enough.

He seem'd to reflect upon himself, that he should be the first person to lead me into that, which he assur'd me he never intended to do himself; and it touch'd him a little, he said, that he should be the cause of his own sin, and mine too. He would often make just reflections also upon the crime itself, and upon the particular circumstances of it, with respect to himself; how

[1] make a living.

wine introduc'd the inclinations, how the Devil led him to the place, and found out an object to tempt him, and he made the moral always himself.

When these thoughts were upon him, he would go away, and perhaps not come again in a month's time or longer; but then, as the serious part wore off, the lewd part would wear in, and then he came prepar'd for the wicked part. Thus we liv'd for some time; tho' he did not keep,[1] as they call it, yet he never fail'd doing things that were handsome, and sufficient to maintain me without working, and, which was better, without following my old trade.

But this affair had its end too; for after about a year I found that he did not come so often as usual, and at last he left it off altogether without any dislike, or bidding adieu; and so there was an end of that short scene of life, which added no great store to me, only to make more work for repentance.

During this interval, I confin'd my self pretty much at home; at least being thus provided for, I made no adventures, no, not for a quarter of a year after; but then finding the fund fail, and being loath to spend upon the main stock, I began to think of my old trade, and to look abroad into the street; and my first step was lucky enough.

I had dress'd myself up in a very mean habit, for, as I had several shapes to appear in, I was now in an ordinary stuff gown, a blue apron and a straw hat; and I plac'd myself at the door of the *Three Cups* inn in St. John's-street. There were several carriers us'd the inn, and the stage coaches for Barnet, for Toteridge, and other towns that way, stood always in the street, in the evening, when they prepar'd to set out; so that I was ready for any thing that offer'd. The meaning was this: people come frequently with bundles and small parcels to those inns, and call for such carriers or coaches as they want to carry them into the country; and there generally attends women, porter's wives or daughters, ready to take in such things for the people that employ them.

It happen'd very oddly that I was standing at the inn-gate, and a woman that stood there before, and which was the porter's wife belonging to the Barnet stage coach, having observ'd me,

1 keep a mistress.

ask'd if I waited for any of the coaches; I told her, yes, I waited for my mistress, that was coming to go to Barnet; she ask'd me who was my mistress, and I told her any madam's name that came next me; [1] but it seem'd I happen'd upon a name, a family of which name liv'd at Hadly near Barnet.

I said no more to her, or she to me a good while, but by and by, some body calling her at a door a little way off, she desir'd me that if any body call'd for the Barnet coach I would step and call her at the house, which it seems was an ale-house; I said yes, very readily, and away she went.

She was no sooner gone, but comes a wench and a child, puffing and sweating, and asks for the Barnet coach. I answer'd presently,[2] Here! Do you belong to the Barnet coach? says she. Yes, sweetheart, said I, what do you want? I want room for two passengers, says she. Where are they, sweetheart? said I. Here's this girl, pray let her go into the coach, says she, and I'll go and fetch my mistress. Make haste then, sweet-heart, says I, for we may be full else. The maid had a great bundle under her arm; so she put the child into the coach; and I said, You had best put your bundle into the coach too. No, said she, I am afraid some body should slip it away from the child. Give it me then, said I. Take it then, says she, and be sure you take care of it. I'll answer for it, said I, if it were twenty pound vallue. There, take it then, says she, and away she goes.

As soon as I got the bundle, and the maid was out of sight, I goes on towards the ale-house, where the porter's wife was, so that if I met her I had then only been going to give her the bundle and to call her to her business, as if I was going away, and could stay no longer; but as I did not meet her I walk'd away, and turning into Charter-house-Lane, made off thro' Charter-house-Yard, and into Long-Lane, then into Bartholomew-Close, so into Little Britain, and thro' the Blue-Coat-Hospital, at Newgate-Street.

To prevent being known, I pull'd off my blue apron, and wrapt the bundle in it, which was made up in a piece of painted callico; I also wrapt up my straw hat in it, and so put the bundle on my head; and it was very well that I did thus, for coming

[1] i.e., the first name that entered my head.
[2] at once.

thro' the Blue-Coat-Hospital, who should I meet but the wench that had given me the bundle to hold; it seems she was going with her mistress, who she had been to fetch to the Barnet coaches.

I saw she was in hast, and I had no business to stop her; so away she went, and I brought my bundle safe to my governess; there was no money, plate, or jewels in it, but a very good suit of Indian damask, a gown and petticoat, a lac'd head and ruffles of very good Flanders lace, and some other things, such as I knew very well the value of.

This was not, indeed, my own invention, but was given me by one that had practis'd it with success, and my governess lik'd it extreamly; and indeed, I try'd it again several times, tho' never twice near the same place; for the next time I try'd in White Chappel, just by the corner of Petti-Coat-Lane, where the coaches stand that go out to Stratford and Bow, and that side of the country; and another time at the *Flying-Horse* without Bishopsgate where the Cheston coaches then lay, and I had always the good luck to come off with some booty.

Another time I placed myself at a warehouse by the water-side, where the coasting vessels from the North come, such as New-Castle upon Tyne, Sunderland, and other places; here the warehouse being shut comes a young fellow with a letter; and he wanted a box, and a hamper that was come from New-Castle upon Tyne. I ask'd him if he had the marks [1] of it, so he shows me the letter, by vertue of which he was to ask for it, and which gave an account of the contents, the box being full of linnen, and the hamper full of glass-ware; I read the letter, and took care to see the name, and the marks, the name of the person that sent the goods, and the name of the person they were sent to; then I bad the messenger come in the morning, for that the warehouse-keeper would not be there any more that night.

Away went I, and wrote a letter from Mr. John Richardson of New-Castle to his dear cousin Jemy Cole, in London, with an account that he had sent by such a vessel (for I remembered all the particulars to a tittle), so many pieces of huckaback [2]

---

[1] i.e., an indication of the ownership.
[2] a rough linen, used for towels etc.

linnen, and so many ells of Dutch holland,[1] and the like, in a box, and a hamper of flint-glasses [2] from Mr. Henzill's glasshouse; and that the box was marked I. C. No. 1., and the hamper was directed by a label on the cording.

About an hour after, I came to the warehouse, found the warehouse-keeper, and had the goods deliver'd me without any scruple; the value of the linnen being about 22 pound.

I could fill up this whole discourse with the variety of such adventures, which daily invention directed to, and which I manag'd with the utmost dexterity, and always with success.

At length, as when does the pitcher come safe home that goes so often to the well, I fell into some broils which tho' they could not affect me fatally, yet made me known, which was the worst thing next to being found guilty that could befal me.

I had taken up the disguise of a widow's dress; it was without any real design in view, but only waiting for any thing that might offer, as I often did. It happen'd that while I was going along a Street in Covent-Garden, there was a great cry of Stop thief! Stop thief! Some artists had it seems put a trick upon a shop-keeper, and being pursued, some of them fled one way, and some another; and one of them was, they said, dress'd up in widow's weeds, upon which the mob gather'd about me, and some said I was the person, others said no. Immediately came the mercer's journey-man, and he swore aloud I was the person, and so seiz'd on me; however, when I was brought back by the mob to the mercer's shop, the master of the house said freely that I was not the woman; and would have let me go immediately; but another fellow said gravely, Pray stay till Mr. —— (meaning the journeyman) comes back, for he knows her; so they kept me near half an hour. They had call'd a constable, and he stood in the shop as my jayler; in talking with the constable I enquir'd where he liv'd, and what trade he was; the man not apprehending in the least what happen'd afterwards, readily told me his name, and where he liv'd; and told me as a jest that I might be sure to hear of his name when I came to the Old-Bayly.

The servants likewise us'd me saucily, and had much ado to keep their hands off me; the master indeed was civiler to me

1 linen.
2 glasses made with ground flint or pebble.

than they, but he would not let me go, tho' he own'd I was not in his shop before.

I began to be a little surly with him, and told him I hop'd he would not take it ill if I made my self amends upon him another time; and desir'd I might send for friends to see me have right done. No, he said, he could give no such liberty, I might ask it when I came before the justice of peace, and seeing I threaten'd him, he would take care of me in the mean time, and would lodge me safe in Newgate. I told him it was his time now, but it would be mine by and by, and govern'd my passion as well as I was able; however, I spoke to the constable to call me a porter, which he did, and then I call'd for pen, ink, and paper, but they would let me have none; I ask'd the porter his name, and where he liv'd, and the poor man told it me very willingly; I bad him observe and remember how I was treated there; that he saw I was detain'd there by force; I told him I should want him in another place, and it should not be the worse for him to speak. The porter said he would serve me with all his heart. But, madam, says he, let me hear them refuse to let you go, then I may be able to speak the plainer.

With that, I spoke aloud to the master of the shop, and said, Sir, you know in your own conscience that I am not the person you look for, and that I was not in your shop before, therefore I demand that you detain me here no longer, or tell me the reason of your stopping me; the fellow grew surlier upon this than before, and said he would do neither till he thought fit. Very well, said I to the constable and to the porter, you will be pleas'd to remember this, gentlemen, another time. The porter said, Yes, madam, and the constable began not to like it, and would have perswaded the mercer to dismiss him, and let me go, since, as he said, he own'd I was not the person. Good sir, says the mercer to him tauntingly, are you a justice of peace, or a constable? I charg'd you with her, pray do your duty. The constable told him, a little mov'd, but very handsomely, I know my duty, and what I am, sir; I doubt you know hardly what you are doing. They had some other hard words, and in the mean time the journey-men, impudent and unmanly to the last degree, used me barbarously, and one of them, the same that first seiz'd upon me, pretended he would search me, and began to lay hands on me; I spit in his face, call'd out to the constable, and bad him take notice of my usage. And pray, Mr. Constable, said I, ask that villain's name, pointing to the man. The constable reprov'd him decently, told him that he did not know what he did, for he knew that his master acknowledg'd I was not the person; and, says the constable, I am afraid your master is bringing himself and me too into trouble, if this gentlewoman comes to prove who she is, and where she was, and it appears that she is not the woman you pretend to. Dam her, says the fellow again, with an impudent harden'd face, she is the lady, you may depend upon it, I'll swear she is the same body that was in the shop, and that I gave the pieces of satin that is lost into her own hand; you shall hear more of it when Mr. William and Mr. Anthony (those were the other journeymen) come back; they will know her again as well as I.

Just as the insolent rogue was talking thus to the constable, comes back Mr. William and Mr. Anthony, as he call'd them, and a great rabble with them, bringing along with them the true widow that I was pretended to be; and they came sweating and blowing into the shop, and with a great deal of triumph dragging the poor creature in a most butcherly manner up towards their master, who was in the back shop, and they cry'd out aloud, Here's the widow, sir, we have catched her at last. What do you mean by that, says the master, why, we have her already, there she sits, and Mr. —— says he can swear this is she. The other man who they call'd Mr. Anthony reply'd, Mr. —— may say what he will, and swear what he will, but this is the woman, and there's the remnant of sattin she stole; I took it out of her cloaths with my own hand.

I now began to take a better heart, but smil'd and said nothing; the master look'd pale; the constable turn'd about and look'd at me. Let 'em alone, Mr. Constable, said I, let 'em go on. The case was plain and could not be denied, so the constable was charg'd with the right thief, and the mercer told me very civilly he was sorry for the mistake, and hop'd I would not take it ill; that they had so many things of this nature put upon them every day, that they could not be blam'd for being very sharp in doing themselves justice. Not take it ill, sir! said I; how can I take it well? if you had dismiss'd me when your insolent fellow seiz'd on me in the street, and brought me to you, and when you your-self acknowledg'd I was not the person, I wou'd have put it by, and not have taken it ill, because of the many ill things I believe you have put upon you daily; but your treatment of me since has been unsufferable, and especially that of your servant; I must and will have reparation for that.

Then he began to parly with me, said he would make me any reasonable satisfaction, and would fain have had me told him what it was I expected; I told him I should not be my own judge, the law should decide it for me, and as I was to be carried before a magistrate, I should let him hear there what I had to say. He told me there was no occasion to go before the justice now, I was at liberty to go where I pleased; and calling to the constable told him, he might let me go, for I was discharg'd. The constable said calmly to him, Sir, you ask'd me just now if I knew whether I was a constable or a justice, and bad me do my duty, and charg'd me with this gentlewoman as a prisoner; now sir, I find you do not understand what is my duty, for you would make me a justice indeed; but I must tell you it is not in my power: I may keep a prisoner when I am charg'd with him, but 'tis the law and the magistrate alone that can discharge that prisoner; therefore 'tis a mistake, sir, I must carry her before a justice now, whether you think well of it or not. The mercer was very high with the constable at first; but the constable happening to be not a hir'd officer, but a good substantial kind of man, I think he was a corn-chandler, and a man of good sense, stood to his business, would not discharge me without going to a justice of the peace, and I insisted upon it too. When the mercer sees that, Well, says he to the constable, you may carry her where you please, I have nothing to say to her. But sir, says the constable, you will go with us, I hope, for 'tis you that charg'd me with her. No, not I, says the mercer, I tell you, I have nothing to say to her. But pray sir, do, says the constable, I desire it of you for your own sake, for the justice can do nothing without you. Prithee fellow, says the mercer, go about your business, I tell you I have nothing to say to the gentle-woman, I charge you in the King's name to dismiss her. Sir, says the constable, I find you don't know what it is to be a constable, I beg of you don't oblige me to be rude to you. I think

I need not; you are rude enough already, says the mercer. No, sir, says the constable, I am not rude; you have broken the peace in bringing an honest woman out of the street, when she was about her lawful occasions, confining her in your shop, and ill using her here by your servants; and now can you say I am rude to you? I think I am civil to you in not commanding you in the King's name to go with me, and charging every man I see that passes your door to aid and assist me in carrying you by force; this you know I have power to do, and yet I forbear it, and once more entreat you to go with me. Well, he would not for all this, and gave the constable ill language. However, the constable kept his temper, and would not be provok'd; and then I put in and said, Come, Mr. Constable, let him alone, I shall find ways enough to fetch him before a magistrate, I don't fear that; but there's that fellow, says I, he was the man that seized on me, as I was innocently going along the street, and you are a witness of his violence with me since; give me leave to charge you with him, and carry him before a justice. Yes, madam, says the Constable; and turning to the fellow, Come young gentleman, says he to the journeyman, you must go along with us; I hope you are not above the constable's power, tho' your master is.

The fellow look'd like a condemn'd thief, and hung back, then look'd at his master, as if he cou'd help him; and he, like a fool, encourag'd the fellow to be rude, and he truly resisted the constable, and push'd him back with a good force when he went to lay hold on him, at which the constable knock'd him down, and call'd out for help; immediately the shop was fill'd with people, and the constable seiz'd the master and man, and all his servants.

The first ill consequence of this fray was, that the woman who was really the thief made off, and got clear away in the crowd, and two others that they had stop'd also; whether they were really guilty or not, that I can say nothing to.

By this time some of his neighbours having come in, and seeing how things went, had endeavour'd to bring the mercer to his senses; and he began to be convinc'd that he was in the wrong; and so at length we went all very quietly before the justice, with a mob of about 500 people at our heels; and all the way we went I could hear the people ask, what was the matter? and others reply and say, a mercer had stop'd a gentlewoman instead of a thief, and had afterwards taken the thief, and now the gentlewoman had taken the mercer, and was carrying him before the justice. This pleas'd the people strangely, and made the crowd encrease, and they cry'd out as they went, Which is the rogue? which is the mercer? and especially the women. Then when they saw him they cryed out, *That's he, that's he!* and every now and then came a good dab of dirt at him; and thus we march'd a good while, till the mercer thought fit to desire the constable to call a coach to protect himself from the rabble; so we rode the rest of the way, the constable and I, and the mercer and his man.

When we came to the justice, which was an ancient gentleman in Bloomsbury, the constable giving first a summary account of the matter, the justice bad me speak, and tell what I had to say; and first he asked my name, which I was very loath to give, but there was no remedy. So I told him my name was Mary Flanders, that I was a widow, my husband being a sea captain, dyed on a voyage to Virginia; and some other circumstances I told which he cou'd never contradict, and that I lodg'd at present in town, with such a person, naming my governess; but that I was preparing to go over to America, where my husband's effects lay, and that I was going that day to buy some cloaths to put my self into second mourning, but had not yet been in any shop, when that fellow (pointing to the mercer's journeyman) came rushing upon me with such fury, as very much frighted me, and carried me back to his master's shop; where, tho' his master acknowledg'd I was not the person, yet he would not dismiss me, but charg'd a constable with me.

Then I proceeded to tell how the journeymen treated me; how they would not suffer me to send for any of my friends; how afterwards they found the real thief, and took the goods they had lost upon her, and all the particulars as before.

Then the constable related his case; his dialogue with the mercer about discharging me, and at last his servant refusing to go with him when I had charg'd him with him, and his master encouraging him to do so; and at last his striking the constable, and the like, all as I have told it already.

The justice then heard the mercer and his man; the mercer indeed made a long harangue of the great loss they have daily by the lifters and thieves; that it was easy for them to mistake, and that when he found it, he would have dismiss'd me, *&c.* as above; as to the journeyman, he had very little to say, but that he pretended other of the servants told him that I was really the person.

Upon the whole, the justice first of all told me very courteously I was discharg'd; that he was very sorry that the mercer's man should in his eager pursuit have so little discretion as to take up an innocent person for a guilty; that if he had not been so unjust as to detain me afterwards, he believ'd I would have forgiven the first affront; that however it was not in his power to award me any reparation, other than by openly reproving them, which he should do; but he suppos'd I would apply to such methods as the law directed; in the mean time he would bind him over.

But as to the breach of the peace committed by the journeyman, he told me he should give me some satisfaction for that, for he should commit him to Newgate for assaulting the constable, and for assaulting of me also.

Accordingly he sent the fellow to Newgate for that assault, and his master gave bail, and so we came away; but I had the satisfaction of seeing the mob wait upon them both, as they came out, holooing, and throwing stones and dirt at the coaches they rode in, and so I came home.

After this hustle, coming home, and telling my governess the story, she falls a laughing at me. Why are you so merry? says I; the story has not so much laughing room in it, as you imagine; I am sure I have had a great deal of hurry and fright too, with a pack of ugly rogues. *Laugh!* says my governess, I laugh, child, to see what a lucky creature you are; why, this jobb will be the best bargain to you that ever you made in your life, if you manage it well: I warrant you, you shall make the mercer pay 500*l.* for damages, besides what you shall get of the journeyman.

I had other thoughts of the matter than she had; and especially because I had given in my name to the justice of peace; and I knew that my name was so well known among the people

at Hicks's-Hall,[1] the Old Baily, and such places, that if this cause
came to be try'd openly, and my name came to be enquir'd
into, no court would give much damages for the reputation of
a person of such a character; however, I was oblig'd to begin
a prosecution in form, and accordingly my governess found me
out a very creditable sort of a man to manage it, being an attorney of very good business, and of good reputation, and she
was certainly in the right of this; for had she employ'd a petty
fogging hedge [2] solicitor, or a man not known, I should have
brought it to but little.

I met this attorney, and gave him all the particulars at large,
as they are recited above; and he assur'd me it was a case, as
he said, that he did not question but that a jury would give very
considerable damages; so taking his full instructions, he began the
prosecution, and the mercer being arrested, gave bail. A few
days after his giving bail, he comes with his attorney to my
attorney, to let him know that he desir'd to accommodate the
matter, that it was all carried on in the heat of an unhappy
passion; that his client (meaning me) had a sharp provoking
tongue, and that I us'd them ill, gibing at them, and jeering them,
even while they believed me to be the very person, and that
I had provok'd them, and the like.

My attorney manag'd as well on my side; made them believe
I was a widow of fortune, that I was able to do myself justice,
and had great friends to stand by me too, who had all made me
promise to sue to the utmost, if it cost me a thousand pound,
for that the affronts I had receiv'd were insufferable.

However, they brought my attorney to this, that he promis'd
he would not blow the coals, that if I enclin'd to an accommodation, he would not hinder me, and that he would rather
perswade me to peace than to war; for which they told him
he should be no looser, all which he told me very honestly,
and told me that if they offer'd him any bribe, I should certainly know it; but upon the whole he told me very honestly that
if I would take his opinion, he would advise me to make it
up with them; for that as they were in a great fright, and were
desirous above all things to make it up, and knew that, let it

---

[1] The Sessions Court of the County of Middlesex, in Clerkenwell.
[2] third-rate.

be what it would, they must bear all the costs, he believed they would give me freely more than any jury would give upon a trial. I ask'd him what he thought they would be brought to; he told me he could not tell, as to that; but he would tell me more when I saw him again.

Some time after this, they came again to know if he had talk'd with me. He told them he had, that he found me not so averse to an accommodation as some of my friends were, who resented the disgrace offer'd me, and set me on; that they blow'd the coals in secret, prompting me to revenge, or to do myself justice, as they call'd it; so that he could not tell what to say to it; he told them he would do his endeavour to persuade me, but he ought to be able to tell me what proposal they made. They pretended they could not make any proposal because it might be made use of against them; and he told them that by the same rule he could not make any offers, for that might be pleaded in abatement of what damages a jury might be inclin'd to give. However, after some discourse and mutual promises that no advantage should be taken on either side by what was transacted then, or at any other of those meetings, they came to a kind of a treaty; but so remote, and so wide from one another, that nothing could be expected from it; for my attorney demanded 500*l*. and charges, and they offer'd 50*l*. without charges; so they broke off, and the mercer propos'd to have a meeting with me myself; and my attorney agreed to that very readily.

My attorney gave me notice to come to this meeting in good cloaths, and with some state, that the mercer might see I was something more than I seem'd to be that time they had me. Accordingly I came in a new suit of second mourning, according to what I had said at the justice's; I set myself out too, as well as a widow's dress would admit; my governess also furnish'd me with a good pearl necklace that shut in behind with a locket of diamonds, which she had in pawn; and I had a very good gold watch by my side: so that I made a very good figure, and as I stay'd till I was sure they were come, I came in a coach to the door, with my maid with me.

When I came into the room, the mercer was surpriz'd; he stood up and made his bow, which I took a little notice of, and but a little, and went and sat down, where my own attorney had

appointed me to sit, for it was his house; after a while, the mercer said he did not know me again, and began to make some
compliments. I told him, I believ'd he did not know me at first,
and that if he had, he would have not treated me as he did.

He told me he was very sorry for what had happen'd, and
that it was to testify the willingness he had to make all possible
reparation that he had appointed this meeting; that he hop'd I
would not carry things to extremity, which might be not only
too great a loss to him, but might be the ruin of his business
and shop, in which case I might have the satisfaction of repaying
an injury with an injury ten times greater; but that I would then
get nothing, whereas he was willing to do me any justice that
was in his power, without putting himself, or me, to the trouble
or charge of a suit of law.

I told him I was glad to hear him talk so much more like a
man of sense than he did before; that it was true, acknowledgment in most cases of affronts was counted reparation sufficient;
but this had gone too far to be made up so; that I was not revenge-
ful, nor did I seek his ruin, or any man's else, but that all my
friends were unanimous not to let me so far neglect my character
as to adjust a thing of this kind without reparation; that to be
taken up for a thief was such an indignity as could not be put up,
that my character was above being treated so by any that knew
me, but because, in my condition of a widow, I had been careless
of myself, I might be taken for such a creature, but that for the
particular usage I had from him afterward — and then I repeated
all as before — it was so provoking I had scarce patience to repeat
it.

He acknowledg'd all, and was mighty humble indeed; he came
up to a hundred pounds and to pay all the law charges, and added
that he would make me a present of a very good suit of cloaths;
I came down to three hundred pounds, and demanded that I
should publish an advertisement of the particulars in the common
news-papers.

This was a clause he never could comply with; however, at last
he came up, by good management of my attorney, to 150*l.* and
a suit of black silk cloaths, and there, as it were at my attorney's
request, I comply'd; he paying my attorney's bill and charges,
and gave us a good supper into the bargain.

When I came to receive the money, I brought my governess

with me, dress'd like an old dutchess, and a gentleman very well dress'd, who we pretended courted me, but I call'd him cousin, and the lawyer was only to hint privately to them that this gentleman courted the widow.

He treated us handsomely indeed, and paid the money chearfully enough; so that it cost him 200*l.* in all, or rather more. At our last meeting, when all was agreed, the case of the journeyman came up, and the mercer beg'd very hard for him, told me he was a man that had kept a shop of his own, and been in good business, had a wife and several children, and was very poor, that he had nothing to make satisfaction with, but should beg my pardon on his knees. I had no spleen at the saucy rogue, nor were his submissions any thing to me, since there was nothing to be got by him; so I thought it was as good to throw that in generously as not, so I told him I did not desire the ruin of any man, and therefore at his request I would forgive the wretch, it was below me to seek any revenge.

When we were at supper he brought the poor fellow in to make his acknowledgment, which he would have done with as much mean humility as his offence was with insulting pride, in which he was an instance of a compleat baseness of spirit, imperious, cruel, and relentless when uppermost; abject and low spirited when down. However, I abated his cringes, told him I forgave him, and desir'd he might withdraw, as if I did not care for the sight of him, tho' I had forgiven him.

I was now in good circumstances indeed, if I could have known my time for leaving off, and my governess often said I was the richest of the trade in England, and so I believe I was; for I had 700*l.* by me in money, besides cloaths, rings, some plate, and two gold watches, and all of them stol'n, for I had innumerable jobbs, besides these I have mentioned. O! Had I even now had the grace of repentance, I had still leisure to have look'd back upon my follies, and have made some reparation; but the satisfaction I was to make for the publick mischiefs I had done was yet left behind; and I could not forbear going abroad again, as I call'd it now, any more than I could when my extremity really drove me out for bread.

It was not long after the affair with the mercer was made up that I went out in an equipage quite different from any I had ever appear'd in before; I dress'd myself like a beggar woman, in the coarsest and most despicable rags I could get, and I walk'd about peering and peeping into every door and window I came near; and indeed I was in such a plight [1] now, that I knew as ill how to behave in, as ever I did in any; I naturally abhor'd dirt and rags; I had been bred up tite and cleanly, and could be no other, whatever condition I was in; so that this was the most uneasy disguise to me that ever I put on. I said presently to my self that this would not do, for this was a dress that every body was shy and afraid of; and I thought every body look'd at me as if they were afraid I should come near them, least I should take something from them, or afraid to come near me, least they should get something from me. I wandred about all the evening the first time I went out, and made nothing of it, and came home again wet, dragl'd, and tired. However I went out again the next night, and then I met with a little adventure, which had like to have cost me dear. As I was standing near a tavern door, there comes a gentleman on horseback, and lights at the door, and wanting to go into the tavern, he calls one of the drawers to hold his horse; he stay'd pretty long in the tavern, and the drawer heard his master call, and thought he would be angry with him; seeing me stand by him, he call'd to me, Here, woman, says he, hold this horse a while, 'till I go in; if the gentleman comes, he'll give you something. Yes, says I, and takes the horse, and walks off with him soberly, and carry'd him to my governess.

This had been a booty to those that had understood it; but never was poor thief more at a loss to know what to do with any thing that was stolen; for when I came home, my governess was quite confounded, and what to do with the creature we neither of us knew; to send him to a stable was doing nothing, for it was certain that notice would be given in the *Gazette,* and the horse describ'd, so that we durst not go to fetch it again.

All the remedy we had for this unlucky adventure was to go and set up the horse at an inn, and send a note by a porter to the tavern that the gentleman's horse that was lost at such a time was left at such an inn, and that he might be had there; that the poor woman that held him, having led him about the street, not being able to lead him back again, had left him there; we

1 dress, attire.

might have waited till the owner had publish'd and offer'd a reward, but we did not care to venture the receiving the reward.

So this was a robbery and no robbery, for little was lost by
it, and nothing was got by it, and I was quite sick of going out
in a beggar's dress; it did not answer at all, and besides I thought
it ominous and threatening.

While I was in this disguise, I fell in with a parcel of folks of
a worse kind than any I ever sorted with, and I saw a little into
their ways too. These were coiners of money, and they made
some very good offers to me, as to profit; but the part they would
have had me embark'd in was the most dangerous; I mean that
of the very working of the dye, as they call it, which, had I been
taken, had been certain death, and that at a stake, I say, to be
burnt to death at a stake; so that tho' I was to appearance but
a beggar, and they promis'd mountains of gold and silver to me,
to engage, yet it would not do; 'tis true, if I had been really a
beggar, or had been desperate as when I began, I might perhaps
have closed with it, for what care they to dye,[1] that cannot tell
how to live? But at present that was not my condition, at least I
was for no such terrible risques as those; besides, the very
thoughts of being burnt at a stake struck terror to my very soul,
chill'd my blood, and gave me the vapours to such a degree as
I could not think of it without trembling.

This put an end to my disguise too, for tho' I did not like the
proposal, yet I did not tell them so, but seem'd to relish it, and
promis'd to meet again; but I durst see them no more; for if I
had seen them, and not comply'd, tho' I had declin'd it with the
greatest assurances of secresy in the world, they would have gone
near to have murder'd me, to make sure work, and make themselves easy, as they call it; what kind of easiness that is, they may
best judge that understand how easy men are that can murder
people to prevent danger.

This and horse stealing were things quite out of my way, and
I might easily resolve I would have no more to say to them; my
business seem'd to lye another way, and tho' it had hazard enough
in it too, yet it was more suitable to me, and what had more of
art in it, and more chances for a coming off, if a surprize should
happen.

[1] A grim pun: to die = to stamp the metal in coining.

I had several proposals made also to me about that time to come into a gang of house breakers,[1] but that was a thing I had no mind to venture at neither, any more than I had at the coining trade; I offer'd to go along with two men and a woman that made it their business to get into houses by stratagem, I was willing enough to venture; but there were three of them already, and they did not care to part,[2] nor I to have too many in a gang, so I did not close with them, and they paid dear for their next attempt.

But at length I met with a woman that had often told me what adventures she had made, and with success, at the water-side, and I clos'd with her, and we drove on our business pretty well. One day we came among some Dutch people at St. Catherine's,[3] where we went on pretence to buy goods that were privately got on shore. I was two or three times in a house where we saw a good quantity of prohibited goods, and my companion once brought away three peices of Dutch black silk that turn'd to good account, and I had my share of it; but in all the journeys I made by myself, I could not get an opportunity to do any thing, so I laid it aside; for I had been there so often that they began to suspect something.

This baulk'd me a little, and I resolv'd to push at something or other, for I was not us'd to come back so often without purchase; so the next day I dress'd myself up fine, and took a walk to the other end of the town. I pass'd thro' the Exchange [4] in the Strand, but had no notion of finding any thing to do there, when on a sudden I saw a great clutter in the place, and all the people, shop-keepers as well as others, standing up, and staring, and what should it be but some great dutchess come into the Exchange; and they said the Queen was coming. I set myself close up to a shop-side with my back to the compter, as if to let the crowd pass by, when, keeping my eye upon a parcel of lace which the shop-keeper was showing to some ladies that stood by me, the shop-keeper and her maid were so taken up with looking to see who was a coming, and what shop they would go to, that I found means to slip a paper of lace into my pocket, and come clear off

1 burglars.   2 go shares.
3 docks near the Tower of London.
4 a famous shopping center.

with it; so the lady millener paid dear enough for her gaping after the Queen.

I went off from the shop, as if driven along by the throng, and mingling myself with the crowd, went out at the other door of the Exchange, and so got away before they miss'd their lace; and because I would not be follow'd, I call'd a coach and shut myself up in it; I had scarce shut the coach doors but I saw the millener's maid and five or six more come running out into the street, and crying out as if they were frighted; they did not cry Stop thief! because no body ran away, but I cou'd hear the word *robb'd*, and *lace*, two or three times, and saw the wench wringing her hands, and run staring to and again,[1] like one scar'd; the coachman that had taken me up was getting up into the box, but was not quite up, and the horses had not begun to move, so that I was terrible uneasy; and I took the packet of lace and laid it ready to have dropt it out at the flap of the coach, which opens before, just behind the coachman; but, to my great satisfaction, in less than a minute the coach began to move, that is to say, as soon as the coachman had got up, and spoken to his horses; so he drove away, and I brought off my purchase, which was worth near twenty pound.

The next day I dress'd me up again, but in quite different cloaths, and walk'd the same way again, but nothing offer'd till I came into St. James's Park. I saw abundance of fine ladies in the Park, walking in the Mall, and among the rest there was a little miss, a young lady of about 12 or 13 years old, and she had a sister, as I suppos'd, with her, that might be about nine. I observ'd the biggest had a fine gold watch on, and a good necklace of pearl, and they had a footman in livery with them; but as it is not usual for the footmen to go behind the ladies in the Mall, so I observ'd the footman stop'd at their going into the Mall, and the biggest of the sisters spoke to him, to bid him be just there when they came back.

When I heard her dismiss the footman, I step'd up to him, and ask'd him what little lady that was, and held a little chat with him about what a pretty child it was with her, and how genteel and well carriag'd the eldest would be; how womanish, and how grave; and the fool of a fellow told me presently who she was,

[1] backwards and forwards.

that she was Sir Thomas ———'s eldest daughter of Essex, and that
she was a great fortune, that her mother was not come to town
yet, but she was with Sir William ———'s lady at her lodgings in
Suffolk Street, and a great deal more; that they had a maid and
a woman to wait on them, besides Sir Thomas's coach, the
coachman and himself, and that young lady was governess to the
whole family, as well here as at home; and told me abundance of
things enough for my business.

I was well dress'd, and had my gold watch, as well as she; so
I left the footman, and I puts myself in a rank with [1] this lady,
having stay'd till she had taken one turn in the Mall, and was
going forward again; by and by, I saluted her by her name, with
the title of Lady Betty: I ask'd her when she heard from her
father? when my lady her mother would be in town and how she
did?

I talk'd so familiarly to her of her whole family that she cou'd
not suspect but that I knew them all intimately: I ask'd her why
she would come abroad without Mrs. Chime with her (that was
the name of her woman) to take care of Mrs. Judith, that was her
sister. Then I enter'd into a long chat with her about her sister,
what a fine little lady she was, and ask'd her if she had learn'd
French, and a thousand such little things, when on a sudden the
Guards came, and the crowd run to see the King go by to the
Parliament-House.

The ladies run all to the side of the Mall, and I help'd my lady
to stand upon the edge of the boards on the side of the Mall,
that she might be high enough to see; and took the little one and
lifted her quite up; during which I took care to convey her gold
watch so clean away from the Lady Betty, that she never miss'd
it till the crowd was gone, and she was gotten into the middle of
the Mall.

I took my leave in the very crowd, and said, as if in haste, Dear
Lady Betty, take care of your little sister, and so [2] the crowd did,
as it were, thrust me away, and that I was unwilling to take my
leave.

The hurry in such cases is immediately over, and the place
clear as soon as the King is gone by; but as there is always a great
running and clutter just as the King passes, so, having drop'd the

1 in line with.   2 as if.

two little ladies, and done my business with them without any miscarriage, I kept hurrying on among the crowd, as if I run to see the King, and so I kept before the crowd 'till I came to the end of the Mall; when the King going on toward the Horse-Guards, I went forward to the passage which went then thro' against the end of the Hay-Market, and there I bestow'd a coach upon myself, and made off; and I confess I have not yet been so good as my word, (*viz.*) to go and visit my Lady Betty.

I was once in the mind to venture staying with Lady Betty 'till she mist the watch, and so have made a great out-cry about it with her, and have got her into her coach, and put my self in the coach with her, and have gone home with her; for she appear'd so fond of me, and so perfectly deceiv'd by my so readily talking to her of all her relations and family, that I thought it was very easy to push the thing farther, and to have got at least the necklace of pearl; but when I consider'd that tho' the child would not perhaps have suspected me, other people might, and that if I was search'd I should be discover'd, I thought it was best to go off with what I had got.

I came accidentally afterwards to hear that when the young lady miss'd her watch she made a great out-cry in the Park, and sent her footman up and down to see if he could find me, she having describ'd me so perfectly that he knew it was the same person that had stood and talked so long with him, and ask'd him so many questions about them; but I was gone far enough out of their reach, before she could come at her footman to tell him the story.

I made another adventure after this, of a nature different from all I had been concern'd in yet, and this was at a gaming house near Covent Garden.

I saw several people go in and out; and I stood in the passage a good while with another woman with me, and seeing a gentleman go up that seem'd to be of more than ordinary fashion, I said to him, Sir, pray don't they give women leave to go up? Yes madam, says he, and to play too if they please. I mean so, sir, said I; and with that, he said he would introduce me if I had a mind. So I follow'd him to the door, and he looking in, There, madam, says he, are the gamesters, if you have a mind to venture. I look'd in, and said to my comerade, aloud, Here's nothing but men, I won't venture; at which one of the gentlemen cry'd out, You need not be afraid, madam, here's none but fair gamesters, you are very welcome to come and set [1] what you please; so I went a little nearer and look'd on, and some of them brought me a chair, and I sat down and see the box and dice go round apace; then I said to my comrade, The gentlemen play too high for us, come let us go.

The people were all very civil, and one gentleman encourag'd me, and said, Come madam, if you please to venture, if you dare trust me I'll answer for it you shall have nothing put upon you here. No sir, said I, smiling, I hope the gentlemen would not cheat a woman; but still I declin'd venturing, tho' I pull'd out a purse with money in it, that they might see I did not want money.

After I had sat a while, one gentleman said to me, jeering, Come madam, I see you are afraid to venture for your self; I always had good luck with the ladies, you shall set for me, if you won't set for yourself. I told him, Sir, I should be very loth to lose your money, tho', I added, I am pretty lucky too; but the gentlemen play so high that I dare not venture my own.

Well, well, says he, there's ten guineas, madam; set them for me. So I took the money and set, himself looking on; I run out the guineas by one and two at a time, and then the box coming to the next man to me, my gentleman gave me ten guineas more, and made me set five of them at once, and the gentleman who had the box threw out, so there was five guineas of his money again; he was encourag'd at this, and made me take the box, which was a bold venture. However, I held the box so long that I gain'd him his whole money, and had a handful of guineas in my lap, and which was the better luck, when I threw out, I threw but at one or two of those that had set me, and so went off easie.

When I was come this length, I offer'd the gentleman all the gold, for it was his own; and so would have had him play for himself, pretending that I did not understand the game well enough. He laugh'd, and said if I had but good luck, it was no matter whether I understood the game or no; but I should not leave off. However, he took out the 15 guineas that he had put in first, and bad me play with the rest. I would have him to have seen how much I had got, but he said, No, no, don't tell [2] them,

[1] stake.   [2] count.

I believe you are very honest, and 'tis bad luck to tell them, so I play'd on.

I understood the game well enough, tho' I pretended I did not, and play'd cautiously, which was to keep a good stock in my lap, out of which I every now and then convey'd some into my pocket; but in such a manner, as I was sure he could not see it.

I play'd a great while, and had very good luck for him, but the last time I held the box, they set me high, and I threw boldly at all, and held the box 'till I had gain'd near fourscore guineas, but lost above half of it back at the last throw; so I got up, for I was afraid I should lose it all back again, and said to him, Pray come, sir, now and take it and play for your self, I think I have done pretty well for you. He would have had me play'd on, but it grew late, and I desir'd to be excus'd. When I gave it up to him, I told him I hop'd he would give me leave to tell it now, that I might see what he had gain'd, and how lucky I had been for him; when I told them there were threescore and three guineas. Ay, says I, if it had not been for that unlucky throw I had got you a hundred guineas; so I gave him all the money, but he would not take it 'till I had put my hand into it, and taken some for my self, and bid me please my self. I refus'd it, and was positive I would not take it my self; if he had a mind to do any thing of that kind it should be all his own doings.

The rest of the gentlemen, seeing us striving, cry'd, Give it her all; but I absolutely refus'd that. Then one of them said, D—n ye, Jack, half it with her, don't you know you should be always upon even terms with the ladies? So, in short, he divided it with me, and I brought away 30 guineas, besides about 43 which I had stole privately, which I was sorry for, because he was so generous.

Thus I brought home 73 guineas, and let my old governess see what good luck I had at play. However, it was her advice that I should not venture again, and I took her council, for I never went there any more; for I knew as well as she, if the itch of play came in, I might soon lose that, and all the rest of what I had got.

Fortune had smil'd upon me to that degree, and I had thriven so much, and my governess too, for she always had a share with me, that really the old gentlewoman began to talk of leaving off while we were well, and being satisfy'd with what we had got; but, I know not what fate guided me, I was as backward to it now as she was when I propos'd it to her before, and so in an ill hour we gave over the thoughts of it for the present, and, in a word, I grew more harden'd and audacious than ever, and the success I had, made my name as famous as any thief of my sort ever had been.

I had sometimes taken the liberty to play the same game over again, which is not according to practice, which however succeeded not amiss; but generally I took up new figures, and contriv'd to appear in new shapes every time I went abroad.

It was now a rambling time of the year, and the gentlemen being most of them gone out of town, Tunbridge and Epsom and such places were full of people, but the city was thin, and I thought our trade felt it a little, as well as others; so that at the latter end of the year I joyn'd my self with a gang, who usually go every year to Sturbridge Fair,[1] and from thence to Bury Fair, in Suffolk. We promised ourselves great things here, but when I came to see how things were, I was weary of it presently; for except meer picking of pockets, there was little worth meddling with; neither, if a booty had been made, was it so easy carrying it off, nor was there such a variety of occasion for business in our way as in London; all that I made of the whole journey, was a gold watch at Bury Fair, and a small parcel of linnen at Cambridge, which gave me occasion to take leave of the place. It was an old bite,[2] and I thought might do with a country shop-keeper, tho' in London it would not.

I bought at a linnen draper's shop, not in the Fair, but in the town of Cambridge, as much fine holland and other things as came to about seven pound; when I had done, I bad them be sent to such an inn, where I had taken up my being the same morning, as if I was to lodge there that night.

I order'd the draper to send them home to me, about such an hour, to the inn where I lay, and I would pay him his money; at the time appointed the draper sends the goods, and I plac'd one of our gang at the chamber door, and when the inn-keeper's maid brought the messenger to the door, who was a young fellow, an

---

[1] A famous fair between Cambridge and Newmarket, said by Defoe in his *Tour through England & Wales* to be "not only the greatest in the whole nation, but in the world."   [2] fraud.

apprentice, almost a man, she tells him her mistress was asleep, but
if he would leave the things, and call in about an hour, I should
be awake, and he might have the money; he left the parcel very
readily, and goes his way, and in about half an hour my maid and
I walk'd off, and that very evening I hired a horse, and a man to
ride before me, and went to New-Market, and from thence got
my passage in a coach that was not quite full to St. Edmund's
Bury; where, as I told you, I could make but little of my trade;
only, at a little country opera house, I got a gold watch from a
ladie's side, who was not önly intollerably merry, but a little
fuddled, which made my work much easier.

I made off with this little booty to Ipswich, and from thence to
Harwich, where I went into an inn, as if I had newly arriv'd from
Holland, not doubting but I should make some purchase [1] among
the foreigners that came on shore there; but I found them generally empty of things of value, except what was in their portmantuas, and Dutch hampers, which were always guarded by
footmen; however, I fairly got one of their portmantuas one
evening out of the chamber where the gentleman lay, the footman being fast asleep on the bed, and I suppose very drunk.

The room in which I lodg'd lay next to the Dutchman's, and
having dragg'd the heavy thing with much ado out of the chamber into mine, I went out into the street, to see if I could find
any possibility of carrying it off; I walk'd about a great while but
could see no probability, either of getting out the thing, or of
conveying away the goods that was in it, the town being so small,
and I a perfect stranger in it; so I was returning with a resolution
to carry it back again, and leave it where I found it. Just in that
very moment I heard a man make a noise to some people to make
haste, for the boat was going to put off, and the tyde would be
spent. I call'd the fellow, What boat is it, friend, said I, that
you belong to? The Ipswich wherry, madam, says he. When do
you go off? says I. This moment, madam, says he; do you want
to go thither? Yes, said I, if you can stay till I fetch my things.
Where are your things, madam? says he. At such an inn, said
I. Well, I'll go with you madam, says he, very civilly, and bring
them for you. Come away then, says I, and takes him with me.

The people of the inn were in a great hurry, the packet-boat

[1] steal some property.

from Holland being just come in, and two coaches just come also with passengers from London for another packet-boat that was going off for Holland, which coaches were to go back next day with the passengers that were just landed. In this hurry it was that I came to the barr, and paid my reckoning, telling my landlady I had gotten my passage by sea in a wherry.

These wherries are large vessels, with good accommodation for carrying passengers from Harwich to London; and tho' they are call'd wherries, which is a word us'd in the Thames for a small boat row'd with one or two men, yet these are vessels able to carry twenty passengers, and ten or fifteen ton of goods, and fitted to bear [1] the sea; all this I had found out by enquiring the night before into the several ways of going to London.

My landlady was very courteous, took my money for the reckoning, but was call'd away, all the house being in a hurry; so I left her, took the fellow up into my chamber, gave him the trunk or portmantua, for it was like a trunk, and wrapt it about with an old apron, and he went directly to his boat with it, and I after him, no body asking us the least question about it; as for the drunken Dutch footman, he was still asleep, and his master with other foreign gentlemen at supper, and very merry below; so I went clean off with it to Ipswich, and going in the night, the people of the house knew nothing but that I was gone to London by the Harwich wherry, as I had told my landlady.

I was plagu'd at Ipswich with the custom-house officers, who stop'd my trunk, as I call'd it, and would open and search it. I was willing, I told them, that they should search it, but my husband had the key, and that he was not yet come from Harwich. This I said, that if, upon searching it, they should find all the things be such as properly belong'd to a man rather than a woman, it should not seem strange to them; however, they being positive to open the trunk, I consented to have it broken open, that is to say, to have the lock taken off, which was not difficult.

They found nothing for their turn, for the trunk had been search'd before; but they discover'd several things much to my satisfaction, as particularly a parcel of money in French pistoles,[2] and some Dutch ducatoons, or rix dollars, and the rest was chiefly two perriwigs, wearing linnen, rasors, wash-balls,[3] perfumes and

---

[1] endure.   [2] gold coins.   [3] cakes of soap.

other useful things necessary for a gentleman; which all pass'd
for my husband's, and so I was quit of them.

It was now very early in the morning, and not light; and I
knew not well what course to take; for I made no doubt but I
should be pursu'd in the morning, and perhaps be taken with the
things about me; so I resolv'd upon taking new measures. I
went publickly to an inn in the town with my trunk, as I call'd
it, and having taken the substance out, I did not think the lumber
of it worth my concern; however, I gave it to the landlady of
the house with a charge to take care of it, and lay it up safe till
I should come again, and away I walk'd into the street.

When I was got into the town a great way from the inn, I
met with an antient woman who had just open'd her door, and
I fell into chat with her, and ask'd her a great many wild questions of things all remote to my purpose and design, but in my
discourse I found by her how the town was situated, that I was
in a street which went out towards Hadly, but that such a street
went towards the water-side, such a street went into the heart
of the town; and at last, such a street went towards Colchester,
and so the London road lay there.

I had soon my ends of [1] this old woman; for I only wanted to
know which was the London road, and away I walk'd as fast as
I could; not that I intended to go on foot, either to London or to
Colchester, but I wanted to get quietly away from Ipswich.

I walk'd about two or three mile, and then I met a plain countryman who was busy about some husbandry work I did not
know what; and I ask'd him a great many questions first, not
much to the purpose; but at last told him I was going for London,
and the coach was full, and I cou'd not get a passage, and ask'd
him if he cou'd not tell me where to hire a horse that would
carry double, and an honest man to ride before me to Colchester,
so that I might get a place there in the coaches; the honest clown
look'd earnestly at me, and said nothing for above half a minute;
when, scratching his poll, A horse say you, and to Colchester
to carry double? why yes, mistress, alack-a-day, you may have
horses enough for money. Well, friend, says I, that I take for
granted, I don't expect it without money. Why but, mistress, says
he, how much are you willing to give? Nay, says I again, friend,

[1] served my purpose with.

I don't know what your rates are in the country here, for I am a stranger; but if you can get one for me, get it as cheap as you can, and I'll give you somewhat for your pains.

Why, that's honestly said too, says the countryman. Not so honest neither, said I, to myself, if thou knewest all. Why, mistress, says he, I have a horse that will carry double, and I don't much care if I go myself with you, an'[1] you like. Will you? says I. Well, I believe you are an honest man; if you will, I shall be glad of it, I'll pay you in reason. Why, look ye, mistress, says he, I won't be out of reason with you, then; if I carry you to Colchester, it will be worth five shillings for myself and my horse, for I shall hardly come back tonight.

In short, I hir'd the honest man and his horse; but when we came to a town upon the road, I do not remember the name of it, but it stands upon a river, I pretended myself very ill, and I could go no farther that night, but if he would stay there with me, because I was a stranger, I would pay him for himself and his horse with all my heart.

This I did because I knew the Dutch gentlemen and their servants would be upon the road that day, either in the stage coaches, or riding post, and I did not know but the drunken fellow, or some body else that might have seen me at Harwich, might see me again, and I thought that in one day's stop they would be all gone by.

We lay all that night there, and the next morning it was not very early when I set out, so that it was near ten a-clock by that time I got to Colchester. It was no little pleasure that I saw the town where I had so many pleasant days, and I made many enquiries after the good old friends I had once had there, but could make little out; they were all dead or remov'd. The young ladies had been all married or gone to London; the old gentleman, and the old lady that had been my early benefactress, all dead; and which troubled me most, the young gentleman, my first lover, and afterwards my brother-in-law, was dead; but two sons, men grown, were left of him, but they too were transplanted to London.

I dismiss'd my old man here, and stay'd incognito for three or four days in Colchester, and then took a passage in a waggon,

[1] if.

because I would not venture being seen in the Harwich coaches; but I needed not have used so much caution, for there was nobody in Harwich but the woman of the house could have known me; nor was it rational to think that she, considering the hurry she was in, and that she never saw me but once, and that by candle light, should have ever discover'd me.

I was now return'd to London, and tho' by the accident of the last adventure I got something considerable, yet I was not fond of any more country rambles; nor should I have ventur'd abroad again if I had carried the trade on to the end of my days. I gave my governess a history of my travels; she lik'd the Harwich journey well enough, and in discoursing of these things between ourselves she observ'd that a thief being a creature that watches the advantages of other people's mistakes, 'tis impossible but that to one that is vigilant and industrious many opportunities must happen, and therefore she thought that one so exquisitely keen in the trade as I was would scarce fail of something wherever I went.

On the other hand, every branch of my story, if duly consider'd, may be useful to honest people, and afford a due caution to people of some sort or other, to guard against the like surprizes, and to have their eyes about them when they have to do with strangers of any kind, for 'tis very seldom that some snare or other is not in their way. The moral indeed of all my history is left to be gather'd by the senses and judgment of the reader. I am not qualified to preach to them; let the experience of one creature compleatly wicked, and compleatly miserable, be a storehouse of useful warning to those that read.

I am drawing now towards a new variety of life. Upon my return, being hardened by a long race of crime and success unparallel'd, I had, as I have said, no thoughts of laying down a trade which, if I was to judge by the example of others, must however end at last in misery and sorrow.

It was on the Christmas-day following, in the evening, that to finish a long train of wickedness, I went abroad to see what might offer in my way; when, going by a working silversmith's in Foster-lane, I saw a tempting bait indeed, and not to be resisted by one of my occupation; for the shop had nobody in it, and a great deal of loose plate lay in the window, and at the seat of the man who, I suppose, work'd at one side of the shop.

I went boldly in and was just going to lay my hand upon a peice of plate, and might have done it, and carried it clear off, for any care that the men who belong'd to the shop had taken of it; but an officious fellow in a house on the other side of the way, seeing me go in, and that there was nobody in the shop, comes running over the street, and without asking me what I was, or who, seizes upon me, and cries out for the people of the house.

I had not touch'd any thing in the shop, and seeing a glimpse of some body running over, I had so much presence of mind as to knock very hard with my foot on the floor of the house, and was just calling out too, when the fellow laid hands on me.

However, as I had always most courage when I was in most danger, so, when he laid hands on me, I stood very high upon it; that I came in to buy half a dozen of silver spoons, and, to my good fortune, it was a silver-smith's that sold plate, as well as work'd plate, for other shops. The fellow laugh'd at that part, and put such a value upon the service that he had done his neighbour, that he would have it be that I came not to buy, but to steal, and raising a great crowd, I said to the master of the shop, who by this time was fetch'd home from some neighbouring place, that it was in vain to make a noise, and enter into talk there of the case; the fellow had insisted that I came to steal, and he must prove it, and I desir'd we might go before a magistrate without any more words; for I began to see I should be too hard for the man that had seiz'd me.

The master and mistress of the shop were really not so violent as the man from t'other side of the way; and the man said, Mistress, you might come into the shop with a good design for ought I know, but it seem'd a dangerous thing for you to come into such a shop as mine is when you see nobody there, and I cannot do so little justice to my neighbour, who was so kind, as not to acknowledge he had reason on his side; tho' upon the whole I do not find you attempt'd to take any thing, and I really know not what to do in it. I press'd him to go before a magistrate with me, and if any thing cou'd be prov'd on me that was like a design, I should willingly submit, but if not I expected reparation.

Just while we were in this debate, and a crowd of people gather'd about the door, came by Sir T. B., an alderman of the city, and justice of the peace, and the goldsmith hearing of it, entreated his worship to come in and decide the case.

Give the goldsmith his due, he told his story with a great deal of justice and moderation, and the fellow that had come over and seiz'd upon me told his with as much heat and foolish passion, which did me good still. It came then to my turn to speak, and I told his worship that I was a stranger in London, being newly come out of the North, that I lodg'd in such a place, that I was passing this street, and went into a goldsmith's shop to buy half a dozen of spoons; by great good luck I had an old silver spoon in my pocket, which I pull'd out, and told him I had carried that spoon to match it with half a dozen of new ones, that it might match some I had in the country.

That seeing nobody in the shop, I knock'd with my foot very hard to make people hear, and had also call'd aloud with my voice. 'Tis true, there was loose plate in the shop, but that nobody cou'd say I had touch'd any of it; that a fellow came running into the shop out of the street, and laid hands on me in a furious manner, in the very moment while I was calling for the people of the house; that if he had really had a mind to have done his neighbour any service, he should have stood at a distance, and silently watch'd to see whether I had touch'd any thing or no, and then have taken me in the fact. That is very true, says Mr. Alderman; and turning to the fellow that stopt me, he ask'd him if it was true that I knock'd with my foot. He said, yes, I had knock'd, but that might be because of his coming. Nay, says the Alderman, taking him short, now you contradict yourself, for just now you said she was in the shop with her back to you, and did not see you till you came upon her. Now it was true that my back was partly to the street, but yet, as my business was of a kind that requir'd me to have eyes every way, so I really had a glance of him running over, as I said before, tho' he did not perceive it.

After a full hearing, the alderman gave it as his opinion that his neighbour was under a mistake, and that I was innocent, and the goldsmith acquiesc'd in it too, and his wife, and so I was dismiss'd; but as I was going to depart, Mr. Alderman said, But hold, madam, if you were designing to buy spoons I hope you will not let my friend here lose his customer by the mistake. I readily answered, No, sir, I'll buy the spoons still if he can match my odd spoon, which I brought for a pattern; and the goldsmith shew'd me some of the very same fashion; so he weigh'd the spoons, and they came to five and thirty shillings, so I pulls out my purse to pay him, in which I had near 20 guineas, for I never went without such a sum about me, whatever might happen, and I found it of use at other times as well as now.

When Mr. Alderman saw my money, he said, Well, madam, now I am satisfy'd you were wrong'd, and it was for this reason that I mov'd you should buy the spoons, and staid till you had bought them, for if you had not had money to pay for them, I should have suspected that you did not come into the shop to buy, for the sort of people who come upon those designs that you have been charg'd with are seldom troubl'd with much gold in their pockets, as I see you are.

I smil'd, and told his worship that then I ow'd something of his favour to my money, but I hop'd he saw reason also in the justice he had done me before. He said, yes, he had, but this had confirm'd his opinion, and he was fully satisfy'd now of my having been injur'd; so I came well off from an affair in which I was at the very brink of destruction.

It was but three days after this that, not at all made cautious by my former danger as I us'd to be, and still pursuing the art which I had so long been employ'd in, I ventur'd into a house where I saw the doors open, and furnish'd myself, as I thought verily without being perceiv'd, with two peices of flower'd silks, such as they call brocaded silk, very rich; it was not a mercer's shop, nor a warehouse of a mercer, but look'd like a private dwelling-house, and was, it seems, inhabited by a man that sold goods for a weaver to the mercer's, like a broker or factor.

That I may make short of the black part of this story, I was attack'd by two wenches that came open-mouth'd at me just as I was going out at the door, and one of them pull'd me back into the room, while the other shut the door upon me. I would have given them good words, but there was no room for it; two fiery dragons cou'd not have been more furious, they tore my cloaths, bully'd and roar'd, as if they would have murther'd me; the mistress of the house came next, and then the master, and all outrageous.

I gave the master very good words, told him the door was open, and things were a temptation to me, that I was poor, and distress'd, and poverty was what many could not resist, and beg'd him with tears to have pity on me. The mistress of the house was mov'd with compassion, and enclin'd to have let me go, and had almost perswaded her husband to it also, but the sawcy wenches were run even before they were sent, and had fetch'd a constable, and then the master said he could not go back, I must go before a justice, and answer'd his wife that he might come into trouble himself if he should let me go.

The sight of a constable indeed struck me, and I thought I should have sunk into the ground; I fell into faintings, and indeed the people themselves thought I would have died, when the woman argued again for me, and entreated her husband, seeing they had lost nothing to let me go. I offer'd him to pay for the two peices, whatever the value was, tho' I had not got them, and argu'd that as he had his goods, and had really lost nothing, it would be cruel to pursue me to death and have my blood for the bare attempt of taking them. I put the constable in mind, too, that I had broke no doors, nor carried any thing away; and when I came to the justice, and pleaded there that I had neither broken any thing to get in, nor carried any thing out, the justice was enclin'd to have releas'd me; but the first sawcy jade that stop'd me affirming that I was going out with the goods, but that she stop'd me and pull'd me back, the justice upon that point committed me, and I was carried to Newgate; that horrid place! my very blood chills at the mention of its name; the place where so many of my comrades had been lock'd up, and from whence they went to the fatal tree; the place where my mother suffered so deeply, where I was brought into the world, and from whence I expected no redemption but by an infamous death. To conclude, the place that had so long expected me, and which with so much art and success I had so long avoided.

I was now fix'd indeed; 'tis impossible to describe the terror of my mind, when I was first brought in, and when I look'd round upon all the horrors of that dismal place. I look'd on my self as lost, and that I had nothing to think of but of going out of the world, and that with the utmost infamy; the hellish noise, the roaring, swearing and clamour, the stench and nastiness, and all the dreadful afflicting things that I saw there, joyn'd to make the place seem an emblem of hell itself, and a kind of an entrance into it.

Now I reproach'd myself with the many hints I had had, as I have mention'd above, from my own reason, from the sense of my good circumstances, and of the many dangers I had escap'd to leave off while I was well, and how I had withstood them all and hardened my thoughts against all fear; it seem'd to me that I was hurried on by an inevitable fate to this day of misery, and that now I was to expiate all my offences at the gallows, that I was now to give satisfaction to justice with my blood, and that I was to come to the last hour of my life, and of my wickedness, together. These things pour'd themselves in upon my thoughts in a confus'd manner, and left me overwhelm'd with melancholly and despair.

Then I repented heartily of all my life past, but that repentance yielded me no satisfaction, no peace, no, not in the least, because, as I said to myself, it was repenting after the power of farther sinning was taken away. I seem'd not to mourn that I had committed such crimes, and for the fact, as it was an offence against God and my neighbour, but that I was to be punish'd for it; I was a penitent, as I thought, not that I had sinn'd, but that I was to suffer, and this took away all the comfort of my repentance in my thoughts.

I got no sleep for several nights or days after I came into that wretch'd place, and glad I wou'd have been for some time to have died there, tho' I did not consider dying as it ought to be consider'd neither; indeed, nothing could be fill'd with more horror to my imagination than the very place, nothing was more odious to me than the company that was there. O! if I had but been sent to any place in the world, and not to Newgate, I should have thought myself happy.

In the next place, how did the harden'd wretches that were there before me triumph over me! What! Mrs. Flanders come to Newgate at last? what, Mrs. Mary, Mrs. Molly, and after that plain Moll Flanders! They thought the Devil had help'd me, they said, that I had reign'd so long. They expected me there many years ago, they said, and was I come at last? Then they flouted me with dejections, welcom'd me to the place, wish'd me joy, bid me have a good heart, not be cast down; things might not be so bad as I fear'd, and the like; then call'd for brandy, and drank to me; but put it all up to my score, for they told me I was but just come to the college, as they call'd it, and sure I had money in my pocket, tho' they had none.

I ask'd one of this crew how long she had been there. She said, four months. I ask'd her how the place look'd to her when she first came into it. Just as it did now to me, says she, dreadful and frightful, that she thought she was in hell. And I believe so still, adds she, but it is natural to me now, I don't disturb myself about it. I suppose, says I, you are in no danger of what is to follow. Nay, says she, you are mistaken there, I am sure, for I am under sentence, only I pleaded my belly, but am no more with child than the judge that try'd me, and I expect to be called down next session. This *calling down* is calling down to their former judgement, when a woman has been respited for her belly, but proves not to be with child, or if she has been with child, and has been brought to bed. Well, says I, and are you thus easy? Ay, says she, I can't help myself; what signifyes being sad? If I am hang'd, there's an end of me; and away she turn'd dancing, and sings as she goes, the following piece of Newgate wit,

If I swing by the string,
I shall hear the bell ring,[1]
And then there's an end of poor Jenny.

I mention this because it would be worth the observation of any prisoner who shall hereafter fall into the same misfortune and come to that dreadful place of Newgate, how time, necessity, and conversing with the wretches that are there familiarizes the place to them; how at last they become reconcil'd to that which at first was the greatest dread upon their spirits in the world, and are as impudently chearful and merry in their misery, as they were when out of it.

I cannot say, as some do, this devil is not so black as he is painted; for indeed no colours can represent that place to the life; nor any soul conceive aright of it but those who have been sufferers there. But how hell should become by degrees so natural,

[1] The bell of St. Sepulchre's, which tolls upon execution-day. [Defoe.]

and not only tollerable, but even agreeable, is a thing unintelligible but by those who have experienc'd it as I have.

The same night that I was sent to Newgate, I sent the news of it to my old governess, who was surpriz'd at it, you may be sure, and spent the night almost as ill out of Newgate as I did in it.

The next morning, she came to see me; she did what she cou'd to comfort me, but she saw that was to no purpose; however, as she said, to sink under the weight was but to encrease the weight. She immediately applied herself to all the proper methods to prevent the effects of it which we fear'd; and first she found out the two fiery jades that had surpriz'd me; she tamper'd with them, persuaded them, offer'd them money, and, in a word, try'd all imaginable ways to prevent a prosecution; she offer'd one of the wenches 100*l.* to go away from her mistress, and not to appear against me; but she was so resolute that tho' she was but a servant maid at 3*l.* a year wages or thereabouts, she refus'd it, and would have refus'd, as my governess said she believ'd, if she had offer'd her 500*l.* Then she attack'd the other maid; she was not so hard-hearted as the other, and sometimes seem'd enclin'd to be merciful; but the first wench kept her up, and would not so much as let my governess talk with her, but threatn'd to have her up for tampering with the evidence.

Then she apply'd to the master, that is to say, the man whose goods had been stol'n, and particularly to his wife, who was enclin'd at first to have some compassion for me; she found the woman the same still, but the man alledg'd he was bound to prosecute, and that he should forfeit his recognizance.

My governess offer'd to find friends that should get his recognizances off of the file, as they call it, and that he should not suffer; but it was not possible to convince him that he could be safe any way in the world but by appearing against me; so I was to have three witnesses of fact against me, the master and his two maids, that is to say, I was as certain to be cast for my life [1] as I was that I was alive, and I had nothing to do but to think of dying. I had but a sad foundation to build upon for that, as I said before, for all my repentance appear'd to me to be only the effect of my fear of death, not a sincere regret for the wicked

[1] condemned to death.

life that I had liv'd, and which had brought this misery upon me, or for the offending my Creator, who was now suddenly to be my judge.

I liv'd many days here under the utmost horror; I had death as it were in view, and thought of nothing night or day but of gibbets and halters, evil spirits and devils; it is not to be expressed how I was harass'd, between the dreadful apprehensions of death, and the terror of my conscience reproaching me with my past horrible life.

The ordinary of Newgate came to me, and talk'd a little in his way, but all his divinity run upon confessing my crime, as he call'd it (tho' he knew not what I was in for), making a full discovery, and the like, without which he told me God would never forgive me; and he said so little to the purpose that I had no manner of consolation from him. And then to observe the poor creature preaching confession and repentance to me in the morning, and find him drunk with brandy by noon, this had something in it so shocking that I began to nauseate the man, and his work too by degrees for the sake of the man; so that I desired him to trouble me no more.

I know not how it was, but by the indefatigable application of my diligent governess I had no bill preferr'd against me the first sessions, I mean to the grand jury, at Guild-Hall; so I had another month, or five weeks, before me, and without doubt this ought to have been accepted by me as so much time given me for reflection upon what was past, and preparation for what was to come; I ought to have esteem'd it as a space given me for repentance, and have employ'd it as such; but it was not in me, I was sorry (as before) for being in Newgate, but had few signs of repentance about me.

On the contrary, like the water in the hollows of mountains, which petrifies and turns into stone whatever they are suffer'd to drop upon, so the continual conversing with such a crew of hell-hounds had the same common operation upon me as upon other people: I degenerated into stone, I turn'd first stupid and senseless, and then brutish and thoughtless, and at last raving mad as any of them were; in short, I became as naturally pleas'd and easy with the place as if indeed I had been born there.[1]

[1] Defoe appears to have forgotten that Moll *was* born in Newgate.

It is scarce possible to imagine that our natures should be capable of so much degeneracy as to make that pleasant and agreeable that in it self is the most compleat misery. Here was a circumstance, that I think it is scarce possible to mention a worse; I was as exquisitely miserable as it was possible for any one to be that had life and health, and money to help them, as I had.

I had a weight of guilt upon me, enough to sink any creature who had the least power of reflection left, and had any sense upon them of the happiness of this life, or the misery of another; I had at first some remorse indeed, but no repentance; I had now neither remorse or repentance. I had a crime charg'd on me, the punishment of which was death; the proof so evident that there was no room for me so much as to plead not guilty; I had the name of an old offender, so that I had nothing to expect but death, neither had I myself any thoughts of escaping, and yet a certain strange lethargy of soul possess'd me; I had no trouble, no apprehensions, no sorrow about me, the first surprize was gone. I was, I may well say, I know not how; my senses, my reason, nay, my conscience, were all asleep; my course of life for forty years had been a horrid complication of wickedness; whoredom, adultery, incest, lying, theft, and, in a word, every-thing but murther and treason, had been my practice, from the age of eighteen, or thereabouts, to threescore; and now I was ingulph'd in the misery of punishment, and had an infamous death at the door, and yet I had no sense of my condition, no thought of heaven or hell, at least, that went any farther than a bare flying touch, like the stitch or pain that gives a hint and goes off; I neither had a heart to ask God's mercy, or indeed to think of it, and in this I think I have given a brief description of the compleatest misery on earth.

All my terrifying thoughts were past, the horrors of the place were become familiar, and I felt no more uneasiness at the noise and clamours of the prison than they did who made that noise; in a word, I was become a meer Newgate-Bird, as wicked and as outragious as any of them; nay, I scarce retain'd the habit and custom of good breeding and manners, which all along 'till now run thro' my conversation; so thorough a degeneracy had possess'd me, that I was no more the same thing that I had been than if I had never been otherwise than what I was now.

In the middle of this harden'd part of my life, I had another sudden surprize, which call'd me back a little to that thing call'd sorrow, which, indeed, I began to be past the sense of before. They told me one night that there was brought into the prison late the night before three highway-men, who had committed a robbery somewhere, on Hounslow-Heath, I think it was, and were pursu'd to Uxbridge by the country, and there taken after a gallant resistance, in which many of the country people were wounded, and some kill'd.

It is not to be wonder'd that we prisoners were all desirous enough to see these brave, topping gentlemen that were talk'd up to be such as their fellows had not been known,[1] and especially because it was said they would in the morning be remov'd into the press-yard,[2] having given money to the head master of the prison to be allow'd the liberty of that better place. So we that were women plac'd ourselves in the way that we would be sure to see them; but nothing could express the amazement and surprize I was in, when the first man that came out I knew to be my Lancashire husband, the same with whom I liv'd so well at Dunstable, and the same who I afterwards saw at Brickhill, when I was married to my last husband, as has been related.

I was struck dumb at the sight, and knew neither what to say, or what to do; he did not know me, and that was all the present relief I had. I quitted my company, and retir'd as much as that dreadful place suffers any body to retire, and cry'd vehemently for a great while. Dreadful creature, that I am, said I, how many poor people have I made miserable? How many desperate wretches have I sent to the devil? This gentleman's misfortunes I plac'd all to my own account. He had told me at Chester he was ruin'd by that match, and that his fortunes were made desperate on my account; for that, thinking I had been a fortune, he was run into debt more than he was able to pay; that he would go into the army, and carry a musquet, or buy a horse and take a tour, as he call'd it; and tho' I never told him that I was a fortune, and so did not actually deceive him my self, yet I did in-

---

[1] i.e., such as were without parallel.
[2] That part of Newgate prison where the punishment of *peine forte et dure* was carried out, but also a place where a prisoner could obtain better quarters by paying the Governor a sum of money.

courage its having it thought so, and so I was the occasion originally of his mischief.

The surprize of this thing only [1] struck deeper in my thoughts, and gave me stronger reflections than all that had befallen me before; I griev'd day and night, and the more for that [2] they told me he was the captain of the gang, and that he had committed so many robberies that Hind, or Whitney, or the Golden Farmer were fools to him; that he would surely be hang'd if there were no more men left in the country; and that there would be abundance of people come in against him.

I was overwhelm'd with grief for him; my own case gave me no disturbance compar'd to this, and I loaded my self with reproaches on his account; I bewail'd my misfortunes, and the ruin he was now come to, at such a rate that I relish'd nothing now as I did before, and the first reflections I made upon the horrid life I had liv'd began to return upon me, and as these things return'd, my abhorrence of the place, and of the way of living in it, return'd also; in a word, I was perfectly chang'd, and became another body.

While I was under these influences of sorrow for him, came notice to me that the next sessions there would be a bill preferr'd to the grand jury against me, and that I should be try'd for my life. My temper was touch'd before, the wretched boldness of spirit which I had acquir'd, abated, and conscious guilt began to flow in my mind. In short, I began to think, and to think indeed is one real advance from hell to heaven; all that harden'd state and temper of soul which I said so much of before is but a deprivation of thought; he that is restor'd to his thinking is restor'd to himself.

As soon as I began, I say, to think, the first thing that occurr'd to me broke out thus: Lord! what will become of me? I shall be cast, to be sure, and there is nothing beyond that but death! I have no friends; what shall I do? I shall be certainly cast! Lord! have mercy upon me! What will become of me! This was a sad thought, you will say, to be the first (after so long time) that had started in my soul of that kind, and yet even this was nothing but fright at what was to come; there was not a word of sincere repentance in it all. However, I was dreadfully

[1] i.e., this thing alone.   [2] because.

dejected, and disconsolate to the last degree; and as I had no friend to communicate my distress'd thoughts to, it lay so heavy upon me that it threw me into fits and swoonings several times a day. I sent for my old governess, and she, give her her due, acted the part of a true friend; she left no stone unturn'd to prevent the grand jury finding the bill; she went to several of the jury men, talk'd with them, and endeavour'd to possess them with favourable dispositions on account that nothing was taken away, and no house broken, &c. But all would not do; the two wenches swore home to the fact, and the jury found the bill for robbery and house-breaking, that is for felony and burglary.

I sunk down when they brought the news of it, and after I came to my self, I thought I should have died with the weight of it. My governess acted a true mother to me, she pitty'd me, she cry'd with me, and for me, but she could not help me; and to add to the terror of it, 'twas the discourse all over the house [1] that I should dye for it; I could hear them talk it among themselves very often, and see them shake their heads, and say they were sorry for it, and the like, as is usual in the place; but still no body came to tell me their thoughts, till at last one of the keepers came to me privately, and said with a sigh, Well, Mrs. Flanders, you will be try'd a Friday (this was but a Wednesday), what do you intend to do? I turn'd as white as a clout, and said, God knows what I shall do; for my part, I know not what to do. Why, says he, I won't flatter you,[2] I would have you prepare for death, for I doubt you will be cast; and as you are an old offender, I doubt you will find but little mercy. They say, added he, your case is very plain, and that the witnesses swear so home against you, there will be no standing it.

This was a stab into the very vitals of one under such a burden, and I could not speak a word good or bad for a great while; at last I burst out into tears, and said to him, O sir, what must I do? Do, says he, send for a minister, and talk with him; for indeed, Mrs. Flanders, unless you have very good friends, you are no woman for this world.

This was plain dealing indeed, but it was very harsh to me, at least I thought it so. He left me in the greatest confusion imaginable, and all that night I lay awake; and now I began to

---

[1] i.e., the prison.   [2] raise your hopes.

say my prayers, which I had scarce done before since my last
husband's death, or from a little while after; and truly I may
well call it *saying my prayers*; for I was in such a confusion,
and had such horror upon my mind, that tho' I cry'd, and repeated several times the ordinary expression of, *Lord, have
mercy upon me*, I never brought myself to any sense of being a
miserable sinner, as indeed I was, and of confessing my sins to
God, and begging pardon for the sake of Jesus Christ; I was
overwhelm'd with the sense of my condition, being try'd for my
life, and being sure to be executed, and on this account I cry'd
out all night, Lord! what will become of me? Lord! what shall
I do? Lord have mercy upon me, and the like.

My poor afflicted governess was now as much concern'd as I,
and a great deal more truly penitent; tho' she had no prospect of
being brought to a sentence, not but that she deserv'd it as much
as I, and so she said herself; but she had not done any thing for
many years other than receiving what I and others had stolen,
and encouraging us to steal it. But she cry'd and took on like a
distracted body, wringing her hands, and crying out that she
was undone, that she believ'd there was a curse from heaven upon
her, that she should be damn'd, that she had been the destruction
of all her friends, that she brought such a one, and such a one,
and such a one to the gallows; and there she reckon'd up ten or
eleven people, some of which I have given an account of that
came to untimely ends, and that now she was the occasion of
my ruin, for she had persuaded me to go on when I would have
left off. I interrupted her there: No, mother, no, said I, don't
speak of that, for you would have had me left off when I got
the mercer's money again, and when I came home from Harwich,
and I would not hearken to you; therefore you have not been to
blame, it is I only have ruin'd myself, I have brought myself to
this misery; and thus we spent many hours together.

Well, there was no remedy; the prosecution went on, and on
the Thursday I was carried down to the sessions-house, where I
was arraign'd, as they call'd it, and the next day I was appointed
to be try'd. At the arraignment I pleaded not guilty, and well I
might, for I was indicted for felony and burglary; that is for
feloniously stealing two pieces of brocaded silk, value 46*l*., the
goods of Anthony Johnson, and for breaking open the doors;

whereas I knew very well they could not pretend I had broken up the doors, or so much as lifted up a latch.

On the Friday I was brought to my tryal, I had exhausted my spirits with crying for two or three days before, that [1] I slept better the Thursday night than I expected, and had more courage for my tryal than I thought possible for me to have.

When the tryal began, and the indictment was read, I would have spoke, but they told me the witnesses must be heard first, and then I should have time to be heard. The witnesses were the two wenches, a couple of hard mouth'd jades indeed, for tho' the thing was truth in the main, yet they aggravated it to the utmost extremity, and swore I had the goods wholly in my possession, that I had hid them among my cloaths, that I was going off with them, that I had one foot over the threshold when they discover'd [2] themselves, and then I put t'other over, so that I was quite out of the house in the street with the goods before they took me, and then they seiz'd me, and took the goods upon me. The fact in general was true, but I insisted upon it that they stop'd me before I had set my foot clear of the threshold: but that did not argue much, for I had taken the goods and was bringing them away, if I had not been taken.

I pleaded that I had stole nothing, they had lost nothing; that the door was open, and I went in with design to buy; if, seeing no body in the house, I had taken any of them up in my hand, it cou'd not be concluded that I intended to steal them, for that I never carried them farther than the door to look on them with the better light.

The court would not allow that by any means, and made a kind of a jest of my intending to buy the goods, that being no shop for the selling of any thing, and as to carrying them to the door to look at them, the maids made their impudent mocks upon that, and spent their wit upon it very much; told the court I had look'd at them sufficiently, and approv'd them very well, for I had pack'd them up, and was a going with them.

In short, I was found guilty of felony, but acquited of the burglary, wich was but small comfort to me, the first bringing me to a sentence of death, and the last would have done no more. The next day, I was carried down to receive the dreadful sen-

[1] i.e., so that.   [2] revealed.

tence, and when they came to ask me what I had to say, why sentence should not pass, I stood mute a while, but some body prompted me aloud to speak to the judges, for that[1] they cou'd represent things favourably for me. This encourag'd me, and I told them I had nothing to say to stop the sentence; but that I had much to say to bespeak the mercy of the court, that I hop'd they would allow something in such a case for the circumstances of it, that I had broken no doors, had carried nothing off, that no body had lost any thing; that the person whose goods they were, was pleas'd to say, he desir'd mercy might be shown, which indeed he very honestly did, that at the worst it was the first offence, and that I had never been before any court of justice before; and, in a word, I spoke with more courage than I thought I cou'd have done, and in such a moving tone, and tho' with tears, (yet not so many tears as to obstruct my speech), that I cou'd see it mov'd others to tears that heard me.

The judges sat grave and mute, gave me an easy hearing, and time to say all that I would, but saying neither yes or no to it, pronounc'd the sentence of death upon me; a sentence to me like death itself, which confounded me; I had no more spirit left in me, I had no tongue to speak, or eyes to look up either to God or man.

My poor governess was utterly disconsolate, and she that was my comforter before wanted comfort now herself, and sometimes mourning, sometimes raging, was as much out of herself as any mad woman in Bedlam. Nor was she only disconsolate as to me, but she was struck with horror at the sense of her own wicked life, and began to look back upon it with a taste quite different from mine; for she was penitent to the highest degree for her sins, as well as sorrowful for the misfortune. She sent for a minister too, a serious pious good man, and apply'd herself with such earnestness by his assistance to the work of a sincere repentance, that I believe, and so did the minister too, that she was a true penitent, and, which is still more, she was not only so for the occasion, and at that juncture, but she continu'd so, as I was inform'd, to the day of her death.

It is rather to be thought of than express'd what was now my condition; I had nothing before me but death; and as I had no

[1] because.

friends to assist me, I expected nothing but to find my name in the dead warrant, which was to come for the execution next Friday of five more and myself.

In the mean time my poor distress'd governess sent me a minister, who at her request came to visit me. He exhorted me seriously to repent of all my sins, and to dally no longer with my soul; not flattering myself with hopes of life, which, he said, he was inform'd there was no room to expect, but unfeign'dly to look up to God with my whole soul, and to cry for pardon in the name of Jesus Christ. He back'd his discourses with proper quotations of Scripture, encouraging the greatest sinner to repent, and turn from their evil way, and when he had done, he kneeled down and pray'd with me.

It was now that for the first time I felt any real signs of repentance; I now began to look back upon my past life with abhorrence, and having a kind of view into the other side of time, the things of life, as I believe they do with every body at such a time, began to look with a different aspect, and quite another shape, than they did before, The views of felicity, the joy, the griefs of life were quite other things; and I had nothing in my thoughts but was so infinitely superiour to what I had known in life, that it appear'd to be the greatest stupidity to lay a weight upon any thing, tho' the most valuable in this world.

The word *eternity* represented it self with all its incomprehensible additions, and I had such extended notions of it that I know not how to express them. Among the rest, how absurd did every pleasant thing look (I mean, that we had counted pleasant before) when I reflected that these sordid trifles were the things for which we forfeited eternal felicity!

With these reflections came in, of meer course, severe reproaches for my wretched behaviour in my past life; that I had forfeited all hope of happiness in the eternity that I was just going to enter into; and, on the contrary, was entitled to all that was miserable; and all this with the frightful addition of its being also eternal.

I am not capable of reading lectures of instruction to any body, but I relate this in the very manner in which things then appear'd to me, as far as I am able, but infinitely short of the lively impressions which they made on my soul at that time; indeed, those impressions are not to be explain'd by words, or if they are, I am not mistress of words to express them; it must be the work of every sober reader to make just reflections, as their own circumstances may direct; and this is what every one at some time or other may feel something of; I mean a clearer sight into things to come than they had here, and a dark view of their own concern in them.

But I go back to my own case. The minister press'd me to tell him as far as I thought convenient, in what state I found myself as to the sight I had of things beyond life; he told me he did not come as ordinary of the place,[1] whose business it is to extort confessions from prisoners for the farther detecting of other offenders; that his business was to move me to such freedom of discourse as might serve to disburthen my own mind, and furnish him to administer comfort to me as far as was in his power; assur'd me that whatever I said to him should remain with him, and be as much a secret as if it was known only to God and myself; and that he desir'd to know nothing of me but to qualifie him to give proper advice to me, and to pray to God for me.

This honest friendly way of treating me unlock'd all the sluices of my passions. He broke into my very soul by it; and I unravell'd all the wickedness of my life to him. In a word, I gave him an abridgment of this whole history; I give him the picture of my conduct for 50 years in miniature.

I hid nothing from him, and he in return exhorted me to a sincere repentance, explain'd to me what he meant by repentance, and then drew out such a scheme of infinite mercy, proclaim'd from heaven to sinners of the greatest magnitude, that he left me nothing to say that look'd like despair or doubting of being accepted, and in this condition he left me the first night.

He visited me again the next morning, and went on with his method of explaining the terms of divine mercy, which, according to him, consisted of nothing more difficult than that of being sincerely desirous of it, and willing to accept it; only a sincere regret for and hatred of those things which render'd me so just an object of divine vengeance. I am not able to repeat the excellent discourses of this extraordinary man; all that I am able to do is to say that he reviv'd my heart, and brought me into such

[1] the chaplain of Newgate.

a condition that I never knew any thing of in my life before. I was cover'd with shame and tears for things past, and yet had at the same time a secret surprizing joy at the prospect of being a true penitent, and obtaining the comfort of a penitent, I mean the hope of being forgiven; and so swift did thoughts circulate, and so high did the impressions they had made upon me run, that I thought I cou'd freely have gone out that minute to execution, without any uneasiness at all, casting my soul entirely into the arms of infinite mercy as a penitent.

The good gentleman was so mov'd with a view of the influence which he saw these things had on me, that he blessed God he had come to visit me, and resolv'd not to leave me till the last moment.

It was no less that 12 days after our receiving sentence before any were order'd for execution, and then the dead warrant, as they call it, came down, and I found my name was among them; a terrible blow this was to my new resolutions, indeed my heart sunk within me, and I swoon'd away twice, one after another, but spoke not a word. The good minister was sorely afflicted for me, and did what he could to comfort me with the same arguments, and the same moving eloquence that he did before, and left me not that evening so long as the prison-keepers would suffer him to stay in the prison, unless he wou'd be lock'd up with me all night, which he was not willing to be.

I wonder'd much that I did not see him all the next day, it being but the day before the time appointed for execution; and I was greatly discourag'd and dejected, and indeed almost sunk for want of that comfort which he had so often, and with such success yielded me in his former visits; I waited with great impatience, and under the greatest oppressions of spirits imaginable till about four a-clock; when he came to my apartment, for I had obtain'd the favour by the help of money, nothing being to be done in that place without it, not to be kept in the condemn'd hole, among the rest of the prisoners who were to die, but to have a little dirty chamber to my self.

My heart leap'd within me for joy when I heard his voice at the door, even before I saw him; but let any one judge what kind of motion I found in my soul, when, after having made a short excuse for his not coming, he shew'd me that his time had been employed on my account; that he had obtained a favourable report from the recorder in my case, and in short that he had brought me a reprieve.

He us'd all the caution that he was able in letting me know what it would have been double cruelty to have conceal'd; for as grief had overset me before, so joy overset me now, and I fell into a more dangerous swooning than at first, and it was not without difficulty that I was recover'd at all.

The good man having made a very Christian exhortation to me not to let the joy of my reprieve put the remembrance of my past sorrow out of my mind, and told me that he must leave me to go and enter the reprieve in the books, and show it to the sheriffs, he stood up just before his going away, and in a very earnest manner pray'd to God for me, that my repentance might be made unfeign'd and sincere; and that my coming back as it were into life again might not be a returning to the follies of life, which I had made such solemn resolutions to forsake; I joyn'd heartily in that petition, and must needs say I had deeper impressions upon my mind all that night of the mercy of God in sparing my life, and a greater detestation of my sins, from a sense of that goodness, than I had in all my sorrow before.

This may be thought inconsistent in itself, and wide from the business of this book; particularly, I reflect that many of those who may be pleas'd and diverted with the relation of the wicked part of my story, may not relish this, which is really the best part of my life, the most advantageous to my self, and the most instructive to others; such however will, I hope, allow me liberty to make my story compleat. It would be a severe satyr on such to say they do not relish the repentance as much as they do the crime; and they had rather the history were a compleat tragedy, as it was very likely to have been.

But I go on with my relation. The next morning there was a sad scene indeed in the prison; the first thing I was saluted with in the morning was the tolling of the great bell at St. Sepulchre's, which usher'd in the day. As soon as it began to toll, a dismal groaning and crying was heard from the condemn'd hole, where there lay six poor souls who were to be executed that day, some for one crime, some for another, and two for murther.

This was follow'd by a confus'd clamour in the house among

the several prisoners, expressing their aukward sorrows for the poor creatures that were to die, but in a manner extreamly differing one from another; some cried for them; some brutishly huzza'd, and wish'd them a good journey; some damn'd and curst those that had brought them to it; many pitying them; and some few, but very few, praying for them.

There was hardly room for so much composure of mind as was requir'd for me to bless the merciful Providence that had, as it were, snatch'd me out of the jaws of this destruction. I remained, as it were, dumb and silent, overcome with the sense of it, and not able to express what I had in my heart; for the passions on such occasions as these are certainly so agitated as not to be able presently to regulate their own motions.

All the while the poor condemn'd creatures were preparing for death, and the ordinary, as they call him, was busy with them, disposing them to submit to their sentence: I say, all this while I was seiz'd with a fit of trembling, as much as I cou'd have been if I had been in the same condition as I was the day before; I was so violently agitated by this surprising fit, that I shook as if it had been in an ague; so that I could not speak or look but like one distracted. As soon as they were all put into the carts and gone, which, however, I had not courage enough to see, I say, as soon as they were gone, I fell into a fit of crying involuntarily, as a meer distemper, and yet so violent, and it held me so long, that I knew not what course to take, nor could I stop, or put a checque to it, no, not with all the strength and courage I had.

This fit of crying held me near two hours, and, as I believe, held me till they were all out of the world, and then a most humble penitent serious kind of joy succeeded; a real transport it was, or passion of thankfulness, and in this I continu'd most part of the day.

In the evening the good minister visited me again, and fell to his usual good discourses; he congratulated my having a space yet allow'd me for repentance, whereas the state of those six poor creatures was determin'd,[1] and they were now past the offers of salvation. He press'd me to retain the same sentiments of the things of life that I had when I had a view of eternity; and at the end of all, told me that I should not conclude that all was over,

[1] ended.

that a reprieve was not a pardon, that he could not answer for the effects of it; however, I had this mercy, that I had more time given me, and it was my business to improve that time.

This discourse left a kind of sadness on my heart, as if I might expect the affair would have a tragical issue still, which, however, he had no certainty of, yet I did not at that time question him about it, he having said he would do his utmost to bring it to a good end, and that he hop'd he might, but he would not have me be secure; [1] and the consequence shew'd that he had reason for what he said.

It was about a fortnight after this that I had some just apprehensions that I should be included in the dead warrant at the ensuing sessions; and it was not without great difficulty, and at last an humble petition for transportation, that I avoided it; so ill was I beholding to fame, and so prevailing was the report of being an old offender, tho' in that they did not do me strict justice, for I was not in the sense of the law an old offender, whatever I was in the eye of the judge; for I had never been before them in a judicial way before, so the judges could not charge me with being an old offender, but the recorder was pleas'd to represent my case as he thought fit.

I had now a certainty of life indeed, but with the hard conditions of being order'd for transportation, which was, I say, a hard condition in it self, but not when comparatively consider'd; and therefore I shall make no comments upon the sentence, nor upon the choice I was put to; we all shall choose any thing rather than death, especially when 'tis attended with an uncomfortable prospect beyond it, which was my case.

The good minister, whose interest, tho' a stranger to me, had obtain'd me the reprieve, mourn'd sincerely for his part; he was in hopes, he said, that I should have ended my days under the influence of good instruction, that I might not have forgot my former distresses, and that I should not have been turn'd loose again among such a wretched crew as are thus sent abroad, where, he said, I must have more than ordinary secret assistance from the grace of God, if I did not turn as wicked again as ever.

I have not for a good while mention'd my governess, who had been dangerously sick, and being in as near a view of death, by

[1] over-confident.

her disease, as I was by my sentence, was a very great penitent; I say, I have not mention'd her, nor indeed did I see her in all this time, but being now recovering, and just able to come abroad, she came to see me.

I told her my condition, and what a different flux and reflux of fears and hopes I had been agitated with; I told her what I had escap'd, and upon what terms; and she was present when the minister express'd his fears of my relapsing again into wickedness upon my falling into the wretch'd company that are generally transported. Indeed, I had a melancholly reflection upon it in my own mind, for I knew what a dreadful gang was always sent away together, and said to my governess that the good minister's fears were not without cause. Well, well, says she, but I hope you will not be tempted with such a horrid example as that, and as soon as the minister was gone, she told me she would not have me discourag'd, for perhaps ways and means might be found to dispose of me in a particular way, by my self, of which she would talk farther with me afterward.

I look'd earnestly at her, and thought she look'd more chearful than she usually had done, and I entertain'd immediately a thousand notions of being deliver'd, but could not for my life imagine the methods, or think of one that was feizible; but I was too much concern'd in it to let her go from me without explaining herself, which, tho' she was very loath to do, yet, as I was still pressing, she answer'd me in a few words, thus: Why, you have money, have you not? Did you ever know one in your life that was transported, and had a hundred pound in his pocket? I'll warrant ye, child, says she.

I understood her presently, but told her I saw no room to hope for any thing but a strict execution of the order, and as it was a severity that was esteem'd a mercy, there was no doubt but it would be strictly observ'd. She said no more but this, We will try what can be done; and so we parted.

I lay in the prison near fifteen weeks after this; what the reason of it was I know not, but at the end of this time I was put on board of a ship in the Thames, and with me a gang of thirteen as harden'd, vile creatures as ever Newgate produc'd in my time; and it would really well take up a history longer than mine to describe the degrees of impudence and audacious

villany that those thirteen were arriv'd to, and the manner of
their behaviour in the voyage; of which I have a very diverting
account by me, which the captain of the ship, who carry'd them
over, gave me, and which he caus'd his mate to write down at
large.

It may perhaps be thought trifling to enter here into a relation of all the little incidents which attended me in this interval
of my circumstances; I mean, between the final order for my
transportation and the time of going on board the ship; and I
am too near the end of my story to allow room for it, but something relating to me and my Lancashire husband I must not omit.

He had, as I have observ'd already, been carry'd from the
master's side [1] of the ordinary prison into the press-yard with
three of his comrades, for they found another to add to them
after some time. Here, for what reason I knew not, they were
kept without being brought to a tryal almost three months; it
seems they found means to bribe or buy off some who were
to come in against them, and they wanted evidence to convict
them. After some puzzle on this account, they made shift to
get proof enough against two of them to carry them off; but
the other two, of which my Lancashire husband was one, lay
still in suspence. They had, I think, one positive evidence against
each of them; but the law obliging them to have two witnesses,
they could make nothing of it; yet they were resolv'd not to
part with the men neither, not doubting but evidence would at
last come in; and in order to this, I think publication was made
that such prisoners were taken, and any one might come to
the prison and see them.

I took this opportunity to satisfy my curiosity, pretending I
had been robb'd in the Dunstable coach, and that I would go
to see the two highway men; but when I came into the press-
yard, I so disguis'd my self, and muffled my face up so, that
he could see little of me, and knew nothing of who I was, but
when I came back, I said publickly that I knew them very well.

Immediately it was all over the prison that Moll Flanders would
turn evidence against one of the highway-men, and that I was
to come off by it from the sentence of transportation.

They heard of it, and immediately my husband desir'd to see

[1] one of the four "sides," or sections, into which Newgate was divided.

this Mrs. Flanders that knew him so well, and was to be an evidence against him, and accordingly I had leave to go to him. I dress'd myself up as well as the best cloaths that I suffer'd myself ever to appear in there would allow me, and went to the press-yard, but had a hood over my face; he said little to me at first, but ask'd me if I knew him. I told him, yes, very well; but as I conceal'd my face, so I counterfeited my voice too, that he had no guess at who I was. He ask'd me where I had seen him; I told him between Dunstable and Brickhill; but turning to the keeper that stood by, I ask'd if I might not be admitted to talk with him alone. He said, yes, yes; and so very civily withdrew.

As soon as he was gone, and I had shut the door, I threw off my hood, and bursting out into tears, My dear, said I, do you not know me? He turn'd pale and stood speechless, like one thunder struck, and not able to conquer the surprize, said no more but this, Let me sit down; and sitting down by the table, leaning his head on his hand, fix'd his eyes on the ground as one stupid. I cry'd so vehemently, on the other hand, that it was a good while e'er I could speak any more; but after I had given vent to my passion, I repeated the same words: My dear, do you not know me? At which he answer'd, Yes, and said no more a good while.

After some time continuing in the surprize, as above, he cast up his eyes towards me and said, How could you be so cruel? I did not really understand what he meant; and I answer'd, How can you call me cruel? To come to me, says he, in such a place as this, is it not to insult me? I have not robb'd you, at least not on the highway.

I perceiv'd by this that he knew nothing of the miserable circumstances I was in, and thought that, having got intelligence of his being there, I had come to upbraid him with his leaving me; but I had too much to say to him to be affronted, and told him in a few words that I was far from coming to insult him, but at best I came to condole mutually; that he would be easily satisfy'd that I had no such view, when I should tell him that my condition was worse than his, and that many ways. He look'd a little concern'd at the expression of my condition being worse than his; but, with a kind of a smile, said, How

can that be? When you see me fetter'd, and in Newgate, and
two of my companions executed already, can you say your condition is worse than mine?

Come, my dear, says I, we have a long piece of work to do,
if I should be to relate, or you to hear, my unfortunate history;
but if you will hear it, you will soon conclude with me that
my condition is worse than yours. How is that possible, says he,
when I expect to be cast for my life the very next sessions?
Yes, says I, 'tis very possible; when I shall tell you that I have
been cast for my life three sessions ago, and am now under
sentence of death, is not my case worse than yours?

Then indeed he stood silent again, like one struck dumb, and
after a little while he starts up. Unhappy couple! says he. How
can this be possible? I took him by the hand. Come, my dear,
said I, sit down, and let us compare our sorrows: I am a prisoner
in this very house, and in a much worse circumstance than you,
and you will be satisfy'd I do not come to insult you when I
tell you the particulars; and with this we sat down together, and
I told him so much of my story as I thought convenient, bringing it at last to my being reduc'd to great poverty, and representing myself as fallen into some company that led me to relieve
my distresses by a way that I had been utterly unacquainted with,
and that they making an attempt on a tradesman's house I was
seiz'd upon, for having been but just at the door, the maid-
servant pulling me in; that I neither had broke any lock, or taken
any thing away, and that, notwithstanding that, I was brought in
guilty, and sentenc'd to die; but that the judges having been
made sensible of the hardship of my circumstances, had obtain'd
leave for me to be transported.

I told him I far'd the worse for being taken in the prison for
one Moll Flanders, who was a famous successful thief that all
of them had heard of, but none of them had ever seen, but that,
as he knew, was none of my name; but I plac'd all to the account
of my ill fortune, and that under this name I was dealt with as
an old offender, tho' this was the first thing they had ever known
of me. I gave him a long account of what had befallen me since
I saw him; but told him I had seen him since he might think I
had; then gave him an account how I had seen him at Brickhill;
how he was pursued, and how, by giving an account that I knew

him, and that he was a very honest gentleman, the hue and cry
was stopp'd, and the high constable went back again.

He listen'd most attentively to all my story, and smil'd at the
particulars, being all of them infinitely below what he had been
at the head of; but when I came to the story of little Brickhill,
he was surpriz'd. And was it you, my dear, said he, that gave
the check to the mob at Brickhill? Yes, said I, it was I indeed.
Then I told him the particulars which I had observ'd of him
there. Why then, said he, it was you that sav'd my life at that
time, and I am glad I owe my life to you, for I will pay the debt
to you now, and I'll deliver you from the present condition you
are in, or I will die in the attempt.

I told him by no means; it was a risque too great, not worth
his running the hazzard of, and for a life not worth his saving.
'Twas no matter for that, he said, it was a life worth all the
world to him; a life that had given him a new life; for, says he,
I was never in real danger but that time till the last minute when
I was taken. Indeed, his danger then lay in his believing he had
not been pursu'd that way; for they had gone off from Hockley
quite another way, and had come over the enclos'd country into
Brickhill, and were sure they had not been seen by any body.

Here he gave a long history of his life, which indeed would
make a very strange history, and be infinitely diverting. He
told me that he took the road about twelve year before he marry'd
me; that the woman which call'd him brother was not any kin
to him; but one that belong'd to their gang, and who, keeping
correspondence with them, liv'd always in town, having great
acquaintance; that she gave them perfect intelligence of persons
going out of town, and that they had made several good booties
by her correspondence; that she thought she had fix'd a fortune
for him when she brought me to him, but happen'd to be disappointed, which he really could not blame her for; that, if I had
had an estate, which she was inform'd I had, he had resolv'd to
leave off the road, and live a new life, but never to appear in
publick till some general pardon had been pass'd, or 'till he
could, for money, have got his name into some particular pardon,
so that he might have been perfectly easy, but that as it had
prov'd otherwise, he was oblig'd to take up the old trade again.

He gave a long account of some of his adventures, and particularly one where he robb'd the West Chester coaches, near Litchfield, when he got a very great booty; and after that, how he robb'd five grasiers in the West, going to Burford Fair in Wiltshire to buy sheep; he told me he got so much money on those two occasions that, if he had known where to have found me, he would certainly have embrac'd my proposal of going with me to Virginia; or to have settled in a plantation on some other of the English colonies in America.

He told me he wrote three letters to me, directed according to my order, but heard nothing from me. This indeed I knew to be true, but the letters coming to my hand in the time of my latter husband, I could do nothing in it, and therefore gave no answer, that so he might believe they had miscarried.

Being thus disappointed, he said, he carry'd on the old trade ever since, tho' when he had gotten so much money, he said, he did not run such desperate risques as he did before; then he gave me some account of several hard and desperate encounters which he had with gentlemen on the road who parted too hardly with their money; and shew'd me some wounds he had receiv'd, and he had one or two very terrible wounds indeed, particularly one by a pistol bullet which broke his arm, and another with a sword which run him quite thro' the body, but that missing his vitals he was cur'd again; one of his comrades having kept with him so faithfully, and so friendly, as that he assisted him in riding near 80 miles before his arm was set, and then got a surgeon in a considerable city, remote from the place where it was done, pretending they were gentlemen travelling towards Carlisle, that they had been attack'd on the road by highwaymen, and that one of them had shot him into the arm.

This, he said, his friend manag'd so well that they were not suspected, but lay still 'till he was cur'd. He gave me also so many distinct accounts of his adventures, that it is with great reluctance that I decline the relating them: but this is my own story, not his.

I then enquir'd into the circumstances of his present case, and what it was he expected when he came to be try'd. He told me that they had no evidence against him, for that of the three robberies which they were all charg'd with, it was his good fortune that he was but in one of them, and that there was but one witness to be had to that fact, which was not sufficient; but that it was expected some others would come in, and that he thought, when he first saw me, I had been one that came of that errand; but that if no body came in against him, he hop'd he should be clear'd; that he had some intimation that if he would submit to transport himself, he might be admitted to it without a tryal, but that he could not think of it with any temper,[1] and thought he could much easier submit to be hang'd.

I blam'd him for that; first, because if he was transported, there might be an hundred ways for him that was a gentleman, and a bold enterprising man, to find his way back again, and perhaps some ways and means to come back before he went. He smil'd at that part, and said he should like the last the best of the two, for he had a kind of horror upon his mind at his being sent to the plantations as the Romans sent slaves to work in the mines; that he thought the passage into another state much more tolerable at the gallows, and that this was the general notion of all the gentlemen who were driven by the exigence of their fortunes to take the road; that at the place of execution there was at least an end of all the miseries of the present state, and as for what was to follow, a man was, in his opinion, as likely to repent sincerely in the last fortnight of his life under the agonies of a gaol and the condemn'd hole as he would ever be in the woods and wildernesses of America; that servitude and hard labour were things gentlemen could never stoop to, that it was but the way to force them to be their own executioners, which was much worse, and that he could not have any patience when he did but think of it.

I used the utmost of my endeavour to persuade him, and joyn'd that known woman's rhetorick to it, I mean that of tears. I told him the infamy of a publick execution was certainly a greater pressure upon the spirits of a gentleman than any mortifications that he could meet with abroad; that he had at least, in the other, a chance for his life, whereas here he had none at all; that it was the easiest thing in the world for him to manage the captain of a ship, who were, generally speaking, men of good humour, and a small matter of conduct, especially if there was any money to be had, would make way for him to buy himself off when he came to Virginia.

[1] equanimity.

He look'd wishfully at me, and I guess'd he meant that he had no money, but I was mistaken; his meaning was another way. You hinted just now, my dear, said he, that there might be a way of coming back before I went, by which I understood you that it might be possible to buy it off here; I had rather give 200*l*. to prevent going, than 100*l*. to be set at liberty when I came there. That is, my dear, said I, because you do not know the place so well as I do. That may be, said he, and yet I believe, as well as you know it, you would do the same, unless it is because, as you told me, you have a mother there.

I told him, as to my mother, she must be dead many years before; and as for any other relations that I might have there, I knew them not; that since my misfortunes had reduc'd me to the condition I had been in for some years, I had not kept up any correspondence with them; and that he would easily believe I should find but a cold reception from them, if I should be put to make my first visit in the condition of a transported felon; that therefore if I went thither, I resolved not to see them; but that I had many views in going there, which took off all the uneasy part of it; and if he found himself oblig'd to go also, I should easily instruct him how to manage himself so as never to go a servant at all, especially since I found he was not destitute of money, which was the only friend in such a condition.

He smil'd, and said he did not tell me he had money. I took him up short, and told him I hop'd he did not understand by my speaking that I should expect any supply from him if he had money; that, on the other hand, tho' I had not a great deal, yet I did not want, and while I had any I would rather add to him than weaken him, seeing, whatever he had, I knew in the case of transportation he would have occasion of it all.

He express'd himself in a most tender manner upon that head; he told me what money he had was not a great deal, but that he would never hide any of it from me if I wanted it, and assur'd me he did not speak with any such apprehensions; that he was only intent upon what I had hinted to him; that here he knew what to do, but there he should be the most helpless wretch alive.

I told him he frighted himself with that which had no terror in it; that if he had money, as I was glad to hear he had, he might not only avoid the servitude, suppos'd to be the consequence of transportation, but begin the world upon such a new foundation as he cou'd not fail of success in, with but the common application usual in such cases; that he could not but call to mind I had recommended it to him many years before, and propos'd it for restoring our fortunes in the world; and I would tell him now that to convince him both of the certainty of it, and of my being fully acquainted with the method, and also fully satisfy'd in the probability of success, he should first see me deliver myself from the necessity of going over at all, and then that I would go with him freely, and of my own choice, and perhaps carry enough with me to satisfy him; that I did not offer it for want of being able to live without assistance from him, but that I thought our mutual misfortunes had been such as were sufficient to reconcile us both to quitting this part of the world, and living where no body could upbraid us with what was past, and without the agonies of a condemn'd hole to drive us to it, where we should look back on all our past disasters with infinite satisfaction, when we should consider that our enemies should entirely forget us, and that we should live as new people in a new world, no body having any thing to say to us, or we to them.

I press'd this home to him with so many arguments, and answer'd all his own passionate objections so effectually, that he embrac'd me, and told me I treated him with such a sincerity as overcame him; that he would take my advice, and would strive to submit to his fate, in hope of having the comfort of so faithful a counsellor, and such a companion in his misery; but still he put me in mind of what I had mention'd before; namely, that there might be some way to get off before he went, and that it might be possible to avoid going at all, which he said would be much better. I told him he should see, and be fully satisfy'd that I would do my utmost in that part too, and if it did not succeed, yet that I would make good the rest.

We parted after this long conference with such testimonies of kindness and affection as I thought were equal, if not superior, to that at our parting at Dunstable; and now I saw more plainly the reason why he then declin'd coming with me toward London; and why, when we parted there, he told me it was not convenient for him to come to London with me, as he would otherwise have done. I have observ'd that the account of his life would have made a much more pleasing history than this of mine; and indeed nothing in it was more strange than this part (*viz.*), that he carried on that desperate trade full five and twenty year, and had never been taken; the success he had met with had been so very uncommon, and such that sometimes he had liv'd handsomely and retir'd in one place for a year or two at a time, keeping himself and a man servant to wait on him, and has often sat in the coffee-houses, and heard the very people who he had robb'd give accounts of their being robb'd, and of the places and circumstances, so that he cou'd easily remember that it was the same.

In this manner, it seems, he liv'd near Liverpool at the time he unluckily married me for a fortune. Had I been the fortune he expected, I verily believe he would have taken up [1] and liv'd honestly.

He had, with the rest of his misfortunes, the good luck not to be actually upon the spot when the robbery was done which they were committed for, and so none of the persons robb'd cou'd swear to him; but it seems, as he was taken with the gang, one hard-mouth'd country man swore home to him; and according to the publication they had made, they expected more evidence against him, and for that reason he was kept in hold.

However, the offer which was made to him of transportation was made, as I understood, upon the intercession of some great person who press'd him hard to accept of it; and as he knew there were several that might come in against him, I thought his friend was in the right, and I lay at him night and day to delay it no longer

At last, with much difficulty, he gave his consent, and as he was not therefore admitted to transportation in court and on his petition, as I was, so he found himself under a difficulty to avoid embarking himself as I had said he might have done; his friend having given security for him that he should transport himself, and not return within the term.

This hardship broke all my measures, for the steps I took afterwards for my own deliverance were hereby render'd wholly ineffectual, unless I would abandon him, and leave him

[1] mended his ways.

to go to America by himself; than which he protested he would much rather go directly to the gallows.

I must now return to my own case. The time of my being transported was near at hand; my governess, who continu'd my fast friend, had try'd to obtain a pardon, but it could not be done unless with an expence too heavy for my purse, considering that to be left empty,[1] unless I had resolv'd to return to my old trade, had been worse than transportation, because there I could live, here I could not. The good minister stood very hard on another account to prevent my being transported also; but he was answer'd that my life had been given me at his first solicitations, and therefore he ought to ask no more; he was sensibly griev'd at my going, because, as he said, he fear'd I should lose the good impressions which a prospect of death had at first made on me, and which were since encreas'd by his instructions; and the pious gentleman was exceedingly concern'd on that account.

On the other hand, I was not so sollicitous about it now, but I conceal'd my reasons for it from the minister, and to the last he did not know that I went with the utmost reluctance and affliction.

It was in the month of February that I was with thirteen other convicts deliver'd to a merchant that traded to Virginia, on board a ship riding in Deptford Reach. The officer of the prison deliver'd us on board, and the master of the vessel gave a discharge for us.

We were for that night clapt under hatches, and kept so close that I thought I should have been suffocated for want of air, and the next morning the ship weigh'd, and fell down the river to a place call'd Bugby's Hole, which was done, as they told us, by the agreement of the merchant, that all opportunity of escape should be taken from us. However, when the ship came thither, and cast anchor, we were permitted to come upon the deck, but not upon the quarter-deck, that being kept particularly for the captain, and for passengers.

When by the noise of the men over my head, and the motion of the ship, I perceiv'd they were under sail, I was at first greatly surpriz'd, fearing we should go away, and that our friends would not be admitted to see us; but I was easy soon after, when

[1] without money.

I found they had come to an anchor, and that we had notice given by some of the men that the next morning we should have the liberty to come upon deck, and to have our friends come to see us.

All that night I lay upon the hard deck, as the other prisoners did, but we had afterwards little cabins allow'd for such as had any bedding to lay in them; and room to stow any box or trunk for cloaths, and linnen if we had it, (which might well be put in) for some of them had neither shirt or shift, linnen or woollen, but what was on their backs, or one farthing of money to help themselves; yet I did not find but they far'd well enough in the ship, especially the women, who got money of the seamen for washing their cloaths, &c., sufficient to purchase any thing they wanted.

When the next morning we had the liberty to come upon deck, I ask'd one of the officers whether I might not be allow'd to send a letter on shore to let my friends know where we lay, and to get some necessary things sent to me. This was the boatswain, a very civil courteous man, who told me I should have any liberty that I desir'd that he could allow me with safety; I told him I desir'd no other; and he answer'd, the ship's boat would go up to London next tide, and he would order my letter to be carry'd.

Accordingly when the boat went off, the boatswain came and told me the boat was going off, that he went in it himself, and if my letter was ready, he would take care of it. I had prepar'd pen, ink, and paper before-hand, and had gotten a letter ready directed to my governess, and enclos'd another to my fellow prisoner, which, however, I did not let her know was my husband, not to the last; in that to my governess I let her know where the ship lay, and press'd her to send me what things she had got ready for me for my voyage.

When I gave the boatswain the letter, I gave him a shilling with it, which I told him was for the charge of a porter, which I had entreated him to send with the letter, as soon as he came on shore, that if possible I might have an answer brought back by the same hand, that I might know what was become of my things. For, sir, says I, if the ship should go away before I have them, I am undone.

I took care, when I gave him the shilling, to let him see I had a little better furniture about me than the ordinary prisoners, that I had a purse, and in it a pretty deal of money, and I found that the very sight of it immediately furnish'd me with very different treatment from what I should otherwise have met with; for tho' he was courteous indeed before, in a kind of natural compassion to me as a woman in distress, yet he was more than ordinarily so afterwards, and procur'd me to be better treated in the ship, than, I say, I might otherwise have been; as shall appear in its place.

He very honestly deliver'd my letter to my governess' own hands, and brought me back her answer; and when he gave it me, gave me the shilling again. There, says he, there's your shilling again too, for I deliver'd the letter my self; I could not tell what to say, I was so surpriz'd at the thing; but after some pause, I said, Sir, you are too kind, it had been but reasonable that you had paid yourself coach hire then.

No, no, says he, I am over paid. What is that gentlewoman? is she your sister?

No, sir, said I, she is no relation to me, but she is a dear friend, and all the friends I have in the world. Well, says he, there are few such friends: why, she crys after you like a child. Ay, says I again, she would give a hundred pound, I believe, to deliver me from this dreadful condition.

Would she so? says he: for half the money, I believe, I could put you in a way how to deliver your self. But this he spoke softly that no body could hear.

Alas! Sir, said I, but then that must be such a deliverance as, if I should be taken again, would cost me my life. Nay, said he, if you were once out of the ship, you must look to yourself afterwards; that I can say nothing to. So we drop'd the discourse for that time.

In the mean time, my governess, faithful to the last moment, convey'd my letter to the prison to my husband, and got an answer to it, and the next day came down herself, bringing me in the first place a sea bed, as they call it, and all its ordinary furniture; she brought me also a sea chest, that is, a chest such as are made for seamen, with all the conveniences in it, and fill'd with every thing almost that I could want; and in one of the corners of the chest, where there was a private drawer, was my bank of money, that is to say, so much of it as I had resolv'd to carry with me; for I order'd part of my stock to be left behind, to be sent afterwards in such goods as I should want when I came to settle; for money in that country is not of much use where all things are bought for tobacco; much more is it a great loss to carry it from hence.

But my case was particular; it was by no means proper for me to go without money or goods, and for a poor convict that was to be sold as soon as I came on shore, to carry a cargo of goods would be to have notice taken of it, and perhaps to have them seiz'd; so I took part of my stock with me thus, and left the rest with my governess.

My governess brought me a great many other things but it was not proper for me to appear too well, at least till I knew what kind of a captain we should have. When she came into the ship, I thought she would have died indeed; her heart sunk at the sight of me, and at the thoughts of parting with me in that condition, and she cry'd so intolerably, I could not for a long time have any talk with her.

I took that time to read my fellow prisoner's letter, which greatly perplex'd me; he told me it would be impossible for him to be discharg'd time enough for going in the same ship, and, which was more than all, he began to question whether they would give him leave to go in what ship he pleas'd, tho' he did voluntarily transport himself; but that they would see him put on board such a ship as they should direct, and that he would be charg'd upon the captain as other convict prisoners were; so that he began to be in dispair of seeing me 'till he came to Virginia, which made him almost desperate; seeing that, on the other hand, if I should not be there, if any accident of the sea or of mortality should take me away, he should be the most undone creature in the world.

This was very perplexing, and I knew not what course to take; I told my governess the story of the boatswain, and she was mighty eager with me to treat with him; but I had no mind to it till I heard whether my husband or fellow prisoner, so she call'd him, could be at liberty to go with me or no; at last I was forc'd to let her into the whole matter, except only that of his being my husband; I told her that I had made a positive agreement with him to go, if he could get the liberty of going in the same ship, and I found he had money.

Then I told her what I propos'd to do when we came there, how we could plant, settle, and, in short, grow rich without any more adventures, and as a great secret, I told her we were to marry as soon as he came on board.

She soon agreed chearfully to my going when she heard this, and she made it her business from that time to get him deliver'd in time, so that he might go in the same ship with me, which at last was brought to pass, tho' with great difficulty, and not without all the forms of a transported convict, which he really was not, for he had not been try'd, and which was a great mortification to him. As our fate was now determin'd, and we were both on board, actually bound to Virginia in the despicable quality of transported convicts, destin'd to be sold for slaves, I for five year, and he under bonds and security not to return to England any more as long as he liv'd, he was very much dejected and cast down; the mortification of being brought on board as he was, like a prisoner, piqu'd him very much, since it was first told him he should transport himself, so that he might go as a gentleman at liberty. It is true he was not order'd to be sold when he came there, as we were, and for that reason he was oblig'd to pay for his passage to the captain, which we were not; as to the rest, he was as much at a loss as a child what to do with himself, but by directions.

However, I lay in an uncertain condition full three weeks not knowing whether I should have my husband with me or no; and therefore not resolv'd how, or in what manner, to receive the honest boatswain's proposal, which indeed he thought a little strange.

At the end of this time, behold my husband came on board. He look'd with a dejected angry countenance, his great heart was swell'd with rage and disdain, to be drag'd along with three keepers of Newgate, and put on board like a convict, when he had not so much as been brought to a tryal. He made loud complaints of it by his friends, for it seems he had some interest; but they got some checque in their application, and were told he had had favour enough, and that they had receiv'd such an account of him since the last grant of his transportation, that he ought to think himself very well treated that he was not prosecuted anew. This answer quieted him, for he knew too much what might have happen'd, and what he had room to expect; and now he saw the goodness of that advice to him which prevail'd with him to accept of the offer of transportation, and after his chagrin at these hell hounds, as he call'd them, was a little over, he look'd more compos'd, began to be chearful, and as I was telling him how glad I was to have him once more out of their hands, he took me in his arms, and acknowledg'd with great tenderness that I had given him the best advice possible. My dear, says he, thou hast twice sav'd my life; from hence forward it shall be employ'd for you, and I'll always take your advice.

Our first business was to compare our stock. He was very honest to me, and told me his stock was pretty good when he came into the prison, but that living there as he did like a gentleman, and, which was much more, the making of friends, and soliciting his case, had been very expensive; and in a word, all his stock left was a hundred and eight pounds, which he had about him in gold.

I gave him an account of my stock as faithfully, that is to say, what I had taken with me; for I was resolv'd, what ever should happen, to keep what I had left in reserve; that in case I should die, what I had was enough to give him, and what was left in my governess' hands would be her own, which she had well deserv'd of me indeed.

My stock which I had with me was two hundred forty six pounds some odd shillings; so that we had three hundred fifty four pound between us, but a worse gotten estate was never put together to begin the world with.

Our greatest misfortune as to our stock was that it was in money, an unprofitable cargoe to be carryed to the plantations; I believe his was really all he had left in the world, as he told me it was. But I, who had between seven and eight hundred pounds in bank when this disaster befel me, and who had one of the faithfulest friends in the world to manage it for me, considering she was a woman of no principles, had still three hundred pounds left in her hand, which I had reserv'd, as above; besides I had some very valuable things with me, as particularly two gold watches, some small peices of plate, and some rings (all stolen goods); with this fortune, and in the sixty-first year of my age, I launch'd out into a new world, as I may call it, in the condition only of a poor convict, order'd to be transported in respite from the gallows; my cloaths were poor and mean, but not ragg'd or dirty, and none knew in the whole ship that I had any thing of value about me.

However, as I had a great many very good cloaths, and linnen in abundance, which I had order'd to be pack'd up in two great boxes, I had them shipp'd on board, not as my goods, but as consign'd to my real name in Virginia, and had the bills of loading in my pocket; and in these boxes was my plate and watches, and every thing of value except my money, which I kept by itself in a private drawer in my chest, and which cou'd not be found, or open'd if found without splitting the chest to peices.

The ship began now to fill; several passengers came on board who were embark'd on no criminal account, and these had accommodations assign'd them in the great cabbin, and other parts of the ship, whereas we as convicts were thrust down below, I know not where. But when my husband came on board, I spoke to the boatswain, who had so early given me hints of his friendship; I told him he had befriended me in many things, and I had not made any suitable return to him, and with that I put a guinea into his hand; I told him that my husband was now come on board, that tho' we were under the present misfortunes, yet we had been persons of a differing character from the wretch'd crew that we came with, and desir'd to know whether the captain might not be mov'd to admit us to some conveniences in the ship, for which we would make him what satisfaction he pleas'd, and that we would gratifie him for his pains in procuring this for us. He took the guinea, as I cou'd see, with great satisfaction, and assur'd me of his assistance.

Then he told us he did not doubt but that the captain, who was one of the best humour'd gentlemen in the world, would be easily brought to accommodate us as well as we cou'd desire; and to make me easie, told me he would go up the next tide on purpose to speak to him about it. The next morning, happening to sleep a little longer than ordinary, when I got up, and began to look abroad, I saw the boatswain among the men in his ordinary

business. I was a little melancholly at seeing him there, and
going forwards to speak to him, he saw me, and came towards
me; but not giving him time to speak first, I said, smiling,
I doubt, sir, you have forgot us, for I see you are very busy.
He return'd presently,[1] Come along with me, and you shall see.
So he took me into the great cabbin, and there sat a good sort
of a gentlemanly man writing, and a great many papers before
him.

Here, says the boatswain to him that was a writing, is the
gentlewoman that the captain spoke to you of; and turning to
me, he said, I have been so far from forgetting your business
that I have been up at the captain's house, and have represented
faithfully what you said, of your being furnish'd with conveniences for your self and your husband; and the captain has sent
this gentleman, who is mate of the ship, down on purpose to
show you every thing, and to accommodate you to your content,
and bid me assure you that you shall not be treated like what
you were expected to be, but with the same respect as other
passengers are treated.

The mate then spoke to me, and not giving me time to thank
the boatswain for his kindness, confirm'd what the boatswain had
said, and added that it was the captain's delight to shew himself
kind and charitable, especially to those that were under any misfortunes; and with that he shew'd me several cabbins built up,
some in the great cabbin, and some partition'd off, out of the
steerage, but opening into the great cabbin, on purpose for
passengers, and gave me leave to choose where I would. I chose
a cabbin in the steerage, in which were very good conveniences
to set our chest, and boxes, and a table to eat on.

The mate then told me that the boatswain had given so good
a character of me and of my husband, that he had orders to tell
me we should eat with him, if we thought fit, during the whole
voyage on the common terms of passengers; that we might lay
in some fresh provisions if we pleas'd; or if not, he should lay
in his usual store, and that we should have share with him. This
was very reviving news to me, after so many hardships and
afflictions; I thank'd him, and told him the captain should make
his own terms with us, and ask'd him leave to go and tell my hus-

[1] answered immediately.

band of it, who was not very well, and was not yet out of his cabbin. Accordingly I went, and my husband whose spirits were still so much sunk with the indignity (as he understood it) offer'd him, that he was scarce yet himself, was so reviv'd with the account I gave him of the reception we were like to have in the ship, that he was quite another man, and new vigour and courage appear'd in his very countenance; so true is it that the greatest spirits, when over whelm'd by their afflictions, are subject to the greatest dejections.

After some little pause to recover himself, my husband came up with me, and gave the mate thanks for the kindness which he had express'd to us, and sent suitable acknowledgments by him to the captain, offering to pay him by advance whatever he demanded for our passage, and for the conveniencies he had help'd us to. The mate told him that the captain would be on board in the afternoon, and that he would leave all that to him; accordingly, in the afternoon, the captain came, and we found him the same courteous obliging man that the boatswain had represented him; and he was so well pleas'd with my husband's conversation that, in short, he would not let us keep the cabbin we had chosen, but gave us one that, as I said before, open'd into the great cabbin.

Nor were his conditions exorbitant, or the man craving and eager to make a prey of us, but for fifteen guineas we had our whole passage and provisions, eat at the captain's table, and were very handsomely entertain'd.

The captain lay himself in the other part of the great cabbin, having let his round house,[1] as they call it, to a rich planter, who went over with his wife and three children, who eat by themselves; he had some other ordinary passengers, who quarter'd in the steerage; and as for our old fraternity, they were kept under the hatches, and came very little on the deck.

I could not refrain acquainting my governess with what had happen'd; it was but just that she, who was really concern'd for me, should have part in my good fortune; besides, I wanted her assistance to supply me with several necessaries, which before I was shy of letting any body see me have; but now I had a cabbin and room to set things in, I order'd abundance of good

---

[1] a cabin, or set of cabins, on the after part of the quarter-deck.

things for our comfort in the voyage, as brandy, sugar, lemons, &c., to make punch, and treat our benefactor, the captain; and abundance of things for eating and drinking; also a larger bed, and bedding proportion'd to it; so that, in a word, we resolv'd to want for nothing.

All this while I had provided nothing for our assistance when we should come to the place, and begin to call ourselves planters; and I was far from being ignorant of what was needful on that occasion; particularly all sorts of tools for the planter's-work, and for building; and all kinds of house-furniture, which, if to be bought in the country, must necessarily cost double the price.

I discours'd that point with my governess, and she went and waited upon the captain, and told him that she hop'd ways might be found out for her two unfortunate cousins, as she call'd us, to obtain our freedom when we came into the country, and so enter'd into a discourse with him about the means and terms also, of which I shall say more in its place; and after thus sounding the captain, she let him know, tho' we were unhappy in the circumstance that occasion'd our going, yet that we were not unfurnish'd to set ourselves to work in the country, and were resolv'd to settle and live there as planters. The captain readily offer'd his assistance, told her the method of entering upon such business, and how easy, nay, how certain it was for industrious people to recover their fortunes in such a manner. Madam, says he, 'tis no reproach to any man in that country to have been sent over in worse circumstances than I perceive your cousins are in, provided they do but apply with good judgment to the business of the place when they come there.

She then enquir'd of him what things it was necessary we should carry over with us, and he, like a knowing man, told her thus: Madam, your cousins first must procure some body to buy them as servants, in conformity to the conditions of their transportation, and then in the name of that person they may go about what they will; they may either purchase some plantations already begun, or they may purchase land of the government of the country, and begin where they please, and both will be done reasonably. She bespoke his favour in the first article, which he promis'd to her to take upon himself, and indeed faithfully perform'd it; and as to the rest, he promis'd to recommend us to such as should give us the best advice, and not to impose upon us, which was as much as could be desir'd.

She then ask'd him if it would not be necessary to furnish us with a stock of tools and materials for the business of planting, and he said, yes, by all means; then she begg'd his assistance in that, and told him she would furnish us with everything that was convenient, whatever it cost her. He accordingly gave her a list of things necessary for a planter, which by his account came to about fourscore, or an hundred pounds; and in short, she went about as dexterously to buy them as if she had been an old Virginia merchant; only that she bought by my direction above twice as much of every thing as he had given her a list of.

These she put on board in her own name, took his bills of loading for them, and endors'd those bills of loading to my husband, ensuring the cargo afterwards in her own name; so that we were provided for all events, and for all disasters.

I should have told you that my husband gave her all his own stock of 108*l.*, which, as I have said, he had about him in gold, to lay out thus, and I gave her a good sum besides; so that I did not break into the stock which I had left in her hands at all, but after all we had near 200*l.* in money, which was more than enough for our purpose.

In this condition, very chearful, and indeed joyful at being so happily accommodated, we set sail from Bugby's Hole to Gravesend, where the ship lay about ten days more, and where the captain came on board for good and all. Here the captain offer'd us a civility which indeed we had no reason to expect, namely, to let us go on shore, and refresh ourselves, upon giving our words that we would not go from him, and that we would return peaceably on board again. This was such an evidence of his confidence in us that it overcame my husband, who in a meer principle of gratitude told him, as he could not be in any capacity to make a suitable return for such a favour, so he could not think of accepting it, nor could he be easy that the captain shou'd run such a risque. After some mutual civilities, I gave my husband a purse, in which was 80 guineas, and he put it into the captain's hand. There captain, says he, there's part of a pledge for our fidelity; if we deal dishonestly with you on any account, 'tis your own; and on this we went on shore.

Indeed, the captain had assurance enough of our resolutions to go, for that having made such provision to settle there, it did not seem rational that we would chuse to remain here at the peril of life, for such it must have been. In a word, we went all on shore with the captain, and supp'd together in Gravesend, where we were very merry, staid all night, lay at the house where we supp'd, and came all very honestly on board again with him in the morning. Here we bought ten dozen of bottles of good beer, some wine, some fowles, and such things as we thought might be acceptable on board.

My governess was with us all this while, and went round with us into the Downs, as did also the captain's wife, with whom she went back; I was never so sorrowful at parting with my own mother as I was at parting with her, and I never saw her more. We had a fair easterly wind the third day after we came to the Downs, and we sail'd from thence the 10th of April; nor did we touch any more at any place, till being driven on the coast of Ireland by a very hard gale of wind, the ship came to an anchor in a little Bay, near a river whose name I remember not, but they said the river came down from Limerick, and that it was the largest river in Ireland.

Here being detain'd by bad weather for some time, the captain, who continu'd the same kind good humour'd man as at first, took us two on shore with him again. He did it now in kindness to my husband indeed, who bore the sea very ill, especially when it blew so hard. Here we bought again store of fresh provisions, beef, pork, mutton, and fowls, and the captain stay'd to pickle up five or six barrels of beef to lengthen out the ship's store. We were here not about five days, when the weather turning mild, and a fair wind, we set sail again, and in two and forty days came safe to the coast of Virginia.

When we drew near to the shore, the captain call'd me to him, and told me that he found by my discourse I had some relations in the place, and that I had been there before, and so he suppos'd I understood the custom in their disposing the convict prisoners when they arriv'd. I told him I did not, and that as to what relations I had in the place, he might be sure I would make

myself known to none of them while in the circumstances of
a prisoner, and that as to the rest, we left ourselves entirely to
him to assist us, as he was pleas'd to promise us he wou'd do. He
told me I must get somebody in the place to come and buy me
as a servant, and who must answer for me to the governor of
the country, if he demanded me. I told him we should do as
he should direct; so he brought a planter to treat with him, as
it were for the purchase of me for a servant, my husband not
being order'd to be sold, and there I was formally sold to him,
and went a shore with him. The captain went with us, and carried us to a certain house, whether it was to be call'd a tavern or
not, I know not, but we had a bowl of punch there made of rum,
&c. and were very merry. After some time the planter gave us a
certificate of discharge, and an acknowledgment of having serv'd
him faithfully, and I was free from him the next morning, to go
whither I would.

For this peice of service the captain demanded of me 6000
weight of tobacco, which he said he was accountable for to his
freighter, and we bought for him, and made him a present of
20 guineas besides; which he was abundantly satisfy'd with.

It is not proper to enter here into the particulars of what part
of the colony of Virginia we settled in, for divers reasons; it
may suffice to mention that we went into the great river of
Potomack, the ship being bound thither; and there we intended
to have settled at first, tho' afterwards we altered our minds.

The first thing I did of moment, after having gotten all our
goods on shore and plac'd them in a store-house, which with
a lodging we hir'd at the small place or village, where we landed;
I say the first thing was to enquire after my mother, and after
my brother (that fatal person who I married as a husband, as I
have related at large). A little enquiry furnish'd me with information that Mrs. ——, that is my mother, was dead; that my
brother (or husband) was alive, and which was worse, I found
he was remov'd from the plantation where I liv'd, and liv'd with
one of his sons in a plantation just by the place where we landed,
and had hir'd a warehouse.

I was a little surpriz'd at first, but as I ventur'd to satisfy
myself that he could not know me, I was not only perfectly
easy, but had a great mind to see him if it was possible, without

his seeing me. In order to that I found out by enquiry the plantation where he liv'd, and with a woman of the place, who I got
to help me, like what we call a chairwoman,[1] I rambl'd about
towards the place, as if I had only a mind to see the country, and
look about me. At last I came so near that I saw the dwelling-
house. I ask'd the woman, whose plantation that was? She said
it belong'd to such a man, and looking out a little to our right
hands, There, says she, is the gentleman that owns the plantation,
and his father with him. What are their Christian names? said
I. I know not, said she, what the old gentleman's name is, but his
son's name is Humphry, and I believe, says she, the father's is so
too. You may guess, if you can, what a confus'd mixture of joy
and fright possest my thoughts upon this occasion, for I immediately knew that this was no body else but my own son, by that
father she shewed me, who was my own brother. I had no mask,
but I ruffled my hoods so about my face, that I depended upon it
that after above 20 years' absence, and withal not expecting any
thing of me in that part of the world, he would not be able to
know me; but I need not have us'd all that caution, for he was
grown dim sighted by some distemper which had fallen upon his
eyes, and could but just see well enough to walk about, and not
run against a tree or into a ditch. As they drew near to us, I
said, Does he know you, Mrs. Owen? (so they call'd the woman).
Yes, she said, if he hears me speak, he will know me; but he can't
see well enough to know me, or any body else; and so she told
me the story of his sight, as I have related. This made me secure,
and so I threw open my hoods again, and let them pass by me.
It was a wretch'd thing for a mother thus to see her own son, a
handsome comely young gentleman in flourishing circumstances,
and durst not make herself known to him, and durst not take any
notice of him; let any mother of children that reads this consider
it, and but think with what anguish of mind I restrain'd myself; what yearnings of soul I had in me to embrace him, and
weep over him; and how I thought all my entrails turn'd within
me, that my very bowels mov'd, and I knew not what to do, as
I now know not how to express those agonies. When he went
from me I stood gazing and trembling, and looking after him as
long as I could see him; then sitting down on the grass, just at a

[1] i.e., charwoman.

place I had mark'd, I made as if I lay down to rest me, but turn'd from her, and lying on my face wept, and kiss'd the ground that he had set his foot on.

I cou'd not conceal my disorder so much from the woman but that she perceiv'd it, and thought I was not well, which I was oblig'd to pretend was true; upon which she press'd me to rise, the ground being damp and dangerous, which I did, and walk'd away.

As I was going back again, and still talking of this gentleman and his son, a new occasion of melancholy offer'd itself thus. The woman began, as if she would tell me a story to divert me: There goes, says she, a very odd tale among the neighbours where this gentleman formerly liv'd. What was that? said I. Why, says she, that old gentleman going to England, when he was a young man, fell in love with a young lady there, one of the finest women that ever was seen here, and married her, and brought her over hither to his mother, who was then living. He liv'd here several years with her, continu'd she, and had several children by her, of which the young gentleman that was with him now was one; but after some time, the old gentlewoman his mother talking to her of something relating to herself, and of her circumstances in England, which were bad enough, the daughter-in-law began to be very much surpriz'd and uneasy, and in short, in examining further into things, it appear'd past all contradiction that she (the old gentlewoman) was her own mother, and that consequently that son was her own brother, which struck the family with horror, and put them into such confusion that it had almost ruin'd them all; the young woman would not live with him, he for a time went distracted, and at last the young woman went away for England, and has never been heard of since.

It is easy to believe that I was strangely affected with this story; but 'tis impossible to describe the nature of my disturbance. I seem'd astonish'd at the story, and ask'd her a thousand questions about the particulars, which I found she was thoroughly acquainted with. At last I began to enquire into the circumstances of the family, how the old gentlewoman, I mean, my mother, died, and how she left what she had; for my mother had promis'd me very solemnly that when she died she would do something for me, and leave it so as that, if I was living, I should one way or other come at it, without its being in the power of her son, my brother and husband, to prevent it. She told me she did not know exactly how it was order'd; but she had been told that my mother had left a sum of money, and had tyed her plantation for the payment of it, to be made good to the daughter, if ever she could be heard of, either in England or elsewhere; and that the trust was left with this son who we saw with his father.

This was news too good for me to make light of, and you may be sure fill'd my heart with a thousand thoughts: what course I should take, and in what manner I should make myself known, or whether I should ever make myself known, or no.

Here was a perplexity that I had not indeed skill to manage myself in, neither knew I what course to take. It lay heavy upon my mind night and day, I could neither sleep or converse, so that my husband perceiv'd it, wonder'd what ail'd me, and strove to divert me, but it was all to no purpose; he press'd me to tell him what it was troubled me, but I put it off, till at last, importuning me continually, I was forc'd to form a story, which yet had a plain truth to lay it upon too. I told him I was troubled because I found we must shift our quarters, and alter our scheme of settling, for that I found I should be known, if I stay'd in that part of the country; for that my mother being dead, several of my relations were come into that part where we then was, and that I must either discover myself to them, which in our present circumstances was not proper on many accounts, or remove; and which to do I knew not, and that this it was that made me melancholly.

He joyned with me in this, that it was by no means proper for me to make myself known to any body in the circumstances in which we then were; and therefore he told me he would be willing to remove to any part of the country, or even to any other country if I thought fit; but now I had another difficulty, which was, that if I remov'd to another colony, I put myself out of the way of ever making a due search after those things which my mother had left. Again, I could never so much as think of breaking the secret of my former marriage to my new husband; it was not a story would bear telling, nor could I tell what might be the consequences of it; it was impossible too, without making it publick all over the country, as well who I was, as what I now was also.

This perplexity continu'd a great while, and made my spouse very uneasy; for he thought I was not open with him, and did not let him into every part of my grievance; and he would often say he wonder'd what he had done, that I would not trust him, whatever it was, especially if it was grievous and afflicting. The truth is, he ought to have been trusted with every thing, for no man could deserve better of a wife; but this was a thing I knew not how to open to him, and yet having no body to disclose any part of it to, the burthen was too heavy for my mind; for let them say what they please of our sex not being able to keep a secret, my life is a plain conviction to me of the contrary; but be it our sex, or the men's sex, a secret of moment should always have a confident, a bosom friend, to whom we may communicate the joy of it, or the grief of it, be it which it will, or it will be a double weight upon the spirits, and perhaps become even insupportable in it self; and this I appeal to human testimony for the truth of.

And this is the cause why many times men, as well as women, and men of the greatest and best qualities other ways, yet have found themselves weak in this part, and have not been able to bear the weight of a secret joy, or of a secret sorrow; but have been oblig'd to disclose it, even for the mere giving vent to themselves, and to unbend the mind, opprest with the weights which attended it; nor was this any token of folly at all, but a natural consequence of the thing; and such people, had they struggl'd longer with the oppression, would certainly have told it in their sleep, and disclos'd the secret, let it have been of what fatal nature soever without regard to the person to whom it might be expos'd. This necessity of nature is a thing which works sometimes with such vehemency in the minds of those who are guilty of any atrocious villany, such as a secret murther in particular, that they have been oblig'd to discover it, tho' the consequence has been their own destruction. Now, tho' it may be true that the divine justice ought to have the glory of all those discoveries and confessions, yet 'tis as certain that Providence, which ordinarily works by the hands of nature, makes use here of the same natural causes to produce those extraordinary effects.

I could give several remarkable instances of this in my long conversation with crime and with criminals. I knew one fellow that, while I was a prisoner in Newgate, was one of those they called then night-fliers, I know not what word they may have understood it by since; but he was one who by connivance was admitted to go abroad every evening, when he play'd his pranks, and furnish'd those honest people they call thief-catchers with business to find out the next day, and restore for a reward what they had stolen the evening before. This fellow was as sure to tell in his sleep all that he had done, and every step he had taken, what he had stolen, and where, as sure as if he had engag'd to tell it waking, and therefore he was oblig'd after he had been out to lock himself up, or be locked up by some of the keepers that had him in fee, that no body should hear him; but on the other hand, if he had told all the particulars, and given a full account of his rambles and success to any comrade, any brother thief, or to his employers, as I may justly call them, then all was well, and he slept as quietly as other people.

As the publishing this account of my life is for the sake of the just moral of every part of it, and for instruction, caution, warning, and improvement to every reader, so this will not pass, I hope, for an unnecessary digression, concerning some people being oblig'd to disclose the greatest secrets either of their own, or other people's affairs.

Under the oppression of this weight, I labour'd in the case I have been naming; and the only relief I found for it was to let my husband into so much of it as I thought would convince him of the necessity there was for us to think of settling in some other part of the world, and the next consideration before us was, which part of the English settlements we should go to. My husband was a perfect stranger to the country, and had not yet so much as a geographical knowledge of the situation of the several places; and I that, till I wrote this, did not know what the word *geographical* signify'd, had only a general knowledge from long conversation with people that came from or went to several places; but this I knew, that Maryland, Pensilvania, East and West Jersy, New York, and New England, lay all north of Virginia, and that they were consequently all colder climates, to which, for that very reason, I had an aversion; for that as I naturally lov'd warm weather, so, now I grew into years, I had a stronger inclination to shun a cold climate. I therefore consider'd of going to Carolina, which is the most southern colony of the English on the continent; and hither I propos'd to go, the rather because I might with ease come from thence at any time, when it might be proper to enquire after my mother's effects, and to demand them.

With this resolution, I proposed to my husband our going away from where we was, and carrying our effects with us to Carolina, where we resolv'd to settle; for my husband readily agreed to the first part (*viz.*) that it was not at all proper to stay where we was, since I had assur'd him we should be known there, and the rest I conceal'd from him.

But now I found a new difficulty upon me. The main affair grew heavy upon my mind still, and I could not think of going out of the country, without some how or other making enquiry into the grand affair of what my mother had done for me; nor could I with any patience bear the thought of going away, and not make my self known to my old husband (brother), or to my child, his son; only I would fain have had it done without my new husband having any knowledge of it, or they having any knowledge of him.

I cast about innumerable ways in my thoughts how this might be done: I would gladly have sent my husband away to Carolina, and have come after my self, but this was impracticable; he would not stir without me, being himself unacquainted with the country, and with the methods of settling any where. Then I thought we would both go first, and that when we were settled I should come back to Virginia; but even then I knew he would never part with me, and be left there alone; the case was plain, he was bred a gentleman, and was not only unacquainted, but indolent, and when we did settle, would much rather go into the woods with his gun, which they call there hunting, and which is the ordinary work of the Indians; I say he would much rather do that than attend the natural business of the plantation.

There were therefore difficulties unsurmountable, and such as I knew not what to do in. I had such strong impressions on my mind about discovering my self to my old husband that I could not withstand them; and the rather, because it run in my thoughts that, if I did not while he liv'd, I might in vain endeavour to convince my son afterward that I was really the same person, and that I was his mother, and so might both lose the assistance and comfort of the relation, and lose whatever it was my mother had left me; and yet on the other hand, I could never think it proper to discover the circumstances I was in; as well relating to the having a husband with me, as to my being brought over as a criminal; on both which accounts it was absolutely necessary to me to remove from the place where I was, and come again to him, as from another place and in another figure.

Upon those considerations, I went on with telling my husband the absolute necessity there was of our not settling in Potomack River; that we should presently be made publick there, whereas if we went to any other place in the world, we could come in with as much reputation as any family that came to plant; that as it was always agreeable to the inhabitants to have families come among them to plant who brought substance with them, so we should be sure of agreeable reception, and without any possibility of a discovery of our circumstances.

I told him, too, that as I had several relations in the place where we was, and that I durst not now let my self be known to them, because they would soon come to know the occasion of my coming over, which would be to expose my self to the last degree; so I had reason to believe that my mother, who died here, had left me something, and perhaps considerable, which it might be very well worth my while to enquire after; but that this too could not be done without exposing us publickly, unless we went from hence; and then, where ever we settled, I might come as it were to visit and to see my brother and nephews, make my self known, enquire after what was my due, be receiv'd with respect, and at the same time have justice done me; whereas if I did it now, I could expect nothing but with trouble, such as exacting it by force, receiving it with curses and reluctance, and with all kinds of affronts; which he would not perhaps bear to see; that in case of being oblig'd to legal proofs of being really her daughter, I might be at a loss, be oblig'd to have recourse to England, and it may be to fail at last, and so lose it.

With these arguments, and having thus acquainted my husband with the whole secret so far as was needful to him, we resolv'd to go and seek a settlement in some other colony, and at first Carolina was the place pitch'd upon.

In order to this we began to make enquiry for vessels going to Carolina, and in a very little while got information that on the other side the bay, as they call it, namely, in Maryland, there was a ship which came from Carolina loaden with rice and other goods, and was going back again thither. On this news we hir'd a sloop to take in our goods, and taking as it were a final farewel of Potomack River, we went with all our cargo over to Maryland.

This was a long and unpleasant voyage, and my spouse said it was worse to him than all the voyage from England, because the weather was bad, the water rough, and the vessel small and inconvenient; in the next place, we were full a hundred miles up Potomack River, in a part they call Westmorland County; and as that river is by far the greatest in Virginia, and I have heard say it is the greatest river in the world that falls into another river, and not directly into the sea; so we had base weather in it, and were frequently in great danger; for tho' they call it but a river, 'tis frequently so broad that, when we were in the middle, we could not see land on either side for many leagues together. Then we had the great Bay of Chesapeake to cross, which is where the River Potomack falls into it, near thirty miles broad, so that our voyage was full two hundred mile, in a poor sorry sloop, with all our treasure, and if any accident had happen'd to us, we might at last have been very miserable; supposing we had lost our goods and saved our lives only, and had then been left naked and destitute, and in a wild strange place, not having one friend or acquaintance in all that part of the world. The very thoughts of it gives me some horror, even since the danger is past.

Well, we came to the place in five days sailing, I think they call it Philip's Point, and behold when we came thither, the ship bound to Carolina was loaded and gone away but three days before. This was a disappointment, but however, I that was to be discourag'd with nothing told my husband that since we could not get passage to Carolina, and that the country we was in was very fertile and good, we would see if we could find out any thing for our turn where we was, and that if he lik'd things we would settle here.

We immediately went on shore, but found no conveniences just at that place, either for our being on shore, or preserving our goods on shore, but was directed by a very honest Quaker who we found there to go to a place, about sixty miles east; that is to say, nearer the mouth of the bay, where he said he liv'd and where we should be accommodated, either to plant, or to wait for any other place to plant in that might be more convenient; and he invited us with so much kindness that we agreed to go, and the Quaker himself went with us.

Here we bought us two servants, (*viz.*) an English woman-servant just come on shore from a ship of Liverpool, and a Negro man-servant, things absolutely necessary for all people that pretended to settle in that country. This honest Quaker was very helpful to us, and when we came to the place that he propos'd, found us out a convenient storehouse for our goods, and lodging for ourselves and servants; and about two months, or thereabout, afterwards, by his direction, we took up a large peice of land from the government of that country, in order to form our plantation, and so we laid the thoughts of going to Carolina wholly aside, having been very well receiv'd here, and accommodated with a convenient lodging till we could prepare things, and have land enough cur'd,[1] and materials provided for building us a house, all which we manag'd by the direction of the Quaker; so that in one year's time we had near fifty acres of land clear'd, part of it enclos'd, and some of it planted with tobacco, tho' not much; besides, we had garden ground and corn sufficient to supply our servants with roots, and herbs, and bread.

And now I perswaded my husband to let me go over the bay again, and enquire after my friends. He was the willinger to consent to it now because he had business upon his hands sufficient to employ him, besides his gun to divert him, which they call hunting there, and which he greatly delighted in; and indeed we us'd to look at one another sometimes with a great deal of pleasure, reflecting how much better that was, not than

[1] cleared.

Newgate only, but than the most prosperous of our circumstances in the wicked trade we had been both carrying on.

Our affair was now in a very good posture. We purchased of the proprietors of the colony as much land for 35 pound, paid in ready money, as would make a sufficient plantation to us as long as we could either of us live; and as for children I was past any thing of that kind.

But our good fortune did not end here. I went, as I have said, over the bay, to the place where my brother, once a husband, liv'd; but I did not go to the same village where I was before, but went up another great river, on the east side of the River Potomack, called Rapahannock River, and by this means came on the back of his plantation, which was large, and by the help of a navigable creek that run into the Rapahannock, I came very near it.

I was now fully resolv'd to go up point-blank to my brother (husband) and to tell him who I was; but not knowing what temper I might find him in, or how much out of temper rather I might make him by such a rash visit, I resolv'd to write a letter to him first to let him know who I was, and that I was come not to give him any trouble upon the old relation, which I hop'd was entirely forgot, but that I apply'd to him as a sister to a brother, desiring his assistance in the case of that provision which our mother at her decease had left for my support, and which I did not doubt but he would do me justice in, especially considering that I was come thus far to look after it.

I said some very tender kind things in the letter about his son, which I told him he knew to be my own child, and that as I was guilty of nothing in marrying him any more than he was in marrying me, neither of us having then known our being at all related to one another, so I hop'd he would allow me the most passionate desire of once seeing my own and only child, and of showing something of the infirmities of a mother in preserving a violent affection for him, who had never been able to retain any thought of me one way or other.

I did believe that having receiv'd this letter he would immediately give it to his son to read; his eyes being, I know, so dim that he cou'd not see to read it; but it fell out better than so, for as his sight was dim, so he had allow'd his son to open

all letters that came to his hand for him, and the old gentleman being from home, or out of the way when my messenger
came, my letter came directly to my son's hand, and he open'd
and read it.

He call'd the messenger in, after some little stay, and ask'd
him where the person was who gave him that letter. The messenger told him the place, which was about seven miles off; so
he bid him stay, and ordering a horse to be got ready, and two
servants, away he came to me with the messenger. Let any one
judge the consternation I was in, when my messenger came
back and told me the old gentleman was not at home, but his
son was come along with him, and was just coming up to me.
I was perfectly confounded, for I knew not whether it was peace
or war, nor cou'd I tell how to behave. However, I had but
a very few moments to think, for my son was at the heels of
the messenger, and coming up into my lodgings, ask'd the fellow at the door something; I suppose it was, for I did not hear it,
which was the gentlewoman that sent him? for the messenger
said, There she is, sir; at which he comes directly up to me, kisses
me, took me in his arms, embrac'd me with so much passion that
he could not speak, but I could feel his breast heave and throb
like a child that cries, but sobs, and cannot cry it out.

I can neither express or describe the joy that touch'd my very
soul, when I found, for it was easy to discover that part, that he
came not as a stranger, but as a son to a mother, and indeed a
son who had never before known what a mother of his own was;
in short, we cryed over one another a considerable while, when
at last he broke out first: My dear mother, says he, are you still
alive! I never expected to have seen your face. As for me, I
cou'd say nothing a great while.

After we had both recover'd ourselves a little, and were able
to talk, he told me how things stood; he told me he had not
shewed my letter to his father, or told him anything about it;
that what his grand-mother left me was in his hands, and that
he would do me justice to my full satisfaction; that as to his
father, he was old and infirm both in body and mind; that he
was very fretful, and passionate, almost blind, and capable of
nothing; and he question'd whether he would know how to act
in an affair which was of so nice a nature as this; and that there-

fore he had come himself, as well to satisfy himself in seeing me, which he could not restrain himself from, as also to put it into my power to make a judgement after I had seen how things were, whether I would discover myself to his father, or no.

This was really so prudently and wisely manag'd that I found my son was a man of sense, and needed no direction from me. I told him I did not wonder that his father was as he had describ'd him, for that his head was a little touch'd before I went away; and principally his disturbance was because I could not be per-swaded to live with him as my husband, after I knew that he was my brother; that as he knew better than I what his father's pres-ent condition was, I should readily joyn with him in such measures as he would direct; that I was indifferent, as to seeing his father, since I had seen him first, and he cou'd not have told me better news than to tell me that what his grand-mother had left me was intrusted in his hands, who I doubted not, now he knew who I was, would, as he said, do me justice. I enquir'd then how long my mother had been dead, and where she died, and told so many particulars of the family that I left him no room to doubt the truth of my being really and truly his mother.

My son then enquir'd where I was, and how I had dispos'd myself. I told him I was on the Maryland side of the bay, at the plantation of a particular friend, who came from England in the same ship with me; that as for that side of the bay where he was, I had no habitation. He told me I should go home with him, and live with him, if I pleas'd, as long as I liv'd; that as to his father, he knew no body, and would never so much as guess at me. I consider'd of that a little, and told him that tho' it was really no little concern to me to live at a distance from him, yet I could not say it would be the most comfortable thing in the world to me to live in the house with him, and to have that unhappy object always before me, which had been such a blow to my peace before; that tho' I should be glad to have his com-pany (my son), or to be as near him as possible, yet I could not think of being in the house where I should be also under constant restraint, for fear of betraying myself in my discourse, nor should I be able to refrain some expressions in my conversing with him as my son that might discover the whole affair, which would by no means be convenient.

He acknowledged that I was right in all this, but then, Dear mother, says he, you shall be as near me as you can. So he took me with him on horseback to a plantation next to his own, and where I was as well entertain'd as I cou'd have been in his own; having left me there, he went away home, telling me he would talk of the main business the next day, and having first called me his aunt, and given a charge to the people, who, it seems, were his tenants, to treat me with all possible respect. About two hours after he was gone, he sent me a maid-servant and a Negro boy to wait on me, and provisions ready dressed for my supper; and thus I was as if I had been in a new world, and began almost to wish that I had not brought my Lancashire husband from England at all.

However, that wish was not hearty neither, for I lov'd my Lancashire husband entirely, as I had ever done from the beginning; and he merited it as much as it was possible for a man to do: but that by the way.

The next morning my son came to visit me again almost as soon as I was up. After a little discourse, he first of all pull'd out a deer-skin bag, and gave it me, with five and fifty Spanish pistoles in it, and told me that was to supply my expences from England, for tho' it was not his business to enquire, yet he ought to think I did not bring a great deal of money out with me, it not being usual to bring much money into that country. Then he pull'd out his grand-mother's will, and read it over to me, whereby it appear'd that she left a plantation on York River to me, with the stock of servants and cattle upon it, and had given it in trust to this son of mine for my use, when ever he would hear of me, and to my heirs, if I had any children, and in default of heirs, to whomsoever I should by will dispose of it; but gave the income of it, till I should be heard of, to my said son; and if I should not be living, then it was to him, and his heirs.

This plantation, tho' remote from him, he said he did not let out, but manag'd it by a head clerk, as he did another that was his father's that lay hard by it, and went over himself three or four times a year to look after it. I ask'd him what he thought the plantation might be worth. He said, if I would let it out, he would give me about sixty pounds a year for it; but if I would live on it, then it would be worth much more, and he believ'd would bring me in about 150*l*. a year; but seeing I was likely either to settle on the other side the bay, or might perhaps have a mind to go back to England, if I would let him be my steward he would manage it for me, as he had done for himself, and that he believ'd he should be able to send me as much tobacco from it as would yield me about a 100*l*. a year, sometimes more.

This was all strange news to me, and things I had not been us'd to; and really my heart began to look up more seriously than I think it ever did before, and to look with great thankfulness to the hand of Providence, which had done such wonders for me, who had been my self the greatest wonder of wickedness, perhaps that had been suffered to live in the world; and I must again observe that not on this occasion only, but even on all other occasions of thankfulness, my past wickedness and abominable life never look'd so monstrous to me, and I never so compleatly abhorr'd it, and reproach'd my self with it, as when I had a sense upon me of Providence doing good to me, while I had been making those vile returns on my part.

But I leave the reader to improve these thoughts, as no doubt they will see cause, and I go on to the fact. My son's tender carriage and kind offers fetch'd tears from me, almost all the while he talk'd with me; indeed, I could scarce discourse with him but in the intervals of my passion; however, at length I began, and expressing my self with wonder at my being so happy to have the trust of what I had left put into the hands of my own child, I told him that as to the inheritance of it, I had no child but him in the world, and was now past having any if I should marry, and therefore would desire him to get a writing drawn, which I was ready to execute, by which I would after me give it wholly to him, and to his heirs; and in the mean time, smiling, I ask'd him, what made him continue a batchelor so long? His answer was kind and ready, that Virginia did not yield any great plenty of wives, and that since I talk'd of going back to England, I should send him a wife from London.

This was the substance of our first day's conversation, the pleasantest day that ever past over my head in my life, and which gave me the truest satisfaction. He came every day after this, and spent a great part of his time with me, and carried me about to several of his friends' houses, where I was entertain'd with great respect; also I dined several times at his own house, when he took care always to see his half-dead father so out of the way that I never saw him, or he me. I made him one present, and it was all I had of value, and that was one of the gold watches, of which I said I had two in my chest, and this I happen'd to have with me, and gave it him at his third visit. I told him, I had nothing of any value to bestow but that, and I desir'd he would now and then kiss it for my sake; I did not indeed tell him that I stole it from a gentlewoman's side, at a meeting house in London; that's by the way.

He stood a little while hesitating, as if doubtful whether to take it or no; but I press'd it on him, and made him accept it, and it was not much less worth than his leather pouch full of Spanish gold; no, tho' it were to be reckon'd, as if at London, whereas it was worth twice as much there; at length he took it, kiss'd it, told me the watch should be a debt upon him, that he would be paying as long as I liv'd.

A few days after, he brought the writings of gift, and the scrivener with him, and I sign'd them very freely, and deliver'd them to him with a hundred kisses; for sure, nothing ever pass'd between a mother and a tender dutiful child, with more affection. The next day he brings me an obligation under his hand and seal, whereby he engag'd himself to manage the plantation for my account, and to remit the produce to my order where ever I should be, and withal, oblig'd himself to make up the produce a hundred pound a year to me. When he had done so, he told me that as I came to demand before the crop was off, I had a right to produce of the current year, and so he paid a hundred pound in Spanish pieces of eight, and desir'd me to give him a receipt for it as in full for that year, ending at Christmas following; this being about the latter end of August.

I stay'd here above five weeks, and indeed had much a-do to get away then. Nay, he would have come over the bay with me, but I would by no means allow it; however, he would send me over in a sloop of his own, which was built like a yacht, and serv'd him as well for pleasure as business. This I accepted of, and so after the utmost expressions both of duty and affection, he let me come away, and I arriv'd safe in two days at my friend's the Quaker's.

I brought over with me for the use of our plantation three

horses with harness and saddles; some hogs, two cows, and a thousand other things, the gift of the kindest and tenderest child that ever woman had. I related to my husband all the particulars of this voyage, except that I call'd my son, my 'cousin'; and first I told him that I had lost my watch, which he seem'd to take as a misfortune; but then I told him how kind my cousin had been, that my mother had left me such a plantation, and that he had preserv'd it for me, in hopes some time or other he should hear from me. Then I told him that I had left it to his management, that he would render me a faithful account of its produce; and then I pull'd him out the hundred pound in silver, as the first year's produce, and then pulling out the deer skin purse with the pistoles, And here, my dear, says I, is the gold watch. Says my husband, So is heaven's goodness sure to work the same effects in all sensible minds, where mercies touch the heart; lifted up both his hands, and with an extasy of joy, What is God a doing! says he, for such an ungrateful dog as I am! Then I let him know what I had brought over in the sloop, besides all this; I mean the horses, hogs, and cows, and other stores for our plantation; all which added to his surprize, and fill'd his heart with thankfulness; and from this time forward I believe he was as sincere a penitent, and as thoroughly a re-form'd man, as ever God's goodness brought back from a pro-fligate, a highway-man, and a robber. I could fill a larger history than this with the evidences of this truth, and but that I doubt that part of the story will not be equally diverting as the wicked part.

But this is to be my own story, not my husband's; I return therefore to my own part. We went on with our own planta-tion, and manag'd it with the help and direction of such friends as we got there, and especially the honest Quaker, who prov'd a faithful, generous, and steady friend to us; and we had very good success; for having a flourishing stock to begin with, as I have said, and this being now encreas'd by the addition of a hun-dred and fifty pound sterling in money, we enlarg'd our number of servants, built us a very good house, and cur'd every year a great deal of land. The second year I wrote to my old gov-erness, giving her part with us of the joy of our success, and order'd her how to lay out the money I had left with her, which was 250*l*. as above, and to send it to us in goods, which she perform'd with her usual kindness and fidelity, and all this arriv'd safe to us.

Here we had a supply of all sorts of cloaths, as well for my husband as for myself; and I took especial care to buy for him all those things that I knew he delighted to have; as two good long wigs, two silver-hilted swords, three or four fine fowling pieces, a fine saddle with holsters and pistols very handsome, with a scarlet cloak; and in a word, everything I could think of to oblige him, and to make him appear, as he really was, a very fine gentleman. I order'd a good quantity of such household-stuff as we wanted, with linnen for us both; as for my self, I wanted very little of cloaths, or linnen, being very well furnish'd before. The rest of my cargo consisted in iron-work of all sorts, harness for horses, tools, cloaths for servants, and woollen-cloth, stuffs, serges, stockings, shoes, hats, and the like, such as servants wear; and whole pieces also, to make up for servants, all by direction of the Quaker; and all this cargo arrived safe, and in good condition, with three woman servants, lusty wenches, which my old governess had pick'd up for me, suitable enough to the place, and to the work we had for them to do, one of which happen'd to come double, having been got with child by one of the seamen in the ship, as she own'd afterwards, before the ship got so far as Gravesend; so she brought us a stout boy, about seven months after our landing.

My husband, you may suppose, was a little surpriz'd at the arriving of this cargo from England, and talking with me one day, after he saw the particulars, My dear, says he, what is the meaning of all this? I fear you will run us too deep in debt. When shall we be able to make returns for it all? I smil'd, and told him that it was all paid for, and then I told him that not knowing what might befal us in the voyage, and considering what our circumstances might expose us to, I had not taken my whole stock with me; that I had reserv'd so much in my friend's hands, which, now we were come over safe, and settled in a way to live, I had sent for, as he might see.

He was amaz'd, and stood awhile telling upon his fingers, but said nothing. At last he began thus: Hold, let's see, says he, telling upon his fingers still; and first on his thumb, There's

246*l*. in money at first; then, Two gold watches, diamond rings and plate, says he, upon the fore finger; then upon the next finger, Here's a plantation on York River, a 100*l*. a year, then 150 in money, then a sloop load of horses, cows, hogs, and stores; and so on to the thumb again. And now, says he, a cargo cost 250*l*. in England, and worth here twice the money. Well, says I, what do you make of all that? Make of it, says he, why, who says I was deceiv'd when I married a wife in Lancashire? I think I have married a fortune, and a very good fortune too, says he.

In a word, we were now in very considerable circumstances, and every year encreasing; for our new plantation grew upon our hands insensibly, and in eight year which we lived upon it we brought it to such a pitch that the produce was, at least, 300*l*. sterling a year: I mean, worth so much in England.

After I had been a year at home again, I went over the bay to see my son, and to receive another year's income of my plantation; and I was surpriz'd to hear, just at my landing there, that my old husband was dead, and had not been bury'd above a fortnight. This, I confess, was not disagreeable news, because now I could appear as I was in a marry'd condition; so I told my son before I came from him that I believ'd I should marry a gentleman who had a plantation near mine; and tho' I was legally free to marry, as to any obligation that was on me before, yet that I was shy of it, least the blot should some time or other be reviv'd, and it might make a husband uneasy. My son, the same kind dutiful and obliging creature as ever, treated me now at his own house, paid me my hundred pound, and sent me home again loaded with presents.

Some time after this, I let my son know I was marry'd, and invited him over to see us, and my husband wrote a very obliging letter to him also, inviting him to come and see him; and he came accordingly some months after, and happen'd to be there just when my cargo from England came in, which I let him believe belong'd all to my husband's estate, and not to me.

It must be observ'd that when the old wretch, my brother (husband) was dead, I then freely gave my husband an account of all that affair, and of this cousin, as I call'd him before, being my own son by that mistaken match. He was perfectly easy in the account, and told me he should have been easy if the old man, as we call'd him, had been alive. For, said he, it was no fault of yours, nor of his; it was a mistake impossible to be prevented. He only reproach'd him with desiring me to conceal it, and to live with him as a wife after I knew that he was my brother; that, he said, was a vile part. Thus all these little difficulties were made easy, and we liv'd together with the greatest kindness and comfort imaginable; we are now grown old, I am come back to England, being almost seventy years of age, my husband sixty eight, having perform'd much more than the limitted terms of my transportation. And now, notwithstanding all the fatigues and all the miseries we have both gone thro', we are both in good heart and health. My husband remain'd there some time after me to settle our affairs, and at first I had intended to go back to him, but at his desire I alter'd that resolution, and he is come over to England also, where we resolve to spend the remainder of our years in sincere penitence for the wicked lives we have lived.

WRITTEN IN THE YEAR 1683.

FINIS.

DEFGHIJ—R—73210/698765

RIVERSIDE EDITIONS

* In preparation